Critical Praise for Robert A. Heinlein's Newest Masterpiece—To Sail Beyond the Sunset . . .

"Thought-provoking . . . considerable wit and energy!"
—**Newsday**

"Admirably successful . . . The autobiographical material is consistently superb. The alternate universes are equally well done . . . The sexuality shows the lusty pleasure in smashing taboos familiar to readers of **Stranger in a Strange Land**."
—**Chicago Sun-Times**

"In **To Sail Beyond the Sunset,** Heinlein continues to assemble most, if not all, the characters he has ever created . . . Heinlein's voice and his prose are stronger and fresher than they have been in some time . . . He remains the master!" —**Locus**

"**To Sail Beyond the Sunset** is an odd and ambitious undertaking, seeking to unite Heinlein's early pulp stories, his later novels and his . . . future history series with autobiographical elements from his childhood. Incredibly, joyfully, the thing works!"
—**Kansas City Star**

"Another major work by the master . . . **To Sail Beyond the Sunset** is both a typical Heinlein work and a work that shows him at the very top of his form . . . Engrossing!" —**San Jose Mercury News**

"His heroine is a feisty, randy, independent woman whose adventures are a must for devotees of the author's Future History series." —**Booklist**

"Entertaining!" —**Fosfax**

Other books by Robert A. Heinlein

ROBERT A. HEINLEIN

TO SAIL BEYOND THE SUNSET

THE LIFE AND LOVES OF MAUREEN JOHNSON
(Being the Memoirs of a Somewhat Irregular Lady)

ACE BOOKS, NEW YORK

This Ace Book contains the complete
text of the original hardcover edition.
It has been completely reset in a typeface
designed for easy reading and was printed
from new film.

TO SAIL BEYOND THE SUNSET

An Ace Book / published by arrangement with
the author

PRINTING HISTORY
Ace/Putnam edition / July 1987
Ace edition / June 1988

ISBN: 0-441-74860-0

To little girls and butterflies and kittens.
To Susan and Eleanor and Chris and (always)
to Ginny.

With my love,
R.A.H.

Contents

Come, my friends,
'Tis not too late to seek a newer world.
Push off, and sitting well in order smite
The sounding furrows; for my purpose holds
To sail beyond the sunset, and the baths
Of all the western stars, until I die.

TENNYSON, "Ulysses"

1

The Committee for Aesthetic Deletions

I woke up in bed with a man and a cat. The man was a stranger; the cat was not.

I closed my eyes and tried to pull myself together—hook "now" to my memory of last night.

No good. There wasn't any "last night." My last clear memory was of being a passenger in a Burroughs irrelevant bus, bound for New Liverpool, when there was a loud bang, my head hit the seat in front of me, then a lady handed me a baby and we started filing out the starboard emergency exit, me with a cat in one arm and a baby in the other, and I saw a man with his right arm off—

I gulped and opened my eyes. A stranger in my bed was better than a man bleeding to death from a stump where his right forearm ought to be. Had it been a nightmare? I fervently hoped so.

If it was not, then what had I done with that baby? And

whose baby was it? Maureen, this won't do. Mislaying a baby is inexcusable. "Pixel, have you seen a baby?" The cat stood mute and a plea of not guilty was directed by the court.

My father once told me that I was the only one of his daughters capable of sitting down in church and finding that I had sat on a hot lemon meringue pie . . . anyone else would have looked. (I *had* looked. But my cousin Nelson— Oh, never mind.)

Regardless of lemon pies, bloody stumps, or missing babies, there was still this stranger in my bed, his bony back toward me—husbandly rather than loverly. (But I did not recall marrying him.)

I've shared beds with men before, and with women, and wet babies, and cats who demand most of the bed, and (once) with a barbershop quartet. But I do like to know with whom I am sleeping (just an old-fashioned girl, that's me). So I said to the cat, "Pixel, who is he? Do we know him?"

"*No-o-o-o.*"

"Well, let's check." I put a hand on the man's shoulder, intending to shake him awake and then ask where we had met—or had we?

His shoulder was cold.

He was quite dead.

This is not a good way to start the day.

I grabbed Pixel and got out of bed by instantaneous translation; Pixel protested. I said sharply, "Shut up, you! Mama has problems." I forced a thalamic pause of at least a microsecond, maybe longer, and decided not to flee headlong outdoors, or out into the hallway, as the case might be . . . but to slow down and attempt to assess the situation, before screaming for help. Perhaps just as well, as I found that I was barefooted all the way up. I am not jumpy about skin but it did seem prudent to dress before reporting a corpse. Police were certain to want to question me and I have known cops who would exploit any advantage in order to throw one off balance.

But first a look at the corpse—

Still clutching Pixel I went around and bent over the other side of the bed. (Gulp.) No one I knew. No one I would choose to bed with, even were he in perfect health. Which he was not; that side of the bed was soggy with blood. (Two gulps and a frisson.) He had bled from his mouth—or his throat had been cut; I was not sure which and was unwilling to investigate.

So I backed away and looked around for my clothes. I knew in my bones that this bedroom was part of a hostelry; rooms for hire do not taste like private homes. It was a luxury suite; it took me a longish time to poke through all the closets and cubbyholes and drawers and cupboards et cetera . . . and then to do it all over again when the first search failed to locate my clothes. The second search, even more thorough, found not a rag—neither his size nor my size, neither women's clothes nor men's.

I decided willy-nilly to telephone the manager, tell him the problem, and let him call the cops—and ask him for a courtesy bathing robe or kimono or some such.

So I looked for a telephone.

Alexander Graham Bell had lived in vain.

I stopped in frustration. "Name of a dog! Where have they hidden that frimping phone?"

A bodyless voice said, "Madam, may we offer you breakfast? We are proud of our Harvest Brunch: a lavish bowl of assorted fresh fruits; a tray of cheeses; a basket of freshly baked hot breads, crisp breads, and soft breads with jams and jellies and syrups and Belgian butter. Basted baby barlops *en brochette;* drawn eggs Octavian; smoked savannah slinker; farkels in sweetsour; Bavarian strudel; your choice of still and sparkling wines, skullbuster Strine beer, Mocha, Kona, Turkish, and Proxima coffees, blended or straight; all served with—"

I repressed a gagging reflex. "I don't want breakfast!"

"Perhaps Madam would enjoy our Holiday Eyeopener: your choice of fruit juice, a roll hot from our oven, your choice of gourmet jams or jellies, your choice in a filling but nonfattening hot cup. Served with the latest news, or background music, or restful silence."

"I don't want to eat!"

The voice answered thoughtfully, "Madam, I am a machine programed for our food and beverage services. May I switch you to another program? Housekeeping? Head porter? Engineering?"

"Get me the manager!"

There was a short delay. "Guest services! Hospitality with a smile! How may I help you?"

"Get me the manager!"

"Do you have a problem?"

"You're the problem! Are you a man, or a machine?"

"Is that relevant? Please tell me how I can help you."

"If you are not the manager, you can't. Do you run on testicles? Or electrons?"

"Madam, I am a machine but a very flexible one. My memories include all curricula of Procrustes Institute of Hotelier Science, including all case studies updated to midnight yesterday. If you will be so good as to state your problem, I will match it at once with a precedent case and show how it was solved to the satisfaction of the guest. Please?"

"If you don't put me through to the manager in nothing flat, I guarantee that the manager will take an axe to your rusty gizzard and install a Burroughs-Libby analog brain in your place. Who shaved the barber? What do your case studies say about that? Moron."

This time I got a female voice. "Manager's office. How may I help you?"

"You can take this dead man out of my bed!"

Short pause— "Housekeeping, Hester speaking. How may we help you?"

"There's a dead man in my bed. I don't like it. Untidy."

Another pause— "Caesar Augustus Escort Service, serving all tastes. Do I understand that one of our gentleman companions died in your bed?"

"I don't know who he is; I just know that he's dead. Who takes care of such things? Room service? Garbage removal? House physician? And I want the sheets changed, too."

This time they gave me background music while I waited . . . and waited—through the first two operas of the *Ring Cycle* and well into the third—

"Accounting and bookkeeping, our Mister Munster speaking. That room was not rented for double occupancy. There will be an additional—"

"Look, buster, it's a corpse. I don't think a corpse counts toward 'double occupancy.' Blood is dripping off the bed and onto your rug. If you don't get somebody up here right away, that rug will be ruined."

"There will be a charge for damage to the rug. That is more than normal wear and tear."

"*Grrrr!*"

"I beg pardon?"

"I am about to set fire to the drapes."

"You're wasting your time; those drapes are fireproof. But your threat has been recorded. Under the Rooming House Act, section seven dee—"

"Get this dead man out of here!"

"Please hold. I'll connect you with the head porter."

"You do and I'll shoot him as he comes through the door. I bite. I scratch. I'm foaming at the mouth. I haven't had my shots."

"Madam, please contain yourself. We pride ourselves on—"

"And then I'll come down to your office and find you, Mister monster Munster, and pull you out of your chair and sit down in it myself and turn you over my knee and take your pants down and— Did I mention that I am from Hercules Gamma? Two and a half gravities surface acceleration; we eat your sort for lunch. So stay where you are; don't make me have to hunt for you."

"Madam, I regret that I must tell you that you cannot sit in my chair."

"Want to bet?"

"I do not have a chair; I am securely bolted to the floor. And now I must bid you good day and turn you over to our security force. You will find the additional charges on your statement of account. Enjoy your stay with us."

They showed up too quickly; I was still eyeing those fireproof drapes, wondering if I could do as well with them as Scarlet O'Hara had with the drapes at Tara, or if I could arrange a simple toga, like Eunice in *The Last Days of Pompeii* (Or was she in *Quo Vadis?*), when they arrived: a house doc, a house dick, and a house ape, the last with a cart. Several more oddments crowded in after them, until we had enough to choose up sides.

I need not have worried about being naked; no one seemed to notice . . . which irked me. Gentlemen should at least leer. And a wolf whistle or other applause would not be out of place. Anything less makes a woman feel unsure of herself.

(Perhaps I am too sensitive. But since my sesquicentennial I have been disposed to check the mirror each morning, wondering.)

There was only one woman in this mob of intruders. She looked at me and sniffed, which made me feel better.

Then I recalled something. When I was twelve, my father told me that I was going to have lots of trouble with men. I said, "Father, you are out of your veering mind. I'm not pretty. The boys don't even throw snowballs at me."

"A little respect, please. No, you aren't pretty. It's the way you smell, my darling daughter. You are going to have to bathe oftener . . . or some warm night you will wind up raped and murdered."

"Why, I bathe every week! You know I do."

"In your case, that's not enough. Mark my words."

I did mark his words and learned that Father knew what he was talking about. My body odor when I'm well and happy is much like that of a cat in heat. But today I was not happy. First that dead man scared me and then those bleeping machines made me angry . . . which adds up to a different sort of stink. A tabby cat not in heat can walk right through a caucus of toms and they will ignore her. As I was being ignored.

They stripped the top sheet off my erstwhile bedmate. The house physician looked over the cadaver without touching it, then looked more closely at that horrid red puddle—leaned down, sniffed it, then made my skin crawl by dipping a finger into the slop and tasting it. "Try it, Adolf. See what you think."

His colleague (I assumed that he was another physician) also tasted the bloody mess. "Heinz."

"No. Skinner's."

"With all due respect, Dr. Ridpath, you have ruined your palate with that cheap gin you guzzle. Heinz. Skinner's catsup has more salt. Which kills the delicate tomato flavor. Which you can't taste, because of your evil habits."

"Ten thousand, Dr. Weisskopf? Even money."

"You're on. What do you place as the cause of death, sir?"

"Don't try to trap me, Doctor. 'Cause of death' is your job."

"His heart stopped."

"Brilliant, Doctor, brilliant! But why did it stop?"

"In the case of Judge Hardacres for some years the question has been: What keeps him alive? Before I express an opinion

I want to place him on a slab and slice him up. I may have
been hasty; he may turn out not to have had a heart."

"Are you going to cut him up to learn something, or to
make certain he stays dead?"

"Noisy in here, isn't it? Do you release the body? I'll have
it taken downtown."

"Hand me a form nine-oh-four and I'll chop it. Just keep
the meat out of sight of our guests. Grand Hotel Augustus
does not have guests dying on its premises."

"Dr. Ridpath, I was handling such things discreetly before
you slid through that diploma mill."

"I'm sure you were, Adolf. Lawn ball later?"

"Thank you, Eric. Yes."

"And dinner after; Zenobia will be expecting you. I'll pick
you up at the morgue."

"Oh, I'm sorry! I'm taking my assistant to the Mayor's
Orgy."

"No fuss. Zenobia would never miss the first big party of
Fiesta; we'll all go together. So bring her with you."

"Him, not 'her.' "

"Pardon my raised eyebrows; I thought you had sworn off.
Very well; bring him."

"Eric, don't you find it depressing to be so cynical? He's
a satyr, not a goose."

"So much the better. With Fiesta starting at sundown Zenobia will welcome any gallant indecency he offers her, as long
as he does not break her bones."

This silly chatter had told me one thing: I was not in New
Liverpool. New Liverpool does not celebrate Fiesta—and this
local festival sounded like *Fasching* in Munich combined with
Carnival in Rio, with a Brixton riot thrown in. So, not New
Liverpool. What city, what planet, what year, and what universe remained to be seen. Then I would have to see what
could be done about my predicament. Clothes. Money. Status. Then, how to get home. But I was not worried. As long
as the body is warm and the bowels move regularly no problem can be other than minor and temporary.

The two doctors were still sneering at each other when I
suddenly realized that I had heard not one word of Galacta.
Not even Spanglish. They were speaking English, almost the

harsh accent of my girlhood, with idiom and vocabulary close to that of my native Missouri.

Maureen, this is ridiculous.

While flunkies were getting ready to move the body (disguised as a nameless something draped in dust covers) the medical examiner (coroner?) got a signed release from the house physician, and both started to leave. I stopped the latter. "Dr. Ridpath!"

"Yes? What is it, Miss?"

"I'm Maureen Johnson Long. You are on the staff of the hotel, are you not?"

"In a manner of speaking. I have my offices here and am available as house physician when needed. Do you wish to see me professionally? I'm in a hurry."

"Just one quick question, Doctor. How does one get the attention of a flesh and blood human being on the staff of this hotel? I can't seem to raise anyone but moronic robots—and I'm stranded here with no clothes and no money."

He shrugged. "Someone is certain to show up before long, once I report that Judge Hardacres is dead. Are you worried about your fee? Why don't you call the talent agency that sent you to him? The judge probably had a running account with them."

"Oh! Doctor, I'm not a prostitute. Although I suppose it does look like it."

He cocked his left brow so high that it disturbed the tilt of his toupée, and changed the subject. "You have a beautiful pussy."

I assumed that he was speaking of my feline companion, who is a most beautiful pussy—a flame-colored tomcat (just the color of my hair) in a striking tiger pattern. He has been much admired in several universes. "Thank you, sir. His name is Pixel and he is a much-traveled cat. Pixel, this is Dr. Ridpath."

The doctor put out a finger close to the little pink nose. "Howdy, Pixel."

Pixel was helpful. (Sometimes he is not—a cat of firm opinions.) He sniffed the proffered finger, then licked it.

The doctor smiled indulgently, then withdrew his finger when Pixel decided that the ritual kiss had gone on long enough. "He's a fine boy, that one. Where did you find him?"

"On Tertius."

"Where's Ontershus? Canada? Mmm, you say you have a money problem. What'll you take for Pixel, cash in hand? My little girl would love him."

(I didn't swindle him. I could have but I didn't. Pixel can't be sold—he can't stay sold—because he can't be locked up. For him, stone walls do not a prison make.) "Oh, I'm sorry! I can't sell him; he's not mine. He's a member of the family of my grandson—one of my grandsons—and his wife. But Colin and Hazel would never sell him. They can't sell him; they don't own him. No one owns him; Pixel is a free citizen."

"So? Then perhaps I can bribe him. How about it, Pixel? Lots of horse liver, fresh fish, cat nibbles, all you want. Plenty of friendly girl cats around and we'll leave your spark plugs right where they are. Well?"

Pixel gave the restless wiggle that means "Let me down," so I did. He sniffed the doctor's legs, then brushed against him. "*Nnnow?*" he inquired.

Dr. Ridpath said to me, "You should have accepted my offer. I seem to have acquired a cat."

"I wouldn't bet on it, Doctor. Pixel likes to travel but he always comes back to my grandson Colin. Colonel Colin Campbell. And his wife Hazel."

For the first time Dr. Ridpath really looked at me. " 'Grandson.' 'Colonel.' Miss, you're hallucinating."

(I suddenly realized how it looked to him. Before I left Tertius, Ishtar had given me a booster treatment—it had been fifty-two years—and Galahad had given me a cosmetic refresher and had overdone it. Galahad likes 'em young, especially redheads—he keeps my twin daughters permanent teenagers, and now we three look like triplets. Galahad cheats. Except for Theodore, Galahad is my favorite husband, but I shan't let anyone find out.)

"Yes, I must be hallucinating," I agreed. "I don't know where I am, I don't know what day this is, I don't know what became of my clothes or my money or my purse, and I don't know how I got here . . . save that I was in an irrelevancy bus for New Liverpool and there was an accident of some sort. If Pixel were not still with me, I would wonder if I were me."

Dr. Ridpath reached down; Pixel allowed himself to be picked up. "What was that bus you mentioned?"

"A Burroughs shifter. I was on Tellus Tertius at Boondock on time line two at Galactic year 2149, or Gregorian 4368 if you like that better. I was scheduled for New Liverpool in time line two, where I was to base for a field trip. But something went wrong."

"Ah, so. Hmm. And you have a grandson who is a colonel?"

"Yes, sir."

"And how old are you?"

"That depends on how you count it, Doctor. I was born on Earth in time line two on the Fourth of July, 1882. I lived there until 1982, one century minus two weeks, whereupon I moved to Tertius and was rejuvenated. That was fifty-two years ago by my personal calendar. I've had a booster just recently, which made me younger than I should be—I prefer to be mature rather than girlish. But I do have grandchildren, lots of them."

"Interesting. Will you come down to my office with me?"

"You think I'm out of my head."

He was not quick to answer. "Let me put it this way. One of us is hallucinating. Tests may show which one. Besides that, I have an exceptionally cynical office nurse who can, without tests, almost certainly spot which one of us has slipped his clutch. Will you come?"

"Yes, certainly. And thank you, sir. But I've got to find some clothes first. I can't very well leave this room until I do." (I wasn't certain that this was true. That crowd that had just left obviously did not have the attitudes on "indecent exposure" that were commonplace in Missouri when I was born. On the other hand, where I now lived on Tertius nudity at home was unremarkable and it didn't cause any excitement even in the most public places—like overalls at a wedding: unusual but nothing to stare at.)

"Oh. But Festival is about to start."

" 'Festival'? Doctor, I'm a stranger in a strange land; that is what I've been trying to say."

"Uh— Our biggest holiday is about to start. Starts at sundown, theoretically, but there are many who jump the gun. By now the boulevard out front will have quite a percentage of naked people, already drunk and looking for partners."

"Partners for what?" I tried to sound innocent. I'm not much for orgies. All those knees and elbows—

"What do you think? It's a fertility rite, my dear girl, to insure fat crops. And fat bellies, for that matter. By now, any virgins left in this fair city are locked up." He added, "But you won't be bothered simply going with me to my office . . . and I promise I'll find you some sort of clothing. A coverall. A nurse's uniform. Something. Does that suit you?"

"Thank you, Doctor. Yes!"

"If I were you and I was still jumpy, I would look for a big beach towel in that bathroom, and make a caftan out of it. If you can do it in three minutes. Don't dilly-dally, dolly; I've got to get back to the grind."

"Yessir!" I hurried into the bathroom.

It really was a bathroom, not a refresher. When I had searched the suite for clothing, I had noticed a stack of Turkish towels in there. Now I looked more closely and spotted two that bulged fat in that stack. I worked one out and unfolded it. Eureka! A towel fit for a rich South American, one at least six feet long and three feet wide. A razor blade from the medicine chest placed a slit big enough for my head spang down the center. Now to find something, anything, to tie around my waist.

While I was doing this, a human head appeared in front of—in place of, rather—the hair dryer. A head female and rather pretty. No body. During my first century this would have made me jumpy. Today I'm used to realistic holos.

"I've been trying to catch you alone," the head said in an organlike baritone. "I speak for the Committee for Aesthetic Deletions. We seem to have caused you some inconvenience. For that we are truly sorry."

"You should be! What became of that baby?"

"Never mind that baby. We'll be in touch." It flickered.

"Hey! Wait!" But I was talking to the hair dryer.

Dr. Ridpath looked up from scratching Pixel's chin. "Five minutes and forty seconds."

"I'm sorry to be late but I was interrupted. A head appeared and spoke to me. Does that happen often around here? Or am I hallucinating again?"

"You really do seem to be a stranger here. That's a telephone. Like this— Telephone, please!"

A head appeared in a frame that had contained a rather dull still-life, a male head in this case. "Your call, sir?"

"Cancel." The head blinked out. "Like that?"

"Yes. But a girl."

"Of course. You're female and the call reached you in a bathroom, so the computer displayed a head matching your sex. The computer matches lip movements to words . . . but the visual stays an impersonal animation unless you elect to be seen. Same for the caller."

"I see. A hologram."

"Yes. Come along." He added, "You look quite fetching in that towel but you looked still better in your skin."

"Thank you." We went out in the hotel corridor; Pixel cut back and forth in front of us. "Doctor, what is 'The Committee for Aesthetic Deletions'?"

"Huh?" He sounded surprised. "Assassins. Criminal nihilists. Where did you hear of them?"

"That head I saw in the bathroom. That telephone." I repeated the call, word for word, I think.

"Hmm. Interesting." He did not say another word until we reached his office suite, ten stories down on the mezzanine.

We ran across several hotel guests who had "jumped the gun." Most were naked save for domino masks but several wore full masks—of animals or birds, or abstract fantasy. One couple was dressed most gaudily in nothing but paint. I was glad that I had my terry cloth caftan.

When we reached Dr. Ridpath's office suite, I hung back in the waiting room while he went on into an inner room, preceded by Pixel. The doctor left the door open; I could hear and see. His office nurse was standing, her back to us, talking "on the telephone"—a talking head. There appeared to be no one else in the suite. Nevertheless I was mildly surprised to find that she had joined the epidemic of skin; she was wearing shoes, minipanties, and a nurse's cap, and had a white nurse's uniform over one arm as if caught by the phone while she was undressing. Or changing. She was a tall and slender brunette. I could not see her face.

I heard her say, "I'll tell him, Doc. Keep your guard up tonight. See you in jail. Bye." She half turned. "That was Daffy Weisskopf, Boss. He has a preliminary report for you. Cause of death, suffocation. But—get this—stuffed down the old bastard's throat, before the catsup was poured in, was a

plastic envelope with a famous—or infamous—card in it:
'The Committee for Aesthetic Deletions.' "

"So I figured. Did he say what brand of catsup?"

"Fer cry eye yie!"

"And what are you doing peeling down? Festival doesn't
start for another three hours."

"Look here, slave driver! See that clock?—ticking off the
precious seconds of my life. See what it says? Eleven past
five. My contract says that I work until five."

"It says that you are on duty until I relieve you, but that
overtime rate starts at five."

"There were no patients here and I was changing into my
festival costume. Wait till you see it, Boss! It 'ud make a
priest blush."

"I doubt it. We do have a patient and I need your help."

"Okay, okay! I'll get back into my Florence Nightingale
duds."

"Don't bother; it would just waste time. Mrs. Long! Come
in, please, and take off your clothes."

"Yes, sir." I came in at once, while peeling off that scrounged
caftan. I could see what he was doing: a prudent male doctor
has a chaperon when examining a female patient; that's a
universal. A multiuniversal. If the circumstances happen to
supply a chaperon in her skin, so much the better; there need
be no time wasted on "angel robes" and other such nonsense.
Having helped my father and having stood years of watches
in the rejuvenation clinic at Boondock and in the associated
hospital I understood the protocol invoked; a nurse in Boondock wears clothes only when the job requires it. Seldom,
that is, as the patient is usually not clothed. "But it's not
'Mrs. Long,' Doctor. I am usually called 'Maureen.' "

" 'Maureen' it is. This is Dagmar. Roast, meet Alice; Alice,
meet Roast. And Pixel, too, Dagmar. He's the one with the
short legs."

"Howdy, Maureen. Hi, Pixel."

"*Mee-ow.*"

"Hi, Dagmar. Sorry to keep you late."

"*De nada,* ducks."

"Dagmar, either I am out of my skull, or Maureen is. Which
is it?"

"Couldn't it be both? I've had my doubts about you for a
long time, Boss."

"Understandable. But she really does seem to have lost a

chunk of her memory. At least. Plus possible hallucinations. You've studied *materia medica* much more recently than I have; if someone wanted to cause a few hours' temporary amnesia, what drug would he choose?"

"Huh? Don't give me your barefoot boy act. Alcohol, of course. But it might be almost anything, the way the kids nowadays eat, drink, snort, smoke, or shoot almost anything that doesn't shoot back."

"Not alcohol. Enough alcohol to do that produces a horrible hangover, with halitosis, twitches and shakes, and bloodshot eyes. But look at her—clear eyes, healthy as a horse, and innocent as a pup in the clean laundry. Pixel! Stay out of that! So what do we look for?"

"I dunno; let's operate and find out. Urine sample. Blood sample. Saliva, too?"

"Certainly. And sweat, if you can find enough."

"Vaginal specimen?"

"Yes."

"Wait," I objected. "If you intend to poke around inside me, I want a chance to douche and wash."

"Not bleedin' likely, ducks," Dagmar answered gently. "What we need is whatever is in there now . . . not after you've washed your sins away. Don't argue; I wouldn't want to break your arm."

I shut up. I do indeed want to smell good, or not smell at all, when being examined. But as a doctor's daughter (and a therapist myself) I knew that what Dagmar said made sense . . . since they were looking for drugs. I didn't expect that they would find any . . . but they might; I certainly was missing some hours. Days? Anything could have happened.

Dagmar had me pee in a cup and took my blood and saliva, then told me to climb onto the table and into the stirrups. "Shall I do it? Or the Boss? Out of the way, Pixel! And stop that."

"Either of you." (A truly considerate nurse. Some female patients can't stand to be touched down below by females, others are shy with males. Me, I was cured of all such nonsense by my father before I was ten.)

Dagmar came back with a dilator . . . and I noticed something. Brunette, I said she was. She had remained undressed save for scanty panties—which were not opaque. She should have shown a dark, built-in fig leaf, no?

No. Just skin shade and a hint of the Great Divide.

A woman who shaves or otherwise depilates her pubic curls has a profound interest in recreational sex. My beloved first husband Brian pointed this out to me in the Mauve Decade, *circa* 1905 Gregorian. I've checked Brian's assertion through a century and a half, endless examples. (I am not counting prepping for surgery or for childbirth.) The ones who did it because they preferred that styling were without exception hearty, healthy, uninhibited hedonists.

Dagmar wasn't prepped for surgery; she (obviously!) was not about to give birth. No, she was about to take part in a saturnalia. QED.

It made me feel warm toward her. Brian, bless his lecherous soul, would have appreciated her.

By now, in the course of chatting while she took samples, she knew the essentials of my "hallucination," so she knew that I was a stranger in town. As she was adjusting that damned dilator (I have always detested them, although this one was blood temperature and was being handled with the gentle care that a woman can bring to the task, having been there herself)—while she was busy with this, I asked a question in order to ignore what she was doing. "Dagmar, tell me about this festival."

"La Fiesta de Santa Carolita? Hey, you clamped down! Watch it, ducks; you'll hurt yourself."

I sighed and tried to relax. Santa Carolita is my second child, born in 1902 Gregorian.

2

The Garden of Eden

I remember Earth.

I knew her when she was clean and green, mankind's beautiful bride, sweet and lush and lovable.

I speak of my own time line, of course, numbered "two" and coded "Leslie LeCroix." But the best known time lines, those policed by the Time Corps for the Circle of Ouroboros, are all one at the time I was born, 1882 Gregorian, only nine years after the death of Ira Howard. In 1882 the population of Earth was a mere billion and a half.

When I left Earth just a century later it had increased to over four billion and that swarming mass was doubling every thirty years.

Remember that ancient Persian parable about doubling grains of rice on a chessboard? Four billion people are a smidgen larger than a grain of rice; you quickly run out of chessboard. On one time line Earth's population swelled to

16

over thirty billion before reaching final disaster; on other time lines the end came at less than ten billion. But on all time lines Dr. Malthus had the last laugh.

It is futile to mourn over the corpse of Earth, as silly as it would be to cry over an empty chrysalis when its butterfly has flown. But I am incurably sentimental and forever sad at how Man's Old Home has changed.

I had a marvelously happy girlhood.

I not only lived on Earth when she was young and beautiful but also had the good fortune to be born in one of her loveliest garden spots, southern Missouri before people and bulldozers ravaged its green hills.

Besides the happy accident of birthplace, I had the special good fortune to be my father's daughter.

When I was still quite young my father said to me, "My beloved daughter, you are an amoral little wretch. I know this, because you take after me; your mind works just the way mine does. If you are not to be destroyed by your lack, you must work out a practical code of your own and live by it."

I thought about his words and felt warm and good inside. "Amoral little wretch—" Father knew me so well.

"What code should I follow, Father?"

"You have to pick your own."

"The Ten Commandments?"

"You know better than that. The Ten Commandments are for lame brains. The first five are solely for the benefit of the priests and the powers that be; the second five are half truths, neither complete nor adequate."

"All right, teach me about the second five. How should they read?"

"Not on your tintype, lazy bones; you've got to do it yourself." He stood up suddenly, dumping me off his lap and almost landing me on my bottom. This was a running game with us. If I moved fast, I could land on my feet. If not, it was one point to him.

"Analyze the Ten Commandments," he ordered. "Tell me how they should read. In the meantime, if I hear just once more that you have lost your temper, then when your mother sends you to discuss the matter with me, you had better have your McGuffey's Reader tucked inside your bloomers."

"Father, you wouldn't."

"Just try me, carrot top, just try me. I will enjoy spanking you."

An empty threat— He never spanked me once I was old enough to understand why I was being scolded. But even before then he had never spanked me hard enough to hurt my bottom. Just my feelings.

Mother's punishments were another matter. The high justice was Father's bailiwick; Mother handled the low and middle—with a peach switch. Ouch!

Father spoiled me rotten.

I had four brothers and four sisters—Edward, born in 1876; Audrey in '78; Agnes in 1880; Tom, '81; in '82 I came along; Frank was born in 1884, then Beth in '92; Lucille, '94; George in 1897—and I took up more of Father's time than any three of my siblings. Maybe four. Looking back on it, I can't see that he made himself more available to me than he did to any of my brothers and sisters. But it certainly worked out that I spent more time with my father.

Two ground-floor rooms in our house were Father's clinic and surgery; I spent a lot of my free time there as I was fascinated by his books. Mother did not think I should read them, medical books being filled with things that ladies simply should not delve into. Unladylike. Immodest.

Father said to her, "Mrs. Johnson, the few errors in those books I will point out to Maureen. As for the far more numerous and much more important truths, I am pleased that Maureen wants to learn them. 'Ye shall know the truth and the truth shall make you free.' John, eight, verse thirty-two."

Mother set her mouth in a grim line and did not answer. For her the Bible was the final word . . . whereas Father was a freethinker, a fact he did not admit even to me at that time. But Father knew the Bible more thoroughly than Mother did and could always quote a verse to refute her—a most unfair way to argue, it seems to me, but an advantage he needed in dealing with her. Mother was strong-willed.

They disagreed on many things. But they had rules that let them live together without bloodshed. Not only live together but share a bed and have baby after baby together. A miracle.

I think Father set most of the rules. At that time and place it was taken for granted that a husband was head of his household and must be obeyed. You may not believe this but the wedding ceremony in those days required the bride to promise to obey her husband—in everything and forever.

If I know my mother (I don't, really), she didn't keep that promise more than thirty minutes.

But they worked out practical compromises.

Mother bossed the household. Father's domain was his clinic and surgery, and the barn and outbuildings and matters pertaining thereto. Father controlled all money matters. Each month he gave Mother a household allowance that she spent as she saw fit. But he required her to keep a record of how she spent it, bookkeeping that Father examined each month.

Breakfast was at seven, dinner at noon, supper at six; if Father's medical practice caused him to need to eat at other times, he notified Mother—ahead of time if possible. But the family sat down on time.

If Father was present, he held Mother's chair for her; she thanked him, he then sat down and the rest of us followed. He said grace, morning, noon, and night. In Father's absence my brother Edward seated Mother and she said grace. Or she might direct one of us to return thanks, for practice. Then we ate, and misbehavior at the table was only one notch below high treason. But a child did not have to sit and squirm and wait for the grownups after he was through eating; he could ask to be excused, then leave the table. He could not return even if he discovered that he had made a horrible mistake such as forgetting that it was a dessert night. (But Mother would relent and allow that child to eat dessert in the kitchen . . . if he had not teased or whined.)

The day my eldest sister, Audrey, entered high school Father added to the protocol: He held Mother's chair as usual. Once she was seated Mother said, "Thank you, Doctor." Then Edward, two years older than Audrey, held her chair for her and seated her just after Mother was seated. Mother said, "What do you say, Audrey?"

"I did say it, Mama."

"Yes, she did, Mother."

"I did not hear it."

"Thank you, Eddie."

"You're welcome, Aud."

Then the rest of us sat down.

Thereafter, as each girl entered high school, the senior available boy was conscripted into the ceremony.

On Sundays dinner was at one because everyone but Father

went to Sunday School and everyone including Father went to morning church.

Father stayed out of the kitchen. Mother never entered the clinic and surgery even to clean. That cleaning was done by a hired girl, or by one of my sisters, or (once I was old enough) by me.

By unwritten rules, never broken, my parents lived in peace. I think their friends thought of them as an ideal couple and of their offspring as "those nice Johnson children."

Indeed I think we were a happy family, all nine of us children and our parents. Don't think for a minute that we lived under such strict discipline that we did not have fun. We had loads of fun, both at home and away.

But we made our own fun, mostly. I recall a time, many years later, when American children seemed to be unable to amuse themselves without a fortune in electrical and electronic equipment. We had no fancy equipment and did not miss it. By then, 1890 more or less, Mr. Edison had invented the electric light and Professor Bell had invented the telephone but these modern miracles had not reached Thebes, in Lyle County, Missouri. As for electronic toys, the word "electron" had yet to be coined. But my brothers had sleds and wagons and we girls had dolls and toy sewing machines and we had many indoor games in joint tenancy—dominoes and checkers and chess and jackstraws and lotto and pigs-in-clover and anagrams . . .

We played outdoor games that required no equipment, or not much. We had a variation of baseball called "scrub" which could be played by three to eighteen players plus the volunteer efforts of dogs, cats, and one goat.

We had other livestock: from one to four horses, depending on the year; a Guernsey cow named Clytemnestra; chickens (usually Rhode Island Reds); guinea fowl, ducks (white domestic), rabbits from time to time, and (one season only) a sow named Gumdrop. Father sold Gumdrop when it developed that we were unwilling to eat pigs we had helped raise. Not that we needed to raise pigs; Father was more likely to receive fees in smoked ham or a side of bacon than he was to be paid in money.

We all fished and the boys hunted. As soon as each boy was old enough (ten, as I recall) to handle a rifle, Father taught him to shoot, a .22 at first. He taught them to hunt, too, but I did not see it; girls were not included. I did not mind that (I refused to have anything to do with skinning and gutting bunny rabbits, that being their usual game) but I did want to learn to shoot . . . and made the mistake of saying so in Mother's hearing. She exploded.

Father told me quietly, "We'll discuss it later."

And we did. About a year later, when it was established that I sometimes drove Father on country calls, unbeknownst to Mother he started taking along in the back of his buggy under gunny sacks a little single-shot .22 . . . and Maureen was taught to shoot . . . and especially how not to get shot, all the rules of firearm safety. Father was a patient teacher who demanded perfection.

Weeks later he said, "Maureen, if you will remember what I've taught you, it may cause you to live longer. I hope so. We won't tackle pistol this year; your hands aren't yet big enough."

We young folks owned the whole outdoors as our playground. We picked wild blackberries and went nutting for black walnuts and searched for pawpaws and persimmons. We went on hikes and picnics. Eventually, as each of us grew taller and began to feel new and wonderful yearnings, we used the outdoors for courting—"sparking," we called it.

Our family was forever celebrating special days—eleven birthdays, our parents' wedding anniversary, Christmas, New Year's Eve and New Year's Day, Valentine's Day, Washington's birthday, Easter, the Fourth of July (a double celebration, it being my birthday), and Admission Day on the tenth of August. Best of all was the county fair—"best" because Father drove in the harness races (and warned his patients not to get sick that week—or see Dr. Chadwick, his exchange). We sat in the stands and cheered ourselves hoarse . . . although Father seldom finished in the money. Then came Halloween and Thanksgiving, which brings us up to Christmas again.

That's a full month of special days, every one of them celebrated with noisy enthusiasm.

And there were nonspecial days when we sat around the dining table and picked the meats from walnuts as fast as Father and Edward could crack them, while Mother or Audrey read aloud from the *Leatherstocking Tales* or *Ivanhoe* or Dickens—or we made popcorn, or popcorn balls (sticky all over everything!), or fudge, or we gathered around the piano and sang while Mother played, and that was best of all.

There were winters when we had a spell-down every night because Audrey was going for it seriously. She walked around with McGuffey's speller under one arm and Webster's *American Spelling Book* under the other, her lips moving and her eyes blank. She always won the family drills; we expected that; family competition was usually between Edward and me for second place.

Audrey made it: First place in Thebes Consolidated Grammar and High School when she was in Sixth Grade, then the following year she went all the way to Joplin for the regional—only to lose to a nasty little boy from Rich Hill. But in her freshman year in high school she won the regional and went on to Jefferson City and won the gold medal for top speller in Missouri. Mother and Audrey went together to the state capital for the finals and the presentation—by stage coach to Butler, by railroad train to Kansas City, then again by train to Jefferson City. I could have been jealous—of Audrey's travel, not of her gold medal—had it not been that by then I was about to go to Chicago (but that's another story).

Audrey was welcomed back with a brass band, the one that played at the county fair, specially activated off season to honor "Thebes' Favorite Daughter" (so it said on a big banner), "Audrey Adele Johnson." Audrey cried. So did I.

I remember especially one hot July afternoon—"Cyclone weather," father decided, and, sure enough, three twisters did touch down that day, one quite close to our house.

We were safe; Father had ordered us into the storm cellar as soon as the sky darkened, and had helped Mother down the steps most carefully—she was carrying again . . . my little sister Beth it must have been. We sat down there for three hours, by the light of a barn lantern, and drank lemonade and ate Mother's sugar cookies, thick and floury and filling.

Father stood at the top of the steps with the slant door open, until a piece of the Ritters' barn came by.

At which point Mother was shrill with him (for the only time that I know of in the presence of children). "Doctor! You come inside at once! I will not be widowed just to let you prove to yourself that you can stand up to anything!"

Father came down promptly, fastening the slant door be-

hind him. "Madam," he stated, "as always your logic is ir-
refutable."

There were hayrides with young people of our own ages,
usually with fairly tolerant chaperonage; there were skating
parties on the Marais des Cygnes; there were Sunday school
picnics, and church ice cream socials, and more and more.
Happy times do not come from fancy gadgets; they come
from "male and female created He them," and from being
healthy and filled with zest for life.

The firm discipline we lived under was neither onerous nor
unreasonable; none of it was simply for the sterile purpose
of having rules. Outside the scope of those necessary rules
we were as free as birds.

Older children helped with younger children, with defined
responsibilities. All of us had assigned chores, from about
age six, on up. The assignments were written down and checked
off—and in later years I handled my own brood (larger than
my mother's) by her rules. Hers were sensible rules; they had
worked for her; they would work for me.

Oh, my rules were not exactly like my mother's rules because our circumstances were not exactly alike. For example,
a major chore for my brothers was sawing and chopping wood;
my sons did not chop wood because our home in Kansas City
was heated by a coal furnace. But they did tend furnace, fill
the coal bin (coal was delivered to the curb, followed by the
backbreaking chore of carrying it a bucket at a time to a chute
that led to the coal bin), and clean out the ashes and haul
them up the basement stairs and out.

There were other differences. My boys did not have to
carry water for baths; in Kansas City we had running water.
And so forth— My sons worked as hard as my brothers had,
but differently. A city house with electricity and gas and a
coal furnace does not create anything like the heavy chores
that a country house in the Gay Nineties did. The house I
was brought up in had no running water, no plumbing of any
sort, no central heating. It was lighted by coal oil lamps and
by candles, both homemade and store-boughten, and it was
heated by wood stoves: a big baseburner in the parlor, a drum
stove in the clinic, monkey stoves elsewhere. No stoves upstairs . . . but grilles set in the ceilings allowed heated air to
reach the upper floor.

Ours was one of the larger houses in town, and possibly

the most modern, as Father was quick to adopt any truly useful new invention as soon as it was available. In this he consciously imitated Mr. Samuel Clemens.

Father judged Mr. Clemens to be one of the smartest and possibly the smartest man in America. Mr. Clemens was seventeen years older than Father; he first became aware of "Mark Twain" with the Jumping Frog story. From that time on Father read everything by Mr. Clemens he could lay hands on.

The year I was born Father wrote to Mr. Clemens, complimenting him on *A Tramp Abroad*. Mr. Clemens sent a courteous and dryly humorous answer; Father framed it and hung it on the wall of his clinic. Thereafter Father wrote to Mr. Clemens as each new book by "Mark Twain" appeared. As a direct result, young Maureen read all of Mr. Clemens's published works, curled up in a corner of her father's clinic. These were not books that Mother read; she considered them vulgar and destructive of good morals. By her values Mother was correct; Mr. Clemens was clearly subversive by the standards of all "right thinking" people.

I am forced to assume that Mother could spot an immoral book by its odor, as she never, never actually read anything by Mr. Clemens.

So those books stayed in the clinic and I devoured them there, along with other books never seen in the parlor—not just medical books, but such outright subversion as the lectures of Colonel Robert Ingersoll and (best of all) the essays of Thomas Henry Huxley.

I'll never forget the afternoon I read Professor Huxley's essay on "The Gadarene Swine." "Father," I said in deep excitement, "they've lied to us all along!"

"Probably," he agreed. "What are you reading?"

I told him. "Well, you've read enough of it for today; Professor Huxley is strong medicine. Let's talk for a while. How are you doing with the Ten Commandments? Got your final version?"

"Maybe," I answered.

"How many are there now?"

"Sixteen, I think."

"Too many."

"If you would just let me chuck the first five—"

"Not while you're under my roof and eating at my table.

You see me attending church and singing hymns, do you not? I don't even sleep during the sermon. Maureen, rubbing blue mud in your belly button is an indispensable survival skill . . . everywhere, anywhen. Let's hear your latest version of the first five."

"Father, you are a horrid man and you will come to a bad end."

"Not as long as I can keep dodging them. Quit stalling."

"Yes, sir. First Commandment: Thou shalt pay public homage to the god favored by the majority without giggling or even smiling behind your hand."

"Go on."

"Thou shalt not make any graven image of a sort that could annoy the powers that be, especially Mrs. Grundy—and, *exempli gratia,* this is why your anatomy book doesn't show the clitoris. Mrs. Grundy wouldn't like it because she doesn't have one."

"Or possibly has one the size of a banana," my father answered, "but doesn't want anyone to find out. Censorship is never logical but, like cancer, it is dangerous to ignore it when it shows up. Darling daughter, the purpose of the second commandment is simply to reinforce the first. A 'graven image' is any idol that could rival the official god; it has nothing to do with sculpture or etchings. Go on."

"Thou shalt not take the name of thy Lord God in vain . . . which means don't swear, not even Jiminy or Golly or darn, or use any of those four-letter words, or anything that Mother might consider vulgar. Father, there is something here that doesn't make sense. Why is 'vagina' a good word while 'cunt' is a bad word? Riddle me that."

"Both are bad words out of your mouth, youngster, unless you are talking to me . . . in which case you will use the medical Latin out of respect for my vocation and my gray hair. You are permitted to say the Anglo-Saxon synonym under your breath if it pleasures you."

"Somehow it does, and I haven't been able to analyze why. Number four—"

"Just a moment. Add to number three: Thou shalt not split infinitives, or dangle participles. Thou shalt shun solecisms. Thou shalt honor the noble English language, speech of Shakespeare, Milton, and Poe, and it will serve thee all the days of thy life. In particular, Maureen, if I ever again hear you say 'different than'—I will beat you about the head and shoulders with an unbated ablative absolute."

"Father, that was an accident! I meant to—"

"Excuses. Let's hear number four."

"Commandment number four. Go to church on Sundays. Smile and be pleasant but don't be too smarmily a hypocrite. Don't let my children, if and when I have any, play out in front on Sunday or make too much noise in back. Support the church by deeds and money but not too conspicuously."

"Maureen, that's well put. You'll be a preacher's wife yet."

"Oh, God, Father, I'd rather be a whore!"

"The two are not incompatible. *Continuez, ma chère enfant.*"

"*Mais oui, mon cher papa.* Honor thy father and thy mother where anyone can see you. But once you leave home, live your own life. Don't let them lead you around by the nose. *Mon papa,* you phrased that one yourself . . . and I don't like it much. I do honor you, because I want to. And I don't have anything against Mother; we just don't sing in the same key. But I'm grateful to her."

"Avoid gratitude, my dear; it can sour your stomach. After you marry and I'm dead, are you going to invite Adele to move in with you?"

"Uh—" I stopped, unable to answer.

"Think about it. Think it through carefully, in advance . . . because any answer you make in a hurry while my grave is still fresh is certain to be a wrong answer. Next item."

"Thou shalt not commit murder. 'Murder' means killing somebody wrongfully. Other sorts of killing come in several flavors and each sort must be analyzed. I'm still working on this one, Father."

"So am I. Just bear in mind that a person who eats meat is on the same moral level as the butcher."

"Yes, sir. Thou shalt not get caught committing adultery . . . and that means don't get pregnant, don't catch a social disease, don't let Mrs. Grundy even suspect you, and above all don't let your spouse find out; it would make him most unhappy . . . and he could divorce you. Father, I don't think I would ever be tempted by adultery. If God had intended a woman to have more than one man he would have supplied more men . . . instead of just enough to go around."

"Who intended? I didn't catch the name."

"I said 'God' but you know what I mean!"

"I do indeed. You are indulging in theology; I would rather see you take laudanum. Maureen, when anyone talks about 'God's' will or God's intentions or Nature's intentions if he is afraid to say 'God,' I know at once that he is selling a gold brick. To himself, in some cases, as you were just doing. To read a moral law into the fact that about as many males are born as females is to make too much stew from one oyster; it's as slippery as '*Post hoc, propter hoc.*'

"As for your belief that you will never be tempted, here you are, barely dry behind the ears and only a year past first onset of menses . . . and you think you know all there is to know about the perils of sex . . . just as every girl your age throughout history has thought. So go right ahead. Jump the fence with your eyes closed. Break your husband's heart and ruin his pride. Shame your children. Be a scandal in the public square. Get your tubes filled with pus, then let some butcher cut them out in some dirty back room with no ether. Go right ahead, Maureen. Count the world well lost for love. For that's what sloppy adultery can get you: The world lost all right and an early grave and children who will never speak your name."

"But, Father, I was saying that I must shun adultery; it's too dangerous. I think I can manage it." I smiled at him and recited:

" 'There was a young lady named Wilde—' "

Father picked it up:

" 'Who kept herself quite undefiled

" 'By thinking of Jesus,

" 'Contagious diseases,

" 'And the dangers of having a child.'

"Yes, I know; I taught you that limerick. Maureen, you failed to mention the safest route to prudent adultery. Yet I know that you've heard of it; I mentioned it the day I tried to give you an estimate of the amount of fence jumping going on in this county."

"I must have missed it, Father."

"I know I mentioned it. If you've just gotta—and the day might come—tell your husband what is biting you, ask his permission, ask for his help, ask him to stand jigger for you."

"Oh! Yes, you did tell me about two couples like that here in our county . . . but I could never figure out who they are."

"I didn't intend you to. So I threw in a few false clues."

"I discounted for that, sir, knowing you. But I still couldn't guess. Father, that seems so undignified. And wouldn't, uh, my husband be terribly angry?"

"He might give you a fat lip; he won't divorce you for asking. Then he might help you anyhow, on the sound theory that you would get into worse trouble if he says No. And—" Father gave a most evil grin. "—he might discover he enjoys the role."

"Father, I find that I'm shocked."

"Then get over it. Complacent husbands are common throughout history; there is a lot of voyeur in everyone . . . especially in males but females weren't left out. He might jump at the chance to help you . . . because you helped him just that way, six weeks earlier. Stood lookout for him and that young schoolteacher, then you lied like a diplomat to cover up for them. Next commandment."

"Wait a minute, please! I want to talk about this one some more. Adultery."

"And that is just what I'm not going to let you do. You think about it but not a word out of you on this subject for at least two weeks. Next."

"Thou shalt not steal. I couldn't improve that one, Father."

"Would you steal to feed a baby?"

"Uh, yes."

"Think about other exceptions; we'll discuss it in a year or two. But it is a good general rule. But why won't you steal? You're smart; you can probably get away with stealing all your life. Why won't you do it?"

"Uh—"

"Don't grunt."

"Father, you're infuriating! I don't steal because I'm too stinkin' proud!"

"Exactly! Perfect. For the same reason you don't cheat in school, or cheat in games. Pride. Your own concept of yourself. 'To thine own self be true, and it must follow, as the night the day—' "

" '—thou canst not then be false to any man.' Yes, sir."

"But you dropped the 'g' from the participle. Repeat it and this time pronounce it correctly: You don't steal because—"

"I am too . . . *stinking* . . . proud!"

"Good. A proud self-image is the strongest incentive you

can have toward correct behavior. Too proud to steal, too proud to cheat, too proud to take candy from babies or to push little ducks into water. Maureen, a moral code for the tribe must be based on survival for the tribe . . . but for the individual correct behavior in the tightest pinch is based on pride, not on personal survival. This is why a captain goes down with his ship; this is why 'The Guard dies but does not surrender.' A person who has nothing to die for has nothing to live for. Next commandment."

"Simon Legree. Thou shalt not bear false witness against thy neighbor. Until you corrupted me—"

"Who corrupted whom? I am the epitome of moral rectitude . . . because I know exactly why I behave as I do. When I started in on you, you had no morals of any sort and your behavior was as naïvely shameless as that of a kitten trying to cover up on a bare floor."

"Yes, sir. As I was saying: Until you corrupted me, I thought the Ninth Commandment meant: Don't tell lies. But all it says is, if you have to go into court and be a witness, then you have to tell the truth."

"It says more than that."

"Yes. You pointed out that it was a special case of a general theorem. I think the general case ought to read: Don't tell lies that can hurt other people—"

"Close enough."

"Father, you didn't let me finish."

"Oh. Maureen, I beg your pardon. Please go on."

"I said, 'Don't tell lies that can hurt other people' but I intended to add, '—but since you can't guess ahead of time what harm your lies may do, the only safe rule is not to tell any lies at all.'"

Father said nothing for quite a long time. At last he said, "Maureen, this one we will not dispose of in an afternoon. A liar is worse to have around than a thief . . . yet I would rather cope with a liar than with a person who takes self-righteous pride in telling the truth, all of the truth and all of the time, let the chips fall where they may—meaning 'No matter who is hurt by it, no matter what innocent life is ruined.' Maureen, a person who takes smug pride in telling the blunt truth is a sadist, not a saint. There are many sorts of lies, untruths, fibs, nonfactual statements, et cetera. As an exercise to stretch the muscles of your mind—"

"The mind has no muscles."

"Smarty. Don't teach Granmaw how to steal sheep. Your mind has no muscles and that's what I'm trying to correct. Try to categorize logically the varieties of not-true statements. Having done so, try to decide when and where each sort may be used morally, if at all . . . and if not, why not. That should keep you out of mischief for the next fourteen, fifteen months."

"Oh, Father, you're so good to me!"

"Stop the sarcasm or I'll paddle your pants. Bring me a preliminary report in a month or six weeks."

"Thy will be done. Papa, I do have one special case. 'Don't tell fibs to Mother lest thy mouth be washed out with lye soap.' "

"Correction: 'Don't tell any fibs to your mother that she can catch you in.' If you ever told her the ungarnished truth about our private talks, I would have to leave home. If you catch Audrey spooning with that unlikely young cub who's been calling on her, what are you going to tell your mother?"

Father took me by surprise on that one. I had indeed caught Audrey spooning . . . and I had an uneasy suspicion that there had been something more than spooning—and it worried me. "I won't tell Mother anything!"

"That's a good answer. But what are you going to tell me? You know that I don't have your mother's moralistic and puritanical attitudes about sex, and you know—I hope you do—that I won't use anything you tell me to punish Audrey but to help her. So what do you tell your father?"

I felt walls closing in on me, caught between loyalty to Father and my love for my oldest sister, who had always helped me and been good to me. "I— I will— I won't tell you a durn thing!"

"Hooraw! You took the hurdle without even ticking the top rail. Dead right, dear one; we don't tell tales out of school, we don't confess on behalf of someone else. But don't say 'durn.' If you need it, say 'damn.' "

"Yes, sir. I won't tell you a damn thing about Audrey and her young man." (And, dear Lord if there is one, don't let my sister get pregnant; Mother would have fits and pray over her and all would be terrible. Thy will be done . . . but not too much of it. Maureen Johnson. Amen.)

"Let's deal with number ten quickly, then move on to the ones Moses neglected to bring down the mountain. Ten doesn't seem to be a problem to you. Coveted anything lately?"

"I don't think I have. Why is there is a rule against coveting your neighbor's wife but not a word about not coveting your neighbor's husband? Was it an oversight on Jehovah's part? Or was it truly open season on husbands in those days?"

"I don't know, Maureen. I suspect that it was simply conceit on the part of some ancient Hebrews who could not imagine their wives wanting to jump the fence when they had such virile heroes at home. The Old Testament doesn't place women very high; it starts right out with Adam putting all the blame on Mother Eve . . . then it gets worse. But here in Lyle County, Missouri, we do have a rule against it . . . and if any wife catches you making eyes at her husband here, she is likely to scratch out your pretty green eyes."

"I don't intend to let her catch me. But suppose it's the other way. Suppose he covets me, or seems to. Suppose he pinches my bottom?"

"Well, well! Who was he, Maureen? Who is he?"

"Hypothetical case, *mon cher père*."

"Very well. If he hypothetically does it again, you may hypothetically respond in several hypothetical fashions. You may hypothetically ignore him, pretend to a hypothetical lack of sensation in your gluteus maximus sinister—or is he left-handed?"

"I don't know."

"Or you can hypothetically whisper, 'Don't do that here. Meet me after church.' "

"Father!"

"You brought it up. Or, if it suits you, you may hypothetically warn him that one more hypothetical pinch will be reported to your hypothetical father who owns both a hypothetical horsewhip and a hypothetical shotgun. You may say this most privately or shout it loudly enough for the congregation and his hypothetical wife to hear it. Lady's choice. Wait one moment. You did say 'husband,' did you not?"

"I did not say. But that was assumed in the hypothesis, I suppose."

"Maureen, a pinch on the bottom is an expression of direct intent. Encouraged, it leads in three short steps to copulation. You are young but you are physically a mature woman capable of pregnancy. Is it your intention to assume full womanhood in the immediate future?"

3

The Serpent in the Garden

Father's question as to whether or not I was thinking about getting rid of my virginity upset me because I had been thinking about nothing else for weeks. Months, maybe. So I answered, "Of course not! Father, how could you think such a thing?"

"Meeting's adjourned."

"Sir?"

"I thought we had cured you of that sort of trivial fibbing. I see we have not, so quit wasting my time. Come back when you feel the need for serious discussion." He swiveled his chair around to face his desk and raised its roll top.

"Father—"

"Eh? Haven't you left?"

"Please, sir. I've been thinking about it all the time."

"Thinking about what?"

"That. Losing my virginity. Breaking my maidenhead."

He glowered at me. " 'Hymen' is the medical term, as you know. 'Maidenhead' is from that list of Anglo-Saxon synonyms, although it doesn't carry quite the curse that the shorter ones do. But don't talk about 'losing' anything, when in fact you will be achieving your birthright, that supreme status of functioning female that your biological inheritance makes possible."

I thought about his words. "Father, you make it sound so desirable that I should run right out at once and find someone to help me break my hymen. Now. Right away. So, if you will excuse me?" I started to stand up.

"Whoa! Steady there! If that is your intention, it won't hurt to wait ten minutes. Maureen, if you were a heifer, I would say that you are ready to be serviced. But you are not; you are a human maiden faced by a world of human men and women, in a complex and often cruel culture. I think that you will be better off if you wait a year or two. You could even go virgin to your marriage bed—although, as a physician, I know that does not happen too often these modern days. But— What's the Eleventh Commandment?"

" 'Don't get caught.' "

"Where do I hide the French purses?"

"Lower right-hand drawer, and the key is in the top left pigeonhole, all the way back."

I did not do it that day, or that week. Or that month. But it was not many months thereafter.

I did it about ten o'clock in the morning on a balmy day the first week of June, 1897, just four weeks before my fifteenth birthday. The place I picked was the floor of the judges' stand at the race track in the county fairgrounds, with a folded horse blanket to pad the bare boards. I knew the area because I had sat up in that judges' stand on many a frosty morning, clocking Father's practice miles, my eyes lined up on the wire and his fat stopwatch in my hand—I had needed both hands to handle that big watch when I had first done this, at six. That was the year that Father bought Loafer, a black stallion sired by the sire of Maud S.—but (sadly!) not as fast as his famous half sister.

In June of 1897 I went there prepared, resolved to do it, with a condom (a "French purse") in my handbag, and a sanitary napkin—homemade, but all of them were in those days—as I knew that I might bleed and, if anything went wrong, I would have to convince my mother that I was simply three days early that month.

My partner in this "crime" was a high school classmate, a boy named Chuck Perkins, a year older and almost a foot taller than I. I was not even in puppy love with him, but we pretended that we were (perhaps he was not pretending, but how is a girl to know?) and we had been progressively seducing each other all that school year—Chuck was the first man (boy) with whom I opened my mouth to a kiss . . . and from that I formulated another "commandment": "Open thy mouth only if thou planneth to open thy limbs"—for I discovered that I liked it.

How I liked it! Chuck's mouth was sweet; he did not smoke, he kept his teeth clean and they were as sound as my own teeth, and his tongue was sweet and loving against mine. At later times I encountered (too often!) men who did not keep their mouths and breaths sweet . . . and I did not open my mouth. Or anything.

To this day I am convinced that tongue kissing is more intimate than coition.

In preparing for this meeting I had followed also my Fourteenth Commandment: "Thou shalt keep thy secret places as clean as a boiled egg lest thou stink in church," to which my lusty father had added: "—and to hold thy husband's love when thou dost catch one." (I told him I had figured that out.)

Keeping really clean in a house not supplied with running water and too well supplied with running children is not easy. But I had worked out expedients from the time Father had warned me some years earlier. One expedient was to sneak in extra washing behind a locked door in Father's surgery. One of my duties was to place a pitcher of hot water in the surgery each morning and again after lunch, and to refill that pitcher as needed. This put me in position to do washing that Mother did not know about. Mother believed that "Cleanliness is next to Godliness"—but I did not dare give her ideas by letting her catch me giving myself extra scrubbing in places I was supposed to be ashamed to touch; Mother didn't approve of too much washing of "those places" as it could lead to "immodest behavior." (It certainly could!)

At the fairgrounds we left Chuck's horse and buggy in one

of the big empty barns, with a nosebag of oats to keep him happy, then we climbed up into the judges' stand. I led the way, up the back stairs, then up a vertical ladder through the roof of the grandstand and to a trap door in the floor of the judges' stand. I tucked up my skirts, and climbed the ladder ahead of Chuck, and I delighted in the scandalous display I was making of myself. Oh, Chuck had seen my legs before—but men always like to peek.

Once we were both inside the stand I had Chuck close the trap door and drag over it a heavy box—heavy with weights used in racing. "Now they can't possibly reach us," I said gleefully, turned and got a key from a ditching place over a locker, opened its padlock.

"But they can see us, Mo'. This front side is wide open."

"Who cares? Just don't stand in front of the judges' bench. If you can't see them, they can't see you."

"Mo', are you sure you want to do this?"

"Isn't that why we came up here? Here, help me spread this blanket. We'll use it doubled. The judges spread it along the bench to protect their tender behinds. It will keep splinters out of my tender behind, and out of your knees."

Chuck didn't say a word as we made our "bed." I straightened up and looked at him. He did not look like a man about to achieve a joyful consummation long desired; he looked like a scared little boy. "Charles . . . are you sure you want to?"

He looked sheepish. "It's bright sunlight, Mo'. This is awfully public. Maybe we could find a quiet place on the Osage?"

"Chiggers, and mosquitoes, and youngsters hunting muskrats. And they'll pop up just when we're busiest. No, thank you, sir. But, Charles—Charles dear—I thought we were agreed on this? I certainly don't want to rush you into anything. Would you mind canceling the trip to Butler?" (A shopping trip to Butler was my excuse to my parents for asking Chuck to drive me that morning—Butler was not much bigger than Thebes, but it had much better shopping. Bennett and Wheeler Mercantile Company was six times as big as our biggest general store. They even stocked Paris styles—or so they claimed.)

"Why, no, Mo', if you don't want to go."

"Then would you mind swinging past Richard Heiser's house? I need to speak to him." (Chuck, I'm smiling and speaking gently . . . but I would like to massage you with a baseball bat!)

"Uh— Something wrong, Mo'?"

"Yes and no. You know why we came up here. If you don't want my cherry, well, Richard let me know that he wanted it. I didn't promise him anything . . . but I did tell him that I would think about it." I looked up at Chuck and then dropped my eyes. "And I did think about it and decided you were the one I wanted . . . had wanted ever since that time you took me up the bell tower. The school Easter party. You know. But, Charles, if you've changed your mind . . . I still don't intend to let the sun set with me still a virgin. So will you drive me to Richard's house?"

Cruel? Not truly so. A few minutes later I delivered what I had promised. But men are far more timid than we are; sometimes the only way you can get one to move is by placing him in sharpest competition with another male. Even a tabby cat knows that. (By "timid" I do not mean "cowardly." A man—what I think of as a man—can face death calmly. But looking ridiculous . . . as when being surprised in copulation . . . can distress him to his marrow.)

"I haven't changed my mind!" Charles was most emphatic.

I gave him my sunniest smile and opened my arms to him. "Then come here and kiss me like you mean it!"

He did, and we both caught fire again. (His backing and filling had cooled me.) At that time I had never heard the word "orgasm"—I am not sure it had been coined by 1897—but I had done some private experimenting and I knew that it was possible for something strongly resembling fireworks to happen inside me. By the end of that kiss I felt myself getting close to that point.

I pulled my face away just far enough to murmur against his lips: "Dear Charles. I'll take off all my clothes . . . if you want me to."

"Huh? Jeepers, yes!"

"All right. Do you want to undress me?"

He undressed me, or tried to, while I unfastened all the snaps and buttons and ties ahead of him. In a few moments I was bare as a frog and ready to burst into flame. I happily struck a pose I had practiced and let him look. He stared and caught his breath; I felt a fine tingle deep inside me.

Then I closed in on him and started unfastening his buttons and things. He was shy and I didn't push it. But I did get him to take off his trousers and his drawers. I put them on top of mine on the box over the trap door, then sank aown on the blankets. "Charles—"

"Coming!"

"You have a safe?"

"A what?"

"A Merry Widow."

"Oh. Gee, Mo', there isn't any way I can buy them. I'm only sixteen. Pop Green is the only one who sells them . . . and he won't unless you're either married or over twenty-one." The poor dear looked woebegone.

I said quietly, "And we aren't married, and don't want to have to get married—not the way Joe and Amelia had to— my mother would have a fit. But— Quit looking grim and hand me my bag."

He did so, and I got out the condom I had fetched. "There are advantages to being a doctor's daughter, Chuck. I swiped this while I was cleaning Father's clinic. Let's see how it fits." (I wanted to check something else. Having become so acutely conscious of my own cleanliness I had become quite critical of cleanliness in others. Some of my classmates, both sexes, could have used Father's advice and some hot soapy water.)

(I'm a decadent today. The best aspect of Boondock aside from its gentle customs is its wonderful plumbing!)

Chuck looked clean and smelled clean—scrubbed as recently as I was, was my guess. A whiff of male musk, but fresh. Even at that age I had learned the difference.

I felt happy and gay. How sweet of him to offer me such a well-kept toy!

It was just inches from my face. I suddenly ducked and planted a quick kiss on it.

"Hey!" Charles almost squealed.

"Did I shock you, dear? It was just so pretty and sweet that I felt like kissing it. I didn't mean to shock you." (No, but I do want to find your shock point.)

"I wasn't shocked. Uh . . . I liked it."

"Cross your heart and shame the Devil?"

"Yes, indeed!"

"Good." I waited while he got ready. "Now, Charles. Take me."

I was clumsy and inexperienced but nevertheless I had to guide him—gently, as his pride had already been hurt once.

Charles was even less skilled than I. Probably what he knew of sex came from barber shops and pool halls and behind barns—the ignorant boasts of bachelor males . . . whereas I had been taught by an old and wise medical doctor who loved me and wanted me to be happy.

I had in my purse a patent medicine, "Vaseline," to use as a lubricant if I needed it. Not necessary!—I was as slippery as boiled flaxseed.

In spite of that— "Charles! Please, dear! Take it easy. Not so fast."

"But I ought to go fast, first push, Mo'. It'll hurt you less. Everybody knows that."

"Charles, I'm not 'everybody'; I'm me. Take it slowly and it won't hurt me at all. I think." I felt eager, terribly excited, and wanted him deep inside me—but he did feel bigger than I had expected. It didn't really hurt. Or not much. But I knew it could hurt plenty if we did this too fast.

Dear Charles did hold still, his face intent. I bit my lip and tried. And again. At last he was firmly against me and all of him that could reach was inside me.

I relaxed and smiled up at him. "There! That's just fine, dear. Now move if you want to. Do it!"

But I had taken too long. He grinned, then I felt a couple of quick twitches and he stopped smiling and looked distressed. He had spent.

So there weren't any fireworks for Maureen that first trip, and not much for Charles. But I wasn't too disappointed; my prime purpose had been achieved; I was no longer a virgin. I made note to ask Father about how to make it last longer— I was certain that I could have reached those fireworks had I been able to stretch it out a little longer. Then I put it out of my mind and was happy with what I had accomplished.

And started a custom that has stood me in good stead for a long lifetime: I smiled up at him and said softly, "Thank you, Charles. You were splendid."

(Men don't expect to be thanked for it. And at that moment a man is always willing to believe any sort of compliment . . . most especially if he hasn't really earned it and is uneasily aware of his shortcoming. To thank him and compliment him is an easy investment that pays high dividends. Believe me, sister mine!)

"Gosh, Maureen. You're swell."

"You are, too, Chuck sweetheart." I hugged him, arms and legs, then relaxed and added, "Maybe we had better get up. This floor is hard, even with a doubled blanket."

Charles was quiet while he drove us on into Butler—not at all the suave Don Juan who has just relieved a maiden of that which enriched her not. I was encountering for the first time that *tristesse* that some males have after intercourse . . . while I myself was bubblingly happy. I no longer minded that I had missed climax—if I had; I was not sure. Maybe those "fireworks" were something one could do only by oneself. We had gotten away with it cold and I felt very grown up. I sat up straight and enjoyed the beautiful day. I didn't hurt, not enough to matter.

I think men often feel buffeted by sex. They often have so much to lose and we often give them little choice. I am minded of a very odd case that involved one of my grandchildren— how he was pushed around by fate and his first wife.

It involved our cat Pixel, too, at that time a small kitten, all fuzz and buzzes.

My grandson, Colonel Campbell, son of my son Woodrow who is also my husband Theodore, but don't let that worry you; Woodrow and Theodore are both Lazarus Long, who is an odd one in any universe—don't let me forget to tell about the time that Lazarus quite unintentionally got three women pregnant at once, a grandmother, her daughter, and her granddaughter . . . and thereby had to make some unusual arrangements with the Time Corps in order to carry out the first commandment in his own private decalogue, which is: Never leave a pregnant woman to face her destiny unsupported.

Since Lazarus has been knocking them up over centuries in several universes this has taken up quite a bit of his time.

Lazarus quite innocently broke his own first commandment with respect to my grandson's mother, and this mishap resulted indirectly in my grandson marrying my sister wife, Hazel Stone, who was on leave of absence from our family for that purpose . . . for you see (or perhaps you don't) Hazel had to marry Colin Campbell so that these two could rescue Mycroft Holmes IV, the computer that led the Lunar Revolution on time line three, code "Neil Armstrong." Let's skip the details; it's all in *Encyclopaedia Galacta* and other books.

"The operation was a success but the patient died." It was almost that way. The computer was saved and is alive and well and happy in Boondock today. All of the raiding party got away without a scratch . . . except Colin and Hazel Campbell and the kitten, Pixel, all of whom were terribly wounded, and were left dying in a cave in Luna.

I must digress again. In that raiding party was a young officer, Gretchen Henderson, great-great-granddaughter of my sister wife Hazel Stone. Gretchen had had a baby boy four months before this raid, which my grandson knew.

What he did not know was that he was the father of Gretchen's son.

In fact he knew beyond doubt that he had never copulated with Gretchen and knew with equal certainty that he had left no sperm in any donor bank anywhere/when.

Nevertheless Hazel, dying, had told him firmly that he was the father of Gretchen's child.

He had asked how; she had answered, "Paradox."

A time paradox Colin could understand. He was a member of the Time Corps; he had been through time loops; he knew that, in a time paradox, it was possible to turn around and bite oneself in the back of one's own neck.

Therefore he now knew that he was going to inseminate Gretchen somewhere forward on his own time line, somewhere backward on her time line—the inverted loop paradox.

But "God helps those who help themselves." That would happen only if he lived through this squeeze and made it happen.

When the three were rescued shortly after this revelation, Colin had piled up new corpses and had been wounded twice more—but all three were still alive. They were flashed two thousand years into the future to the greatest physicians in any universe: Ishtar and her staff. My sister wife Ishtar won't let a patient die as long as the body is warm and the brain is intact. It took some doing, Pixel especially. The baby creature was held at Kelvin ought point three for several months while Doctor Bone was fetched from another universe and a dozen of Ishtar's best including Ishtar herself were put through a crash course in feline medicine, surgery, physiology, etc. Then they raised Pixel to simple hypothermia, rebuilt him, brought him to blood temperature and wakened him. So today he is a strong, healthy tom, still traveling as he pleases and making kittens wherever he goes.

In the meantime Hazel arranged the time loop and Colin encountered and wooed and won and tumbled and impregnated a somewhat younger Gretchen. So she had her baby, and later on (by her personal time line) she joined Hazel and Colin in saving the computer Mycroft Holmes.

But why such extreme effort over a kitten? Why not give a dying kitten the release he needs to end his pain?

Because, without Pixel and his ability to walk through walls, Mycroft Holmes would not have been rescued, all of the raiding party would have died, and the future of the entire human race would have been placed at risk. The chances were so evenly balanced that in half of the futures they died, in half of them they succeeded. A few ounces of kitten made the difference. He warned them, with the only word he had mastered: "*Blert!*"

On the way back from Butler Charles had recovered from his postcoital depression; he wanted to do it again. Well, so did I, but not that day. That buggy ride over dirt roads had reminded me that what I was sitting on was just a leetle tender.

But Charles was raring to go; he wanted an encore right now. "Mo', there is a spot just ahead there where we can get a buggy clear off the road and out of sight. Quite safe."

"No, Chuck."

"Why not?"

"It's not perfectly safe; anybody else could pull off there, too. We're late now and I don't want to have to answer questions today. Not this day. And we don't have another Merry Widow and that settles it because while I do plan to have children, I don't want to have them at fifteen."

"Oh."

"Quite so. Be patient, dear, and we will do it again . . . another day, with careful arrangements . . . which you might be thinking about. Now take your hand away, please; there is a rig coming down the road—see the dust?"

Mother did not scold me over being a half hour late. But she did not press Charles when he refused her offer of lemonade, on the excuse that he had to get Ned (his gelding) home and curried and the buggy wiped down because his parents were going to need it. (A too complex lie—I'm sure he simply did not want to meet Mother's eye, or be questioned by her. I'm glad Father taught me to avoid fancy lies.)

Mother went upstairs as soon as Chuck left; I went out back.

Two years earlier Father had indulged us in a luxury many of our church members felt was sinfully wasteful: two outhouses, one for the boys and one for us girls, just like at school. In fact we truly needed them. That day I was delighted to find the girls' privy empty. I flipped the bar to lock, and checked up.

Some blood, not much. No problems. Slightly sore, nothing more.

So I sighed with relief and peed and reassembled myself, and went back to the house, picking up a piece of stove wood for the kitchen as I passed the wood pile—a toll each of us paid for each trip out back.

I dropped off the wood and stopped in the wash shed adjoining the kitchen, washed my hands and sniffed them. Clean. Just my guilty conscience. I went to the clinic, stopping only to tousle Lucille's strawberry hair and pat her bottom. Lucy was three, I think—yes, she was born in '94, the year after Father and I went to Chicago. She was a little doll, always merry. I decided that I wanted one just like her . . . but not this year. But soon. I was feeling very female.

I reached the clinic just as Mrs. Altschuler was leaving. I spoke politely; she looked at me and said, "Audrey, you've been out in the sun without a sunbonnet again. Don't you know any better than that?"

I thanked her for her interest in my welfare and went on in. According to Father all she suffered from was constipation and lack of exercise . . . but she showed up at least twice a month and had not, since the first of the year, paid a single penny. Father was a strong man, firm-minded, but not good at collecting money from people who owed it to him.

Father entered her visit in his book and looked up. "I'm taking your bishop, young lady."

"Sure you don't want to change your mind, sir?"

"No. I may be wrong but I'm certain. Why? Have I made a mistake?"

"I think so, sir. Mate in four moves."

"Eh?" Father stood up, went over to his chess table. "Show me."

"Shall we simply play it out? I may be mistaken."

"Grrummph! You'll be the death of me, girl." He studied the board, then went back to his desk. "This will interest you. This morning's mail. From Mr. Clemens—"

"Oh, my!"

I remember especially one paragraph:

"I agree with you and the Bard, sir; let's hang them. Hanging its lawyers might not correct all of this country's woes but it would be lots of fun and could do no harm to anyone.

"Elsewhere I have noted that the Congress is the only distinct criminal class this country has. It cannot be mere coincidence that 97 percent of Congress are lawyers."

Mr. Clemens added that his lecture agency had scheduled him for Kansas City next winter. "I recall that four years ago we failed of rendezvous in Chicago by a week. Is it possible that you will be in K.C. January tenth, next?"

"Oh, Father! Could we?"

"School will be in session."

"Father, you know that I made up all time lost by going to Chicago. You know, too, that I am first among the girls in my class . . . and could be first including the boys if you hadn't cautioned me about the inadvisability of appearing too smart. But what you may not have noticed is that I have enough credits and could have graduated—"

"—with Tom's class last week. I noticed. We'll work on it. *Deus volent* and the crick don't rise. Did you get what you wanted in Butler?"

"I got what I wanted. But not in Butler."

"Eh?"

"I did it, Father. I am no longer virgin."

His eyebrows shot up. "You have managed to surprise me."

"Truly, Father?" (I didn't want him to be angry with me . . . and I thought that he had implied long back that he would not be.)

"Truly. Because I thought that you had managed it last Christmas vacation. I have been waiting the past six months, hoping that you would decide to trust me with it."

"Sir, I didn't even consider keeping it from you. I depend on you."

"Thank you. Mmm, Maureen, freshly deflowered, you should be examined. Shall I call your mother?"

"Oh! Does Mother have to know?"

"Eventually, yes. But you need not have her examining you if it frets you—"

"It does!"

"In that case I'll take you over to see Dr. Chadwick."

"Father, why must I see Dr. Chadwick? It is a natural event, I was not hurt, and I feel no need."

We had a polite argument. Father pointed out that an ethical doctor did not treat members of his own family, especially his womenfolk. I answered that I was aware of that . . . but that I needed no treatment. And back and forth.

After a bit, having made sure that Mother was upstairs for her nap, Father took me into the surgery, locked the door, and helped me up onto the table, and I found myself in much the position for examination that I had been in earlier for Charles, except that this time I had removed only my bloomers.

I suddenly realized that I had become excited.

I tried to suppress it and hoped that Father would not notice it. Even at fifteen I was not naïve about my unusual and possibly unhealthy relation with my father. As early as twelve I had had the desert-isle daydream with my father as the other castaway.

But I also knew how strong the taboo was from the Bible, from classic literature, and from myth. And I remembered all too well how Father quit letting me sit on his lap, had stopped it completely and utterly, once I reached menarche.

Father put on a pair of rubber gloves. This was something he had started as a result of the Chicago trip . . . which had not been to allow Maureen to enjoy the Columbian Exposition but to permit Father to attend school at Northwestern University in Evanston in order to get up to date on Professeur Pasteur's germ theories.

Father had always been strong for soap and water, but he had had no science to back up his attitudes. His preceptor, Dr. Phillips, had started practice in 1850, and (so said Father) regarded the rumors from France as "just what you could expect from a bunch of Frogs."

After Father returned from Evanston, nothing ever again

could be clean enough to suit him. He started using rubber gloves and iodine, and boiling and sometimes burning used instruments, especially anything used with lockjaw.

Those impersonal clammy rubber gloves cooled me down . . . but I was embarrassed to realize that I was quite wet.

I ignored it, Father ignored it. Shortly he helped me down and turned away to strip off his gloves while I got back into my bloomers. Once I was "decent" he unlocked and opened the door. "Healthy, normal woman," he said gruffly. "You should have no trouble bearing offspring. I recommend that you refrain from intercourse for a few days. I conclude that you used a French purse. Correct?"

"Yes, sir."

"Good. If you will continue to use them . . . every time! . . . and are discreet about your public conduct, you should have no serious problems. Hmm— Do you feel up to another buggy ride?"

"Why, certainly, sir. Is there any reason why I should not?"

"No. Word came in that Jonnie Mae Igo's latest baby is ailing; I promised to try to get out there today. Will you ask Frank to hitch up Daisy?"

It was a long drive. Father took me along to tell me about Ira Howard and the Foundation. I listened, unable to believe my ears . . . save that Father, the only utterly dependable source of information, was telling me.

After a long stretch I at last spoke up. "Father, I think I see. How does this differ from prostitution? Or does it?"

4

The Worm in the Apple

Father let Daisy amble on quite a piece before he answered, "I suppose it is prostitution, if you want to stretch the definition to cover it. It does involve payment, not for intercourse per se, but for the result of that intercourse, a baby. The Howard Foundation will not pay you to marry a man on their list, nor is he paid for marrying you. In fact you are never paid; he is paid . . . for every baby you bear, sired by him."

I listened and found myself humiliated by these arrangements. I was never one of those women demanding the vote . . . but fair is fair! Somebody was going to inseminate me . . . then, when I groaned and moaned the way Mother does and gave birth to a baby, he got paid. I fumed to myself.

"It still sounds like whoring, Father, from where I sit. What's the going rate? How much does my hypocritical, hypothetical husband get paid for each set of my labor pains and one smelly baby?"

"No set price."

"What? *Mon papa,* that is a hell of a way to run a business. I lie down and spread my legs, by contract. Nine months later my husband is paid . . . five dollars? Fifty cents? This is not a good bet. I think I would be better off to move to Kansas City and walk the streets."

"Maureen. Behave yourself."

I took a deep breath, and held it. Then I lowered my voice an octave, the way I had been practicing lately. (I had promised myself never to let my voice get shrill.) "I'm sorry, sir. I guess I'm just another vaporish ex-virgin—I had thought I was more grown up." I sighed. "But it does seem crass."

"Yes, perhaps 'crass' is *le mot juste.* But let me tell you how it works. No one will ask you to marry anyone. If you consent, your mother and I will submit your name to the Foundation, along with a questionnaire that I will help you fill out. In return they will send you a list of young men. Each man on that list will be what is called an 'eligible bachelor'— eligible quite aside from the Foundation and its money.

"He will be young, not more than ten years older than you are, but more likely about your age—"

"Fifteen?" I was amazed. Shocked.

"Simmer down, flame top. Your name is not yet on the list. I'm telling you this now because it is not fair not to let you know about the Howard Foundation option once you have graduated to functioning woman. But you're still too young to marry."

"In this state I can marry at twelve. With your permission."

"You have my permission to marry at twelve. If you can manage it."

"Father, you're impossible."

"No, merely improbable. He'll be young but older than fifteen. He will be of good health and of good reputation. He will be of adequate education—"

"He had better be able to speak French, or he won't fit into this family." The Thebes school system offered French and German; Edward had picked French, then Audrey also, because both Father and Mother had studied French, and made a habit of shifting to French when they wanted to talk privately in front of us. Audrey and Edward established a precedent; we all followed. I started on French before I could take it in school; I did not like having words talked in front of me that I did not understand.

This precedent affected my whole life—but, again, that's another story.

"You can teach him French—including that French kissing you asked me about. Now this faceless stranger who ruined our Nell— Can he kiss?"

"Gorgeously!"

"Good. Was he sweet to you, Maureen?"

"Quite sweet. A bit timid but he'll get over that, I think. Uh, Father, it wasn't as much fun as I think it could be. And will be, next time."

"Or maybe the time after that. What you're saying is that today's trial run was not as satisfying as masturbation. Correct?"

"Well, yes, that is what I meant. It was over too fast. He— Goodness, you know who drove me to Butler. Chuck. Charles Perkins. He's sweet, *cher papa*, but . . . he knows less about it than I do."

"So I would expect. I taught you, and you were an apt student."

"Did you teach Audrey . . . before she got married?"

"Your mother taught her."

"So? I suspect that you taught me more. Uh, was Audrey's marriage sponsored by the Howard Foundation? Is that how she met Jerome?"

"That is a question never asked, Maureen. It would be polite not even to speculate."

"Well, excuse my bare face!"

"I won't excuse your naked manners. I never discuss your private affairs with your siblings; you should not ask me about theirs."

I suddenly felt the curb bit. "I'm sorry, sir. This is all new to me."

"Yes. This young man—these young men—will all be acceptable prospects . . . or, if I don't approve of one, I'll tell you why and not permit him in my house. But in addition to everything else, each one will have four living grandparents."

"What's special about that? I not only have four living grandparents but also eight living great-grandparents. Have I not?"

"Yes. Although Grampaw McFee is a waste of space. If he had died at ninety-five he would have been better off. But that is what this is all about, dear daughter; Ira Howard wanted his fortune used to extend human life. The Foundation trustees have chosen to treat it as if it were a stock breeding problem. Do you recall the papers on Loafer, and the reason I paid a high price for him? Or the papers on Clytemnestra? You have long life in your ancestry, Maureen, all branches. If you marry a young man on the list, your children will have long life in all their branches."

Father turned in his seat and looked me in the eye. "But nobody—nobody!—is asking you to do anything. If you authorize me to submit your name—not today but let's say next year—it simply means that you will have six or eight or ten or more additional suitors to choose from, instead of being effectively limited to the few young men near your age in Lyle County. If you decide to marry Charles Perkins, I won't say a word. He's healthy, he's well behaved. And he's not my cup of tea. But he may be yours."

(He was not my cup of tea, either, Papa. I guess I was just using him. But I'd promised him a return match . . . so I would have to.)

"Father, suppose we hold off until next year?"

"I think that is sound judgment, Maureen. In the meantime, don't get pregnant and try not to get caught. Oh, by the way— If you submit your name and a young man on the list comes along, if you wish, you can try him out on the parlor sofa." He smiled. "More convenient and safer than the judges' stand."

"Mother would have heart failure!"

"No, she would not. Because that is exactly the arrangement her mother provided for her . . . and that is why Edward was officially a premature baby. Because it is stupid to go the Howard route, then find out after you're committed by marriage vows that the two of you are infertile with each other."

I had no answer. Mother . . . my mother who thought "breast" was a dirty word and that "belly" was outright profanity . . . Mother with her bloomers off, bouncing her bawdy buttocks on Grandma Pfeiffer's sofa, making a baby out of wedlock, while Grandma and Grandpa pretended not to know what was going on! It was easier to believe in virgin birth and transubstantiation and resurrection and Santa Claus and the Easter Bunny. We are strangers, all of us, family most of all.

Shortly we pulled into the Jackson Igo place, eighty acres, mostly rocks and hills, a shack and a sorry barn. Mr. Igo cropped it a bit but it didn't seem possible that the place supported him and his thin, tired wife and his swarm of dirty children. Mostly Jackson Igo cleaned cesspools and built privies.

Some of those children and half a dozen dogs gathered round our buggy; one boy ran shouting into the house. Presently Mr. Igo came out. Father called out, "Jackson!"

"Yeah, Doc."

"Get these dogs away from my rig."

"They ain't no harm."

"Do it. I won't have them jumping up on me."

"Jest as you say, Doc. Cleveland! Jefferson! Get them hounds! Take 'em around back."

The order was carried out; Father got down with a quiet word over his shoulder, "Stay in the buggy."

Father was inside their shack only a short time, which suited me, as the oldest boy, Caleb, my age or near it, was pestering me to get down and come see a new litter of pigs. I knew him from school, where he had attended fifth grade for some years. He was, in my opinion, a likely candidate for lynching if some father did not kill him first. I had to tell him to get away from Daisy and quit bothering her; he was causing her to toss her head and back away from him. I took the whip out of its socket to point up my words.

I was glad to see Father reappear.

He climbed into the buggy without a word. I clucked to Daisy and we got out of there. Father was frowning like a thunder cloud, so I kept quiet.

A quarter of a mile down the road he said, "Please pull over onto the grass," so I did, and said to Daisy, "Whoa, girl," and waited.

"Thank you, Maureen. Will you help me wash, please?"

"Certainly, sir." This buggy, used for his country calls and specially built by the carriage wrights who built his racing sulkies, had a larger baggage space in back, with a rain cover. In it were carried a number of items that Father might need on a call but which did not belong in his black bag. One was a coal oil can with a spout, filled with water, and a tin basin, and soap and toweling.

This time he wanted me to pour water over his hands. Then he soaped them; I rinsed them by pouring. He shook them dry; then washed them all over again in the basin and dried them after shaking, on clean toweling.

He sighed. "That's better. I did not sit down in there, I did not touch anything I could avoid touching. Maureen, remember that bathtub we used in Chicago?"

"I certainly do!" The World's Fair had been an endless wonder and I'll never forget my first view of the Lake and my first ride on a railroad train up high in the air . . . but I dreamed about that tub, all white enamel, and hot water up to my chin. I could be seduced for a hot bath. They say every woman has her price. That's mine.

"Mrs. Malloy charged us two bits for each bath. This minute I would happily pay her two dollars. Maureen, I need glycerine and rose water. In my bag. Please."

Father compounded this lotion himself and it was intended primarily for chapped hands. Right now he needed it to soothe his hands against the strong lye soap he had just used.

Once back on the road he said, "Maureen, that baby was dead long before Jackson Igo sent for me. Since last night, I estimate."

I tried to feel sorry about that baby. But growing up in that household was no fate to wish on anyone. "Then why did he send for you?"

"To bless the death. To get me to write a death certificate, to keep him from trouble with the law when he buries it . . . which he is probably doing this very minute. Primarily to cause me—and you—to make a six-mile round trip to save himself the trouble of harnessing his mule and coming into town." Father laughed without mirth. "He kept pointing out that I couldn't charge him for a call since I didn't get there before the baby died. I finally said, 'Shut up, Jackson. You haven't paid me a cent since Cleveland beat Harrison.' He said something about hard times and how this administration never does anything for the farmer."

Father sighed. "I didn't argue with him; he had a point. Maureen, you've been keeping my books this past year; would you say these were hard times?"

That brought me up sharp. I had been thinking about the Howard Foundation and Chuck's pretty penis. "I don't know, Father. But I know that you have far more on the books than you ever get paid. I've noticed something else, too: the worst of the deadbeats would rather owe you a dollar for a house call than fifty cents for an office visit. Like Jackson Igo."

"Yes. He could have fetched that little cadaver in—never saw a child so dehydrated!—but I'm relieved that he did not; I don't want him in my clean clinic . . . or Adele's clean house. You've seen the books; do you estimate that collections are enough to support our family? Food, clothing, shelter, oats and hay, and a nickel for Sunday School?"

I thought about it. I knew my multiplication tables through twenty times twenty, same as everybody, and in high school I had been learning the delights of more advanced ciphering. But I had never applied any of it to our household affairs. Now I drew a blackboard in my mind and did some hard calculating.

"Father . . . if they all paid you what they owe you, we would be quite comfortable. But they don't pay you, not enough of them." I thought. "Nevertheless we are comfortable."

"Maureen, if you don't want the Howard option, better marry a rich man. Not a country doctor."

Presently he shrugged and smiled. "Don't worry about it. We'll keep food on the table even if I have to slide over into Kansas and rustle cattle. Shall we sing? 'Pop Goes the Weasel' would be appropriate today. How is your weasel by now, dear? Sore?"

"Father, you are a dirty old man and you will come to a bad end."

"I've always hoped so, but I've been too busy raising *Kinder* to raise Cain. Meant to tell you: Someone else is interested in your welfare. Old lady Altschuler."

"So I know." I told him about her remark. "She thinks I'm Audrey."

"That unspeakable old cow. But she may not really think you are Audrey. She asked me what you were doing in the grandstand at the fairgrounds."

"Well! What did you tell her?"

"I told her nit. Silence is all a snoopy question deserves . . . just fail to hear it. But the insult direct is still better. Which I handed that snapping turtle by ignoring her question and telling her next time to bathe before she comes to see me, as I found her personal hygiene to be less than adequate. She was not pleased." He smiled. "She may be so angry that she will switch to Dr. Chadwick. One may hope."

"One may. So somebody saw us go up. Well, sir, they did

not actually see us doing it." I told Father about the box heavy with weights. "Spectators would have to have been in a balloon."

"I would say so. Safe enough if not very comfortable. I wish I could extend to you the courtesy of the sofa . . . but I can't until you take up the Howard option. If you do. In the meantime let's think about it. Safe places."

"Yes, sir. Thank you. What I can't figure out is this: We trimmed the trip to Butler short, in order to conceal the time used up in unscheduled activity. I've been figuring times and distances in my head. *Cher papa,* unless my arithmetic is wrong—"

"It never is."

"Whoever spotted us climbing up into my hideaway must then have proceeded at a fast trot to the Altschuler place, reported my sins, then the Ugly Duchess must have been already dressed, with her buggy hitched and ready, to hurry over to see you. When did she show up?"

"Let me see. When she arrived, three patients were waiting. I made her wait her turn . . . so she came in already angry. I sent her out boiling mad. Mmm . . . she must have arrived at least an hour before you showed up and bumped into her coming out."

"Father, it won't work. Physically impossible. Unless she herself was at the fairgrounds, then drove straight to our house on the pretense of needing to see you."

"That's possible. Quite unlikely. But, Maureen, you have just encountered a phenomenon that you will see again and again all your life after this red-letter day: the only thing known to science faster than the speed of light is Mrs. Grundy's gossip."

"I guess so."

"I know so. When you next encounter it, how will you handle it? Do you have that in your commandments?"

"Uh, no."

"Think about it. How will you defend yourself?"

I thought about it for the next half mile. "I won't."

"Won't what?"

"I won't defend myself against gossip; I will ignore it. At most I will look her—or him—in the eye and state loudly, 'You are a filthy-minded liar.' But it's usually best to ignore it entirely. I think."

"I think so, too. People of that sort want to be noticed.

The cruelest thing you can do to them is to behave as if they did not exist."

During the remaining half of 1897 I ignored Mrs. Grundy while trying to avoid being noticed by her. My public persona was straight out of Louisa M. Alcott while in private I tried to learn more about this amazing new art. I don't mean to imply that I spent much time on my back, sweating away for the mutual pleasure of Maureen and His Name Is Legion. Not in Lyle County, not in 1897. Too hard to find a place to do it!

"Conscience is that little voice that tells you that someone may be watching." (Anon. and Opcit.)

And there was the problem of a satisfactory partner. Charles was a nice boy and I did offer him that encore, and even a third try at it for good measure. The second and third attempts were more comfortable but even less exciting—cold mush without sorghum and cream.

So after the third one I told Charles that someone had seen us on top of Marston Hill and had told one of my sisters . . . and a good thing that it hadn't been one of my brothers, because I had been able to cool things down with my sister. But he and I had better act as if we had quarreled . . . or next time the word might get all the way to my mother, who would tell my father, and then there was just no telling. So you had better leave me alone until school starts, huh? You see, don't you, dear?

I learned that the hardest problem of all in dealing with a man is how to stop dealing with him when he does not want to stop. A century and a half of quite varied experience has not given me any answer that is totally satisfactory.

One partly satisfactory answer that I did not learn until much later than 1897 requires considerable skill, great self-control, and some sophistication: the intentional "dead arse." Lie there like a dead woman and, above all, let your inner muscles be utterly relaxed. If you combine that with garlic on your breath, it is likely—although not certain—that he will save you the trouble of thinking of a reason to break off. Then, when he initiates a break, you can be brave about it. A "good sport."

I am not suggesting that lively hips and tight muscles constitute "sex appeal." Such qualities, while useful, are merely equivalent to sharp tools for a carpenter. My sister wife Tamara, mother of our sister wife Ishtar and at one time the most celebrated whore in all Secundus, is the epitome of sex appeal . . . yet she is not especially pretty and no one who has slept with her talks about her technique. But their faces light up when they see her and their voices throb when they speak of her.

I asked Jubal Harshaw about Tammy because Jubal is the most analytical of my husbands. He said, "Mama Maureen, quit pulling my leg. You of all people know the answer."

I denied it.

"All right," he said, "but I still think you are fishing. Sex appeal is the outer evidence of deep interest in your partner's pleasure. Tammy's got it. So have you and just as strongly. It is not your red hair, wench, or even the way you smell, which is yummy. It is the way you give . . . when you give."

Jubal got me so stirred up that I tripped him, then and there.

But in Lyle County in 1897 one cannot simply trip a darling man and have at it; Mrs. Grundy is sitting up in every tree, eager to catch you and publish it. So the preliminaries must be more complex. There are plenty of eager males (about twelve in every dozen) but it is necessary to pick the one you want—age, health, cleanliness, personal charm, discretion (if he gossips to you, he will gossip about you), and other factors that vary with each candidate. Having selected him for the slaughter you must cause him to decide that he wants you while letting him know silently that it is possible. That is easy to phrase but to put it into practice— You'll be honing your skills for a lifetime.

So you reach an agreement . . . but you still haven't found a place.

After picking a place to shed my virginity I resigned that aspect of the problem. If a boy/man wanted my immoral carcass, he would get his gray matter churning and solve it. Or he could go chase flies.

But I did risk chiggers and (once) poison ivy. He caught it; I seem to be immune.

From June to January three boys ranging sixteen to twenty had me, and one married man of thirty-one. I added him in on the assumption (false) that a married man would be so skilled that he could set off those fireworks without fail.

Total copulations: nine. Orgasms: three—and one was wonderful. Time actually spent copulated: an average of five minutes per go, which is not nearly enough. I learned that life can be beautiful indeed . . . but that the males of my circle ranged from clumsy to awkward.

Mrs. Grundy apparently did not notice me.

By New Year's Eve I had decided to ask Father to submit my name to the Howard Foundation . . . not for the money (I still did not know that the payments could amount to enough to matter) but because I would welcome a chance to meet more eligible males; the hunting in Lyle County was too poor to suit Maureen. I had firmly made up my mind that, while sex might not be the be all and end all, I did want to marry and it had to be a man who would make me eager to go to bed early.

In the meantime I kept on trying to make Maureen as desirable a female animal as I could manage and I listened most carefully to my father's advice. (I knew that what I really wanted was a man just like my father, but twenty-five years younger. Or twenty. Make that fifteen. But I was prepared to settle for the best imitation I could find.)

There were two hundred days left in 1897 from that day Chuck and I climbed up into the judges' stand; that makes 200 x 24 x 60 = 288,000 minutes. Circa 45 of those minutes I spent copulated; that leaves 199 days, 23 hours, 15 minutes. It is obvious that I had time for other things.

That summer was one of the best of my life. While I did not get laid very often or very effectively, the idea was on my mind awake and asleep. It brightened my eyes and my days; I shed female pheromones like a female moth and I never stopped smiling—picnics, swimming parties in the Osage (you wouldn't believe what we wore), country dances (frowned on by the Methodist and Baptist churches but sponsored by Jack Mormons who welcomed gentiles who might be converted—Father overruled Mother; I went and learned to swing on the corners and dosey-doh), watermelon contests, any excuse to get together.

I stopped thinking about the University of Missouri at Columbia. From Father's books I could see that there just wasn't money to put me through four years of college. I was not anxious to be a nurse or a school teacher, so there seemed to be little point in my aspiring to formal (and expensive) higher education. I would always be a bookworm but that does not require a college degree.

So I decided to be the best housewife I could manage—starting with cooking.

I had always taken my turn in the kitchen along with my sisters. I had been assistant cook for the day in rotation since my twelfth birthday. By fifteen I was a good plain cook.

I decided to become a good fancy cook.

Mother remarked on my increased interest. I told her the truth, or some of it. "*Chère mama,* I expect to be married someday. I think the best wedding present I can bring my future husband is good cooking. I may not have the talent to become a gourmet chef. But I can try."

"Maureen, you can be anything you want to be. Never forget that."

She helped me, and she taught me, and she sent away to New Orleans for French cookbooks, and we pored over them together. Then she sent me for three weeks to stay with Aunt Carole, who taught me Cajun skills. Aunt Carole was a Johnny Reb, married after the War to—Heavens!—a damn Yankee, Father's eldest brother, Uncle Ewing, now deceased. Uncle Ewing had been in the Union occupation of New Orleans, and had poked a sergeant in the nose over a distressed Southern girl. It got him a reduction from corporal to private, and a wife.

In Aunt Carole's house we never discussed the War.

The War was not often discussed in our own house as the Johnsons were not native to Missouri, but to Minnesota. Being newcomers, by Father's policy we avoided subjects that might upset our neighbors. In Missouri sympathies were mixed—a border state and a slave state, it had veterans from both sides. But that part of Missouri had been "local option"—some towns never had had any slaves and now permitted no colored people; Thebes was one such. But Thebes itself was so small and unimportant that the Union troops had ignored it when they came through there in '65, burning and looting. They burned Butler to the ground and it never fully recovered. But Thebes was untouched.

Even though the Johnsons had come down from the North,

we were not carpetbaggers as Missouri never seceded; Reconstruction did not touch it. Uncle Jules, Father's cousin in Kansas City, explained our migration this way:

"After fighting four years in Dixie, we went back home to Minnesota . . . and stayed just long enough to pack up again and git. Missourah ain't as hot as Dixie but it ain't so cold that the shadows freeze to the sidewalks and the cows give ice cream."

Aunt Carole put a polish on my cooking and I was in and out of her kitchen quite a lot until I married. It was during that three weeks that the matter of the lemon pie took place— I think I mentioned it earlier.

I baked that pie. It was not my best work; I had burned the crust. But it was one of four, and the other three were all right. Getting the temperature just right on a wood range is tricky.

But how did my cousin Nelson get that pie into church without anyone seeing it? How did he slide it under me without my noticing it?

He made me so furious that I went straight home (to Aunt Carole's house), then, when Nelson showed up to apologize, I burst into tears and took him straight to bed . . . and had one of those three fireworks occasions.

Sudden impulse and quite reckless and we got away with it cold.

Thereafter I let Nelson have me from time to time when we could figure out a safe way right up to my wedding. Which did not quite finish it, as years later he moved to Kansas City.

I should have behaved myself with Nelson; he was only fourteen.

But a smart fourteen. He knew that we didn't dare get caught; he knew that I couldn't marry him no matter what and he realized that he could get me pregnant and that a baby would be disaster for each of us.

That Sunday morning he held still while I put a French purse on him, grinned and said, "Maureen, you're smart." Then he tackled me with unworried enthusiasm and brought me to orgasm in record time.

For the next two years I kept Nelson supplied with Merry Widows. Not for me; I carried my own. For his harem. I started him off; he took up the sport with zeal and native genius, and never got into trouble. Smart.

•   •   •

Besides cooking, I endeavored to straighten out Father's accounts receivable, with less success. After consulting with Father I sent out some polite and friendly dunning letters. Have you ever written over one hundred letters, one after another, by hand? I found out why Mr. Clemens had grabbed the first opportunity to shift from pen to typewriter—first author to do so.

"Dear Mr. Deadbeat:

"In going over Dr. Johnson's books I find that your account stands at umpteen dollars and that you have made no payment on it since March 1896. Perhaps this is an oversight. May we expect payment by the first of the month?

"If it is not possible for you to pay the full amount at once, will you please call at the clinic this Friday the tenth so that we can work out arrangements mutually satisfactory?

"The Doctor sends his good wishes to you and to Mrs. Deadbeat, and also to Junior and the twins and little Knothead.

> "I remain,
>> "Faithfully yours,
>>> "Maureen Johnson
>>> "(On behalf of Ira Johnson, M.D.)"

I showed Father sample letters ranging from gentle to firm to tough; the sample above shows what we used on most of them. With some he said, "Don't dun them. They would if they could, but they can't." Nevertheless I sent out more than a hundred letters.

For each letter postage was two cents, stationery about three. Can we reckon my time as worth five cents per letter? If so, each letter comes to a dime, and the whole mailing cost slightly over ten dollars.

Those hundred letters did not bring in as much as ten dollars in cash.

About thirty patients came in to talk to us about it. Perhaps half of those fetched some payment in kind—fresh eggs, a ham, side meat, garden truck, fresh bread, and so forth. Six or seven arranged schedules of payment; some of those actually met their promises.

But over seventy totally ignored the letters.

I was upset and disappointed. These were not shiftless peckerwoods like Jackson Igo; these were respectable farmers and townspeople. These were people for whom my father had gotten up in the middle of the night, dressed, then driven or ridden horseback through snow or rain, dust or mud or frozen ruts, to attend them or their children. And when he asked to be paid, they ignored it.

I couldn't believe it.

I asked, "Father, what do I do now?" I expected him to tell me to forget it, as he had been dubious as to the usefulness of these letters. I awaited his response with anticipated relief.

"Send each of them the tough one and mark it, 'Second Notice.' "

"You think that will do it, sir?"

"No. But it will do some good. You'll see."

Father was right. That second mailing brought in no money. It fetched a number of highly indignant replies, some of them scurrilous. Father had me file each with its appropriate case record, but make no reply.

Most of those seventy patients never showed up again. This was the good result Father expected. He was cheerful about it. "Maureen, it's a standoff; they don't pay me and I don't do them much good. Iodine, calomel, and Aspirin—that's about all we have today that isn't a sugar pill. The only times I'm certain of results are when I deliver a baby or set a bone or cut off a leg.

"But, damn it all, I'm doing the best I know how. I do try. If a man gets angry at me simply because I ask him to pay for my services . . . well, I see no reason why I should get out of a warm bed to physic him."

Eighteen ninety-seven was the year that the Katy ran a line not a mile from our town square, so the council extended the city limits and that put Thebes on the railroad. That brought the telegraph to Thebes, too, which enabled the *Lyle County Leader* to bring the news to us direct from Chicago. But still only once a week; the *Kansas City Star* by mail was usually quicker. The Bell telephone reached us, too, although at first only from nine to nine and never on Sunday mornings, because the switchboard was in the Widow Loomis's parlor and service stopped when she was not there.

The *Leader* published a glowing editorial: "Modern Times."

Father frowned. "They point out that it will soon be possible, as more people subscribe, to call for a doctor in the middle of the night. Yes, yes, surely. Today I make night calls because somebody is in such trouble that some member of the patient's family has hitched up in the middle of the night and driven here to ask me to come.

"But what happens when he can rout me out of bed just by cranking a little crank? Will it be for a dying child? No, Maureen, it will be for a hangnail. Mark my words; the telephone signals the end of the house call. Not today, not tomorrow, but soon. They will ride a willing horse to death . . . and you will see the day when medical doctors will refuse to make house calls."

At New Year's, I told Father that I had made up my mind: I wanted him to put my name in to the Howard Foundation.

Before the end of January I received the first of the young men on my list.

By the end of March I had received all seven of them. In three cases I did go so far as to avail myself of the privilege of the sofa . . . although I used the couch in Father's office, and locked the door.

Wet firecrackers.

Decent enough young men, those three, but . . . to marry? No.

Maureen felt glum about the whole matter.

But on Saturday the second of April Father received a letter from Rolla, Missouri:

"My dear Doctor:

"Permit me to introduce myself. I am a son of Mr. and Mrs. John Adams Smith of Cincinnati, Ohio, where my father is a tool and die maker. I am a senior at the School of Mines of the University of Missouri at Rolla, Missouri. I was given your name and address by Judge Orville Sperling, of Toledo, Ohio, Executive Secretary of the Howard Foundation. Judge Sperling tells me that he has written to you about me.

"If I may do so, I will call on you and Mrs. Johnson on Sunday afternoon the seventeenth of April. Then, if you permit, I ask to be presented to your daughter Miss Maureen

Johnson for the purpose of offering myself as a possible suitor for her hand in marriage.

"I welcome any investigation you care to make of me and I will answer fully and frankly any questions you put to me.

"I look forward to your reply.

> "I remain, sir,
> "Faithfully your servant,
> "Brian Smith"

Father said, "See, my dear daughter? Your knight comes riding."

"Probably has two heads. Father, it's no good. I shall die an old maid, at the age of ninety-seven."

"Not a fussy old maid, I trust. What shall I tell Mr. Smith?"

"Oh, tell him Yes. Tell him I'm drooling with eagerness."

"Maureen."

"Yes, Father. I'm too young to be cynical, I know. *Quel dommage.* I will straighten up and give Mr. Brian Smith my best smile and approach the meeting with cheerful optimism. But I have grown a bit jaundiced. That last orangutan—"

(That ape had tried to rape me, right on Mother's sofa, just as soon as Mother and Father went upstairs. He then left abruptly, clutching his crotch. My study of anatomy had paid off.)

"I'll tell him that we will welcome him. Sunday the seventeenth. That's two weeks from tomorrow."

I greeted Sunday the seventeenth with little enthusiasm. But I did stay home from church and prepared a picnic lunch, and grabbed the chance for an extra bath. Mr. Smith turned out to be presentable and well spoken, if not especially inspiring. Father grilled him a bit and Mother offered him coffee; about two we got away—Daisy and a family buggy, with his livery stable nag left in our barn.

Three hours later I was certain that I was in love.

Brian made a date to come back on the first of May. He had final examinations to get out of the way in the meantime.

One week later, Sunday the twenty-fourth of April, 1898, Spain declared war on the United States.

5

Exit from Eden

This is not a bad jail, as jails go. I was in a much worse one, in Texas, seventy-odd years back on my personal time line. In that one the cockroaches slugged it out with each other for a thin chance of finding a few crumbs on the floor, there was no hot water at any time, and the screws were all cousins of the sheriff. Bad as that joint was, wetbacks used to sneak across the Rio and break a window or two in order to get themselves locked up, so they could fatten up for the winter. That says something about Mexican jails that I don't care to investigate.

Pixel comes to see me almost every day. The guards can't figure out how he does it. They all like him and he has given several of them his conditional approval. They fetch tidbits in to him; he deigns to eat some of their tribute.

The warden heard about Pixel's Houdini talents, came to my cell, happened to show up when Pixel was making a call

on me, tried to pet him and got nipped for his presumption—
not hard enough to break the skin, but the message was clear.

The warden told me (ordered me) to be sure to let him
know ahead of time when Pixel went in or out; he wanted to
see how Pixel managed to sneak past and not set off alarms.
I told him that no mortal man or woman could predict what
a cat would do next, so don't hold your breath, buster. (Guards
and trusties are okay, in their place, but a warden is not my
social equal. Apparently Pixel realizes this.)

Dr. Ridpath has been in a couple of times, to urge me to
plead guilty and throw myself on the mercy of the court. He
says that I would be certain to get no worse than a suspended
sentence, if I convinced the tribunal that I was truly con-
trite.

I told him that I was not guilty and would rather be a *cause
célèbre* and sell my memoirs for an outrageous sum.

He told me that I was apparently unaware that the College
of Bishops had passed a law years back under which any
profits arising out of a case of sacrilege went to the Church,
after the fee for disposing of the body was paid. "Look,
Maureen, I'm your friend, although you don't seem to know
it. But there is nothing I or anyone can do for you if you
won't cooperate."

I thanked him and told him that I was sorry that he was
disappointed in me. He said to think it over. He didn't kiss
me when he left, so I conclude that he really is vexed with
me.

Dagmar has been in almost daily. She doesn't try to coerce
me into confessing, but what she did do last time had more
effect on me than Dr. Eric's reasonableness: She smuggled
in a Last Friend. "If you are going to be stubborn about
confessing, this will help. Just break off the tip and inject it
anywhere. Once it takes hold—five minutes or less—even a
slow fire won't hurt . . . or not much. But for Santa Carolita's
sake, ducks, don't let anyone find it!"

I'll try not to.

I would not be dictating this if I were not in jail. I don't
necessarily have publication in mind, but the discipline of
sorting it all out may show me where I went wrong . . . and
that may show me how to straighten out the mess and go
right.

•   •   •

The Battle of New Orleans was fought two weeks after the War of 1812 was over. Poor communications— But in 1898 the Atlantic Cable was in use. The news of Spain's declaration of war went from Madrid to London to New York to Chicago to Kansas City to Thebes almost with the speed of light— only the delays of retransmission. Thebes is about eight hours west of Madrid, so the Johnson family was in church when the dreadful news arrived.

The Reverend Clarence Timberly, our pastor at Cyrus Vance Parker Memorial Methodist Episcopal Church, was preaching and had just finished fourthly and was digging into fifthly when someone started ringing the big bell in the county courthouse cupola.

Brother Timberly stopped preaching. "Let us suspend services for a few moments while the Osage Volunteers and members of the bucket brigades withdraw."

Ten or a dozen of the younger men got up and left. Father picked up his bag and followed them. Being a doctor Father did not serve on the volunteer fire team but, being a doctor, he usually did go to fires if not actively engaged in treating a patient when the bell rang.

As soon as Father closed the church door behind him our preacher got back to work on "fifthly"—what it was I don't know; during sermons I always tried to look alert and attentive, but I rarely listened.

On down Ford Street someone was shouting; he could be heard right through Brother Timberly's loud voice. Those shouts came closer.

Presently Father came back into the church. Instead of returning to his pew he walked up to the chancel rail and handed a sheet of newspaper to our pastor.

I should interject that the *Lyle County Leader* was a four-page single sheet, printed on what was then called "boiler plate"—newsprint printed on one side with international and national and state news, and shipped that way to small country papers, which would then fill the inside pages with local news and local advertising. The *Lyle County Leader* bought "boiler plate" from the *Kansas City Star* with the *Leader*'s own masthead printed on it.

The sheet Father handed to Brother Timberly was of that sort, with the same local stuff inside as had been in the *Leader*'s weekly edition dated Thursday, April twenty-first, 1898, except that the upper half of page two had been reset in large type with one short news story:

SPAIN DECLARES WAR!!!

By wire from the *New York Journal* April 24 Madrid—Today our Ambassador was summoned to the office of the Premier and was handed his passport and a curt note stating that the "crimes" of the United States against His Most Catholic Majesty have forced His Majesty's government to recognize that a state of war exists between the Kingdom of Spain and . . .

Reverend Timberly read that one new story aloud from the pulpit, put the paper down, looked solemnly at us, took out his handkerchief and wiped his brow, then blew his nose. He said hoarsely, "Let us pray."

Father stood up, the rest of the congregation followed. Brother Timberly asked Lord God Jehovah to lead us in this time of peril. He asked Divine guidance for President McKinley. He asked the Lord's help for all our brave men on land and sea who now must fight for the preservation of this sacred, God-given land. He asked mercy for the souls of those who would fall in battle, and consolation and help in drying the tears of widows and orphans and of the fathers and mothers of our young heroes destined to die in battle. He asked that right prevail for a speedy end to this conflict. He asked for help for our friends and neighbors, the unfortunate people of Cuba, oppressed for so long by the iron heel of the king of Spain. And more, about twenty minutes of it.

Father had long since cured me of any belief in the Apostles' Creed. In its place I held a deep suspicion, planted by Professor Huxley and nurtured by Father, that no such person as Jesus of Nazareth had ever lived.

As for Brother Timberly, I regarded him as two yards of noise, with his cracks filled with unction. Like many preachers in the Bible Belt, he was a farm boy with (I strongly suspected) a distaste for real work.

I did not and do not believe in a God up there in the sky listening to Brother Timberly's words.

Yet I found myself saying "Amen!" to his every word, while tears streamed down my cheeks.

At this point I must drag out my soap box.

In the twentieth century Gregorian, in the United States of America, something called "revisionist history" became popular among "intellectuals." Revisionism appears to have been based on the notion that the living actors present on the spot never understood what they were doing or why, or how they were being manipulated, being mere puppets in the hands of unseen evil forces.

This may be true. I don't know.

But why are the people of the United States and their government always the villains in the eyes of the revisionists? Why can't our enemies—such as the king of Spain, and the kaiser, and Hitler, and Geronimo, and Villa, and Sandino, and Mao Tse-tung, and Jefferson Davis—why can't these each take a turn in the pillory? Why is it always our turn?

I am well aware that the revisionists maintain that William Randolph Hearst created the Spanish-American War to increase the circulation of his newspapers. I know, too, that various scholars and experts later asserted that the USS *Maine,* at dock in Havana harbor, was blown up (with loss of 226 American lives) by faceless villains whose purpose was to make Spain look bad and thereby to prepare the American people to accept a declaration of war against Spain.

Now look carefully at what I said. I said that I know that these things are asserted. I did not say that they are true.

It is unquestionably true that the United States, acting officially, was rude to the Spanish government concerning Spain's oppression of the Cuban people. It is also true that William Randolph Hearst used his newspapers to say any number of unpleasant things about the Spanish government. But Hearst was not the United States and he had no guns and no ships and no authority. What he did have was a loud voice and no respect for tyrants. Tyrants hate people like that.

Somehow those masochistic revisionists have turned the War of 1898 into a case of imperialistic aggression by the United States. How an imperialist war could result in the freeing of Cuba and of the Philippines is never made clear. But revisionism always starts with the assumption that the United States is the villain. Once the revisionist historian proves this assumption (usually by circular logic) he is granted his Ph.D. and is well on his way to a Nobel peace prize.

In April 1898 to us benighted country people certain simple facts were true. Our battleship *Maine* had been destroyed, with great loss of life. Spain had declared war on us. The president had asked for volunteers.

The next day, Monday the twenty-fifth of April, came the president's call asking the state militias to furnish 125,000 volunteers to augment our almost-nonexistent army. That morning Tom had ridden over to Butler Academy as usual. The news reached him there and he came trotting back at noon, his roan gelding Beau Brummel in a lather. He asked Frank to wipe Beau down for him and hurried into the house, there to disappear into the clinic with Father.

They came out in about ten minutes. Father told Mother, "Madam, our son Tom is about to enlist in the service of his country. He and I will be leaving for Springfield at once. I must go with him in order to swear that he is eighteen years old and has parental approval."

"But he is not eighteen!"

"That is why I must go with him. Where is Frank? I want him to hitch Loafer."

"I'll hitch him, Father," I put in. "Frank just now left for school, in a rush. He was a bit late." (Tending Beau had made Frank late, but it wasn't necessary to say so.)

Father looked worried. I insisted, "Loafer knows me, sir; he would never hurt me."

I had just returned to the house when I saw Father standing at the new telephone instrument, which hung in the hallway we used as a waiting room for patients. Father was saying, "Yes . . . yes, I understand . . . Good luck, sir, and God speed. I will tell her. Good-bye." He took the receiver away from his ear, stared at it, then remembered to hang it up.

He looked at me. "That was for you, Maureen."

"For me?" I had never had a telephone call.

"Yes. Your young man, Brian Smith. He asks you to forgive him but he will not be able to call on you next Sunday. He is catching a train for St. Louis at once in order to return to Cincinnati, where he will be enlisting in the Ohio State Militia. He asks to be permitted to call on you again as soon as the war is over. Acting for you, I agreed to that."

"Oh." I felt an aching tight place under my wishbone and I had trouble breathing. "Thank you, Father. Uh . . . could you show me how to call him, call Rolla I suppose I mean, and speak to Mr. Smith myself?"

Mother interrupted. "Maureen!"

I turned to face her. "Mother, I am not being forward, or unladylike. This is a very special circumstance. Mr. Smith is going off to fight for us. I simply wish to tell him that I will pray for him every night while he is gone."

Mother looked at me, then said gently, "Yes, Maureen. If you are able to speak to him, please tell him that I shall pray for him, too. Every night."

Father cleared his throat, loudly. "Ladies—"

"Yes, Doctor?" Mother answered.

"The matter is academic. Mr. Smith told me that he could talk only a few moments because there was a long line of students waiting to use the telephone. Similar messages, I assume. So there is no use in trying to reach him; the telephone wire will be in use . . . and he will be gone. Which in no way keeps you two ladies from praying for his safety. Maureen, you can tell him so in a letter."

"But I don't know how to write to him!"

"Use your head, daughter. You know at least three ways."

"Doctor Johnson, please." Mother then said gently, to me, "Judge Sperling will know."

" 'Judge Sperling.' Oh!"

"Yes, dear. Judge Sperling always knows where each of us is."

A few minutes later we all kissed Tom good-bye, and Father also while we were about it although he was coming back . . . and, so he assured us, it was extremely likely that Tom would be back . . . sworn in, then told what day to return for duty, as it was most unlikely that the state militia could accept a thousand or more new bodies all on the same day.

They drove off. Beth was crying quietly. Lucille was not— I don't think she understood any of it—but was solemn and round-eyed. Mother did not cry and neither did I . . . not then. But Mother went upstairs and closed her door . . . and so did I. I now had a room to myself, ever since Agnes married, so I threw the latch and lay down and let myself cry.

I tried to tell myself that I was crying over my brother, Thomas. But I knew better; it was Mr. Smith who was causing that ache in my heart.

I wished, with all my soul, that I had not caused him to use a French purse in making love to me a week earlier. I had been tempted—I knew, I was certain, that it would be ever so much nicer just to forget that rubber sheath and be bare to him, inside and out.

But I had told Father solemnly that I would always use a sheath . . . until the day when, after sober discussion with the man concerned, I omitted it for the purpose of becoming pregnant . . . under a mutual firm intention of marrying if we succeeded.

And now he was going off to war . . . and I might never see him again.

I dried my eyes and got up and took down a little volume of verse, Professor Palgrave's *Golden Treasury*. Mother had given it to me on my twelfth birthday, and it had been given to her on her twelfth birthday, in 1866.

Professor Palgrave had found 288 lyrics which were fine enough, in his exquisite taste, for his treasury; that day I wanted just one: Richard Lovelace's "To Lucasta, Going to the Warres."

"I could not love thee (Deare) so much,
"Lov'd I not Honour more."

Then I cried some more, and after a while I slept. When I woke up, I got up and did not let myself cry again. Instead I slipped a note under Mother's door, telling her that I would get supper for all of us by myself . . . and she could have supper in bed if it pleased her to do so.

She let me cook supper but she came down and presided and, for the first time, Frank seated Mother and sat opposite her. She looked at me. "Maureen, will you return thanks?"

"Yes, Mother. Dear Lord, we thank Thee for that which we are about to partake. Please bless this food to our use and bless all our brothers and sisters in Jesus everywhere, both known to us and unknown." I gulped and added, "And on this day we ask a special blessing for our beloved brother, Thomas Jefferson, and for all other young men who have gone to serve our beloved country." (*Et je prie que le bon Dieu garde bien mon ami!*) "In Jesus' Name. Amen."

"Amen," Mother said firmly. "Franklin, will you carve?"

Father and Tom returned the next day, late in the afternoon. Beth and Lucille threw themselves on Tom and Father, and I wanted to, but could not, as I was carrying George and he had picked that moment to wet a diaper. But I just held him and let him wait, so that I wouldn't miss any news—a spare diaper under him; I knew George. That baby peed more than all the rest put together.

Beth demanded, "Did you do it, Tommy, did you do it, did you do it, did you?"

"Of course he did," Father answered. "He's Private Johnson now; next week he'll be a general."

"He will?"

"Well, maybe not that fast." Father stopped to kiss Lucille and Beth. "But they do promote them fast in wartime. Take me, for example. I'm a captain."

"Doctor Johnson!"

Father straightened up. "Captain Johnson, Madam. Both of us enlisted. I am now Acting Surgeon, Medical Detachment, Second Missouri Regiment, with assigned rank of captain."

At this point I ought to say something about the families of my parents, especially Father's brothers and sisters, as what happened that week in April 1898 in Thebes had its roots a century earlier.

Father's grandparents were:
George Edward Johnson (1795–1897) and Amanda Lou Fredericks Johnson (1798–1899)
Terence McFee (1796–1900) and Rose Wilhelmina Brandt McFee (1798–1899)
Both George Johnson and Terence McFee served in the War of 1812.
Father's parents were:
Asa Edward Johnson (1813–1918) and Rose Altheda McFee Johnson (1814–1918)
Asa Johnson served in the War with Mexico, a sergeant in the Illinois militia.

Mother's grandparents were:
Robert Pfeiffer (1809–1909) and Heidi Schmidt Pfeiffer (1810–1912)

Ole Larsen (1805–1907) and Anna Kristina Hansen Larsen (1810–1912)
and her parents were:
Richard Pfeiffer (1830–1932) and Kristina Larsen Pfeiffer (1834–1940)

Father was born on his grandfather Johnson's farm in Minnesota, in Freeborn County, near Albert, on Monday, August second, 1852, the youngest of four boys and three girls. His grandfather George Edward Johnson (my great-grandfather) was born in 1795, in Bucks County, Pennsylvania. He died in a nursing home in Minneapolis in December 1897, and the newspapers made a to-do over the fact that George Washington was still alive when he was born. (We had nothing to do with this publicity. While I was not aware of the policy until I was married, even at that time Howard Foundation families avoided public mention of ages.)

George Edward Johnson married Amanda Lou Fredericks (1798–1899) in 1813 and took her to Illinois, where she had her first child, Asa Edward Johnson, my grandfather, that same year. It seems likely that Grampaw Acey was the same sort of "premature" baby as was my oldest brother, Edward. After the War with Mexico the Johnson family migrated west and homesteaded in Minnesota.

There was no Howard Foundation in those days, but all of my ancestors appear to have started breeding young, had lots of children, were healthy despite the uncontrolled diseases of those times, and lived long lives, mostly to a hundred and more.

Asa Edward Johnson (1813–1918) married Rose Altheda McFee (1814–1918) in 1831. They had seven children:

1. Samantha Jane Johnson, 1831–1915 (died from injuries suffered while breaking a horse)
2. James Ewing Johnson, 1833–1884 (killed attempting to ford the Osage during spring flood. I barely remember him. He married Aunt Carole Pelletier of New Orleans.)
3. Walter Raleigh Johnson, 1838–1862 (killed at Shiloh)
4. Alice Irene Johnson, 1840–? (I don't know what became of Aunt Alice. She married back east.)
5. Edward McFee Johnson, 1844–1884 (killed in a train wreck)
6. Aurora Johnson 1850–? (last heard of in California ca. 1930) (married several times)

7. Ira Johnson, August 2, 1852–1941 (reported missing in the Battle of Britain)

When Fort Sumter fell in April 1861, Mr. Lincoln asked for volunteers from the militias of the several states (just as Mr. McKinley would do in a later April). On the Johnson farm in Freeborn County, Minnesota, the call was answered by Ewing (twenty-eight), Walter (twenty-three), Edward (seventeen)—and Grampaw Acey, at that time forty-eight years old, thus producing a situation that utterly humiliated Ira Johnson, nine years old and a grown man in his own estimation. He was going to be left home to do chores, while all the other men went to war. His sister Samantha (whose husband had volunteered) and his mother would run the farm.

Small comfort to him that his father returned home almost at once, turned down for something, I do not know what.

Father endured this humiliation for three long years . . . and at twelve ran away from home to enlist as a drummer boy.

He found his way down the Mississippi on a barge, managed to locate the encampment of the Second Minnesota before it joined Sherman's drive to the sea. His cousin Jules vouched for him and he was tentatively accepted (subject to training; he knew nothing of drums, or of bugles) and was assigned quarters and rations with headquarters company.

Then his father showed up and fetched him home.

So Father's service in the War was about three weeks and he was never in combat. He was not credited even with those three weeks . . . as he learned to his dismay when he attempted to join the Union veterans' organization, the Grand Army of the Republic.

There was no record of his service, as the regimental adjutant had "discharged" him and let Grampaw Acey take him home simply by destroying the paper work.

I think it is necessary to assume that Father was marked for life.

During the nine days that Father and Tom waited at home before they could be inducted into army life I saw no indication that Mother disapproved (other than her first expression of surprise). But she never smiled. One could feel the tension between our parents . . . but they did not let it be seen.

Father did say something to me that, I think, had some

bearing on this tension. We were in his clinic and I was helping him to thin out and update his patients' records so that he could turn them over to Dr. Chadwick for the duration of the war. He said to me, "Why no smiles, Turkey Egg? Worried about your young man?"

"No," I lied. "He had to go; I know that. But I wish you weren't going. Selfish, I guess. But I'll miss you, *cher papa*."

"I'll miss you, too. All of you." He was silent for several minutes, then he added, "Maureen, someday you may be faced—will be faced, I think—with the same thing: your husband going off to war. Some people say—I've heard talk—that married men should not go. Because of their families.

"But this involves a contradiction, a fatal one. The family man dare not hang back and expect the bachelor to do his fighting for him. It is manifestly unfair for me to expect a bachelor to die for my children if I am unwilling to die for them myself. Enough of that attitude on the part of married men and the bachelor will refuse to fight if the married man stays safe at home . . . and the Republic is doomed. The barbarian will walk in unopposed."

Father looked at me—looked worried. "Do you see?" I think he was honestly seeking my opinion, my approval.

"I—" I stopped and sighed. "Father, I think I see. But at times like these I am forced to realize that I am not very experienced. I just want this war to be over so that you will come home and Tom will come home . . . and—"

"And Brian Smith? I agree."

"Well, yes. But I was thinking of Chuck, too. Chuck Perkins."

"Chuck is going? Good lad!"

"Yes, he told me today. His father has agreed and is going to Joplin with him tomorrow." I sniffed back a tear. "I don't love Chuck but I do feel sort of sentimental about him."

"That's understandable."

Later that day I let Chuck take me up on Marston Hill and defied chiggers and Mrs. Grundy and told Chuck I was proud of him and demonstrated it the very best I knew how. (I did use a sheath; I had promised Father.) And an amazing thing happened. I had gone up there simply intending to run through some female calisthenics to demonstrate to Chuck that I was proud of him and appreciated his willingness to fight for us. And the miracle happened. Fireworks, big ones! I got all blurry and my eyes squinched shut and I found I was making loud noises.

And about half an hour later the miracle happened again. Amazing!

Chuck and his father caught the eight-oh-six out of Butler the next morning and were back that same afternoon—Chuck sworn in and assigned to the same company (C Company, Second Regiment) Tom was in, and with similar delay time. So Chuck and I went to another (fairly) safe spot, and I told him good-bye again, and again the miracle overtook me.

No, I did not decide I was in love with him, after all. Enough men had had me by then that I was not inclined to mistake a hearty orgasm for eternal love. But it was nice that they happened since I intended to tell Chuck good-bye as often and as emphatically as possible, come what might. And did, right up to the day, a week later, when it really was good-bye.

Chuck never came back. No, he was not killed in action; he never got out of Chickamauga Park, Georgia. It was the fever, whether malaria or yellow jack, I'm not sure. Or it could have been typhoid. Five times as many died of the fevers as were lost in combat. They are heroes, too. Well, aren't they? They volunteered; they were willing to fight . . . and they wouldn't have caught the fever if they had hung back, refused to answer the call.

I've got to drag out that soap box again. All during the twentieth century I've run into people who either have never heard of the War of 1898, or belittle it. "Oh, you mean that one. That wasn't a real war, just a skirmish. What happened? Did he stub his toe, running back down San Juan Hill?"

(I should have killed them! I did throw an extra dry martini into the eyes of one man who talked that way.)

Casualties are just as heavy in one war as in another . . . because death comes just one to the customer.

And besides— In the summer of 1898 we did not know that the war would be over quickly. The United States was not a superpower; the United States was not a world power of any sort . . . whereas Spain was still a great empire. For all we knew our men might be gone for years . . . or not come back. The bloody tragedy of 1861–1865 was all we had to go by, and that had started just like this one, with the president calling for a few militiamen. My elders tell me that no one dreamed that the rebel states, half as big and less than half as populous and totally lacking in the heavy industry on which modern war rests—no sensible person dreamed that they could hold out for four long, dreary, death-laden years.

With that behind us, we did not assume that beating Spain would be easy or quick; we just prayed that our men would come back . . . someday.

The day came, the fifth of May, when our men left . . . on a special troop train, down from Kansas City, a swing over to Springfield, then up to St. Louis, and east—destination: Georgia. All of us went over to Butler, Mother and Father in the lead, in his buggy, drawn by Loafer, while the rest of us followed in the surrey, ordinarily used only on Sundays, with Tom driving Daisy and Beau. The train pulled in, and we made hurried good-byes as they were already shouting "All abo . . . ard!" Father turned Loafer over to Frank, and I inherited the surrey with the gentle team.

They didn't actually pull out all that quickly; baggage and freight had to be loaded as well as soldiers. There was a flatcar in the middle of the train, with a brass band on it, supplied by the Third Regiment (Kansas City) and it played all the time the train was stopped, a military medley.

They played, "Mine eyes have seen the glory—" and segued right into "I wish I was in de land ob cotton—" and from that into "Tenting tonight, tenting tonight—" and "—stuck a feather in his cap and called it macaroni!" Then they played "In my prison cell I sit—" and the engine gave a toot and the train started to move, and the band scrambled to get off the flatcar and into the coach next to it, and the man with the tuba had to be helped.

And we started home and I was still hearing "Tramp, tramp, tramp, the boys are marching—" and that tragic first line, "In my prison cell I sit—" Somebody told me later that the man who wrote that knew nothing about it, because wartime prison camps don't have anything as luxurious as cells. He cited Andersonville.

As may be, it was enough to make my eyes blur up and I couldn't see. But that didn't matter; Beau Brummel and Daisy needed no help from me. Just leave the reins slack and they would take us home. And they did.

I helped Frank unharness both rigs, then went in and upstairs. Mother came to my room just as I closed the door, and tapped on it. I opened it. "Yes, Mother?"

"Maureen, your *Golden Treasury*— May I borrow it?"

"Certainly." I went and got it; it was under my pillow. I handed it to her. "It's number eighty-three, Mother, on page sixty."

She looked surprised, then thumbed the pages. "So it is," she agreed, then looked up. "We must be brave, dear."

"Yes, Mother. We must."

Speaking of prison cells, Pixel has just arrived in mine, with a present for me. A mouse. A dead mouse. Still warm. He is so pleased with himself and clearly he expects me to eat it. He is waiting for me to eat it.

How am I going to get out of this?

6

"When Johnny Comes Marching Home—"

The rest of 1898 was one long bad dream. Our men had gone to war but it was difficult to find out what was happening in that war. I remember a time, sixty-odd years later, when the malevolent eye of television turned war into a spectator sport, even to the extent (I hope that this is not true!) that attacks were timed so that the action could be shown live on the evening news. Can you imagine a more ironically horrible way to die than to have one's death timed to allow an anchor man to comment on it just before turning the screen over to the beer ads?

In 1898 the fighting was not brought live into our living rooms; we had trouble finding out what had happened even long after the fact. Was our Navy guarding the east coast (as eastern politicians were demanding), or was it somewhere in the Caribbean? Had the *Oregon* rounded the Horn and would it reach the Fleet in time? Why was there a second battle at

Manila? Hadn't we won the battle of Manila Bay weeks ago?

In 1898 I knew so little about military matters that I did not realize that civilians should not know the location of a fleet or the planned movements of an army. I did not know that anything known to an outsider will be known by enemy agents just minutes later. I had never heard of the public's "right to know," a right that cannot be found in the Constitution but was sacrosanct in the second half of the twentieth century. This so-called "right" meant that it was satisfactory (regrettable perhaps but necessary) for soldiers and sailors and airmen to die in order to preserve unblemished that sacred "right to know."

I had still to learn that neither Congressmen nor newsmen could be trusted with the lives of our men.

Let me try to be fair. Let us assume that over 90 percent of Congressmen and of newsmen are honest and honorable men. In that case, less than 10 percent need be murderous fools indifferent to the deaths of heroes for that minority to destroy lives, lose battles, turn the course of a war.

I did not have these grim thoughts in 1898; it would take the War of 1898 and two world wars and two undeclared wars ("police actions," for God's sake!) to make me realize that neither our government nor our press could be trusted with human lives.

"A democracy works well only when the common man is an aristocrat. But God must hate the common man; He has made him so dadblamed common! Does your common man understand chivalry? Noblesse oblige? Aristocratic rules of conduct? Personal responsibility for the welfare of the State? One may as well search for fur on a frog." Is that something I heard my father say? No. Well, not exactly. It is something I recall from about two o'clock in the morning in the Oyster Bar of the Benton House in Kansas City after Mr. Clemens's lecture in January 1898. Maybe my father said part of it; perhaps Mr. Clemens said all of it, or perhaps they shared it—my memory is not perfect after so many years.

Mr. Clemens and my father were indulging in raw oysters, philosophy, and brandy. I had a small glass of port. Both port and raw oysters were new to me; I disliked both . . . not helped by the odor of Mr. Clemens's cigar.

(I had assured Mr. Clemens that I enjoyed the aroma of a good cigar; please do smoke. A mistake.)

But I would have endured more than cigar smoke and raw oysters to be present that night. On the platform Mr. Clemens had looked just like his pictures: a jovial Satan with a halo of white hair, in a beautifully tailored white suit. In person he was a foot shorter, warmly charming, and he made of me an even more fervent admirer by treating me as a grown lady.

I was up hours past my bedtime and had to keep pinching myself not to fall asleep. What I remember best was Mr. Clemens's discourse on the subject of cats and red-heads . . . composed on the spot for my benefit, I think—it does not appear anywhere in his published works, not even those released by the University of California fifty years after his death.

Did you know that Mr. Clemens was a redhead? But that must wait.

News of the signing of the peace protocol reached Thebes on the twelfth of August, a Friday. Mr. Barnaby, our principal, called us all into the lecture hall and told us, then dismissed school. I ran home, found that Mother already knew. We cried on each other a little while Beth and Lucille were noisy around us, then Mother and I started in on a complete, unseasonal spring cleaning so that we would be ready when Father and Tom (and Mr. Smith?—I did not voice it) got home sometime next week. Frank was told to cut the grass and to do anything else that needed doing outdoors—don't ask; just do it.

Church on Sunday was a happy Praise-the-Lord occasion, with Reverend Timberly being even more long-windedly stupid than usual but nobody minded, least of all me.

After church Mother said, "Maureen, are you going to school tomorrow?"

I had not thought about it. The Thebes school board had decided to offer summer high school (in addition to the usual make-up session for grammar school dullards) as a patriotic act to permit older boys to graduate early and enlist. I had signed up for summer school both to add to my education (since I had given up the idea of college) and to fill that aching emptiness caused by Father and Tom (and Mr. Smith) being away at war.

(I have spent the longest years of my life waiting for men

to come back from war. And for some who did not come
back.)

"Mother, I had not thought about it. Do you really think
there will be school as usual tomorrow?"

"There will be. Have you studied?"

(She knew I hadn't. You can't do much with Greek irregular verbs when you are down on your knees, scrubbing the
kitchen floor.) "No, Ma'am."

"Well? What would your father expect of you?"

I sighed. "Yes, Ma'am."

"Don't feel sorry for yourself. Summer school was your
idea. You should not waste that extra tuition. Now git! I will
get supper by myself tonight."

They did not come home that week.
They did not come home the following week.
They did not come home that fall.
They did not come home that year.

(Chuck's body came home. The GAR provided a firing
squad and I attended my first military funeral and cried and
cried. A bugler with white hair played for Charles: "—sleep
in peace, soldier brave, God is nigh."

(If I ever come close to believing, it is when I hear "Taps."
Even today.)

After that summer session in 1898, when September came
it was necessary to make a choice: go to school or not, and
if so, where? I did not want to remain home, doing little but
play nursemaid to George. Since I could not go to Columbia,
I wanted to go to Butler Academy, a two-year private school
that offered a liberal arts course acceptable at Columbia or
at Lawrence in lieu of lower division. I pointed out to Mother
that I had saved Christmas and birthday presents and "egg
money" ("egg money" was any earned money—taking care
of neighbors' children, minding a stand at the county fair,
and so forth—not much and quite seldom)—I had saved enough
for my tuition and books.

Mother said, "How will you get back and forth?"

I answered, "How does Tom get back and forth?"

"Don't answer a question with a question, young lady. We
both know how your brother did it: By buggy in good weather,
on horseback in bad weather . . . and he stayed home in the

very worst weather. But your brother is a grown man. Tell me how you will do it.''

I thought about it. A buggy was no problem; the Academy had a barn for horses awaiting their masters. Horseback? I could ride almost as well as my brothers . . . but girls do not arrive at school wearing overalls, and sidesaddle was not a good idea for weather not suited to a buggy. But even good weather and a buggy— From late in October to early in March I would have to leave home before daylight and return home after dark.

In October 1889 Sarah Trowbridge had left her father's farm to go four miles by buggy to Rich Hill. Her horse and buggy came home. Sarah was never seen again.

Ours was a quiet countryside. But the most dangerous animal in all history walks on two legs . . . and sometimes slinks along country roads.

"I am not afraid, Mother."

"Tell me what your father would advise you to do."

So I gave up, and prepared to go back to high school for another semester, or more. School was less than a mile away and there were people we knew within shouting distance the whole way. Best of all, our high school had courses I had not had time to take. I continued Greek and another year of Latin and started differential equations and first-year German and audited geology and medieval history instead of study hall those two hours. And of course I still continued piano lessons on Saturday mornings—Mother had taught me for three years, then she had decided that I could profit from more advanced training than she could give me. It was an "in kind" deal; Miss Primrose owed Father both for herself and for her ailing and ancient mother.

So that kept me out of mischief the school year starting September 1898 while still leaving me plenty of time to write a newsy unsentimental letter to Mr. Smith (*Sergeant* Smith!) each week, and another to Tom, and another to Father, and another to Chuck . . . until one came back to me the week before Chuck came back to us, forever.

I didn't see boys or young men any to speak of. The good ones had gone to war; those who remained behind struck me, mostly, as having drool on their chins. Or as too impossibly young for me. I was not consciously being faithful to Mr. Smith. He had not asked me to be, and I would not expect him to be faithful to me. We had had one—just one—highly successful first meeting. But that did not constitute a betrothal.

Nor was I faithful. But it was just my young cousin Nelson, who hardly counts. Nelson and I had one thing in common: We both were as horny as a herd of goats, all the time. And another thing— We were both cautious as a vixen with kits in coping with Mrs. Grundy.

I let him pick the times and places; he had a head for intrigue. Between us, we kept each other toned down to a pleasant simmer without waking Mrs. Grundy. I could happily have married Nelson, despite his being younger than I, had we not been so closely related. A dear boy. (Except for that lemon pie!)

They were not home for Christmas. But two more bodies came home. I attended each funeral, for Chuck's sake.

In January my brother Tom came marching home with his regiment. Mother and Frank went to Kansas City to see the troop train arrive and the parade down Walnut, and the countermarch back to the depot where most of them got back aboard to go on terminal furlough at their home towns. I stayed home to take care of my sisters and George, and thought privately that it was pretty noble of me.

Tom had a hand-carried letter for Mother:

"Mrs. Ira Johnson
"Courtesy of Lance Corporal T. J. Johnson,
"C Company, Second Missouri Regiment.

"Dear Madam:
    "I had hoped and expected to return home in the same train as our son Thomas. Indeed, by the terms of enrollment under which I accepted appointment as surgeon in our state militia on federal duty, I cannot be held more than 120 days beyond the proclamation of peace, *id est,* the twelfth of December last, or the sixth of January, this current month—the difference in dates being a legal technicality now moot.

    "I regret that I must inform you that the Surgeon General of the Army has asked me and my professional colleagues to continue on duty here on a day to day basis until our services can be spared, and that I have accepted.

"We had thought that we had these devastating fevers under control and that we could dismantle the field hospitals here and send our remaining patients to Fort Bragg. But, with the arrival three weeks ago of casuals and casualties from Tampa, our hopes were dashed.

"In short, Madam, my patients need me. I will come home as quickly as the Surgeon General decides that I can be spared . . . under the spirit of the Oath of Hippocrates rather than through any quibble over the letter of the contract.

"I trust that you will understand, as you have so many times in the past.

> "I remain, faithfully yours,
> Your loving husband,
> Ira Johnson, M.D.,
> Captain (M.C.) AUS

Mother did not cry where anyone could see her . . . and I didn't cry where anyone could see me.

Late in February I received a letter from Mr. Smith . . . postmarked Cincinnati!

"Dear Miss Maureen,
"By the time this reaches you I will have laid aside my Army blues and resumed wearing mufti; our engineering battalion, Ohio militia, is rolling west as I write this.

"It is my dearest wish to see you and to resume my suit for your hand in matrimony. With that prime purpose in mind, after a few days at home with my family, I purpose going at once to Rolla with the intention of re-enrolling. Although I was granted my degree in April last year about six weeks early, that sheepskin does not supply me with academic work that I missed. So I intend to make up what I lost, plus a bit more for good measure—which puts me close to Thebes for each weekend [which is what the wily fellow had in mind all along!].

"May I hope to see you on Saturday afternoon March fourth, and again on Sunday, March fifth? A postal card should reach me at School of Mines—but if I do not hear from you, I shall assume that your answer is Yes.

"This train is moving too slowly to suit me!

"My respects to your parents and my greetings to all your family.

> "While looking forward eagerly to the fourth,
> I remain faithfully yours,
> Brian Smith, B.S.,
> Sergeant, Eng. Battalion,
> Ohio Militia (Federal Duty)

I reread it, then took a deep breath and held it, to slow my heart. Then I found Mother and asked her to read it. She did so, and smiled. "I'm happy for you, dear."

"I don't have to tell him to wait until Father gets home?"

"Your father has already expressed his approval of Mr. Smith . . . in which I concur. He is welcome." Mother looked thoughtful. "Will you ask him to consider fetching with him his uniform?"

"Really?"

"Truly. So that he can wear it in church on Sunday. Would you like that?"

Would I! I told her so. "Like Tom did, his first Sunday home. Goody!"

"We will be proud of him. I intend to ask your father to wear his uniform his first Sunday home, too." She looked thoughtful. "Maureen, there is no reason why Mr. Smith should have to put up with Mrs. Henderson's boarding house, or drive clear back to Butler to the Mansion House. Frank can sleep in the other bed in Tom's room and Mr. Smith can have Edward's old room."

"Oh, that would be nice!"

"Yes, dear. But— Look at me, Maureen." She held my eyes. "Don't let his presence under this roof cause either of you to permit any of the children—including Thomas, I must add—to see, or even to suspect, any impropriety."

I blushed clear to my collarbones. "I promise, *chère mama*."

"No need for promises; just be discreet. We are women together, dear daughter; I want to help you."

March came in like a lamb, which just suited me, as I did not want to spend a long afternoon being primly proper in our parlor. The weather was warm and sunny, with no breeze to speak of. So on Saturday the fourth I was the perfect shy young maiden, with parasol and leg o' mutton sleeves and a silly number of petticoats . . . until Daisy had us a hundred yards from the house and out of earshot of anyone. "Briney!"

"Yes, Miss Maureen?"

" 'Miss Maureen,' my foot. Briney, you've had me in the past; you can stop being formal, now that we are alone. Do you have an erection?"

"Now that you mention it—Yes!"

"If you had said No, I would have burst into tears. Look, darling, I've found the loveliest place—"

(Nelson had found it.) There seemed to be evidence that no one else knew of it. Daisy had to be led through two tight spots, then she could be unharnessed and allowed to graze— while we two turned the buggy around. Impossible for the mare to do it; not enough room for her to back and fill.

I spread the blanket down on a grassy spot separated from the bank by a thick bush . . . and undressed while Brian watched me—right to my skin, right to stockings and shoes.

That spot was certainly private but anyone within a quarter mile must have heard me. I fainted on that first one, then opened my eyes to find my Briney boy worried. "Are you all right?" he asked.

"I've never been more all right in my life! Thank you, sir! You were splendid! Terrific. I've died and gone to heaven."

He smiled at me. "You aren't dead. You're here and you're wonderful and I love you."

"Do you, truly? Brian, are you honestly intending to marry me?"

"I am."

"Even with me disqualified for the Howard Foundation?"

"Redhead, the Foundation introduced us . . . but it had nothing to do with me coming back. I would happily indenture myself for seven years, like what's-his-name in the Bible, for the privilege of marrying you."

"I hope you mean that. Do you want to hear how I'm disqualified?"

"No."

"So? I'm going to tell you anyhow, because I need your help."

"At your service, Ma'amselle!"

"I'm disqualified because I'm not pregnant. If you will raise up just a little, I will take that rubber mockery off you. Then, sir, if you please, as soon as you are rested enough, I ask you to qualify me. Briney, let's start our first baby!"

He surprised me . . . by being ready again almost at once. Even Nelson could not manage it that quickly. My Brian was a remarkable man.

Bareness to bareness was just as perfect as I always knew it would be. This time I was even louder. I have since learned to have an orgasm silently . . . but I would much rather sound off, if conditions permit. Most men like applause. Especially Briney.

At last I sighed. "That did it. Thank you, sir. I am now an expectant mother. I felt it hit the target. *Spung!*"

"Maureen, you're wonderful."

"I'm dead. I died happy. Are you hungry? I made some tiny cream puffs for our lunch and filled them just before you arrived."

"I want you for lunch."

"Blarney. We must keep up your strength. You won't be deprived." I told him about the arrangements we would have that night—and other nights. "Of course Mother knows all about it; she was a Howard bride herself. She just asks that we keep a good face on things. Briney, are your parents redheaded?"

"Mother is. Dad's hair is as dark as mine. Why?"

I told him about Mr. Clemens's theory. "He says that while the rest of the human race are descended from monkeys, redheads derive from cats."

"Seems logical. By the way, I forgot to tell you. If you marry me, my cat is part of the package."

"Shouldn't you have mentioned that before you knocked me up?"

"Perhaps I should have. You object to cats?"

"I don't even speak to people who object to cats. Briney, I'm cold. Let's go home." The sun had gone behind a cloud and the temperature suddenly dropped—typical March weather for Missouri.

While I dressed, Briney got Daisy backed into the shafts and hitched up. Brian has that gentle but firm touch that horses (and women) understand; Daisy obeyed him as readily as she obeyed me, although she was usually terribly shy with strangers.

By the time we were home my teeth were chattering. But Frank had the baseburner in the parlor fired up; we had my picnic lunch next to it. I invited Frank to share. He had had lunch, but he found room for cream puffs.

My period was due on March eighteenth; I missed it. I told Briney but no one else. "Father says that to miss just one is nothing. We should wait."

"We'll wait."

Father got home on the first of April, and the house was in a happy uproar for days. My next period should have been April fifteenth—I didn't even spot. Briney agreed that it was time I told my father, so I did, that same Saturday afternoon. Father looked at me solemnly. "How do you feel about it, Maureen?"

"I'm utterly happy about it, sir. I did it on purpose—we did it on purpose. Now I would like to marry Mr. Smith as soon as possible."

"Reasonable. Well, let's call in your young man. I want to speak to him privately."

"I can't be present?"

"You may not be present."

I was called back in, then Father stepped out. I said, "I don't see any blood on you, Briney."

"He didn't even get out his shotgun. He just explained your trifling ways to me."

"*What* trifling ways?"

"Now, now. Simmer down."

Father came back in with Mother. He said to us, "I have explained to Mrs. Johnson about the skipped periods." He turned to Mother. "When do you think they should get married?"

"Mr. Smith, when is your last class at Rolla?"

"I have my last examination on Friday, May nineteenth, Ma'am. Commencement isn't until June second, but that doesn't affect me."

"I see. Would Saturday, May twentieth, suit you two? And, Mr. Smith, do you think your parents will be able to come here for the wedding?"

· · ·

At seven-thirteen P.M. on May twentieth my husband and I were rolling north from Butler on the Kansas City Southern Express . . . "express" meaning that it stopped for cows, milk cans, and frogs, but not for fireflies. I said, "Briney, my feet hurt."

"Take your shoes off."

"In public?"

"You no longer have to pay attention to any opinion but mine . . . and durned little to mine."

"Thank you, sir. But I don't dare take them off; my feet would swell and I would never get them back on. Briney, the next time we get married, let's elope."

"Suits. We should have this time. What a day!"

I chose to have a noon wedding. I was overruled by my mother, my prospective mother-in-law, the minister, the minister's wife, the organist, the church janitor, and anyone else who cared to speak up. I had thought that the bride was supposed to get her own way about her wedding (if what she wanted was not too dear for her father's purse), but apparently I had been reading too many romantic stories. I wanted a noon wedding so that we could reach Kansas City before dark. When I found myself frustrated on every side, I spoke to Father about it.

He shook his head. "I'm sorry, Maureen, but it is written right here in the Constitution that the father of the bride has no rights whatever in a wedding. He gets to pay the bills and he must give the bride away. Otherwise they don't let him out of his cage. Did you tell your mother why you wanted to catch the earlier train?"

"Yes, sir."

"What did she say?"

"She said that all the planning had been done on the assumption that the Smiths would arrive on the ten-forty-two, soon enough for a four o'clock wedding but not for a noon wedding. I said, 'But, Mother, they are already here.' And she said that it was too late to change everything. And I said, 'Who says so? And why wasn't I consulted?' And she said, 'Keep quiet and stop wiggling. I've got to pin this over again.' Father, this is dreadful. I'm being treated like a prize cow about to be shown at the fair. And I'm listened to just as much as that cow."

"Maureen, it probably is too late to change anything now.

Stipulated, your wishes should have been followed. But now it is less than forty-eight hours till your wedding and when Adele takes the bit in her teeth, she doesn't listen. I wish I could help you. But she won't listen to me, either." Father looked as unhappy as I felt. "Grit your teeth and wait it out. Once Brother Timberly says, 'I pronounce you man and wife,' you no longer have to pay any attention to anyone but Brian. And I see that you have a ring in his nose; you won't find that too difficult."

"I don't think I have a ring in his nose."

The Reverend Timberly had been told that the Methodist Episcopal service was to be followed exactly, none of these modern innovations. He had been told also that it would be a single-ring ceremony. The muttonhead didn't listen on either point. He stuck in all sorts of stuff (from his lodge rituals, I think; he was a Past Grand Chancellor of the Knights and Lords of the High Mountain), stuff that had not been in the rehearsal, questions and responses I didn't recognize. And he preached, telling each of us things we didn't need to hear, matters not in the wedding service.

This went on and on, while my feet hurt (Don't buy shoes by mail order!) and my corset was stifling me. (I had never worn one before. But Mother insisted.) I was about to tell Brother Timberwolf to stick to the book, stop improvising (it was getting closer and closer to train time) when he reached the point where he wanted two rings and there was of course but one.

He wanted to back up and start over.

Brian spoke up (and a groom isn't supposed to say anything but "I will" and "I do") and said in a whisper that could not be heard more than a hundred yards, "Reverend, stop stalling and stick to words in the book . . . or I won't pay you a red cent."

Brother Timberly started to expostulate and looked at Briney—and stopped suddenly, and said, "ByAuthorityvested-inmebythesovereignstateofMissouri I pronounce you man and wife!" And thereby saved his own life. I think.

Brian kissed me and we turned and started down the aisle and I tripped on my train. Beth was carrying my train and was supposed to move it off to the left.

It wasn't her fault; I turned the wrong way.

•   •   •

"Briney, did you get any wedding cake?"

"Never had time."

"Me, too. I suddenly realize that I haven't eaten anything since breakfast . . . and not much then. Let's find that dining car."

"Suits. I'll inquire." Briney got up, was gone a few moments. When he came back he leaned over me. "I found it."

"Good. Is it in front of us, or behind us?"

"Behind us. Quite a bit behind us. They left it off in Joplin."

So our wedding supper was two stale ham sandwiches from the news butcher and a bottle of soda pop, split.

About eleven o'clock we finally reached the Lewis and Clark, where Briney had a reservation for us. The hack driver had apparently never heard of that hotel but was willing to search for it as long as his horse held out. He started away from the depot in the wrong direction. Briney spotted this and stopped him; the driver gave him an argument and some lip. Briney said, "Back to the depot; we'll get another hack." This ultimatum finally got us there.

I suppose that it was only to be expected that the night clerk had never heard of Briney's reservation. But Brian can't be pushed around and he won't be intimidated. He said, "I made my reservation by mail three weeks ago with a postal money order deposit. I have my receipt right here along with a letter of confirmation signed by your manager. Now wake him up and put a stop to this nonsense." Briney shoved the letter under the clerk's nose.

The clerk looked at it and said, "Oh, *that* Mr. Smith! And the bridal suite. Why didn't you say so?"

"I did say so, ten minutes ago."

"I am very sorry, sir. Front!"

Twenty minutes later I was in a wonderful tub of hot, soapy water, just like Chicago six years earlier. I almost fell asleep in the tub, then realized that I was keeping my bridegroom out of the bath, and pulled myself together. "Briney! Shall I fill a tub for you?"

No answer. I dried off a bit, wrapped the towel around me, aware that I was a scandalous sight (and a provocative one, I hoped).

My gallant knight was fast asleep, still in his clothes, lying across the bedspread.

There was a silver bucket just inside the door—ice and a bottle of champagne.

I got out my nightgown (virginal white and perfumed; it had been Mother's bridal nightgown) and a pair of bunny slippers. "Brian. Briney. Please wake up, dear. I want to help you undress, and open the bed, and get you into it."

"Murrf."

"Please, dear."

"I wasn't asleep."

"No, of course not. Let me help you off with your boots."

"I c'n get'em." He sat up and reached for them.

"All right, dear. I must let the water out of the tub, then I'll run a bath for you."

"Your water is still in the tub?"

"Yes."

"Let it be; I'll use it. Mrs. Smith, you couldn't get a tub of water dirty; you would just impart a delicious flavor."

Sure enough, my gallant knight did bathe in my bath water (still lukewarm). I climbed into bed . . . and was sound asleep when he came to bed. He did not wake me.

I woke up in darkness about two or three, frightened to find myself in a strange bed—then remembered. "Briney?"

"You awake now?"

"Awake some." I snuggled closer.

Then I sat up and got rid of that nightgown; I was getting bound up in it. And Briney took off his nightshirt, and for the first time both of us were bare all over and it was wonderful and I knew that all my life had just been preparation for this moment.

After an unmeasured time that had started out slowly, we both took fire together—after that, I was lying quietly under him, loving him. "Thank you, Briney. You are wonderful."

"Thank you. Love you."

"Love you, my husband. Briney. Where's your cat? In Cincinnati? In Rolla?"

"Eh? No, no. In Kansas City."

"Here? Boarded with someone?"

"I don't know."

"I don't understand."

"You haven't picked it out yet, Mo'. It's the kitten you're going to give me. Bride's present to the bridegroom."

"Oh! Briney, you're a scamp!" I tickled him. He tickled me. It resulted, by stages, in Maureen being disgracefully noisy again. Then I got my back scratched. Having your back scratched is not the only reason to be married, but it is a good one, especially for those spots that are so hard to reach by yourself. Then I scratched his back. We finally went to sleep all tangled up in each other like a basket of kittens.

Maureen had at last found out what she was good for, her true destiny.

We had champagne for breakfast.

7

Ringing the Cash Register

From having read candid autobiographies written by liberated women in the twentieth century, especially those published after the second phase of the Final Wars, ca. 1950 et seq., I know that I am now expected to tell in detail all aspects of my first pregnancy and of the birth of my first child—all about morning sickness and my cyclic moods and the tears and the loneliness . . . then the false labor, the unexpected breaking of the bag of waters, followed by eclampsia and emergency surgery and the secrets I spilled under anesthesia.

I'm sorry but it wasn't that way at all. I've seen women with morning sickness and it's obviously horrible, but I've never experienced it. My problem has always been to "stay on the curve," not gain more weight than my doctor thought was healthy for me. (There have been times when I would have killed for a chocolate éclair.)

With my first baby labor lasted forty minutes. If having

babies in hospitals had been the expected thing in 1899, I would have had Nancy on the way to the hospital. As it was, Brian delivered Nancy, under my direction, and it was much harder on him than it was on me.

Dr. Rumsey arrived and retied the cord and cut it, and told Brian he had done an excellent job (he had). Then Dr. Rumsey took care of the delivery of the afterbirth, and Briney fainted, poor lamb. Women are more rugged than men; they have to be.

I've had longer labors than that one but never a terribly long one. I did not have an episiotomy with the first one (obviously!) and I did not need a repair afterward, so on later births I never allowed a knife to be used on me down there and so I have no scar tissue there, just undamaged muscle.

I'm a brood mare, built for it, wide in my thighs and with a birth canal made of living rubber elastic. Dr. Rumsey told me that it was my attitude that made the difference but I know better; my ancestors gave me the genetic heritage that makes me a highly efficient female animal, for which I am grateful . . . as I have seen women who were not, and they suffered terribly and some of them died. Yes, yes, "natural selection" and "survival of the fittest" and Darwin was right—stipulated. But it is no joke to attend the funeral of a dear friend, dead in her golden youth because her baby killed her. I was at such a funeral in the twenties and heard a sleek old priest talk about "God's will." At the graveside I managed to back away from the coffin such that I got him proper in his instep with a sharp heel. When he yelped, I told him it was God's will.

Once I had a baby in the middle of a bridge game. Pat it was, Patrick Henry Smith, so that makes it 1932 and that makes it contract we were playing, not auction, and that all fits together, as Justin and Eleanor Weatheral taught us contract after they learned it and we were playing at their house. Eleanor and Justin were parents of Jonathan Weatheral, husband of my first born, so the Weatherals were a Howard marriage themselves, but they were our friends long before we knew that about them. We did not learn it until the spring Jonathan showed up on Nancy's Howard Foundation list of young male eligibles.

In this bridge game I was Justin's partner; Eleanor was Briney's partner. Justin had dealt; contract had been reached and we were about to play, when I said, "Put your hands face down and put paperweights on them; I'm having a baby!"

"Forget the hand!" said my husband.

"Of course," agreed my partner.

"Hell, no!" I answered in my ladylike way, "I bid the bloody thing; I'm damn well going to play it! Help me up from here!"

Two hours later we played the hand. Dr. Rumsey, Jr., had come and gone; I was on Eleanor's bed with the table, legs collapsed and supported by pillows, across my lap, and my new son was in my partner's arms. El and Briney were on each side of me, half seated on the bed. I had bid a small slam in spades, doubled and redoubled, vulnerable.

I went down one trick.

Eleanor tilted her nose at me and pushed it up with the tip with her finger. "Smarty, smarty, missed the party!" Then she looked very startled. "Mo'! Move over, dear! I'm about to have mine!"

So Briney delivered two babies that night and Junior Doc had to come back just as soon as he reached home and grumbled at us that he did wish we would make up our minds; he was going to charge us mileage and overtime. Then he kissed us and left—by that time we had long known that the Rumseys were Howards, too, which made Junior Doc a member of the family.

I called Ethel, told her we were staying overnight, and why. "Is everything all right, dear? Can you and Teddy manage? (Four younger ones at home. Five? No, four.)

"Certainly, Mama. But is it a boy or a girl? And how about Aunt Eleanor?"

"Both. I had a boy, Eleanor just had a girl. You youngsters can start working on names . . . for mine, at least."

But the best joke was another matter entirely, something we didn't tell Junior Doc or the children: Briney put that little girl into my sweetheart Eleanor, and her husband Justin put Pat into me . . . all at a weekend in the Ozarks to celebrate Eleanor's fifty-fifth birthday. The birthday party got a bit relaxed and our husbands decided that, since all four of us were Howards, there was no sense in bothering with these pesky rubber sheaths . . . when we could be ringing the cash register.

(Cultural note: I mentioned that Eleanor got pregnant on

her fifty-fifth birthday. But the age of the mother on the birth certificate Junior Doc filed was "forty-three," or close to that. And the age filed on mine was thirty-eight, not fifty. In 1920 all of us had received a warning from the Howard Foundation trustees, delivered by word of mouth, to trim years off our official ages at every opportunity. Later that century we were encouraged and helped to acquire new identities every thirty years or so. Eventually this became the full "Masquerade" that saved the Howard Families during the Crazy Years and following. But I know of the Masquerade only from the Archives, as I was taken out of that turmoil—thank Heaven and Hilda!—in 1982.)

We rang the cash register five times, Brian and I, during the Mauve Decade—five babies in ten years, 1900–1910 Gregorian. I was the first to call it "ringing the cash register" and my husband went along with my crass and vulgar jest. It was after I had recovered from unloading my first one (our darling Nancy) and had been cleared by Dr. Rumsey to resume "family duties" (so help me, that's what they called it then) if we so pleased.

I came home from that visit to Dr. Rumsey, started dinner, then took another bath and used some scandalous perfume Briney had given me for Christmas, got into a lime-green negligee Aunt Carole had given me as a wedding present, checked dinner and turned down the gas—I had it all planned— and was ready when Briney got home.

He let himself in; I was posed. He looked me up and down, and said, "Joe sent me. Is this the right address?"

"Depends on what you are looking for, Sport," I answered in a deep sultry voice. "May I offer you the specialty of the house?" Then I broke my pose and dropped my act. "Briney! Dr. Rumsey says that it is all right!"

"You'll have to speak more plainly, little girl. What is all right?"

"Anything is all right. I'm all back together again." I suddenly dropped the negligee. "Come on, Briney! Let's ring the cash register!"

So we did, although it didn't work that time—I didn't catch again until early in 1901. But it was always delirious fun to try, and try we did, again and again. As Mammy Della once told me, "Lawsy a mercy, chile, jes hunnuds an' hunnuds a times ain't nuffin happen a tall."

How did Mammy Della get in here? Brian found her, that's how, when I started being too big to do a washing easily. Our first house, a tiny one on Twenty-sixth Street, was only a short distance from darktown; Della lived within walking distance, and she would work all day for a dollar and carfare. That she didn't use the streetcar was irrelevant; that dime was part of the bargain. Della had been born a slave and could not read or write . . . but she was as fine a lady as I have ever known, with a heart full of love for all who would accept her love.

Her husband was a roustabout with Ringling Brothers; I never laid eyes on him. She continued to come to see me—or to see Nancy, "her" baby—after I no longer needed help, sometimes bringing along her latest grandchild . . . then she would drop her grandchild in with Nancy and insist on doing my work. Sometimes I could nail her down with a cup of tea. Not often. Later she went back to work for me with Carol. Then with each baby, up to 1911, when "the Lord took her in His arms." If there is a heaven, Della is there.

Can it be that Heaven is as real as Kansas City to those who believe in Heaven? This would fit, it seems to me, the World-as-Myth cosmology. I must ask Jubal about this, when I get out of this jail and back to Boondock.

In gourmet restaurants in Boondock "Potatoes à la Della" are highly esteemed, as are some others of her recipes. Della taught me a great deal. I don't think that I was able to teach her anything, as she was far more sophisticated and knowledgeable than I in the subjects we had in common.

These were my first five "cash register" babies:

Nancy Irene, December 1, 1899 or January 5, 1900

Carol (Santa Carolita) (named for my Aunt Carole) January 1, 1902

Brian, Jr., March 12, 1905

George Edward, February 14, 1907

Marie Agnes, April 5, 1909

After Marie I did not catch again until the spring of 1912. That one was my spoiled brat and favorite child, Woodrow Wilson . . . who was later my lover, Theodore Bronson . . . and much later, my husband Lazarus Long. I don't know why I didn't catch sooner, but it was not from lack of trying; Briney and I tried to ring the cash register at every opportunity. We did not care whether I caught or not; we did it for fun . . . and if we missed, that simply postponed those several weeks when we would have to refrain before and after each birth. Oh, not refrain from everything; I became quite skilled with hands and mouth and so did Briney. But for solid day in and day out happy fun, we both preferred the old-fashioned sport, whether it was missionary style or eighteen other ways.

Perhaps I could account for all the times I failed to catch if I had a calendar of the Mauve Decade, with a record of my menstrual periods. The calendar would be no problem, but a record of my menses, while I did keep one at that time, is long gone and irretrievable—or nearly so; it would take a Time Corps operation to retrieve it. But here is my theory: Briney was often away on business; he was "ringing the cash register" his own way, as an analyst and planner for corporate mining ventures, one whose exceptional talents were increasingly in demand.

Neither of us had heard of the simple fourteen-day rule for ovulation, or the thermometer check, much less the more subtle and more reliable techniques developed in the latter half of the twentieth century. Dr. Rumsey was as good a family doctor as you could find at that time and he was not constrained by the taboos of the time—he had been sent to us by the Howard Foundation—but Dr. Rumsey knew no more about this than we did.

If it were possible to prepare a calendar showing my menses 1900–1912, then mark on it by the fourteen-day rule my probable dates of ovulation, then mark the dates that Briney was away from Kansas City, it is long odds that such a chart would show that those little wigglers never had a target to shoot at on those occasions that I failed to catch. This seems certain, as Briney was a prize stallion and I was Myrtle the Fertile Turtle.

But I am glad that I did not know the rules of ovulation at that time, because there is nothing that beats the tingling excitement of lying back, legs open and eyes closed and bare to the possibility of impregnation. And I know that this is not just one of Maureen's many eccentricities; I have checked this with endless other women: the knowledge that it can happen adds to the zest.

I am not running down contraception; it's the greatest boon to women in all history, as efficient contraception frees women from that automatic enslavement to men that has been the norm through all histories. But the ancient structure of our female nervous systems is not tuned to contraception; it is tuned to getting pregnant.

So it was grand for Maureen that, once I ceased being a bawdy schoolgirl, I almost never needed to use contraception.

One unusually balmy February day in 1912 Briney nailed me to the ground on a bank of the Blue River, almost exactly duplicating an earlier occasion, March fourth, 1899, on a bank of the Marais des Cygnes. We both delighted in making love outdoors, especially with a spice of danger. On the occasion of that 1912 prank I was wearing opera-length silk hose and green round garters, and my husband photographed me so, standing, naked in the sunlight, facing the camera and smiling—and that picture played a major part in my life six years later, and seventy years later, and over two thousand years later.

That picture, I am told, changed the entire history of the human race in several time lines.

Maybe so, maybe not. I'm not fully sold on World-as-Myth even though I am a Time Corps field agent, even though the smartest people I know tell me it's the real McCoy. Father always required me to think for myself, and Mr. Clemens urged me to, also. I was taught that the one Unforgivable Sin, the offense against one's own integrity, was to accept anything at all simply on authority.

Nancy has two birthdays: the day I bore her, which was registered with the Foundation, and the date we handed out to the world, the day that matched more properly the date of my marriage to Brian Smith. That was easy to do at the end of the nineteenth century, as in Missouri vital statistics were just beginning to be taken. Most records were still of the family-Bible sort. The county clerk of Jackson County recorded births and deaths and marriages if offered to him, but nothing happened if such milestones were not reported.

Nancy's birth was reported correctly to the Foundation, a report signed by me and by Brian, and certified by Dr. Rumsey, then a month later Dr. Rumsey filed a birth certificate with the county clerk, with the false date.

Easy to do—Nancy was born at home; all my babies were born at home until the middle thirties. So there were no hospital records to confuse the issue. On January eighth I wrote the happy news (false date) to several people in Thebes and sent an announcement to the *Lyle County Leader*.

Why such a silly hooraw to fuzz the date of birth of a baby? Because the customs of those times were cruel, cruel, harshly cruel. Mrs. Grundy would have counted on her fingers and whispered that we had to get married to give our sinful bastard a name she shouldn't bear. Yes. It was all a part of the nastiness of the grim age of Bowdler, Comstock, and Grundy, the vultures that corrupted what could have been a civilization.

Near the end of that century single women openly gave birth to babies whose fathers might or might not be around. But this was not the behavior of a truly free culture; it was the other swing of the pendulum and not easy for mother or child. The old rules were being broken but no workable new code had as yet evolved.

Our expedient kept everyone in Thebes County from knowing that sweet little Nancy was a "bastard." Of course Mother knew the date was false . . . but Mother was not in Thebes; she was in St. Louis with Grandpa and Grandma Pfeiffer. And Father had gone back into the Army.

I still don't know how to look at this. A girl should not pass judgment on her parents . . . and I shan't.

The Spanish-American War had brought me closer to Mother. Her worry and grief made me decide that she really did love Father; they just kept it private from the children.

Then, on the day of my wedding, while Mother was dressing me, she gave me that motherly advice that traditionally the bride's mother gives the bride to insure matrimonial tranquility.

Can you guess what she told me? Better sit down to hear this:

She told me that I must be prepared to endure without resentment submission to my husband for "family duties." It was the Lord's plan, explained in Genesis, and was the price that women must pay for the privilege of having children . . . and if I would just look at it that way, I could submit cheerfully. But I must realize also that men have needs different from ours; you must expect to meet his needs. Don't think of it as animal, or ugly—just remember your dear children.

I said, "Yes, Mother. I will remember."

So what happened? Did Mother cut Father off? Whereupon he went back into the Army? Or did he tell her that he wanted to get out of that little town, so deep in the gumbo mud, and try a second career in the Army?

I don't know. I don't need to know; it's not my business. Father did go back into the Army, so quickly after my wedding that I feel sure he had it planned before then. His letters showed that he was in Tampa for a while, then Guantánamo in Cuba . . . then clear out in the Philippines, in Mindanao, where the Moslem Moros were killing more of our soldiers than the Spaniards had ever managed . . . and then he was in China.

After the Boxer Rebellion I thought my father was dead, for I did not hear for a long time. Then at last he was at the Presidio in San Francisco and his letter from there referred to other letters I had never received.

He left the Army in 1912. He was sixty that year—was he retired on age? I don't know. Father always told you what he wanted you to know; if you crowded him, he might treat you to some creative fiction . . . or he might tell you to go straight to hell.

He came to Kansas City. Brian invited him to come live with us, but Father had already found himself a flat and settled into it before he let us know that he was in town, indeed before we knew that he had left the Army.

Five years later he did move in with us because we needed him.

In the 1900s Kansas City was an exciting place. Despite three months in Chicago ten years earlier I was not used to a big city. When I went there as a bride, Kansas City had 150,000 people in it. There were electric streetcars, almost as many automobiles as horse-drawn vehicles, trolley wires and telephone wires and power wires everywhere. All of the main streets were paved and more of the side streets were being paved each year; the park system was already famous worldwide and still not finished. The public library had (unbelievable!) nearly half a million volumes.

Kansas City's Convention Hall was so big that the Democratic party was scheduled to hold its 1900 presidential nominating convention in it—then it burned down overnight and its reconstruction was under way before the ashes were cold and the Democrats nominated William Jennings Bryan in that hall just ninety days after it burned down.

Meanwhile the Republicans renominated President McKinley and, with him, Colonel Teddy Roosevelt, hero of San Juan Hill. I don't know for whom my husband voted . . . but it never seemed to displease him when someone would notice a resemblance between him and Teddy Roosevelt.

I think Briney would have told me, had I asked—but in 1900 politics was not a woman's business, and I was doing my utter best to simulate publicly the perfect modest housewife, interested only in kirk, kitchen, and kids, as the kaiser put it. (*"Kirche, Küche, und Kinder."*)

Then in September 1901, only six months into his second term, our president was murdered most vilely . . . and the dashing young war hero was precipitated into the highest office.

There are time lines in which Mr. McKinley was not assassinated and Colonel Roosevelt was never president, and his distant cousin was not nominated in 1932, which utterly changes the patterns of wars, both in 1917 and 1941. Our Time Corps mathematicians deal with these matters, but the structural simulations are large even for the new computer complex combining Mycroft Holmes IV with Pallas Athene, and are quite beyond me. I'm a baby factory, a good cook, and I aim to be a panic in bed. It seems to me that the secret of happiness in life is to know what you are and then be content to be that, in style, head up and proud, and not yearn to be something else. Ambition can never change a sparrow into a hawk, or a wren into a bird of paradise. I'm a Jenny Wren; it suits me.

Pixel is a fine example of being what he is in style. His tail is always up and he is always sure of himself. Today he brought me still another mouse, so I praised him and petted him, and kept the mouse until he left, then flushed it away.

A midnight thought finally surfaced. These mice are the first proof anyone has had (I'm almost sure) that Pixel can take anything with him when he grasps a probability and walks through walls (if that describes what he does) (well, at least it labels it).

What message can I send, and to whom, and how can I fasten it to him?

In shifting from schoolgirl to housewife I had to add to Maureen's private decalogue. One was: Thou shalt always live within thy household allowance. Another I formulated earlier: Thou shalt not let thy children see thee cry—and when it became clear that Brian would have to be away frequently, I added him in. Never let him see me cry and be sure to offer him a smiling face when he returns . . . don't, Don't, DON'T sour his return with fiddling details about how a pipe froze, or the grocer boy was rude, or see what that dadratted dog did to my pansy bed. Make him happy to come home, sorry to have to leave.

Do let children welcome him; don't let them smother him. He wants a mother for his children . . . but he wants a willing and available concubine, too. If you are not she, he will find one elsewhere.

Another commandment— Promises must be kept—especially ones made to children. So think three times before making one. In case of tiniest doubt, don't promise.

Above all, don't save up punishments "until your father comes home."

Many of these rules did not yet apply when I had only one baby and that one still in diapers. But I did think out most of my rules ahead of time and then wrote them down in my private journal. Father had warned me that I had no moral sense; therefore it would be necessary to anticipate decisions I would have to make. I could not depend on that little voice of conscience to guide me on an ad hoc basis; I did not have that little voice. Therefore I would have to reason things out instead, ahead of time, forming rules of conduct somewhat like the Ten Commandments, only more so, and without the glaring defects of an ancient tribal code intended only for barbaric herdsmen.

But none of my rules were really difficult and I had a wonderfully good time!

I never tried to find out how much Briney was paid whenever I had a baby; I did not want to know. It was more fun to believe that it was a million dollars each time, paid in red-gold ingots the color of my hair, each golden ingot too heavy for one man to lift. A king's favorite, lavished with jewels, is proud of her "fallen" state; it is the poor drab on the street, renting her body for pennies, who is ashamed of her trade. She is a failure and she knows it. In my daydream I was a king's mistress, not a sad-faced mattress-back.

But the Foundation must have paid fairly well. Attend me— Our first house in Kansas City was close to minimum for respectable middle class. It was near the colored district; in 1899 this made it a cheap neighborhood even though it was segregated for whites. Besides, it was on an east-west street and faced north, two more points against it. It was on a high terrace with a long flight of steps to climb. It was a one-story frame house, built in 1880 with its plumbing added as an afterthought—the bath opened directly off the kitchen. It had no dining room, no hallway, just one bedroom. It had no proper basement, just a dirt-floor cellar for the furnace and coal bin. It had no attic, just a low, unfinished space.

But houses for rent that we could afford were scarce; Briney had been lucky to find it. I had thought for a while that I was going to have my first baby in a boarding house.

Briney took me to see it before he closed the deal, a courtesy I appreciated as married women could not sign contracts in those days; he did not have to consult me. "Think you could live here?"

Could I! Running water, a flush toilet, a bathtub, a gas range, gas lamp fixtures, a furnace— "Briney, it's lovely! But can we afford it?"

"That's my problem, Mrs. S., not yours. The rent will be paid. In fact you will pay it for me, as my agent, the first of every month. Our landlord, a gentleman named Ebenezer Scrooge—"

" 'Ebenezer Scrooge' indeed!"

"I think that was the name. But there was a streetcar going by; I may have misunderstood. Mr. Scrooge will collect in person, the first of every month, except Sundays, in which case he will collect on the Saturday preceding, not the Monday following; he was firm about that. And he wants cash; no checks. He was firm about that, too. Real cash, silver cartwheels, not banknotes."

Despite the house's many shortcomings its rent was high. I gasped when Briney told me: Twelve dollars a month. "Oh, Briney!"

"Get your feathers down, freckled one. We're going to be in it just one year. If you think you can stand it that long, you won't have to deal with dear Mr. Scrooge—his name is O'Hennessy—as I can tie it down for twelve months with a discount of four points. Does that mean anything to you?"

I thought about it. "Mortgage money is six percent today . . . so three points represents the average cost of hiring the money, since you are paying in advance and they don't own the money until they have earned it, month by month. One point must be because Mr. O'Hennessy Scrooge won't have to make twelve trips here to collect his rent. So that comes to a hundred and thirty-eight dollars and twenty-four cents."

"Flame Top, you continue to amaze me."

"But they really ought to give you another point, for administrative overhead."

"How is that?"

"For the bookkeeping they don't have to do because you are paying it all in a lump. That brings it down to a hundred thirty-six eighty. Offer him a hundred and thirty-five, Briney. Then settle for one thirty-six."

My husband looked at me in astonishment. "To think I married you for your cooking. Look, I'll stay home and have the baby; you go do my job. Mo', where did you learn that?"

"Thebes High School. Well, sort of. I worked awhile on Father's accounts, then I found a textbook at home that my brother Edward had used, *Commercial Arithmetic and Introduction to Bookkeeping.* We had our schoolbooks in common; there were shelves of them in the back hallway. So I didn't take the course but I read the book. But it's silly to talk about me doing your job; I don't know beans about mining. Besides, I don't want that long streetcar ride down to the west bottoms."

"I'm not sure I can have a baby, either."

"I'll do that, sir; I'm looking forward to it. But I would like to ride downtown with you each morning as far as McGee Street."

"You are more than welcome, Madam. But why McGee Street?"

"Kansas City Business College. I want to spend the next few months, before I get too big, learning to use a typewriter and to take Pittman shorthand. Then, if you ever become ill, dearest man, I could work in an office and support us . . . and if you ever go into business for yourself, I could do your office work. That would save you hiring a girl and maybe get us past that tight spot the books say every new business has."

Briney said slowly, "It was your cooking and one other talent; I remember clearly. Who would have guessed it?"

"Do you mean I may?"

"Better figure up what it will cost in tuition and carfare and lunch money—"

"I'll pack lunches for both of us."

"Tomorrow, Mo'. Or the next day. Let's settle this house."

We took the house, although that skinflint held out for a hundred and thirty-eight dollars. We stayed in it two years and another girl baby, Carol, then moved around the corner onto Mersington and into a slightly larger house (same landlord), where I had my first boy, Brian Junior, in 1905 . . . and learned what had become of the Howard bonuses.

It was the spring of 1906, a Sunday in May. We often took a streetcar ride on Sundays, to the far end of some line we had never explored before—our two little girls in their Sunday best and Briney and me taking turns holding Junior. But this time he had arranged to leave our three with the lady next door, Mrs. Ohlschlager, a dear friend who was correcting and extending my German.

We walked up to Twenty-seventh Street and caught the streetcar heading west; Briney asked for transfers as usual, as on Sundays we might change anywhere, wind up anywhere. This day we rode only ten blocks when Briney pushed the button. "It's a lovely day; let's walk the boulevard awhile."

"Suits."

Brian handed me down; we crossed to the south side, headed south on the west side of Benton Boulevard. "Sweetheart, would you like to live in this neighborhood?"

"I would like it very much and I'm sure we will, in twenty years or so. It's lovely." It truly was—every house on a double lot, each house ten or twelve rooms at least, each with its carriage drive and carriage house (barn, to us country jakes). Flower beds, stained-glass fan lights over the doors, all the houses new or perfectly kept up—from the styles I guessed 1900; I seemed to recall building going on here the year we came to K.C.

"Twenty years in a pig's eye, my love; don't be a pessimist. Let's pick out one and buy it. How about that one with the Saxon parked at the curb?"

"Must I take the Saxon, too? I don't like that door that opens to the rear; a child could fall out. I prefer that phaeton with the matched blacks."

"We're not buying horses, just houses."

"But, Brian, we can't buy a house on Sunday; the contract would not be legal."

"We can, my way. We can shake hands on it; then sign papers on Monday."

"Very well, sir." Briney loved games. Whatever they were, I went along with them. He was a happy man and he made me happy (in or out of bed).

At the end of the block we crossed over to the east side and continued south. In front of the third house from the corner he stopped us. "Mo', I like the looks of this one. It feels like a happy house. Does it to you?"

It looked much like the houses around it, big and comfortable and handsome—and expensive. Not as inviting as the others, as it seemed to be unoccupied—no porch furniture, blinds drawn. But I agreed with my husband whenever possible . . . and it was no fault of the house that it was unoccupied. If it was. "I'm sure it could be a happy house with the right people in it."

"Us, for instance?"

"Us, for instance," I agreed.

Brian started up the walk toward the house. "I don't think there is anyone at home. Let's see if they left a door unlocked. Or a window."

"Brian!"

"Peace, woman."

Willy-nilly, I followed him up the walkway, with a feeling that Mrs. Grundy was staring at me from behind curtains all up and down the block (and learned later that she was).

Brian tried the door. "Locked. Well, let's fix that." He reached into his pocket, took out a key, unlocked the door, held it open for me.

Breathless and frightened, I went in, then was slightly relieved when bare floors and echoes showed that it was empty. "Brian, what is this? Don't tease me, please."

"I'm not teasing, Mo'. If this house pleases you . . . it's my long-delayed wedding present from the groom to the bride. If it does not please you, I'll sell it."

I broke one of my rules; I let him see me cry.

8

Seacoast Bohemia

Brian held me and patted my back, then said, "Stop that infernal blubbering. Can't stand a woman's tears. Makes me horny."

I stopped crying and snuggled up close to him. Then my eyes widened. "Goodness! A real Sunday special." Brian maintained that the only effect church had on him was to arouse his passion, because he never listened to the service; he just thought about Mother Eve, who (he says) has red hair.

(I did not need to tell him that church had a similar effect on me. Every Sunday after church a "special" was likely to happen, once we got the children down for their naps.)

"Now, now, my lady. Don't you want to look around your house first?"

"I wasn't suggesting anything, Briney. I wouldn't dare do it here. Somebody might walk in."

"Nobody will. Didn't you notice that I bolted the front door? Maureen . . . I do believe that you didn't believe me when I said that I was giving this house to you."

I took a deep breath, held it, let it out slowly. "My husband, if you tell me that the sun rises in the west, I will believe you. But I may not understand. And this time I do not understand."

"Let me explain. I can't really give this house to you, because it's already yours; you've paid for it. But, as a legality, title still rests in me. Sometime this coming week we'll change that, vest title in you. It is legal for a married woman to own real property in her own name in this state as long as the deed describes you as a married woman and I waive claim . . . and even that last is no more than a precaution. Now as to how you bought it—"

I bought it flat on my back, I did, "ringing the cash register." The down payment was money Brian had saved while in the Army, plus money from a third mortgage his parents had accepted from him. This let him make a sizable down payment, with a first mortgage at the usual 6 percent, and a second mortgage at 8.5 percent. The house was rented when he bought it; Brian kept the tenants, invested the rent to help pay off the mortgages.

The Howard bonus for Nancy cleared that too-expensive second mortgage; Carol's birth paid off Brian's parents. The Foundation's payment for Brian Junior let Brian Senior refinance the first mortgage down to the point where the rental income let him at last clear the property in May 1906, only six and a half years after he had assumed this huge pyramid of debt.

Briney is a gambler; I told him so. "Not really," he answered, "as I was betting on you, darling. And you delivered. Like clockwork. Oh, Brian Junior was a little later than I expected but the plan had some flexibility in it. While I had insisted on the privilege of paying off the first mortgage ahead of time, I didn't actually have to pay it earlier than June first, 1910. But you came through like the champion you are."

A year ago he had discussed his projected program with his tenants; a date was agreed on: they had moved out quite amicably just the Friday past. "So it's yours, darling. I did not renew our lease this time; Hennessy O'Scrooge knows we are leaving. We can move out tomorrow and move in here, if this house pleases you. Or shall we sell it?"

"Don't talk about selling our house! Briney, if this truly is your wedding present to me, then at last I can make my bride's present to you. Your kitten."

He grinned. "Our kitten, you mean. Yes, I had figured that out." We had postponed getting a kitten because there were dogs on both sides of the little house on Twenty-sixth—and one of them was a cat killer. By moving around the corner we had not gotten away from that menace.

Brian showed me around the place. It was a wonderful house: upstairs a big bathroom and a smaller one, a little bathroom downstairs adjacent to a maid's room, four bedrooms and a sleeping porch, a living room, a parlor, a proper dining room with a built-in china closet and a plate rail, a gas log in the parlor in what could be a fireplace for logs if the gas log was removed, a wonderful big kitchen, a formal front staircase and a convenient back staircase leading from the kitchen, privately—oh, just everything and anything that a family with children could want, including a fenced back yard just right for children and pets . . . and for croquet and picnic dinners and a vegetable garden and a sand pile. I started to cry again.

"Stop it," ordered Briney. "This one is the master bedroom. Unless you prefer another room."

It was a fine, big, airy room, with that sleeping porch off it. The house was empty and reasonably clean (I looked forward to scrubbing every inch), but some items not worth hauling away had been left here and there. "Briney, that old porch swing out there has a pad on it. Would you please bring that pad in?"

"If you wish. Why?"

"Let's ring the cash register!"

"Right away, Madam! Honey, I wondered how long it would take you to decide to baptize your new home."

That pad didn't look too clean and wasn't very big, but I didn't care about trifles; it would keep my spine from being ground into the bare boards. As Briney was fetching it in and placing it on the floor, I was getting out of the last of my clothes. He called out, "Hey! Leave your stockings on."

"Yes, sir. Right away, Mister. Aintchu gonna buy a drink first, dearie?" Drunk with excitement, I took a deep breath and got down on my back. "What's your name, Mister?" I said huskily. "Mine's Myrtle; I'm fertile."

"I'll bet you are." Briney finished getting out of his clothes, hung his coat on a hook behind the bathroom door, started to mount me. I reached for him. He stopped me, paused to kiss me. "Madam, I love you."

"I love you, sir."

"I'm pleased to hear it. Brace yourself."

Then he said, "*Unh!* Ease off a notch."

I relaxed a little. "Better?"

"Just dandy. You're wonderful, lady mine."

"So are you, Briney. Now? Please!"

I started to peak almost at once, then the skyrockets took off and I was screaming and just barely conscious when I felt him let go, and I fainted.

I'm not a fainter. But I did that time.

Two Sundays later I missed my period. The following February (1907) I had George Edward.

Our next ten years were idyllic.

Our life may have looked dull and humdrum to other people since all we did was live quietly in a house in a quiet neighborhood and raise children . . . and cats and guinea pigs and rabbits and snakes and goldfish and (once) silkworms on top of my piano—a project of Brian Junior when he was in fourth grade. That required mulberry leaves, silkworms being fussy eaters. Brian Junior made a deal with a neighbor who had a mulberry tree. Quite early he displayed his father's talent for always finding a way to work out a deal to accomplish his ends, no matter how unlikely they seemed at first.

A deal for mulberry leaves was big excitement the way we lived those years.

We had kindergarten Crayola pictures with stars on them posted in my kitchen, and tricycles on the back porch, and roller skates beside them, and fingers that had to be kissed well and bandaged, and special projects to do at home and take to school, and lots of shoes to be shined to get our tribe ready for Sunday School on time, and noisy arguments over who got the buttonhook next—until I got shoe buttonhooks for each child and put names on them.

All the while Maureen's belly waxed and waned like the round belly of the Moon: George in 1907, Marie in 1909,

Woodrow in 1912, Richard in 1914, and Ethel in 1916 . . . which by no means ended it but brings us up to the War that changed the World.

But endless things happened before then, some of which I should mention. We moved from the church we had attended while we were tenants of "Scrooge" soon after we moved to our new neighborhood. In part we were upgrading in churches just as we were upgrading in houses and neighborhoods. In the United States at that time Protestant denominations were closely linked to economic and social status, although it was never polite to say so. At the top of the pyramid was high-church Episcopalian; at the bottom were several pentecostal fundamentalist sects whose members piled up treasures in Heaven because they were finding it impossible to pile up treasures on Earth.

We had been attending a middle-level church selected largely because it was close by. We would have moved eventually to a more prosperous boulevard church now that we had moved to a more prosperous neighborhood . . . but we moved when we did because Maureen got herself quasi-raped.

My own silly fault. In any century rape is the favorite sport of large numbers of men when they can get away with it, and any female under ninety and over six is at risk anywhere and at all times . . . unless she knows how to avoid it and takes no chances—which is close to impossible.

On second thought forget that bracket of six and ninety; there are crazies out there who will rape any female of any age. Rape is not intercourse; it is murderous aggression.

On third thought what happened to me was not even quasi-rape, as I knew better than to place myself unchaperoned in private with a preacher yet I had gone ahead and done so, knowing quite well what would happen. Reverend Timberly (the slob!) had managed to let me know when I was fourteen that he felt that he could teach me a great deal about life and love . . . while patting my fanny in a fatherly (!) way. I had complained to my father about it without quite naming him, and Father's advice had enabled me to put a stop to it.

But this Biblethumper— It was six weeks after we moved into our new house; I knew I was pregnant, and I was horny; Brian was away. I'm not complaining; Brian had to go where business took him and this is true of endless trades and professions; the breadwinner must go where the bread is. This time he was in Denver; then, when I had expected him home, he sent me a telegram (night letter) telling me that he must go to Montana—just three or four days, a week at the most. Love, Brian.

Spit. Dirty drawers. Garbage. But I kept my smile because Nancy was watching me and at six she was hard to fool. I read her a revised version, then put the typed sheet where she could not get at it; she had taught herself to read.

At three that afternoon, bathed, dressed, and wearing no drawers, I tapped at the door of the study of the Reverend Doctor Ezekiel "Biblethumper." My usual baby watcher was with my three, with written instructions including where I was going and the Home system telephone number of the pastor's study.

The reverend doctor and I had been doing a silent and inconspicuous barnyard dance ever since he had been called to that pulpit three years earlier. I didn't like him all that much, but I was acutely aware of him and his deep, organlike voice and clean masculine odor. It is too bad that he didn't have bad breath or smelly feet or something like that to put me off. But physically I could not fault him—good teeth, sweet breath, bathed and shampooed regularly.

My excuse for going to his study was that I needed to confer with him because I was chairman of the ladies auxiliary committee for the forthcoming whoop-te-do—I don't remember what. But twentieth-century Protestant churches were always preparing for the next whoop-te-do. Yes, I do remember; a citywide revival. Billy Sunday? I think he was the one—a ball player and reformed drunkard who had found Jesus in a big way.

Dr. Zeke let me in; we looked at each other and we both knew; we didn't need to say anything. He put his arms around me; I turned my face up. He put his mouth to mine—and my mouth came open as my eyes closed. In scant seconds after he answered his door he had me down on the couch back of his desk, my skirts up, and he was trying to couple with me.

I reached down and took hold of him and got him aimed properly; he had been about to make his own hole.

Big! With a lost feeling of "Briney is not going to like this," I took him. He had no finesse; he just romped on home. But I was so excited that I was teetering on the edge and ready to explode when I felt him spend—

—just as someone knocked at his study door and he pulled out of me.

The bleeping affair had lasted under a minute . . . and my orgasm had shut down like a frozen pipe.

But all was not lost. Or should not have been. Once that jack rabbit jumped off me, I simply stood up and was immediately presentable. In 1906 skirts came down to the ankles and I had picked a dress that would stand up under crushing. I had left my drawers off not alone for his convenience (and mine) but because, if you are not wearing drawers and encounter an emergency, you don't have to scramble to put them on.

As for Dr. Zeke the stupid geek, all he needed to do before he answered that door was to button his pants . . . which he had to do anyhow.

We could have brazened it out. We could have looked them in the eye, refused to look guilty, invited them into our conference.

But what he did was grab my arm, shove me into his coat closet, and turn the key on me.

I stood in there, in the dark, for two solid hours that seemed like two years. I kept my sanity by thinking up painful ways to kill him. "Hoisting him by his own petard" was the simplest. Some of the others are too nasty to think about.

Finally he unlocked that door, looked at me, and whispered hoarsely, "They're gone now. Let's slip you out the back door."

I didn't spit in his face. I said, "No, Doctor, we will now have our conference. Then you will escort me out the front door of the church, and you will stand there, chatting with me, until several people have seen us."

"No, no, Mrs. Smith! I think—"

"You didn't think. Doctor, the only alternative is for me to run screaming out of here shouting 'Rape!' . . . and what a police matron will find inside me that you left there will prove rape to a jury."

When Brian got home, I told him about it. I had considered keeping it to myself. But we had reached a friendly agreement three years earlier concerning how and when we each could adulterate our marriage without offending or damaging the other. So I decided to make a clean breast of it and accept a spanking if he thought I rated it. I thought I did rate a spanking . . . and if it was a truly hard spanking, that would be an excuse to cry and that would probably wind up wonderfully.

So I wasn't too worried. But I did want to confess and be shrived.

That friendly agreement for prudent adultery— We had resolved to operate together whenever possible, and always to help each other, cover up for each other, and help the other make the kill. The discussion had come about through Dr. Rumsey's confirming that I was pregnant again (with Brian Junior) and I was feeling especially sentimental. That, plus an incitement: we had received a pianissimo "mixed doubles" invitation from a couple we liked.

I started in by telling Briney solemnly that I intended to be utterly faithful to him. I had been faithful for four years and now that I knew that I could be, I would be, till death do us part.

He had answered, "Look, Stupid, you're sweet but not smart. You started in at fourteen—"

"Almost fifteen!"

"Short of fifteen. You told me that twelve other men and boys had sampled your sweetness—but you wanted to know if I thought that the candidates on your Howard list need be counted? Then you revised the tally, telling me that a couple of minor incidents had slipped your mind. You also told me that you had learned to enjoy it almost at once . . . but you wanted me to know that I was the best. Swivel Hips, do you really think that it changed you and your happy loving ways forever just because that bonehead preacher said some magic words over you? Truth will out, the leopard does not change his spots, and the day inevitably comes. When it does, I want you to enjoy it but to stay out of trouble . . . for your sake, for my sake, and especially for our children's sake. But I do not expect you to be what society calls 'faithful' forever amen. I do expect you not to get pregnant, not to catch some filthy disease, not to cause a scandal, not to shame me or yourself, not to risk the welfare of our children. Mostly that means using common sense and always pulling down the shades."

I gulped. "Yes, sir."

"Now, my love, if it is true, as you assert, that Hal Andrews causes your gizzard to throb but that you are avoiding the temptation on my account, then be assured that your forbearance gains you no stars in your crown. We both know Hal; he's a gentleman and he keeps his nails clean. He's polite to his wife. If you don't mean business, quit flirting with him. But if you do want him, go get him! Don't mind me; I'll be busy. Jane is as delectable a piece as I've seen in a long time. I've hankered to bisect her angle from the day we met them.''

"Briney! Is that true? You never showed it. Why didn't you tell me?"

"And give you a chance to go female and jealous and possessive? Sweetheart, I've had to wait until you admitted out loud, with no coaxing or coaching from me, that you were feeling a deep curiosity about another man . . . with a suggestion that perhaps I might feel the same way about his wife. It turns out that I do. So call Jane and accept their dinner invitation. We'll see what develops."

"But what if it turns out that you like Jane more than you like me?"

"Impossible. I love you, my lady."

"I mean what she's sitting on. How she makes love."

"Possible, but unlikely. If I did, I would not stop loving you or lose interest in what you are sitting on; it's special. But that doesn't mean I don't want to try Jane; she smells good." He licked his lips and grinned.

He did and she did and we four did and they remained our loving friends for years although they moved to St. Joe two years later when he got a better offer from the school board there. That put them too far away for quiet family orgies, mostly.

Over the course of time Brian and I worked out detailed rules about how to handle sex, all of them intended to avoid the hazards while leaving both of us free to "sin"—not carelessly but prudently, so that we could always look Mrs. Grundy in the eye and tell her to peddle her papers elsewhere.

Brian made no concessions whatever to the prevalent belief that sex was in some way innately sinful. He was utterly contemptuous of popular opinion. "If a thousand men believe something and I believe otherwise, then it's a thousand to one that they are wrong. Maureen, I support us by having contrary opinions."

When I told Briney about being locked in that closet, he sat up in bed. "That bastard! Mo', I'm going to break both his arms."

"Then you had better break mine, too, as I went there intending to do it. I did it. The rest derived from that bald, inexcusable fact. I took a risk I should not have taken. My fault at least as much as his."

"Yes, yes, but that's not the point. Sweetheart, I'm not faulting him for screwing you; any man not castrated will screw you if he has a clear chance at you. So your only protection is not to give him that chance if you don't want him to take it. What I'm angry about is his shoving my poor baby into a closet, into the dark, locking her in, frightening her. I'll kill him slowly. God damn him. I'll nut him first. I'll take his scalp. And cut off his ears."

"Briney—"

"I'll drive a stake— What, dear?"

"I've been a bad girl, I know, but I got away with it cold. I didn't get pregnant because I am pregnant. No disease . . . or I don't think so. I'm almost certain nobody twigged, no scandal. I would like to watch you do all those things to him; I despise him. But, if you hurt him even a little bit, even punch his nose, it's no longer a secret . . . and that could hurt our children. Couldn't it?"

Briney conceded the pragmatic necessity. I wanted us to leave that church. Briney agreed. "But not right away, love. I'll be home for the next six weeks at least. We'll go to church together—" We got there early and sat down front, facing the pulpit. Briney caught Dr. Zeke's eye and held it, all through the sermon, Sunday after Sunday.

Dr. Zeke had a nervous breakdown and had to take a leave of absence.

Briney and I did not work out all our rules for sex and love and marriage too easily. We were trying to do two things at once: create a whole new system of just conduct in marriage— a code that any civilized society would have taught us as children—and create simultaneously an arbitrary and utterly pragmatic set of rules for public conduct to protect us from the Bible-Belt arbiters of morals and conduct. We were not missionaries trying to convert Mrs. Grundy to our way of thinking; we simply wanted to hold up a mask so that she would never suspect that we did not agree with her way of thinking. In a society in which it is a mortal offense to be different from your neighbors your only escape is never to let them find out.

Slowly over the years we learned that many Howard families had been forced to face up to the fact that the Howard Foundation program simply did not fit the midwestern Bible Belt . . . yet the majority of Howard candidates came from the middle west. Eventually these conflicts and contradictions resulted in most Howards either dropping out of organized religion, or paying it lip service as Brian and I did, until we left Kansas City in the late thirties and quit pretending.

So far as I know, there are no organized religions in Boondock, or anywhere on Tellus Tertius. Question: Is this an inevitable evolutionary development as mankind approaches true civilization? Or is that wishful thinking?

Or did I die in 1982? Boondock is so utterly unlike Kansas City that I have trouble believing that they are in the same universe. Now that I am locked up incommunicado in what appears to be a madhouse run by its inmates it is easy to believe that a traffic accident that hit an old, old woman in 1982 was fatal . . . and that these dreams of weirdly different worlds are merely delirium of dying. Am I heavily sedated and on IC life support in some Albuquerque hospital while they decide whether or not to pull the plug? Are they waiting to hear from Woodrow for authorization? As I recall, I listed him as "Next of Kin" in my wallet.

Are "Lazarus Long" and "Boondock" a senile fantasy?

Must ask Pixel next time he visits me. His English is scarce but I've no one else to ask.

One fine thing we did even before we got our new house furnished: We got the rest of our books out of storage. In the crackerbox we had been living in we had had room for only a couple of dozen volumes, and that precious few only by storing them on the top shelf in the kitchen, a spot I could reach only by standing on a stool—something I did not risk when I was big with child. Once I waited three days for Brian to come home from Galena, intending to ask him to reach down for me my *Golden Treasury*—I could see it; couldn't reach it—then, when he did get home, I forgot it.

I had two boxes of books in storage, Brian had more than that . . . and I had "inherited" case after case of my father's books. He had written to me when he went back into the

Army to tell me that he had had them packed and shipped to Kansas City Storage and Warehousing—receipts enclosed. His bank was instructed to keep the storage paid up . . . but if I wanted to give them a home, that would please him. Perhaps someday he might ask for some of them back, but in the meantime treat them as my own. "Books are meant to be read and loved, not stored."

So we got our printed friends out of bondage and into the light and air—although we had no bookcases as yet. Briney got boards and bricks and set up temporary shelves . . . and I learned what my husband liked better than sex.

Books.

Almost any books but what hooked him that weekend were Professor Huxley's essays . . . which I hardly noticed because I had my hands on Father's Mark Twain collection, Mr. Clemens's books, for the first time since May 1898—everything of his up to that date, mostly first editions and four of them signed by Mr. Clemens and by "Mark Twain"— signed on that great night in January 1898 when I fought to stay awake in order not to miss any of Mr. Clemens's words.

For perhaps two hours Brian and I took turns touching the other one's elbow and saying, "Listen to this!"—then reading aloud. It turned out that Brian had never read "The £1,000,000 Bank-Note" or "The Facts Concerning the Recent Carnival of Crime in Connecticut." I was astonished. "Dear, I love you—but why did they let you graduate?"

"I don't know. The War, probably."

"Well, I'll just have to tutor you. We'll start with the *Connecticut Yankee*."

"I've read it. What's that fat one?"

"That's not Mark Twain; that's one of Father's medical books." I handed it to him, returned to *The Prince and the Pauper*.

A couple of moments later I looked up when Briney said, "Hey, this plate is not correct."

I answered, "Yes, I know. As I know what plate you are looking at. Father says that any layman who gets his hands on that book invariably looks at that plate first. Shall I take off my drawers so that you can check it?"

"Quit trying to divert me, wench; I have an excellent memory." He thumbed on through. "Fascinating. One could study these plates for hours."

"I know. I have."

"Amazing how much machinery can be packed into one set of skin." He went on thumbing through, then got hooked by a work on obstetrics, shuddered at parts of that one (Brian was a good jackleg midwife, but he didn't like blood), put it aside and picked up another one. "Whee!"

"What is it this time, dear? Oh. '*What Every Young Girl Should Know.*' " (He had picked up the Forberg etchings, *Figuris Veneris*. I was startled, too, the first time I opened it.)

"That's not its name. Here's the title page: *Figures of Venus*."

"Joke, dear. Father's joke. He had me study it as a sex instruction manual, then we discussed each picture and he answered any questions I asked. Lots of questions, that is. He said that Mr. Forberg's pictures were anatomically correct . . . which is more than we can say about that censored plate you complained about. Father said that these pictures should be used in school, because they were far superior to the behind-the-barn cartoons or photographs that were the only thing most young people get to look at—until they were confronted by the real thing and were frightened and sometimes hurt." I sighed. "Father says that this so-called civilization is sick throughout but nowhere more so than about sex, every aspect of sex."

"Your father is dead right, I think. But, Maureen, do I understand that Dr. Johnson gave this to you as an instruction manual? My revered father-in-law endorsed everything in these pictures? *Everything?*"

"Oh, heavens, no. Just most of them. But in general Father says that anything two—or more—people want to do is all right as long as it does no physical harm. He felt that the words 'moral' and 'immoral' were ridiculous when applied to sexual relations. Right and wrong were the correct words, used exactly as they would be used in any other human relation."

"*Mon beau-père a raison*. And my wife is a smart cookie, too."

"I had tutoring by a wise man all my life, until he turned me over to you. At least I think my father is wise. Here, let me sit beside you and I'll point out what he approved of, what he didn't."

I moved across beside him; he put his arm around me and

I held the book on his lap. "The title page— Note the date, 1824. But the pictures are mostly classic Greece and Rome, except one in Egypt. Father said that, despite that date less than a hundred years back, these pictures match murals in whorehouses in Pompeii . . . except that these are artistically much superior to the Pompeii paintings."

"Dr. Johnson has been to Pompeii?"

"No. Well, I don't think he has. With Father it is sometimes hard to be sure. He did tell me that he had seen photographs of Pompeii murals in Chicago. At Northwestern or in some museum."

"But how did he get these pictures? I hate to tell you, my sweet innocent, but I'm certain that these pictures would get us a long rest at federal expense . . . under the Comstock Act. If we were caught with them."

" 'If we were caught.' 'Caught' is the important word. Father urged me to know the Law as thoroughly as possible . . . so as not to get caught when I broke one. Father never felt that any law applied to him . . . other than in that sense."

"I think it is clear that your father is a subversive character, a bad influence, a wicked old man . . . and I admire him without limit and hope to grow up like him."

"I love him all to pieces, *mon homme*. He could have had my maidenhead just by lifting his eyebrow. He wouldn't take it."

"I know that, beloved. I've known it since I first met you."

"Yes, I'm a woman scorned . . . and someday he'll pay. But I want to take his advice about the Law. Briney, do you suppose I could attend classes at the Kansas City School of Law . . . if I could squeeze the tuition out of my household allowance?"

"Perhaps. But you won't have to squeeze it out of your housekeeping money; any schooling you want we now can afford. But never mind such trivial matters; we're talking about sex. S-E-X, the stuff that makes the world go around. Next picture, please."

"Yes, sir. Missionary style. Approved even by priests. The next picture is almost as widely accepted, although perhaps Mrs. Grundy never gets on top. This next one is certainly not used by Mrs. Grundy although by everybody else—says Father. But he noted that a gentleman, in coupling with a lady from behind and standing up, will reach under and find her button, so that she is insured a good time, too. Now the next— Oh! Briney, someday, when we can afford it, I want a bed just the right height so that you can put me on it in that position, on my back, legs up—just the right height so that you can stand up and enter me without crouching. I like that position, so do you—but the last time we used it, you got cramps in your legs and were trembling toward the last, you got so tired. Darling, I want you to enjoy it as much as I do. Loads, that is."

"Lady, you're a gentleman."

"Why, thank you, sir! If that is not a jest."

"No jest. Most ladies are not gentlemen; they will pull stunts that would get a man ten days in the stocks . . . and walk on, with their noses in the air. But not my Mo'. With you, fair is fair and you don't expect to get by on your sex."

"Ah, but I do. By 'ringing the cash register.' "

"Don't confuse me with logic. You treat everyone decently, that's all, even your poor old husband. Yes, I'll build you that bed. Not only the right height but one guaranteed not to squeak. I'll get busy on the design. Mmm, Mo', how would you like a really big bed? Say one that would hold you and me and Hal and Jane—or playmates of your choice—all at once."

"Goodness, what a thought! I hear that Annie Chambers has a bed like that."

"But I'll design a better one. Mo', where did you hear of K.C.'s top Madam?"

"At a Ladies' Aid meeting. Mrs. Bunch was deploring the open immorality of this city. I kept my ears open and my mouth closed. Darling, I'll love that bed when it's built . . . and in the meantime I'll be happy with any reasonably level place or even a pile of coal if Briney puts me on it."

"Go along with you. Next picture."

"Then quit teasing my right nipple. Young man masturbating, his daydreams in the background. Father strongly approved of masturbation. He said that all the stories about it were nonsense. He urged me to masturbate all I want to and whenever I want to, all my life, and to be no more ashamed of it than I am of peeing—just close the door, as I do when peeing."

"They told me that it would make me go blind. But it didn't. Next."

"He's an irrumator and she is a fellatrix and that's Vesuvius in the background. Only Father says that those names are silly; it's just two youngsters discovering that sex can be fun. He pointed out that not only is it fun for both of them but also there is a major advantage. If she discovers that it smells bad, she can suddenly remember that it's bedtime; goodnight, Bill—and, No, I can't see you next Saturday. Don't come back at all; I'm entering a nunnery. Briney, I've done that—tossed a boy out because I didn't like the way his penis smelled. One was a Howard candidate. *Phew!* Father told me that a penis that smelled bad was not necessarily diseased, but that was the way to bet . . . and in any case if it wasn't sweet enough to kiss, it wasn't sweet enough to put inside me."

I moved on to the next one. "Same situation, *comme ci* instead of *comme ça*. Cunnilingus. Another silly word, says Father; it's just a kiss. The sweetest kiss of all . . . unless you combine this one with the one we just looked at, to make a sixty-nine. *Soixante-neuf*. Although there is much to be said for taking the two sorts of kisses one at a time, and concentrating."

I turned the page. "Oh, oh! Here's one that Father did not care for."

"Me, too. I prefer girls."

"Yes, but you can do it to a woman, too. Father said that someday some man was going to want to do that to me . . . and that I should think about it ahead of time and be prepared to cope with it. He said that it was not immoral, or wrong, but that it was dirty and physically risky—" (This was in 1906, long before AIDS showed that buggery could be a special and deadly hazard.)

"—but that if I got curious and just had to try it, make him use a sheath and get him to be ultra slow and extra gentle—or I would wind up buying fur coats for proctologists' wives."

"Seems likely. Next, please."

"Beloved—"

"Yes, Mo'?"

"If you want to do that to me, I'm willing. I'm not in the least afraid that you would hurt me."

"Thank you. You're a silly little wench, but I love you. I'm not yet tired of your other hole. Next picture, please; there are people queued up for the second show."

"Yes, sir. I think this one is meant to be funny: husband surprises wife playing happy games with the housewife next door—look at the expression on his face! Briney, I had never suspected that a woman could be so much fun until that time Jane made a grab for me. She's real cuddly. Or anything."

"Yes, I know. Or anything. So is Hal. Or anything."

"Well! I must have slept through something. This next one— Briney, I can't see why women would use dildoes when there are so many live, warm ones around attached to men. Do you?"

"They don't all have your opportunities, my love. Or your talents."

"Thank you, sir." I moved on. "Cunnilingus again, but two women. Briney, why are mermaids used as a symbol of Lesbos?"

"I don't know. What did your Father say?"

"Just what you did. Oh, this next one does show something Father disapproves of. He says that anyone who mixes whips and chains, or either, with sex, is crazy as a pet coon and should be kept away from healthy people. Mmm, the next one is nothing special, just a different position, one that we've tried. Fun for variety, I think, but not for every day. And now— Oh, this one Father called, 'the hetaera's examination, or three ways for a dollar.' Do you think Annie Chambers's girls are examined this way? I hear that they are top quality this side of Chicago. Maybe New York."

"Look, my sweet, I know nothing of Madam Chambers, or her girls. I can't support both you and Annie Chambers, not even with the help of the Foundation. So I don't patronize brothels."

"What do you do in Denver, Briney? Cancel that—under our agreement, I'm not supposed to ask."

"That wasn't in the agreement; of course you can ask. You tell me your bedtime stories and I'll tell you mine—then we'll play doctor. Denver— I'm glad you asked that. In Denver I met this young fat boy—"

"Briney!"

"—who has the most gorgeous big sister, a grass widow a little younger than you are, with long slender legs, natural-blonde, honey-colored hair down to her waist, a sweet disposition, and big, firm tits. I asked her, 'How about it?' " Briney stopped.

"Well? Go on. What did she say?"

"She said No. Hon, in Denver I'm usually too tired for anything more adventurous than Mother Thumb and her four daughters. They are faithful to me in their own fashion and they don't expect me to take them out to dinner and a show first."

"Oh, piffle! What is the blonde's name?"

"What blonde?"

I've just figured out how to get a message out via Pixel. So, if you will excuse me, I'll get it ready at once so that I will have it ready the next time he shows up.

9

Dollars and Sense

Where is that damned cat?

No, no, cancel that. Pixel, Mama Maureen didn't mean that; she's just worried and upset. Pixel is a good boy, a fine boy; everybody knows that.

But, damn it, where are you when I need you?

As soon as we were settled into our new home we shopped for Briney's kitten, but not in pet shops. I'm not sure that there was such a thing as a pet shop in K.C. in 1906; I don't recall ever having seen one that far back . . . and I do remember that we bought goldfish at Woolworth's or at Kresge's, not at a pet shop. Special items for cats, such as flea powder, we bought at the Dog and Cat Hospital at Thirty-first and Main. But finding a kitten required asking the wind.

First I got permission to put a notice on the bulletin board at Nancy's school. Then I told our grocer that we were looking

127

for a kitten, and left the same word with our huckster—a greengrocer who stopped his wagon in our block every week-day morning to offer fresh fruits and vegetables.

The Great Atlantic and Pacific Tea Company peddled its wares the same way but its sales wagon called only once a week since it carried only tea and coffee, sugar and spices. But that meant it covered a larger area with more customers and therefore greater chances of finding kittens. So I gave their driver our telephone number, Home Linwood 446, and asked him to call me if he heard of a litter of kittens, and then (having asked a favor) I bought his special for the week, twenty-five pounds of sugar for a dollar.

A mistake— He insisted on carrying it in for me, asserting that twenty-five pounds was much too heavy for a lady . . . and I learned that what he really wanted was to get me alone. I evaded his hands by picking up Brian Junior, a tactic Mrs. Ohlschlager had taught me when Nancy was tiny. It works best with a small and very wet baby but any child small enough to pick up will throw a hopeful male off his stride and cool him down. Oh, it won't stop a crazy rapist, but most deliverymen (and plumbers, repairmen, etc.) are not rapists; they are simply ordinary rutty males who will go for it if offered. The problem is simply to turn him down firmly but gently, without causing him to lose face. Picking up a child does this.

It was bad judgment also because a whole dollar was too much of my household budget to tie up in sugar, and (worse) I did not have antproof storage for that much sugar . . . so I wound up spending another sixty cents on a sugar safe as big as my flour bin—which left me so short on cash a week later that I served fried mush for supper when my "plan ahead" called for ground beef patties. It was almost the end of the month, so it was serve mush or ask Briney for an advance . . . which I would not do.

With fried mush I served two strips of bacon to Brian and one to me, and one strip, fried crisp and crumbled, divided for Carol and Nancy. (Brian Junior still regarded Cream o' Wheat as a gourmet dish, so he got that plus what milk I had left in my breasts.) Fresh dandelion greens helped to fill out the menu, and their butter-yellow blooms I floated in a shallow dish as a centerpiece. (Can anyone tell me why such pretty flowers are considered weeds?)

It was a skimpy supper but I ended it with a substantial

dessert I could make with what I had on hand, plus two cooking apples picked up cheap that morning from my huckster: apple dumplings with hard sauce.

Hard sauce should be made with confectioners' sugar—but Aunt Carole had taught me how to crush and crush and keep on crushing granulated sugar, using a big spoon and a bowl, to achieve a fair imitation of powdered sugar. I had enough butter on hand and vanilla extract, and I used one teaspoon of cooking brandy—also on hand; Aunt Carole had given it to me on my wedding day. (It was now half gone. I tasted it once—horrible! But a smidgen of it at the right time and place certainly enhanced the flavor of food.)

Brian made no comment on fried mush, but complimented me on the dumplings. On the first of the month following he said, "Mo', the papers say that food prices are up even though the farmers are squawking. And I'm certain that this bigger house is costing you more to run, if only in electricity, gas, and Sapolio. How much more each month do you need?"

"Sir, I'm not asking for more money. We'll get by."

"I'm sure we will but the hot weather will be with us next month. I don't want you paying the iceman the way some housewives do. Let's raise your allowance by five dollars."

"Oh, I don't need that much!"

"My lady, let's do raise it that much, and see how it works out. If you have money left over at the end of the month, tuck it away. At the end of the year you can buy me a yacht."

"Yes, sir. What color?"

"Surprise me."

I managed to add pennies and nickels and dimes to that "egg money" over the months by never using a charge account, even with my grocer—which was just as well, as Brian was in business for himself sooner than he had anticipated.

His employer, Mr. Fones, had made him a junior associate after two years, then assistant manager in 1904. Six months after we moved into our wonderful new house Mr. Fones decided to retire and offered Brian a chance to buy him out.

It was one of the few times I have seen my husband in a quandary. He usually made decisions quickly with the icy calm of a riverboat gambler; this time he seemed bemused—sugaring his coffee twice, then forgetting to drink it.

At last he said, "Maureen, I'm going to have to consult you on a business matter."

"But, Brian, I don't know anything about business."

"Listen to me, my love. Ordinarily I will not bother you about business. *Deus volent*, I will not need to do so again. But this affects you and our three children and the one that has caused you to get out your fat clothes again." He told me in detail what Mr. Fones had offered.

I thought hard about it, then said, "Brian, under this agreement you are to pay this—'drawing account,' you called it— to Mr. Fones each month?"

"Yes. If the business makes more profit than the average of the last few years, his share increases."

"Suppose it makes less. His share goes down?"

"Not below that drawing account figure."

"Even if the business loses money?"

"Even if it loses money. Yes, that's part of the proposal."

"Briney, just what is it he is selling you? You are contracting—will be contracting if you accept—to support him indefinitely—"

"No, just twelve years. His life expectancy."

"If he dies, it ends? Hmmm! Does he know about my great-aunt Borgia?"

"No, it doesn't end if he dies, so get that gleam out of your eye. If he dies, it goes to his estate."

"All right, twelve years. You support him for twelve years. What do you get out of it?"

"Well . . . I receive a going business. Its files, its records, and, principally, its good will. I'll have the right to use the name 'Fones and Smith, Mining Consultants.' " He stopped.

"What else?" I asked.

"The office furniture, and the lease. You've seen the office."

Yes, I had. Down in the west bottoms, across from International Harvester. In the spring flood of 1903 when the Missouri River again failed to turn that corner and tried to run up the Kaw almost to Lawrence, Briney had to go to work in a rowboat. I had wondered then why a mining company would be down there—no mining in the west bottoms, just black mud clear down to China. And the heavy stink of the stockyards.

"Brian, why are the offices there?"

"Cheap rent. It would cost us four times as much to get the same space on Walnut or Main, even clear out at Fifteenth. I take over the lease, of course."

I thought about it hard for several minutes. "Sir, how much of the firm's traveling has Mr. Fones been doing?"

"Originally? Or recently? When I first went to work for him, both he and Mr. Davis made field trips; I stayed in the office. Then he broke me in on what he expected from a survey—that was before Mr. Davis retired. Then—"

"Excuse me, sir. I mean, 'How much traveling has Mr. Fones done this past year?' "

"Eh? Mr. Fones has not made a field survey for more than two years. He's made a couple of money trips. Two to St. Louis, one to Chicago."

"While you made all the muddy-boots trips?"

"You could call it that."

"That's what you call it, Briney. Dear, you do want to go into business for yourself, don't you?"

"You know that I do. This is just sooner than I had thought I could manage it."

"Are you seriously asking me to say what I think you should do? Or are you just using me as a sounding board to get your thoughts straight?"

He gave me his endearing grin. "Maybe some of both. I'll make the decision. But I do want you to tell me what to do, just as if it were entirely up to you."

"Very well, sir. But I need more information. I have never known the amount of your salary—and I don't want to know now; it's not fitting for a wife to ask—but tell me this. Is that drawing account figure more or less than your salary?"

"Eh? More. Quite a bit more. Even with the bonuses I have received on some deals."

"I see. All right, Briney; I'll express my advice in the imperative. Refuse his offer. Go down tomorrow morning and tell him so. At the same time hit him for a raise. Ask him—no, tell him—that you expect a salary equal to that drawing account he was proposing to siphon out of the business."

Briney looked startled, then laughed. "He'll have a stroke."

"Perhaps, perhaps not. But he is certain to be angry. Count on that and be braced for it. Don't let him get you even the least bit angry. Just tell him calmly that fair is fair. For the last two years you have been doing all the hard and dirty work. If the business can afford to pay Mr. Fones that big a drawing account for not working at all, it can certainly pay you the same amount for working very hard indeed. True?"

"Well . . . yes. Mr. Fones won't like it."

"I don't expect him to like it. He's trying to hornswoggle you; he's certain not to like it when the same swindle is offered to him. Briney, that's a touchstone for a fair deal that my father taught me: Does it feel like a fair deal if it's turned the other way around, mirror image? Point this out to him."

"All right. When he comes down off the ceiling. Mo', he won't pay me that much. Wouldn't it be better for me to resign?"

"Truly, Briney, I don't think so. If you simply quit, he will make loud squawks about your disloyalty—how he took you on as a youngster with no experience and taught you the trade—"

"There's some truth in that. Before he hired me, I had had practical experience underground in lead and zinc and in coal through working summers while I was going to school. But no experience with precious metals, just book learning. So I've learned quite a lot while working for him."

"Which is why you must not resign. Instead you are simply asking to be paid what you are worth. What the proposition he offered you shouts aloud that you are worth. Fair is fair. He can go ahead and retire, and pay you that amount to run the business, while he enjoys the net profit himself."

"He'll give birth to a porcupine. Breech presentation."

"No, he'll fire you. Oh, he may possibly offer you a counterproposal; it may take a while. But he will fire you. Briney, would it suit you to stop on your way home at Wyandotte Office Supply and buy a second-hand Oliver typewriter? Pretty please? No, best to rent one for a month with privilege of applying rent on purchase; I should try it out before we tie up so much money. In the meantime we'll design some stationery. 'Brian Smith Associates,' I think. Mining Consultants. No, Business Consultants. Mining Properties. Farms and Ranches. Mineral Rights. Petroleum Rights. Water Rights."

"Hey, I don't know all those things."

"You will." I patted my tummy. "Three months from now this little boiled pig will ring the cash register for us." I thought about the double eagle Father had slipped into my purse on our wedding day. I had never spent it; I was fairly sure Briney did not know that I had it. Father's formal wedding present to us had been a check that had gone into furniture for that little crackerbox we had first lived in. "Dear, I guarantee to keep us fed until you can report this baby to Judge Sperling. Then the Foundation's payment for this baby ought to keep us going for a while . . . and you and I can try to ring the cash register a fifth time before the cash from number four runs out."

I went on, "If the business isn't making money by then, it might be time for you to look for a job. But I'm betting that from now on you will always be your own boss . . . and that we will wind up rich. I have confidence in you, sir. That's why I married you."

"Really? I thought there was another reason. That wee bit of proud flesh."

"There's that, I admit. A contributing factor. But don't change the subject. You've given Mr. Fones more than six hard-working years—much of your time away from home—and now he wants to indenture you, make you his bound boy, for a pittance. He's trying to milk you like a cow. Let him know that you know it . . . and that you won't let him get away with it."

My husband nodded soberly. "I won't let him. Beloved, I knew what he was trying to do. But I had to think of you and our children."

"You do. You will. You always have."

Brian came home early the next day, carrying a battered Oliver typewriter. He put it down and kissed me. "Madam, I have joined the ranks of the unemployed."

"Really? Oh, goodie!"

"I am an ungrateful wretch. I am no better than a Wobbly and I probably am one. He has treated me like his own son, his own flesh and blood. And now I do this to him. Smith, get out of here! Leave these premises; I don't want to see your face again. Don't you dare take even a piece of paper out of this office. You are through as a mining consultant; I'm going to let the whole mining community know how thoroughly unreliable, completely undependable, utterly ungrateful you are."

"Doesn't he owe you some salary?"

"Salary and two weeks notice and earned participation in that Silver Plume Colorado deal. I declined to budge until he paid up. He did, reluctantly, with more comments on my character." Briney sighed. "Mo', it upset me to listen to what he said. But I feel relieved, too. Free, for the first time in more than six years."

"Let me draw you a tub. Then dinner in your robe and then to bed. Poor Briney! I love you, sir."

My sewing room became an office and we installed a Bell telephone in addition to our Home instrument and put the two side by side near my typewriter. Our letterhead carried both numbers and a post office box number. I kept a baby bed in there and a couch I used for quick naps. Mr. Fones's animosity did not seem to hurt us, and it may have helped simply by emphasizing that Brian was no longer working for Davis and Fones—a fact Brian advertised in all the trade journals. My first job with the typewriter was to write to about 150 people and/or firms, announcing that Brian Smith Associates was now in business . . . and announcing a new policy.

"The idea is, Mo', that I am betting on my own judgment. I'll confer with anyone, first visit free, here in Kansas City. If I travel, it's my railroad ticket, two dollars a night for a hotel room, three dollars a day for food, costs such as livery stable rents as required by the survey, plus per diem consulting fee . . . all in advance. In advance because I saw while working for Mr. Fones how nearly impossible it is to get a client to pay for a dead horse. Fones did it by refusing to budge until he had a retainer in hand equal to his projected expenses, applied overhead, and expected minimum profit . . . more, if he could squeeze it out.

"It's on that per diem that I'll differ in my methods from Davis and Fones. I will use a formal, signed contract, with two options, the client to make his choice ahead of time. Forty dollars a day—"

"What!!"

But Briney had spoken seriously. "Mr. Fones charged a client that much for my services. My dear, there are plenty of lawyers who get paid that much per diem for nice clean work in a warm courtroom. I want to be paid at that rate for trudging and sloshing and sometimes crawling through mines that are always cold and usually wet. For that price they'll get my best professional judgment as to how much it will cost to work that mine, including capital investment required before they ship their first ton of ore . . . and my best guess, based on assays, geology, and other factors, as to whether or not the claim can be worked at a profit . . . for it is a sad fact that, in the mining business as a whole, more money goes into the ground than ever is taken out.

"That's the business I'm in, Mo'. Not in mining. I get paid for telling people not to mine. To cut their losses and run. They often don't believe me, which is why I must insist on being paid in advance.

"But once in a while I have had the happy privilege of telling someone, 'Go ahead, do it! It will cost you this big wad of money . . . but you should get it all back and more.'

"And that is where the second option comes in, the one I really prefer. Under the second option I gamble with the client. I lower my per diem and instead take some points on the net, if and when. I won't take more than five points at most, and I won't do a field survey for less than expenses plus a per diem of fifteen dollars a day, minimum. That bracket leaves room to dicker.

"Now— Can you write a model letter for me, explaining the tariff schedule? How they can have our best work, at our standard fee. Or we'll gamble with them at a much lower fee, and they will still have our best work."

"I'll try, Mister Boss Man, sir."

It paid. It made us rich. But I did not suspect how well it paid until forty years later when circumstances caused my husband and me to count up all our assets and figure their worth. But that is forty years later and this account may not go on that long.

It paid especially well through an oddity of human psychology . . . or an oddity of persons seized by the mining mania, which may not be the same thing. Like this—

The compulsive gamblers, the sort who try to beat lotteries or slot machines or other house games, almost always were betting on striking it rich on some claim that could not be worked at a profit. Each of these saw himself as another Cowboy Womack . . . and did not want to share his lucky star with some hireling, even at only five points. So, if he could scrape it up, he paid the full fee, grumbling.

After a survey (when I was my husband's secretary) I would prepare a letter along these lines, telling this optimist that his best vein was "—surrounded by country rock that has to be dug out to get at the high grade. The mine cannot be worked successfully without drifting a new tunnel out to the north to the highway, through a right of way still to be negotiated via the third level of the claim to the north of yours.

"In addition, your claim requires a blacksmithy, a tool repair shop, a new pumping system, new ties and rails for approximately two hundred yards of track, etc., etc.—plus wages for eighty shifts per month as required by the bond-and-lease for an estimated three years before appreciable pay tonnage could be taken to the mill, etc., etc., see enclosures A, B, and C.

"In view of the state of the claim and the capital investment required to work it, we regret to have to report that we recommend against attempting to work this claim.

"We agree with your arithmetic as to the effect on the commercial feasibility of processing low-grade ore if the new Congress does in fact pass legislation requiring free and unlimited coinage of silver at sixteen to one. But we are not as sanguine as you are that such legislation will indeed pass.

"We are forced to recommend that you sell your bond-and-lease for whatever it will bring. Or cut your losses and surrender it.

> "We remain, sincerely at your service,
> "Brian Smith Associates
> "by
> "Brian Smith, President"

This report was typical for an old claim being reopened by a new optimist—the commonest situation in mining. (The West is pocked with holes where some prospector ran out of money and luck.)

I wrote many letters like that one. They hardly ever believed unfavorable reports. They frequently demanded their money back. Then a client often took the bit in his teeth and went ahead anyhow . . . and went broke trying to satisfy a bond-and-lease on country rock assaying only enough silver per ton to go broke on, plus a trace of platinum and a whiff of gold.

The clients attempting to mine gold were even worse. There is something about gold that has an effect on human judgment similar to that of heroin or cocaine.

But there were also a few rational investors—gamblers, but gambling the odds correctly. Offered a chance to reduce up-front expenses in exchange for points, they often took that option . . . and the claims selected by these more level-headed people were more likely to merit a go-ahead from Brian.

Even these worthwhile mining claims usually lost money in the long run, through failure of their owners/operators to shut down soon enough when the operations stopped paying their costs. (Brian did not lose when that happened; he simply stopped making money from his percentage of the net.) But some of them made money and some of them made lots of money and some of them were still making money regularly forty years later. Brian's willingness to postpone his return other than a modest fee put our children into the best schools and Brian's quondam secretary, Mama Maureen, into big, fat emeralds. (I don't like diamonds. Too cold.)

I see that I've missed telling about Nelson and Betty Lou and Random Numbers and Mr. Renwick. That's what comes of being a Time Corps operative; all times look alike to you, and temporal sequence becomes unimportant. All right, let's fill in.

Random Numbers may have been the silliest cat I've ever lived with—although all cats are sui generis, and Pixel has his supporters for the title of funniest cat, unlimited, all times, all universes. But I'm sure Betty Lou would vote for Random Numbers. Theoretically title to Random lay in Brian, since the cat was his bride's wedding present to him, somewhat delayed. But it is silly to talk of title to a cat, and Randie felt that Betty Lou was his personal slave, available at all hours to scratch his skull, cuddle him, and open doors for him, a conviction she supported by her slavish obedience to his tiniest whim.

Betty Lou was Brian's favorite sweetheart for, oh, pretty steadily for three years, then as circumstances brought them together for years and years. Betty Lou was Nelson's wife, Nelson being my cousin who played fast and loose with a lemon meringue pie. My past had come back to haunt me.

Nelson showed up in December of 1906, shortly after Brian had decided to strike out on his own. Brian had met Nelson once, at our wedding, and neither of us had seen him since that day.

He had been fifteen then, no taller than I; now he was a tall, handsome young man of twenty-three, who had earned a master's degree in agronomy at Kansas State University, Manhattan . . . and was as charming as ever, or more so. I felt that old tingle deep inside me and those cold lightnings at the base of my spine. I said to myself, Maureen, as a dog returneth to its vomit, you are in trouble. The only thing protecting you is that you are seven months gone, big as a house, and as seductive as a Poland China sow. Tell Briney in bed tonight and get him to keep a close eye on you.

Big help! Nelson showed up in the afternoon, Brian invited him to stay for dinner. When he learned that Nelson had not checked into a hotel, he invited Nelson to stay overnight. That was to be expected; at that year and in that part of the country, people never stayed in hotels when homes of kinfolk were at hand. We had had overnighters several times even in our first crackerbox; if you didn't have a spare bed, you made up a pallet on the floor.

I didn't say anything to Brian that night. While I was sure that I had told Briney the lemon-pie story, I wasn't sure that I had mentioned Nelson by name. If I had not—or if Brian had not made the connection—then let sleeping dogs bury their own bones. It was swell to have an understanding and tolerant husband but, Maureen, don't be a greedy slut! Don't stir it up again.

Nelson was still there the next day. Brian was his own boss now, but not overwhelmed by clients; he had no need to leave the house that day other than to check our post office box at the Southside substation. Nelson had arrived in an automobile, a smart four-passenger Reo runabout. Nelson offered to drive Brian to the post office.

He offered to take me, too. I was glad that I had the excuse of a little girl—Nancy was at school; Carol at home—and a baby boy not to accept. I had never ridden in an automobile and, to tell the truth, I was scared. Surely, I expected to ride in one someday; I could see a time coming when they would be commonplace. But I was always more timid when I was pregnant, especially toward the end—my worst nightmare concerned miscarriage.

Brian said, "Can't you get the Jenkins girl to come over for an hour?"

I said, "Thank you, another time, Nelson. Brian, paying for a baby watcher is an unnecessary expense."

"Penny pincher."

"I surely am. As your office manager I intend to pinch every penny so hard that the Indian will scream in pain. Go along, gentlemen; I'll get the breakfast dishes done while you're out."

They were gone three hours. I could have walked to the post office and back in less time. But, following a corollary in my expanded Ten Commandments, I said nothing and did not mention my frets about accidents. I smiled and said happily, "Welcome home, gentlemen! Lunch will be ready in twenty minutes."

Briney said, "Mo', meet our new partner! Nel is going to justify our letterhead. He's going to teach me farms and ranches and which end of a cow the milk comes out of . . . and I'm going to teach him how to tell fool's gold from fools."

"Oh, wonderful!" (One fifth of zero is zero; one sixth of zero is still zero—but it's what Brian wants.) I gave Nelson a quick peck. "Welcome to the firm!"

"Thank you, Maureen. It should be a good team," Nelson said solemnly. "Brian tells me he is too lazy to swing a pick, and you know I'm too lazy to pitch manure . . . so we'll both be gentlemen and tell other people how to do it."

"Logical," I agreed.

"Besides, I don't own a farm and I haven't been able to find a job as a county agent—or even as the boy who opens the mail for a county agent. I'm looking for a job to let me support a wife. Brian's offer is heaven sent."

"Brian is paying you enough to support a wife?" (Oh, Briney!)

"That's just it," Brian answered. "I'm not paying him anything. That's why we can afford to hire him."

"Oh." I nodded agreement. "Seems a fair arrangement. Nelson, after a year, if your performance is still satisfactory, I'll recommend to Brian that we double your wages."

"Maureen, you always were a dead game sport."

I did not ask him what he meant by that. I had a bottle of

muscatel tucked away, bought by Briney for Thanksgiving. It was full, save for a little used for one toast. I fetched it for that purpose. "Gentlemen, let us toast the new partnership."

"Hear, hear!"

So we did and the gentlemen drank and I touched my lips to mine, then Nelson offered another toast: " 'Life is short.' "

I looked at him, kept surprise out of my face, but answered, " 'But the years are long.' "

He answered, just as Judge Sperling had given it to us: "Not 'While the evil days come not.' "

"Oh, Nelson!" I spilled my glass. Then I threw myself on him and kissed him properly.

There was no mystery, truly. Nelson was of course eligible on one side of his family; we shared Johnson grandparents (and great-grandparents, although three of four were dead now—all at past a hundred). My father had written to Judge Sperling (I learned later) and said that it had come to his attention that his sister-in-law, Mrs. James Ewing Johnson of Thebes, née Carole Yvonne Pelletier of New Orleans, had living parents; therefore his nephew Nelson Johnson might be eligible for Howard Foundation benefits, stipulating that he married an eligible.

It took them awhile, as they check health and other things, and in particular in Nelson's case that his father actually had died by mischance (drowning) and not through other cause.

Nelson was in Kansas City because Thebes and its environs had no Howard-listed young females. So he was given a list for Kansas City—both Kansas Cities, Missouri and Kansas.

And that's how we met Betty Lou—Miss Elizabeth Louise Barstow. Nelson did his final courting—got her pregnant, I mean—under our roof, while Maureen played shut-eye chaperon, a role I would fill repeatedly for my own girls in future years.

This protected me from my own folly—and I felt rather grumpy about it. Nelson had been my personal property before Betty Lou ever set eyes on him. But Betty Lou is a darling; I couldn't stay grumpy. Eventually I had no need to feel grumpy.

Betty Lou was from Massachusetts. She had been attending KU, God knows why—Massachusetts has some adequate schools. But it worked out that we stood in for her parents as they could not come out for her wedding; they were taking care of their parents. Theoretically Nelson and Betty Lou should have gone back to Boston to be married. But they did not want to spend the money. The Gold Panic was getting under way, and, while that would make a boom in Brian's business, as yet it just meant that money was tight.

Her wedding took place in our parlor on February fourteenth, a blustery cold day. Our new pastor, Dr. Draper, tied the knot, I presided over the reception, with too much help from Random Numbers, who was convinced that the party was in his honor.

Then, when Dr. and Mrs. Draper had left, I went slowly upstairs, with Brian and Dr. Rumsey helping me . . . the first time and almost the last time that I waited long enough for my doctor to arrive.

George Edward weighed seven pounds three ounces.

10

Random Numbers

Pixel went away, wherever it is that he goes, with my first attempt to call for help. Now I can only keep my fingers crossed—

My beloved friend and shared husband Dr. Jubal Harshaw I once heard define happiness. "Happiness, " Jubal stated, "lies in being privileged to work hard for long hours in doing whatever you think is worth doing.

"One man may find happiness in supporting a wife and children. Another may find it in robbing banks. Still another may labor mightily for years in pursuing pure research with no discernible result.

"Note the individual and subjective nature of each case. No two are alike and there is no reason to expect them to be. Each man or woman must find for himself or herself that occupation in which hard work and long hours make him or her happy. Contrariwise, if you are looking for shorter hours and longer vacations and early retirement, you are in the wrong job. Perhaps you need to take up bank robbing. Or geeking in a sideshow. Or even politics."

For the decade 1907–1917 I was privileged to enjoy perfect happiness by Jubal's definition. By 1916 I had borne eight children. During those years I worked harder and for longer hours than I ever have before or since, and I was bubbling with happiness the whole time save for the fact that my husband was away oftener than I liked. Even that had its compensations, as it made our marriage a series of honeymoons. We prospered, and the fact that Briney was oftenest away when business was best resulted in our never experiencing what the Bard called so aptly: "—the tired marriage sheets."

Briney always tried to telephone to let me know exactly when he would be home . . . and then he would tell me: "B.i.b.a.w.y.l.o and I w.w.y.t.b.w." Day or night I would do my best to follow his instructions exactly; I would be in bed asleep with my legs open and wait for him to wake me the best way, but I always took the precaution of bathing first and my sleep might be only that I closed my eyes and held still when I heard him unlock the front door. Then as he got into bed with me he might call me by some outlandish name, "Mrs. Krausemeyer," or "Battleship Kate," or "Lady Plush-bottom"—and I would pretend to wake up, and call him anything but Brian—"Hubert" or "Giovanni" or "Fritz"—and perhaps inquire, still with my eyes closed, whether or not he had placed five dollars on the dresser . . . whereupon he would scold me for trying to run up the price of tail in Missouri and I would get busier than ever, trying to prove that I was so worth five dollars.

Then, sated but still coupled, we would argue over whether or not I had put on a five-dollar performance. Which could result in tickling, biting, wrestling, spanking, laughing, and another go at it, with much bawdy joking throughout. I delighted in trying to be that duchess in the drawing room, economist in the kitchen, and whore in the bedroom that is the classic definition of the ideal wife. Perhaps I was never perfect at it, but I was happiest working hard at all three aspects of that trinity.

Brian also enjoyed singing bawdy songs while coupling, songs with plenty of rhythm to them, a beat that could be matched to the tempo of coition and speeded up or slowed down at will, songs like:

> *"Bang away, my Lulu!*
> *"Bang away good and strong!*
> *"Oh, what'll I do for a bang away*
> *"When my Lulu's dead and gone!"*

Then endless verses, each bawdier than the last:

> *"My Lulu had a chicken,*
> *"My Lulu had a duck.*
> *"She took them into bed with her*
> *"And taught them how to—*
>
> *"BANG! away my Lulu!*
> *"Bang away good and strong!"*

Until at last Briney couldn't stretch it out any longer and had to spend.

While he was resting and recovering, he might demand of me a bedtime story, wanting to know how I had improved each shining hour with a little creative adultery.

He didn't mean what I might have done with Nelson and/ or Betty Lou; that was all in the family and didn't count. "What's new, Mo'? Are you getting to be a dead arse in your old age? You, the Scandal of Thebes County? Tell me it's not true!"

Now believe me, friends, between dishes and diapers, cooking and cleaning, sewing and darning, wiping noses and soothing children's tragedies, I didn't have time to commit enough adultery to interest even a young priest. After that ridiculous and embarrassing contretemps with Reverend Zeke I can't recall any illicit bed bouncing Maureen did between 1906 and 1918 that my husband did not initiate and condone in advance . . . and not much of that as Briney was if anything even busier than I.

I must have been a great disappointment to Mrs. Grundy (several of her lived in our block, many of her went to our church) as, during those ten years leading up to the war that eventually was called "World War I" or "War of the Collapse, First Phase"—during that decade I not only tried to simulate the perfect, conservative, Bible-Belt lady and housewife, I actually was that sexless, modest, church-oriented creature—except in bed with the door locked, alone or with my husband or, on rare and utterly safe occasions, in bed with someone else but with my husband's permission and approval and usually with his chaperonage.

Besides which, only a robot can stay coupled enough hours out of the year to matter. Even Galahad, tireless as he is, spends most of his time being the leader of Ishtar's best surgical team. (Galahad— Galahad reminds me of Nelson. Not just in appearance; the two are twins in temperament and attitudes—even in body odor now that I think of it. When I get home, I must ask Ishtar and Justin how much of Galahad derives from Nelson. Since we Howards started with a limited gene pool, convergence, along with probability and chance, often comes close to physically reincarnating a remote ancestor in some descendant on Tertius or Secundus.)

Which reminds me of what I did with part of my time and how Random Numbers got his name.

I don't think there was ever a month in the first half of the twentieth century but what both Briney and I were studying something . . . and usually studying a language besides, which hardly counts; we had to stay ahead of our children. We usually did not study the same thing—Briney did not study shorthand or ballet; I did not study petroleum extraction methods or evaporation control in irrigation. But study we did. I studied because I had been left with a horrid feeling of intellectual coitus interruptus through not being able to go on to college at least through a bachelor's degree, and Brian studied because, well, because he was a Renaissance man with all knowledge his field. According to the Archives my first husband lasted 119 years. It is a cinch bet that he was studying some subject new to him the last few weeks of his life.

Sometimes we studied together. In 1906 he started in on statistics, probability, and chance by mail, the ICS school—and here were the books and the lessons in our house, so Maureen did them too, all but mailing my work in. So we both were immersed in this most fascinating field of mathematics when our kitten, Random Numbers, joined our lives, courtesy of Mr. Renwick, driver salesman for the Great Atlantic and Pacific Tea Company.

The kitten was an adorable mass of silver-gray fluff and was at first named Fluffy Ruffles through an error in sex; she was a he. But he demonstrated such lightning changes in mood, direction, speed, and action that Brian remarked, "That kitten doesn't have a brain; he just has a skull full of random numbers, and whenever he bangs his head into a chair or ricochets off a wall, it shakes up the random numbers and causes him to do something else."

So "Fluffy Ruffles" became "Random Numbers" or "Random" or "Randie."

As soon as the snow was gone in the spring of '07 we installed a croquet court in our back yard. At first it was played by us four adults. (Over the years it was played by everyone.) Then it was four adults and Random Numbers. Every time a ball was hit that kitten would draw his sword and CHARGE! He would overtake the ball and throw himself on it, grabbing it, all four limbs. Imagine, please, a grown man stopping a rolling hogshead by throwing himself around it. Better imagine football pads and a helmet for him.

Random wore no pads; he went into action wearing nothing but fluff and his do-or-die attitude. That ball must be stopped, and it was up to him to do it—*Allah il Allah Akbar!*

Only one solution— Lock up the cat while playing croquet. But Betty Lou would not permit that.

Very well, add to the rules this special ground rule: Anything done to a croquet ball by a cat, good or bad, was part of the natural hazards; you played it that way.

I remember one day when Nelson picked up the cat and cradled it in his left arm, then used his mallet with one hand. Not only did it not help him—Random jumped out of his arm and landed ahead of the ball, causing Nelson to accomplish nothing—but also we convened a special session of the Supreme Croquet Court and ruled that picking up a cat in an attempt to influence the odds was unfair to cats and an offense against nature and must be punished by flogging the villain around the regimental square.

Nelson pleaded youth and inexperience and long and faithful service and got off with a suspended sentence, although a minority opinion (from Betty Lou) called for Nelson to drive to a drugstore and fetch back six ice cream cones. Somehow the minority opinion prevailed, although Nelson complained that fifteen cents was too heavy a fine for what he had done and the cat should pay part of it.

Eventually Random Numbers grew up, became sedate, and lost his enthusiasm for croquet. But the cat rule remained and was adjudged to apply to any cat, be he resident or traveling salesman, and to puppies, birds, and children under the age of two. At a later time I introduced this rule onto the planet Tertius.

Did I mention the transaction under which I obtained Random Numbers from Mr. Renwick? Perhaps I didn't. He wanted to "swap a little pussy for a little pussy"—that's the way he expressed it. I walked right into that because I asked what he wanted for the kitten?—expecting him to say that there was no charge as the kitten hadn't cost him anything. I did not expect anything else because, while I was aware that some pedigreed cats were bought and sold, I had never actually encountered one. In my experience kittens were always given away, free.

I had not intended ever again to let Mr. Renwick inside the house; I remembered the first time. But I was unexpectedly confronted with a fact: Mr. Renwick carrying a cardboard shoe box with a kitten in it. Grab the box and shut the door in his face? Open the box on the front porch when he was warning me that the kitten was eager to escape, and scraping, scrambling sounds confirmed it? Lie to him, tell him, sorry, we have already acquired a kitten?

When the telephone rang—

I wasn't really used to having a telephone. I felt that a ringing telephone meant either bad news or that Briney was calling; either way, I had to answer it at once. I said, "Excuse me!" and fled, leaving him standing in our open door.

He followed me in, through the central hall, and into my sewing room/office/chore room, where I was on the phone. There he put the shoe box down in front of me, and opened it . . . and I saw this adorable gray kitten while I was talking with my husband.

Brian was on his way home and had called to ask if there was anything I wanted him to pick up.

"I don't think so, dear. But do hurry home; I have your kitten. She's a little beauty, just the color of a pussywillow. Mr. Renwick brought her, the driver for the Great Atlantic and Pacific Tea Company. He's trying to screw me, Briney, in exchange for the kitten . . . No, I'm quite certain. He not only said so, but he has come up behind me and put his arms around me and is now playing with my breasts . . . What? . . .

No, I didn't tell him anything of the sort. So do hurry. I won't fight with him, dear, because I'm pregnant, I'll just give in . . . Yes, sir; I will. *Au 'voir.*" I hung up the receiver . . . although I had thought of using it like a policeman's truncheon. But I truly was unwilling to fight while I had a baby inside me.

Mr. Renwick did not let go of me, but when what I was saying penetrated his head, he held still. I turned around in his arms. "Don't try to kiss me," I said. "I don't want to risk so much as a cold while I'm pregnant. Do you have a rubber? A Merry Widow?"

"Uh— Yes."

"I thought you would have; I'm sure I'm not the first housewife you've tried this with. All right; do please use it, as I don't want to contract a social disease, and neither do you. Are you married?"

"Yes. Christ, you're a cool one!"

"Not at all. I simply won't risk being raped while I'm carrying a baby; that's all. Since you are married, you don't want to catch anything, either, so put on that rubber. How long does it take to drive from Thirty-first and Woodland?" (Brian had called from Twelfth and Walnut, much farther away.)

"Uh— Not very long."

"Then you'd better hurry or my husband will catch you at it. If you really do mean to do this to me."

"Oh, the hell with it!" He abruptly let go of me, turned away, headed for the front door.

He was fumbling with the latch when I called out, "You forgot your kitten!"

"Keep the damned cat!"

That is how I "bought" Random Numbers.

Raising kittens is fun, but raising children is the most fun— if the children happen to be your own—if you happen to be the sort of person who enjoys bearing and rearing children. For Jubal was right; it is subjective, a matter of one's individual disposition. I had seventeen children on my first go-around and greatly enjoyed rearing all of them—each different, each individual—and I've had more since my rescue and rejuvenation, and have enjoyed them even more because Lazarus Long's household is organized so that taking care of babies is easy for everyone.

But I often find other people's children repulsive and their mothers crashing bores, especially when they talk about their disgusting offspring (instead of listening to me talking about mine). It seems to me that many of those little monsters should have been drowned at birth. They strike me as compelling arguments for birth control. As my father pointed out years ago, I am an amoral wretch . . . who does not necessarily regard an unfinished human being, wet and soiled and smelly at one end and yelling at the other, as "adorable."

In my opinion many babies are simply bad-tempered, mean little devils who grow up to be bad-tempered, mean big devils. Look around you. The "sweet innocence" of children is a myth. Dean Swift had an appropriate solution for some of them in "A Modest Proposal." But he should not have limited it to the Irish, as there are many scoundrels who are not Irish.

Now you may be so prejudiced and opinionated that you feel that my children are less than perfect—despite the overwhelming evidence that mine were born with halos and cherubs' wings. So I won't bore you with every time Nancy brought home straight A's on her report cards. Practically every time, that is. My kids are smarter than your kids. Prettier, too. Is that enough? All right, I'll drop the matter. My kids are wonderful to me, and your kids are wonderful to you, and let's leave it at that, and not bore each other.

I mentioned the Panic of 1907 when I told about Betty Lou's marriage to Nelson but at the time I had no idea that a panic was coming. Nor did Brian, or Nelson, or Betty Lou. But history does repeat itself, somewhat and in some ways, and something that happened in early 1907 reminded me of something that happened in 1893.

After the birth of Georgie on Betty Lou's wedding day, I stayed home as usual, for a while, but as soon as I felt up to moving around, I left my brood with Betty Lou and went downtown. I planned to go by streetcar, was unsurprised when Nelson volunteered to drive me down in his Reo runabout. I accepted and bundled up warm; the Reo was rather too well ventilated; it had an open buggy somewhere in its ancestry.

My purpose was to move my savings account. I had placed it in the Missouri Savings Bank in 1899, when we married and settled in Kansas City, by a draft on the First State Bank of Butler (the booming metropolis of Thebes had no banks), where Father had helped me to open a savings account when we came back from Chicago. By the time I was married, it had grown to more than a hundred dollars.

Footnote: If I had more than a hundred dollars in a savings account, why did I serve my family fried mush for their evening meal? Answer: Do you think I am crazy? In 1906 in the American middle west, a sure way for a wife to castrate spiritually her husband would be to suggest that he was incapable of keeping food on the table; I didn't need Dr. Fraud to tell me that. Males live by pride. Kill their pride and they won't support wives and children. It would be some years before Brian and I would learn how to be utterly open and easy with each other. Brian knew that I had a savings account but he never asked me how much I had in it, and I would serve fried mush or do any symbolic equivalent as often as needed before I would buy groceries with my own money. Savings were for "a rainy day." We both knew this. If Brian fell ill, had to go to a hospital, I would use my savings as needed. We had no need to talk about it. Meanwhile Brian was the breadwinner; I did not intrude into his responsibility. Nor he into mine.

But what about Foundation monies? Didn't that hurt his pride? Perhaps it did. It may be indicative to take a look into the future: In the long run every dime we received from "ringing the cash register" wound up with our children, as each got married. Brian never mentioned to me any such intention. In 1907 it would have been silly to do so.

By early 1907 my savings account had grown to over three hundred dollars, by nickels and pennies and tightest economies. Now that I was working at home and could no longer go to school downtown it seemed smart to me to move my account to a little neighborhood bank near the southside post office substation. One of us four had to go to our post office box each day; whoever did it could make deposits for me. If ever I had to withdraw money, then that one could be I.

Nelson parked his runabout on Grand Avenue and we walked around to 920 Walnut. I took my passbook to a teller—did not have to wait; the bank was not crowded—and told the teller that I wanted to withdraw my account.

I was referred to an officer of the bank, over behind the railing, a Mr. Smaterine. Nelson put down the newspaper he had been glancing at, stood up. "Difficulty?"

"I don't know. They don't seem to want to let me have my money. Will you come with me?"

"Sure thing."

Mr. Smaterine greeted me politely, but raised his brows at Nelson. I introduced them. "This is Mr. Nelson Johnson, Mr. Smaterine. He is my husband's business partner."

"How do you do, Mr. Johnson. Please sit down. Mrs. Smith, our Mr. Wimple tells me that you need to see me about something."

"I suppose I do. I attempted to withdraw my account. He told me that I must see you."

Mr. Smaterine gave a smile that displayed his false teeth. "We are always sorry to lose an old friend, Mrs. Smith. Has our service been unsatisfactory?"

"Not at all, sir. But I wish to move my account to a bank closer to my home. It is not too convenient to come all this way downtown, especially in this cold weather."

He picked up my passbook, glanced at the address in the front, then at the current amount farther on. "May I ask where you propose to transfer your account, Mrs. Smith?"

I was about to tell him, when I caught Nelson's eye. He didn't actually shake his head . . . but I've known him a long time. "Why do you ask that, sir?"

"It is part of a banker's professional duty to protect his customers. If you wish to move your account—fine! But I want to see you go to an equally reliable bank."

My wild animal instincts were aroused. "Mr. Smaterine, I have discussed this in detail with my husband"—I had not—"and I do not need to seek advice elsewhere."

He made a tent of his fingers. "Very well. As you know, the bank can require three weeks' notice on savings accounts."

"But, Mr. Smaterine, you yourself were the officer I dealt with when I opened my account here. You told me that that fine print was just a formality, required by the state banking act, but that you personally assured me that any time I wanted my money, I could have it."

"And so you can. Let's change that three weeks to three days. Just go home and write us a written notice of intent, and three business days later you can close your account."

Nelson stood up, put his hands flat on Mr. Smaterine's desk. "Now just one moment," he drawled loudly, "did you or did you not tell Mrs. Smith that she could have her money any time she wanted it?"

"Sit down, Mr. Johnson. And lower your voice. After all, you are not a customer here. You don't belong here."

Nelson did not sit down, did not lower his voice. "Just answer yes or no."

"I could have you evicted."

"Try it, just try it. My partner, Mr. Brian Smith, this lady's husband, asked me to come with Mrs. Smith"—Brian had not—"because he had heard that your bank was just a leetle bit reluctant—"

"That's slander! That's criminal slander!"

"—to be as polite to ladies as you are to businessmen. Now— Do you keep your promise to her? Right now? Or three days from now?"

Mr. Smaterine was not smiling. "Wimple! Let's have a check for Mrs. Smith's account."

We all kept quiet while it was made out; Mr. Smaterine signed it, handed it to me. "Please see that it is correct. Check it against your passbook."

I agreed that it was correct.

"Very well. Just take that to your new bank and deposit it. You will have your money as soon as it clears. Say about ten days." He smiled again, but there was no mirth in it.

"You said I could have my money now."

"You have it. There's our check."

I looked at it, turned it over, endorsed it, handed it to him. "I'll take it now."

He stopped smiling. "Wimple!"

They started counting out banknotes. "No," I said, "I want cash. Not paper issued by some other bank."

"You are hard to please, Madam. This is legal tender."

"But I deposited real money, every time. Not bank notes." And I had—nickels and dimes and quarters and sometimes pennies. Once in a while a silver cartwheel. "I want to be paid back in real money. Can't you pay me in real money?"

"Of course we can," Mr. Smaterine answered stiffly. "But you will find, ah, over twenty-five pounds of silver dollars quite cumbersome. That's why bank certificates are used for most transactions."

"Can't you pay me in gold? Doesn't a great big bank like this one carry any gold in its vaults? Fifteen double eagles would be ever so much easier to carry than would be three hundred cartwheels." I raised my voice a little and projected it. "Can't you pay me in gold? If not, where can I take this to change it for gold?"

They paid in gold, with the odd change in silver.

Once we were headed south Nelson said, "Whew! What bank out south do you want? Troost Avenue Bank? Or Southeast State?"

"Nellie, I want to take it home and ask Brian to take care of it."

"Huh? I mean, 'Yes, Ma'am. Right away.' "

"Dear, something about this reminds me of 1893. What do you remember about that year?"

"Eighteen ninety-three— Let me see. I was nine and just beginning to notice that girls are different. Uh, you and Uncle Ira went to the Chicago Fair. When you got back I noticed that you smelled good. But it took another five years to get you to notice me, and I had to slide a pie under you to manage it."

"You always were a bad boy. Never mind my folly in '98; what happened in '93?"

"Hmm— Mr. Cleveland started his second term. Then banks started to fail and everybody blamed it on him. Seems a bit unfair to me—it was too soon after he was sworn in. The Panic of '93, they called it."

"So they did and my father did not lose anything in it, for reasons he described as pure dumb luck."

"Nor did my mother, because she always did her banking in a teapot on the top shelf."

"Father accidentally did something like that. He left Mother a four-months allowance, in cash, in four sealed envelopes, each with a date. He took with him cash, in gold, in a money belt. And he left money behind—whatever it was beyond what we needed—in a lockbox, again in gold.

"Nelson, he told me later that he had not guessed that banks were about to fail; he did it just to annoy Deacon Houlihan—Deacon 'Hooligan,' Father called him. Do you remember him? President of Butler State Bank."

"No, I guess he died without my permission."

"Father told me that the Deacon had remonstrated with him for drawing out cash. The Deacon said it was poor business practice. Just leave instructions to pay Mrs. Smith— Mother I mean—so much each month. Father should leave his money where it was and use checks—the modern way to do business.

"Father got balky—he's good at that—and consequently the bank failures never touched him. Nelson, I don't think Father did business with any bank after that. He just kept cash in a lockbox in his surgery. I think. Although with Father one is never sure."

We had a conference about it when we got home, Brian, me, Nelson, Betty Lou. Nelson told them what had happened. "Getting money out of that bank was like pulling teeth. This boiled shirt certainly did not want to part with Mo's money. I don't think he would have done so if I had not made a loud, obnoxious nuisance out of myself. But that is only partly the point. Mo', tell 'em about Uncle Ira and a similar case."

I did so. "Dears, I don't claim to know anything about finance. I'm so stupid that I never have understood how a bank can print paper money and claim that it is just the same as real money. But today felt like 1893 to me . . . because it is just the sort of thing that happened to Father just before the banks started to fail. He didn't get caught by bank failures because he was balky and stopped using banks. I don't know, I just don't know . . . but I felt uneasy and decided not to put my egg money back into a bank. Brian, will you keep it for me?"

"Here in the house it could be stolen."

Nelson said, "And if it's in a bank, the bank can fail."

"Are you getting jumpy, Nel?"

"Maybe. Betty Lou, what do you think?"

"I think I'm going to draw out my thirty-five cents and find a Mason jar and bury it in the back yard." She paused. "And then I'm going to write to my father and tell him what I've done and why. He won't listen—he's a Harvard man. But I'll sleep better if I tell him."

Brian said, "Some others also we must tell."

"Who?" said Nelson.

"Judge Sperling. And my own folks."

"We don't want to shout it from the house tops. That could start a run."

"Nel, it's our money. If the banking system can't afford to let us draw out our own money and sit on it, then maybe there is something wrong with the banking system."

"Tsk, tsk. You some kind of an anarchist or something?

Well, let's get busy. The first ones in line always get the biggest pieces."

Brian was so serious about it that he made a trip back to Ohio, expensive though it was for him to travel without a client to pay for it. There he talked to Judge Sperling and to his parents. I do not know details . . . but neither the Foundation nor Brian's parents were hurt by the Panic of 1907. Later on we all saw the United States Treasury saved by the intervention of J. P. Morgan . . . who was vilified for it.

In the meantime the assets of Brian Smith Associates were not buried in the back yard . . . but were locked up in the house, and we started keeping guns.

Correction: So far as I know, that was when we started keeping guns. I may be mistaken.

While Brian went to Ohio, Nelson and I tried a project: articles for trade journals such as *Mining Journal*, *Modern Mining*, and *Gold and Silver*. Brian Smith Associates ran small display advertisements in each of these each issue. Nelson had pointed out to Brian that we could get major advertising free by Brian writing articles for these journals—each of them carried about the same number of pages of articles and editorials as it did of advertisements. So instead of a little bitty one-column three-inch display card—no, not "instead of" but "in addition to"—in addition to advertising Brian should write articles. "Lord knows that the stuff they print is dull as ditch water; it can't be hard to write." So said Nelson.

So Brian tried and the result was dull as ditch water.

Nelson said, "Brian old man, you are my revered senior partner— Do you mind if I take a swing at this?"

"Help yourself. I didn't want to do it, anyhow."

"I have the advantage of not knowing anything about mining. You supply the facts—you have; I have them in my hand—and I will slide in some mustard."

Nelson rewrote Brian's sober factual articles about what a mining consultant's survey could accomplish in a highly irreverent style . . . and I drew little pictures, cartoons, styled after Bill Nye, to illustrate them. Me an artist? No. But I had taken Professor Huxley's advice ("A Liberal Education") seriously and had learned to draw. I was not an artist but I was a competent draftsman, and I stole details and tricks from Mr. Nye and other professionals without a qualm—without realizing that I was stealing.

Nelson's first attempt retitled Brian's rewritten article as "How to Save Money by Skimping" and featured all sorts of grisly mining accidents—which I illustrated.

The *Mining Journal* not only accepted it; they actually paid for it, five dollars, which none of us had expected.

Nelson eventually worked it into a deal in which Brian's by-line (ghosted by Nelson) appeared in every issue, and a quarter-page display for Brian Smith Associates appeared in a good spot.

At a later time a twin of that article appeared in *The Country Gentleman* (*The Saturday Evening Post*'s country cousin) telling how to break your neck, lose a leg, or kill your worthless son-in-law on a farm. But the Curtis Publishing Company refused to dicker. They paid for the article; Brian Smith Associates paid for their display cards.

In January 1910 a great comet appeared and soon it dominated the evening sky in the west. Many people mistook it for Halley's Comet, due that year. But it was not; Halley's Comet came later.

In March 1910 Betty Lou and Nelson set up their own household—two adults, two babies—and Random Numbers had a bad time trying to decide where he lived, at The Only House, or with his slave, Betty Lou. For a while he shuttled between the two households, riding any automobile going his way.

In April 1910 the real Halley's Comet began to be prominent in the night sky. In another month it dominated the sky, its head as bright as Venus and its tail half again as long as the Great Dipper. Then it got too close to the Sun to be seen. When it reappeared in the morning sky in May it was still more magnificent. On May fifteenth Nelson drove us out to Meyer Boulevard before dawn so that we could see the eastern horizon. The comet's great tail filled the sky, slanting up from the east to the south, pointing down at the Sun below the horizon, an incredible sight.

But I got no joy from it. Mr. Clemens had told me that he had come in with Halley's Comet and he would go out with it . . . and he did, on April twenty-first.

When I heard—it was published in the *Star*—I shut myself in our room, and cried.

11

A Dude in a Derby

They took me out of my cell today and led me, cuffed and hoodwinked, into what was probably a courtroom. There they removed the hoodwink and the cuffs . . . which left me the only one out of step; my guards were hooded and so were the three who (I think) were judges. Bishops, maybe, they were wearing fancy robes with that sacerdotal look.

Other flunkies here and there also were hooded—put me in mind of a Ku Klux Klan meeting, so I tried to check their shoes—Father had pointed out to me during the recrudescence of the Klan in the twenties that those hooded "knights" showed under their sheets the cracked, scuffed, cheap, and worn-out shoes of the social bottom layer who could manage to feel superior to somebody only by joining a racist secret society.

I could not use that test on these jokers. The three "judges" were behind a high bench. The court clerk (?) had his recording equipment on a desk, his feet under it. My guards were behind me.

They kept me there about two hours, I think. All I gave them was "name, rank, and serial number"—"I am Maureen Johnson Long, of Boondock, Tellus Tertius. I am a distressed traveler, here by misadventure. To all those silly charges: Not guilty! I demand to see a lawyer."

From time to time, I repeated "Not guilty" or stood mute.

After about two hours, judged by hunger and bladder pressure, we had an interruption: Pixel.

I didn't see him come in. Apparently he had come to my cell as usual, failed to find me, and went looking—found me.

I heard behind me this "*Cheerlup!*" with which he usually announces his arrival; I turned and he jumped into my arms, started head bumping and purring, while demanding to know why I wasn't where I was supposed to be.

I petted him and assured him that he was a fine cat, a good boy, the best!

The middle ghost behind the bench ordered: "Remove that animal."

One of the guards attempted to comply by grabbing Pixel.

Pixel has absolutely no patience with people who do not observe correct protocol. He bit the guard in the fleshy part of his left thumb, and got him here and there with his claws. The guard tried to drop him; Pixel did not let go.

The other guard tried to help—now two wounded. But not Pixel.

That middle judge used some language quite colorful, got down and came around, saying: "Don't you know how to grab a cat?"

—and proved at once that he did not. Now three wounded. Pixel hit the deck, running.

I then saw something that had been known to me only through inference, something that none of my friends and family claimed to have seen. (Correction: Athene has seen it, but Athene has eyes everywhere. I mean meat-and-bone people.)

Pixel headed straight for a blank wall at emergency full speed—and just as he seemed about to crash headlong into it, a round cat door opened in front of him, he streaked through it, and it closed instantly behind him.

After a bit, I was returned to my cell.

·   ·   ·   ·

In 1912 Brian bought an automobile, a car—somewhere during that decade "automobile carriage" changed to "automobile," and then to "auto," and then to "motor car," or "car"—the ultimate name for the horseless carriage, as it could not get any shorter.

Brian bought a Reo. Nelson's little Reo runabout had proved most durable and satisfactory; after five years of hard wear it was still a good vehicle. The firm used it for many things, including dusty drives to Galena and Joplin and other towns in the white metals area, and records were kept and Nelson was paid mileage and wear-and-tear.

So when Brian decided to buy a car for his family he bought another Reo, but a family car, a five-passenger touring car, a beauty and one that I could see was safe for children, as it had doors and a top—the runabout had neither. Mr. R. E. Olds called the 1912 Reo his "Farewell Car," claiming that it was the best car that he could design with his twenty-five years of experience, and the best that could be built, in materials and workmanship.

I believed him, and (far more important) Brian believed him. It may have been the "farewell" Reo but, when I left Earth in 1982, Mr. Olds's name was still famous in autos, in "Oldsmobile."

Our luxury car was quite expensive—more than twelve hundred dollars. Brian did not tell me what he had paid, but the Reo was widely advertised and I can read. But we got a lot for our money; it was not only a handsome, roomy touring car but also it had a powerful engine (thirty-five horsepower) and a top speed of forty-five miles per hour. It was never driven at that speed, I think—the speed limit in the city was seventeen miles per hour, and the rutted dirt roads outside the city were quite unsuited to such high speed. Oh, Brian and Nelson may have tried it—opened the throttle wide on some freshly graded, level road out in Kansas somewhere; neither of them believed in bothering ladies with things that might worry them. (Betty Lou and I did not believe in worrying our husbands unnecessarily, either; it evens out.)

Brian outfitted the basic car with all sorts of luxuries that would make it pleasant for his wife and family—a windshield, a self-starter, a top, a set of side curtains, a speedometer, a spare tire, an emergency gas tank, etc. The tires had demountable rims and only rarely did Brian have to patch a tire beside the road.

It did have one oddity; its top could predict the weather. Put the top down; it rained. Put the top up; the sun came out.

It was a one-man top, just as the ads claimed. That one man was Briney—assisted by his wife, two half-grown girls, and two small boys, all of us straining and sweating and Brian nobly repressing the language he wanted to use. But eventually Brian figured out how to outsmart that top: Leave it up all the time. This insured good weather for motoring.

We surely did enjoy that car. Nancy and Carol named it "El Reo Grande." (Brian and I had lately taken up Spanish; as usual our children were trying to outwit us. Pig Latin never did work; they cracked the code at once. Alfalfa speech did not last much longer.) We had established early in our marriage that some occasions were for the entire family . . . and some were for Mama and Papa alone—children would stay home and not whine about it, lest the middle justice be invoked. (Mother had used a peach switch; I found that one from an apricot tree worked just as well.)

By 1912, with Nancy a responsible twelve-year-old girl, it was possible to leave the youngsters at home in her charge for a couple of hours or more in the daytime. (This was before Woodrow was born. Once he was big enough to walk, controlling him called for an Oregon boot and a morningstar.) This let Briney and me have some precious outings alone— and one of them got me Woodrow, as I have mentioned. Briney delighted in making love outdoors, and so did I; it gave a spice of danger to what was otherwise a sweet but lawful occasion.

But when the whole family went for a joy ride, we piled Nancy and Carol, Brian Junior and George, into the roomy tonneau . . . with Nancy charged with seeing that no one stood up on the back seat (not to save the leather upholstery but to protect the child); I sat up front with Marie, and Brian drove.

The picnic basket and the lemonade jug were carried in the tonneau, Carol being charged with keeping her brothers out of the picnic. We would drive out to Swope Park, picnic there, and see the zoo animals, then joy ride again after the picnic, perhaps clear out to Raytown or even Hickman Mills . . . then home with the children falling asleep, to a supper of picnic remains and cups of hot soup.

Nineteen twelve was a good year, despite a blizzard touted as the "worst since '86" (it may have been; I don't remember the '86 blizzard too clearly). It was a campaign year, with a noisy three-sided race, Mr. Taft running for reelection, Teddy Roosevelt at outs with his former protégé Mr. Taft and running on his own "Bull Moose" (Progressive Republican) ticket, and Professor Wilson of Princeton, now governor of his state, running on the Democratic ticket.

That last was a surprise outcome to an unbelievable month-long convention in which it seemed for days that Missouri's favorite son, Mr. Champ Clark, Speaker of the House, would be nominated. Mr. Clark led for twenty-seven ballots and had a clear majority on several but not the two-thirds majority the Democrats required. Then Mr. William Jennings Bryan made a bargain with Dr. Wilson, to be named secretary of state, and Governor Wilson was nominated on the forty-sixth ballot after many of the delegates had gone home.

I followed all this in the *Star* with deep interest as I had read Dr. Wilson's monumental (eighteen volumes!) *A History of the American People*, borrowing it a volume at a time from the Kansas City Public Library. But I did not mention my interest to my husband as I suspected that he favored Colonel Roosevelt.

The election day was the fifth but we did not learn the outcome at once—three days I think it was. Woodrow was born Monday the eleventh at 3:00 P.M., and arrived squalling. Betty Lou midwifed me; as usual I was too fast for my doctor and this time Briney was at work, as I had told him that it couldn't be sooner than the end of that week.

Betty Lou said, "Have you picked a name for this one?"

I said, "Yes. Ethel."

She held the baby up. "Take another look; that name doesn't match this tassel; better save it. Why don't you name him after our new president? That should give him a running start."

I don't remember what I said as Brian arrived about then, Betty Lou having telephoned him. She greeted him at the door with, "Come meet Woodrow Wilson Smith, president of the United States in 1952."

"Sounds good." Brian marched into our bedroom, imitating a brass band. The name stuck; we registered it with the Foundation and with the County.

When I thought it over, the name pleased me. I wrote a note to Dr. Wilson, telling him of his namesake and saying that I was praying for the success of his administration. I received back, first, a note from Mr. Patrick Tumulty, acknowledging my letter and saying that it was being brought to the attention of the president elect "but you will understand, Madam, that recent events have flooded him with mail. It will be several weeks before all of it can be answered personally."

Shortly after Christmas I did receive a letter from Dr. Wilson, thanking me for having honored him in the naming of my son. I framed it and had it for years. I wonder if it is still in existence somewhere on time line two?

The 1912 presidential campaign had been fought on the issue of the "High Cost of Living." The Smith family was not suffering but prices, food prices especially, were indeed rising—while as usual the farmers were complaining that they were not receiving even cost-of-production prices for what they grew. This may well have been so—I recall that wheat was less than a dollar a bushel.

But I did not buy wheat by the bushel; I bought food at a local grocery store and from my huckster and my milkman and so forth. Again Brian asked me if I needed a raise in household allowance.

"Possibly," I answered. "We are getting by, but prices are going up. A dozen freshly gathered eggs cost five cents now, and so does a quart of grade A. The Holsum Bread Company is talking about changing from two sizes at a nickel and a dime to two sizes at ten cents and fifteen cents. Want to bet that this does not mean a raise in price by the pound—I repeat, by the pound, not by the loaf—of at least twenty percent?"

"Find yourself another sucker, sister; I already bet on the election. I was thinking about meat prices."

"Up. Oh, just a penny or two a pound, but it goes on. But I've noticed something else. Mr. Schontz used to include a soup bone without being asked. And some liver for Random. Suet for birds in the winter. Now those things happen only if I ask for them and, when I do, he doesn't smile. Just this week he said that he was going to have to start charging for liver as people were beginning to eat it, not just cats. I don't know how I'm going to explain this to Random."

"Let's keep first things first, my love; my wedding present must be fed. How you behave toward cats here below determines your status in Heaven."

"Really?"

"That's straight out of the Bible; you can look it up. Have you talked to Nelson about cat food?"

"It would not occur to me to do so. Betty Lou, yes; Nelson, no."

"Just remember that he is a professional economist concerning the growing and marketing of foodstuffs and he has a handsome sheepskin to prove it. Nel tells me that, starting anytime now, cats and dogs are going to have their own food industry—fresh food, packaged food, canned food, special stores or special departments in stores, and national advertising. Big business. Millions of dollars. Even hundreds of millions."

"Are you sure he wasn't joking? Nelson will joke about anything."

"I don't think he was. He was quite serious and he had figures to back his remarks. You have seen how gasoline-powered machinery has been displacing horses, not just here in the city, but on farms—slowly but more each year. So we have out-of-work horses. Nelson says not to worry about those horses; the cats will eat them."

"What a horrid thought!"

At Brian's urging I worked up a chart that told me how grocery prices were rising. Fortunately I had thirteen years of exact records of what I had spent on food, what items, how much per peck, or pound, or dozen, etc. Briney had never required me to do it but it matched what my mother had done and it truly was a great help to me during those years of pinching every penny to know just what return I had received in food for each cent I had spent.

So I worked up this big chart, then figured out what a year's "ration" was, per person, as if I were feeding an army—so many ounces of flour, so many ounces of butter, of sugar, of meat, of fresh vegetables, of fresh fruits—not much for canned goods as I had learned, early on, that the only economical way to get canned goods was by canning stuff myself.

Eventually I produced a curve, the cost of a ration for one adult, 1899–1913.

It was a fairly smooth curve, trending steadily up, and with inflexure upward. There were minor discontinuities but, on the whole, it was a smooth first-order curve.

I looked at that curve and it tempted me. I got down my old text for analytical geometry, from Thebes High School, measured some ordinates, abscissas, and slopes—plugged in the figures and wrote down the equation.

And stared at it. Had I actually derived a formula by which food prices could be predicted? Something the big brains with Ph.D.s and endowed chairs could not agree on?

No, no, Maureen! There is not a crop failure on there, not a war, not any major disaster. Not enough facts. "Figures don't lie, but liars figure." "There are lies, damned lies, and statistics." Don't make too much stew from one oyster.

I put my analytical work away where no one would find it. But I kept that chart. I did not use it for prediction but I did keep plotting that curve because it let me go to Briney and show him exactly why I needed a larger allowance, whenever I did—instead of waiting until it reached the "fried mush" situation. I did not hesitate to ask because Brian Smith Associates were prosperous.

I no longer was secretary-bookkeeper of our family firm; I had relinquished that status when Nelson, Betty Lou, and our business office had all moved out of the house together, two years earlier. No friction between us, not at all, and I had urged them to stay. But they wanted to be on their own and I understood that. Brian Smith Associates took an office near Thirty-first and Paseo, second floor, over a haberdashery, a location near the Troost Avenue Bank and the PO substation. It was a good neighborhood for an office outside the downtown financial district. The Nelson Johnsons had their first home of their own about a hundred yards south on a side street, South Paseo Place.

This meant that Betty Lou could handle the records and go to the bank and pick up the mail, while still taking care of her two children, i.e., the back room of the company's "palatial suite" was converted into a day nursery.

Yet I was only twenty minutes away and could relieve her if she needed me, straight down Thirty-first by trolley car, good neighborhoods at both ends, where I need not feel timid even after dark.

We continued this way until 1915, when Brian and Nelson hired a downy duckling fresh out of Spaulding's Commercial College, Anita Boles. Betty Lou and I continued to keep an eye on the books and one of us would be in the office if both men were out of town, as this child still believed in Santa Claus. But her typing was fast and accurate. (We had a new Remington now. I kept my old Oliver at home—a loyal friend, grown feeble.)

So I continued to know our financial position. It was good and got steadily better. Brian accepted points in lieu of full fee several times in the years 1906–1913; five of these enter-prises had made money and three had paid quite well: a reopened zinc mine near Joplin, a silver mine near Denver, and a gold mine in Montana . . . and Briney was just cynical enough that he paid freely under the table to keep a close check on both the silver mine and the gold mine. He told me once, "You can't stop high-grading. Even your dear old grandmother can be tempted when gold ore gets so heavy that you can simply pick it up and know that it is loaded. But you can make stealing difficult if you are willing to pay for service."

By 1911 there was plenty of money coming in, but I could not tell where much of it was going—and I would not ask Briney. It came in, it showed in the books; Nelson drew out some of it, Brian drew out more of it. Some of it wound up in my hands and in Betty Lou's hands to support our two households. But that did not account for all of it. The firm's checking account was simply an aid to bookkeeping, a means to pay Anita and to pay by check other expenses; it was never allowed to grow larger than was needed for those purposes.

It was many years before I learned more than that.

On June 28,1914, in Sarajevo, Serbia, the heir to the throne of the Austro-Hungarian Empire was assassinated. He was Archduke Franz Ferdinand, an otherwise useless piece of royalty, and to this day I have never been able to understand why this event could cause Germany to invade Belgium a month later. I read carefully all the newspapers at the time;

I've studied all the books I could lay hands on since, and I still can't see it. Sheer folly. I can see why, by a sort of insane logic, the Kaiser would attack his first cousin in St. Petersburg—a network of "suicide-compact" alliances.

But why invade Belgium?

Yes, yes, to get at France. But why get at France at all? Why go out of your way to start wars on two fronts? And why do it through Belgium when that would drag in the one nation on Earth with a navy big enough to bottle up the German High Seas Fleet and deny it the high seas?

I heard my father and my husband talking about these matters on August 4, 1914. Father had come over for dinner but it was not a merry occasion—it was the day of the invasion of Belgium and there had been extras out on the streets.

Brian asked, "*Beau-père,* what do you think about it?"

Father was slow to answer. "If Germany can conquer France in two weeks, Great Britain will drop out."

"Well?"

"Germany can't win that fast. So England will come in. So it will be a long, long war. Write the ending yourself."

"You mean we will be in it."

"Be a pessimist and you will hardly ever be wrong. Brian, I know little or nothing about your business. But it is time for all businesses to get on a war footing. What do you deal in that is bound to get involved?"

Briney said nothing for several moments. "All metals are war materials. But— *Beau-père,* if you have some money you want to risk, let me point out that mercury is indispensable for munitions. And scarce. Mostly they mine it in Spain. A place called Almaden."

"Where else?"

"California. Some in Texas. Want to go out to California?"

"No. Been there. Not my taste. I think I'll go back to my digs and get off a letter to Leonard Wood. Damn it, he made the switch from medical corps to line officer—he ought to be able to tell me how I can do it."

Briney looked thoughtful. "I don't want to be in the engineers again, either. I don't belong there."

"You'll be a pick-and-shovel soldier again if you wait and join up here."

"How's that?"

"The old Third Missouri is going to be reorganized as an

engineer regiment. Wait around long enough and they'll hand you a shovel."

I kept my best unworried mask on, and kept on knitting. It felt like the end of April 1898.

The European War dragged along, horribly, with stories of atrocities in Belgium and of ships being sunk by German submarine boats. One could feel a division building up in America; the sinking of the *Lusitania* in May 1915 brought the dichotomy sharply to the fore. Mother wrote from St. Louis about the strong sentiment there for the Central Powers. Her parents, my grandpa and grandma Pfciffcr, apparently took it for granted that all decent people supported "the Old Country" in this struggle—this, despite the fact that *Grossvater's* parents had come to America in 1848 to get away from Prussian imperialism, along with their son, who was just the right age to be conscripted if they had not emigrated. (Grandpa was born in 1830.)

But now it was "*Deutschland Über Alles*" and everybody knew that the Jews owned France and ran everything there, and if those American passengers had minded their own business and stayed home where they belonged, out of the war zone, they wouldn't have been on the *Lusitania*—after all, the emperor had warned them. It was their own fault.

My brother Edward in Chicago reported much the same sentiment there. He did not sound pro-German himself, but he did express a fervent hope that we would stay out of a war that wasn't any of our business.

This was not what I heard at home. When President Wilson made his famous (infamous?) speech about the sinking of the *Lusitania*, the "too proud to fight" speech, Father came over to see Brian and sat there, smoldering like a volcano, until all the children were in bed or elsewhere out of earshot. Then he used language that I pretended not to hear. He applied it mainly to the cowardly tactics of the Huns but he saved a plentiful portion for that "pusillanimous Presbyterian parson" in the White House. " 'Too proud to fight'! What sort of talk is that? It requires pride in order to fight. A coward slinks away with his tail between his legs. Brian, we need Teddy Roosevelt back in there!"

My husband agreed.

In the spring of 1916 my husband went to Plattsburg, New

York, where the previous summer General Leonard Wood had instituted a citizens training camp for officer candidates—Brian had been disappointed not to be able to attend it in 1915, and planned ahead not to miss it in 1916. Ethel was born while Brian was away, through some careful planning of my own. When he returned at the end of August, I had the property back in shape and ready to welcome him, i.b.a.w.m.l.o. so that he could w.m.t.b.w.— and "Mrs. Gillyhooley" did her best to be worth more than five dollars.

I suspect that I was, as my biological pressure was far up past the danger line.

It was the longest dry spell of my married life, in part because I was thoroughly chaperoned at home. At Brian's request Father lived with us while Brian was away. No harem guard ever took his duties more seriously than Father did. Brian had often "chaperoned" me as a shut-eye sentry, protecting me from the neighbors, not from my own libidinous nature.

Father included protecting me from himself. Yes, I tested the water. I had known way back when I was still *virgo intacta* how thoroughly incestuous were my feelings toward my father. Furthermore I was certain that he was just as moved by me.

So about ten days after Brian drove away, when my animal nature was crawling up on me, I arranged it so that I missed saying goodnight to Father, then came into his room right after he had gone to bed, dressed in a low-cut nightgown and a not too opaque peignoir—freshly bathed and smelling good ("April Showers," a euphemism)—and said that I had come in to say goodnight, which he echoed. So I leaned over to kiss him, exposing my breasts and producing a wave of that sinful scent.

He pulled his face back. "Daughter, get out of here. And don't come around me again half naked."

"All naked, perhaps? *Mon cher papa, je t'adore.*"

"You shut t' door . . . behind you."

"Oh, Papa, don't be mean to me. I need to be cuddled. I need to be hugged."

"I know what you need but you are not going to get it from me. Now get out."

"What if I won't? I'm too big to spank."

He sighed. "So you are. Daughter, you are an enticing and amoral bitch, we both know it, we have always known it.

Since I can't spank you, I must warn you. Get out this instant . . . or I will telephone your husband right now, tonight, and tell him that he must come home at once as I am unable to carry out my responsibilities to him and to his family. Understand me?"

"Yes, sir."

"Now get out."

"Yes, sir. May I make a short statement first?"

"Well—make it march."

"I did not ask you to couple with me but if you had—if we had done so, it would have done no harm; I am pregnant."

"Irrelevant."

"Let me finish, please, sir. Ages ago, back when you were requiring me to work out my own personal commandments, you defined for me the parameters of prudent adultery. I have conformed meticulously to your definition, for it turned out that my husband's values in this matter match yours exactly."

"I am pleased to know that . . . but, possibly, not pleased that you told me. Did your husband specifically authorize you to tell me that?"

"Uh— No, sir. Not specifically."

"Then you have told me a bedroom secret without the consent of the other person affected by the secret. Materially affected, as it is his reputation at risk as well as yours. Maureen, you have no right to place another person at risk without his knowledge and consent and you know it."

I kept quiet a long, cold moment. "Yes. I was wrong. Goodnight, sir."

"Goodnight, my darling daughter. I love you."

When Brian returned, he told us that he would be going back to Plattsburg again in 1917—if we were not already at war by then. "They want some of us to get there early and turn instructor to help train the new ones with no military experience . . . and if I will, I go from second to first lieutenant in a hurry. No promise in writing. But that's the policy. *Beau-père,* can you be here next year? Why don't you just stay on? No point in your opening up your flat again, and I'll bet that Mo's cooking is better than the restaurant cooking at that Greek joint under your flat. Isn't it? Careful how you answer."

"It's somewhat better."

" 'Somewhat'! I'll burn your toast!"

We had a small war on our southern border in 1916; "General" Pancho Villa raided across the border again and again, killing and burning. "Black Jack" Pershing, of Mindanao fame, who had been jumped by President Roosevelt from captain to brigadier general, was sent by President Wilson to find and seize Villa. Father had known Pershing when they both were captains in the fight against the Moros; Father thought well of him and was delighted with his meteoric rise (with more to come).

Father pacified a small war at home, for he did stay on with us, and took Woodrow largely out of my hands, with full authority to exercise on Woodrow the low, the middle, and the high justice without consulting either of Woodrow's parents. Both Brian and I were relieved.

Father took a shine to my sixth child, and that left me free to hold Woodrow my favorite in my heart, with no need or temptation to let it show. (My children were all different, and I liked each one of them differently, just as with other people . . . but I did my utter best to treat them all with even justice, without any favoritism in act or manner. I tried. Truly I tried.)

At this great distance, more than a century, I think I at last know why my least likable son was my favorite:

Because he was most like my father, both in his good points and his bad. My father was by no means a saint . . . but he was "my kind of a scoundrel" . . . and my son Woodrow was almost his replica, sixty years younger, the same faults, the same virtues—and the two most stubborn males I have ever met.

Perhaps an unbiased judge might think that we three were "triplets"—aside from the unimportant fact that we were father, daughter, and daughter's son . . . and that they each were as emphatically male as I am female (I am so totally every minute a set of female glands and organs, that I can cope with it only by carefully simulating the sort of "lady" approved by Mrs. Grundy and Queen Victoria).

But those two males were stubborn. Me? *Me* stubborn? How could you think such a thing?

Father clobbered Woodrow as necessary (frequently), took over his education as he had taken over mine, taught him to play chess at four, did not need to teach him to read—like Nancy, Woodrow taught himself. It left me free to rear my other, civilized, well-behaved children with no difficulty and with no need to raise my voice. (Woodrow could have pushed me into being the sort of screaming scold I despise.)

Father's "adoption" of Woodrow left me more time with my lovely and loving and lovable husband. All too soon it was time for him to leave again for Plattsburg. Then I settled down for a truly dry spell. Nelson had been in town part of the time the year before. But now "Brian Smith Associates" had moved its physical location to Galena where Nelson was supervising a new mine that Brian had bought into, when his survey showed its worth but its developer needed more capital. Anita Boles had married and left us; our K.C. office was now just a post office box number, a telephone number transferred back to our house, and a little clerical work I could handle with ease, as my biggest boy, Brian Junior, now twelve, picked up the mail from the box on his bicycle each day on his way home from school.

So Nelson, my only utterly safe "relief husband," was too far away . . . and my father, the puritanical shikepoke, was watching me closely . . . so Maureen resigned herself to four, five, possibly six months in a nunnery.

Father often spent a couple of hours in the evening at a pool hall he called his "chess club." On a rainy night at the end of February he surprised me by bringing home with him a stranger.

He thereby subjected me to the greatest emotional shock of my life.

I found myself offering my hand and greeting a young man who matched in every way (even to his body odor, which I caught quite clearly—clean male, in fresh rut)—a man who was my father as my earliest memory recalled him.

While I smiled and made small talk, I said to myself, "Don't faint. Maureen, you must not faint."

For I had immediately gone into high readiness to receive a male. This male. This male who looked like my father, thirty years younger. I forced myself not to tremble, to keep my voice low, to treat him exactly like any other welcome guest brought to my house by husband or father or child.

Father introduced him as Mr. Theodore Bronson. I heard Father say that he had promised Mr. Bronson a cup of coffee, which gave me the respite I needed. I smiled and said, "Yes, indeed! For a cold and rainy night. Gentlemen, do be seated"—and I fled into the kitchen.

The time I spent in the kitchen, slicing pound cake, dishing up mints, setting out coffee service, cream and sugar, transferring coffee from the kitchen range coffeepot into a silver "company" serving pot—this busyness gave me time to pull myself together, not expose my own rut and (I hoped) cover some of my body odor simply by the odors of food and the fact that female clothing in those days was all-encompassing. I hoped that Father would not notice what I had been sure of, that Mr. Bronson felt the same about me.

I carried in the tray; Mr. Bronson jumped up and helped me with it. We had coffee and cake and small talk. I need not have worried about Father; he was busy with an idea of his own. He too had seen the family resemblance . . . and had formed a theory: Mr. Bronson was a by-blow of his brother Edward, killed in a train wreck not long after I was born. Father had us stand up, side by side, then look in the mirror over the mantelpiece together.

Father trotted out this possible theory of Mr. Bronson's "orphan" origin. It was many months before he admitted to me that he suspected that Mr. Bronson was not my cousin through my rakehell Uncle Edward, but my half brother through Father himself.

The talk that night let me, with all propriety and right under my father's nose, tell Mr. Bronson that I looked forward to seeing him at church on Sunday and that my husband expected to be home for my birthday and we would expect him for dinner . . . since it was Mr. Bronson's birthday, too!

He left soon after that. I bade Father goodnight and went up to my lonely room.

First I took a bath. I had bathed before supper but I needed another one—I reeked of rut. I masturbated in the tub and my breasts stopped hurting. I dried down and put on a nightgown and went to bed.

And got up and locked my bedroom door and took off my gown and got naked back into bed, and masturbated again, violently, thinking about Mr. Bronson, how he looked, the way he smelled, the timbre of his voice.

I did it again and again, until I could sleep.

12

"Hang the Kaiser!"

I'm wondering whether Pixel will come back at all, so disastrous was his last visit.

I tried an experiment today. I called out, "Telephone!" just as I had heard Dr. Ridpath do. Sure enough, a hologram face appeared . . . of a police matron. "Why are you asking for a telephone?"

"Why not?"

"You don't have telephone privileges."

"Who says so? If that is true, shouldn't someone have told me? Look, I'll bet you fifty octets that you're right and I'm wrong."

"Huh? That's what I said."

"So prove it. I won't pay until you prove it."

She looked puzzled and blinked out. We shall see.

Mr. Bronson was at church on Sunday. After the services, at the huddle at the front entrance where church members say nice things to the minister about his sermon (and Dr. Draper did preach a fine sermon if one simply suspended critical faculty and treated it as art)—at the door I spoke to him. "Good morning, Mr. Bronson."

"Good morning, Mrs. Smith. Miss Nancy. Fine weather for March, is it not?"

I agreed that it was, and introduced him to the others of my tribe who were present, Carol, Brian Junior, and George. Marie, Woodrow, Richard, and Ethel were home with their grandfather—I do not think Father ever entered a church after he left Thebes other than to get some friend or relative married or buried. Marie and Woodrow had been at Sunday School but were, in my opinion, too young for church.

We chatted inanities for a few moments, then he bowed and turned away and so did I. Neither of us showed in any fashion that the meeting had any significance to either of us. His need for me burned with a fierce flame, as did mine for him and we both knew it and neither acknowledged it.

Day after day we conducted our love affair wordlessly, never touching, not even a lover's glance, right under my father's eyes. Father told me later that he had had his suspicions—"smelled a rat"—at one point, but that both Mr. Bronson and I had behaved with such propriety that Father had had no excuse to clamp down on us. "After all, my darling, I can't condemn a man for wanting you as long as he behaves himself— we both know what you are—and I can't scold you for being what you are—you can't help it— as long as you behave like a lady. Truth is, I was proud of both of you, for behaving with such civilized restraint. It's not easy, I know."

Through playing chess with my father and, shortly, with Woodrow as well, Mr. Bronson managed to see me, en passant, almost every day. He volunteered as assistant scoutmaster for the troop at our church . . . then drove Brian Junior and George home after Scout meeting the next Friday night— which resulted in a date with Brian Junior for the following afternoon to teach him to drive. (Mr. Bronson owned a luxury model of Ford automobile, a landaulet, always shining and beautiful.)

The following Saturday he took my five older children on a picnic; they were as charmed by him as I was. Carol confided to me afterward: "Mama, if I ever get married, Mr. Bronson is just the sort of man I want to marry."

I did not tell her that I felt the same way.

The Saturday after that one Mr. Bronson took Woodrow downtown to a Hippodrome Theater matinee to see the magician Thurston the Great. (I would have been delighted to be invited along; stage magic fascinates me. But I didn't dare even hint with Father watching me.) When Mr. Bronson returned the child, asleep in his arms, I was able to invite him inside as Father was with me, lending his sanction to the meeting. Never once during that strange romance did Mr. Bronson enter our house without Father being there and then publicly present.

Once when Mr. Bronson fetched Brian Junior back from a driving lesson, I invited him in for tea. He inquired about Father. Learning that Father was not home, Mr. Bronson discovered that he was already late for an appointment. Men are more timid than women . . . at least in my experience.

Brian arrived home on Sunday the first of April, and on the same day Father left on a short visit to St. Louis—to see my mother I assume, but Father never discussed his reasons. I could have wished that Father had stayed home, so that Brian and I could have taken a little journey to nowhere, while Father guarded the teepee and Nancy did the cooking.

But I said nothing about this to anyone, as the children were as anxious to see their father and visit with him as I was to get him alone and take him to bed. Besides— Well, we no longer had an automobile. Before leaving for Plattsburg this time Brian had sold "El Reo Grande."

"Mo'," he had said, "last year, leaving in April, it made sense to drive to Plattsburg; I got lots of use out of the Reo there. But only a fool would attempt to drive from Kansas City to upstate New York in February. Last year in April I had to be pulled out of the mud three times; had it been February I simply would not have made it.

"Besides," Briney had added, with his best Teddy Roosevelt grin, "I'm going to buy us a ten-passenger car. Or eleven. Shall we try for eleven?"

We tried for eleven but failed to ring the cash register that time. Briney went off to Plattsburg by train, with a promise to me that when he got back, he intended to buy the biggest passenger car available—a seven-passenger, if that was the biggest—and what did I think of a closed car this time? A Lexington seven-passenger sedan, for example? Or a Marmon? Or a Pierce-Arrow? Think about it, dear one.

I gave it little thought as I knew that, when the time came, Brian would make his own decision. But I was glad to know that we were going to have a bigger motor car. A five-passenger car is a bit cramped for a family of ten. (Or eleven when I managed to catch.)

So when Brian got home on April first, 1917, we stayed home and did our lovemaking in bed. After all, it isn't necessary to do it in the grass.

That night, when we were tired but not ready to go to sleep, I asked, "When must you return to Plattsburg, my love?"

He was so long in answering I added, "Was that an improper question, Brian? It has been so long since '98 that I am unused to the notion of questions that may not be asked."

"My dearest, you may ask any question. Some I may not be able to answer because the answer is restricted but far more likely I won't be able to answer because a first lieutenant isn't told very much. But this one I can answer. I don't think I'll be going back to Plattsburg. I'm sufficiently sure of it that I didn't leave anything there, not even a toothbrush."

I waited.

"Don't you want to know why?"

"My husband, you will tell me if it suits you. Or when you can."

"Maureen, you're too damned agreeable. Don't you ever have any female-type nosiness?"

(Of course I have, dear man—but I get more out of you if I am not nosy!) "I would like to know."

"Well— I don't know what the papers here have been saying but the so-called 'Zimmerman telegram' is authentic. There is not a chance that we can stay out of the war more than another month. The question is: Do we send more troops to the Mexican border? Or do we send troops to Europe? Or both? Do we wait for Mexico to attack us, or do we go ahead and declare war on Mexico? Or do we declare war first on the kaiser? If we do, do we dare turn our backs on Mexico?"

"Is it really that bad?"

"A lot depends on President Carranza. Yes, it's that bad; I already have my mobilization assignment. All it takes is a telegram and I'm on active duty and on my way to my point of mobilization . . . and it's not Plattsburg." He reached out and caressed me. "Now forget war and think about me, Mrs. MacGillicuddy."

"Yes, Clarence."

Two choruses of "Old Riley's Daughter" later Brian said, "Mrs. Mac, that was acceptable. I think you've been practicing."

I shook my head. "Nary a bit, my love; Father has watched me unceasingly— he thinks I'm an immoral woman who sleeps with other men."

"What a canard! You never let them sleep. Never. I'll tell him."

"Don't bother; Father made up his mind about me before you and I ever met. How are the Plattsburg pussies? Tasty? Affectionate?"

"Hepzibah, I hate to admit this but— Well, the fact is . . . I didn't get any. Not any."

"Why, Clarence!"

"Honey girl, they worked my tail off. Field instruction and drills and lectures in the daytime, six days a week—and surprise drills on Sundays. More lectures in the evenings and always more book work than we could possibly handle. Stagger to bed around midnight, reveille at six. Feel my ribs; I'm skinny. Hey! That's not a rib!"

"So it isn't; it's not a bone of any sort. Hubert, I'm going to keep you in bed until we get you fatted up and stronger; your story has touched my heart."

"It's a tragic one, I know. But what's your excuse? Justin would have offered you a little gentle exercise, I'm certain."

"Dearest man, I did have Justin and Eleanor over for dinner, yes. But with a house full of youngsters and Father a notorious night owl I didn't even get my bottom patted. Nothing but a few gallant indecencies whispered into my horrified ear."

"Your what? You should have gone over there."

"But they live so far away." It was a far piece even by automobile, an interminable distance by streetcar. We had first met the Weatherals at our new church, the Linwood Methodist, when we moved into our home on Benton Boulevard. But that same year, after we got on friendly but not intimate terms with the Weatherals, they moved far out south into the new J. C. Nichols subdivision, the Country Club district, and there they switched to an Episcopalian church near their new home, which put them clear out of our orbit.

Briney and I had discussed them—they both smelled good—but they moved too far away for much socializing, and they were older than we and clearly quite well to do. All these factors left me a bit intimidated, so I had moved the Weatherals to the inactive file.

Then Brian ran into them again when Justin tried to get accepted for Plattsburg; Justin had given Brian as a reference, which flattered him. Justin was turned down for officer-candidate training—a damaged foot, an accident that had maimed him before he learned to walk. He limped but it was hardly noticeable. Brian wrote a letter, urging a waiver; it was not granted. But as a consequence Eleanor had invited us to dinner in January, a week before Brian left for Plattsburg.

A fine big house and even more children than we had—Justin had incorporated into the house design an elegant but expensive idea: Justin and Eleanor occupied not just a master bedroom but the entire upper floor of one wing, a master suite consisting of a sitting room (in addition to a formal parlor and a family sitting room downstairs), a huge bedroom with a pantry and wine safe in one corner, a bath broken into units: a tub, a shower, and two closets, one of the latter having in addition to its WC a fixture I had heard of but never seen before: a fountain bidet.

Eleanor helped me try out the latter and I was delighted! Just what Maureen, with her give-away body odor, needed. I told her so, and told her why.

"I think your natural fragrance is delightful," Eleanor told me seriously, "and so does Justin."

"Justin said that about me?"

Eleanor took my face between her hands and kissed me, softly and gently, her mouth slack—not a tongue kiss but not totally dry. "Justin said that. He said considerably more than that. Dear, he feels enormous attraction to you"—I knew that—"and so do I. And so I do for your husband. Brian affects me all through. If by any chance you two share our feelings . . . Justin and I are willing and eager to realize our feelings in acts."

"You mean a trade off? All the way?"

"All the way! 'A fair exchange is no robbery.' "

I didn't hesitate. "Yes!"

"Oh, good! Do you want a chance to consult Brian?"

"Not necessary. I know. He wants to eat you, raw." I took her face between my palms, kissed her deeply. "How do we go about this?"

"Whatever is easiest for you, Maureen little love. My sitting room converts into a second bedroom in only seconds, and it has its own little powder room. So it can be either two couples, or all four of us together."

"Briney and I don't hide from each other. Eleanor, I have found in the past that, if I simply take my clothes off, it saves time and words."

Her mouth twitched. "I've found it so. Maureen, you astound me. I've known you ten years, I think. Back when we still lived on South Benton and we all attended Linwood Boulevard Methodist, Justin and I discussed you two as possible playmates. I told Justin that Brian had that look in his eyes but I couldn't see any way to crack your armor. The perfect lady, right out of *Godey's Lady's Book*. Since in order to be safe this sort of family seduction has to be negotiated between wives, we simply moved you to the Too-Bad list."

I was unhooking and unbuttoning, while chuckling. "Eleanor love, I broke my maidenhead at fourteen and I've been in heat ever since. Brian knows it and understands me, and loves me anyhow."

"Oh, delightful! Sweetheart, I gave away my cherry at twelve to a man four times my age."

"Then it couldn't have been Justin."

"Heavens, no!" She stepped out of her drawers; it left her in opera-length hose and evening slippers. "I'm ready."

"So am I." I was eyeing her and was sorry Briney hadn't shaved me, as she was as smooth as a grape—Briney was going to love her! Tall, statuesque, blonde.

A few minutes later Justin placed me on the Persian rug in front of the fire in their upstairs sitting room. Eleanor was beside me, with my husband. She turned her head toward me and smiled and took my hand, as we each received the other's husband.

I've heard formal discussions at salons in Boondock, complete with Stimulator and Interlocutor, debating the ideal number for polymorphous sensuality. There were some who favored trios, each of the four sorts or all four or any, and some who favored high numbers, and some who insisted that any odd number could produce maximum pleasure but no even number. Me, I still think that a foursome of families, all loving and lovable, cannot be beaten. I'm not running down any other combination and I like them all. I'm simply naming what I like best, year in and year out.

Later that night Brian telephoned Father and explained that the streets were getting icy; would he mind being zoo-keeper for us tonight?

Brian looked down at me. "What was the faraway look in your eye?"

"I was thinking about your favorite girl—"

"You're my favorite girl."

"Favorite blonde girl. Eleanor."

"Oh. Granted."

"And your favorite oldest daughter."

"Something ambivalent there. Positional grammar? Oldest favorite daughter. Favorite oldest daughter. Yes, I guess they both mean Nancy. Continue."

"News I couldn't put into a letter. Nancy did it."

"Did what? If you mean she did it with that pimply kid, I seem to recall that you concluded that a year ago. How many times can she stop being a virgin?"

"Briney, Nancy finally decided to tell me. She had a scare and that pimply kid doesn't come here anymore, because he wouldn't stop after a rubber broke. So she told Mama. So I douched her and checked her calendar with her and she came around just fine three days later, and she stopped being scared. But at last we were women together and we talked. I gave her some hurry-up Father-Ira instruction, including the lecture that goes with the Forberg etchings—hey, that thing does have a bone in it after all!"

"What do you expect? You're talking about Nancy's fancy; did you think I could stay limp? While Nancy's pretty fancy is *verboten* to me, I can dream, can't I? If you can dream about your father, I can dream about my daughter. Go ahead, hon; get to the good parts."

"Nasty man. Lecher. Brian, don't tempt Nancy unless you mean business or she will turn and sink her fangs into you; she's in an unstable state.

"And now to the good parts. Brian, as we agreed, I told Nancy about the Howard Foundation, and promised that you would talk to her about it, too . . . and I telephoned Judge Sperling. He referred me to a lawyer here in town, Mr. Arthur J. Chapman. Do you know him?"

"I know who he is. Corporation lawyer, never goes into court. Very expensive."

"And a trustee of the Howard Foundation."

"So I inferred from your remark. Interesting."

"I called on him, identified myself, and he gave me Nancy's list. For this area, I mean: Jackson and Clay counties, and Johnson County in Kansas."

"Good hunting?"

"I think so. On the list is Jonathan Sperling Weatheral, son of your favorite blonde."

"I'll be a brass-balled baboon!"

Later on that night Brian said, "So Ira thinks this city slicker is his brother's woods-colt?"

"Yes. You will think so, too, when you see him. Dear one, he and I look so much alike that you would swear that we are brother and sister."

"And you have an acute case of flaming drawers about him."

"That's a mild way of putting it. I'm sorry, dear."

"What is there to be sorry about? If your interest in sex were so mild that you never thought about any man but your poor, old, tired, worn out—*Ouch!*"—I had pinched him—"husband, you wouldn't be half as good tail as you are. As it is, you are quite lively, Mrs. Finkelstein. I prefer you as you are, good points and bad."

"Will you sign a certificate to that effect?"

"Certainly. You want it to show to your customers? Darling girl, I slipped the leash on you years ago, as I knew then and know now that you would never do anything that could risk the welfare of our children. You never have, you never will."

"My record isn't all that good, dearest. What I did with the Reverend Doctor Ezekiel was stupidly reckless. I blush whenever I think of it."

"Zeke the Greek was your rite of passage, my love. It scared the hell out of you and you'll never take a chance on a second-rater again. That's the acid test for adult adultery, my true love: what sort of person you select with whom to share your escapades. All other factors follow naturally from that choice. This Bronson who may or may not be your cousin: Would you be proud to have him here in bed with us tonight? Or would it embarrass you? Would you be happy about it? How does this bloke measure up?"

I thought about Briney's acid test and checked over Mr. Bronson in my mind. "Brian, I can't pass judgment. My head is spinning and I haven't any sense about him."

"Want me to talk to Father Ira about him? Nobody can pull the wool over Ira's eyes."

"I wish you would. Oh, don't suggest that I want to go to bed with Mr. Bronson; it would embarrass Father and he would say *Mrrrph!* and grunt and stalk out of the room. Besides, he knows it. I can feel it."

"I can understand that. Of course Ira is jealous of this city slicker, over you. So I'll stay away from that aspect of the subject."

" 'Jealous'? Father? Over *me?* How could he be?"

"My love, your great sweetness makes up for your slight stupidness. Ira can be—is—jealous over you for the same reason that I can be jealous over Nancy and her little pink fancy. Because I can't have her. Because Ira wants you himself and can't have you. Whereas I have no need to be jealous over you as I do have you and know that your riches are an inexhaustible bonanza. That beautiful flower between your sweet thighs is the original horn of plenty; I can share it endlessly with no possibility of diminishing its wealth. But for Ira it's the unattainable, the treasure that can never be reached."

"But Father can have me any time!"

"Wups! Did you finally get past his guard?"

"No, damn it! He won't give."

"Oh. Then the situation is unchanged; Ira won't touch you for the same reason I won't touch Nancy—although I'm not dead sure I'm as noble as Ira. You had better warn Nancy to stay covered up and downwind when dealing with her poor, old, frail pop."

"I'm damned if I'll warn her, Briney. You are the only male in the whole world I am absolutely certain would not hurt our Nancy in any way. If she can get past your guard, I'll cheer her on—I might learn something from her about how to cope with my own chinchy, impossible-to-seduce father."

"Okay, you redheaded baggage—I'll sniff Nancy and jump you. That'll larn yuh!"

"I'm skeered. Want a giggle? Brian Junior wanted to look. Nancy let him."

"Be damned."

"Yes. I kept my face straight; I neither laughed nor pretended to be shocked. B. Junior told her that he had never had a chance to see just how girls are different from boys—"

"What nonsense! All our kids have been naked in front of each other from time to time; we brought them up that way."

"But, dear, he really did have a point. A boy's differences hang right out where they can be seen; a girl's girlishness is mostly inside and doesn't show unless she lies down and makes it show. That is what Nancy did for him. Lay down, pulled up her robe—she was just out of her bath—spread her thighs wide, pulled her lips apart and showed him the baby hole. Probably winked at him with it. Probably enjoyed it herself. I would have—but none of my brothers asked me to."

"Wench, we haven't found anything yet that you don't enjoy."

I thought about that. "I think you're right, Brian. Some things hurt a little but mostly I have a wonderfully good time. Even this frustration over Mr. Bronson pleasures me more than it hurts . . . since I can tell my beloved husband all about it without causing him to stop loving me."

"Do you want me to tell Ira to lay off? Ask him to give you the shut-eye chaperonage that I would give you?"

"Uh, let's wait until you have sized up Mr. Bronson. If you approve of him, I'll have my drawers off in a jiffy. If you don't, I'll continue my best Vestal Virgin act, which is what he has been getting. But, as I told you, my head is in a whirl and my judgment is no good. I need your cool head."

On Tuesday the *Post* and the *Star* each reported that President Wilson had asked the Congress to declare that a state of war exists between the United States of America and the German Empire. Wednesday we waited for the shout of "Extra!" in the street, or for the telephone to ring, or both— and neither happened. We required the children to go to school although they did not want to, Brian Junior especially. Woodrow was utterly unbearable; I had to refrain from switching him too often.

On Thursday Father returned home, in a state of tense excitement. He and Brian kept their heads together, and I stayed with them, mostly, while delegating all that I could. Woodrow demanded that his grandfather—or someone—play chess with him, until Father turned him over his knee and walloped him, then made him stand in a corner.

On Friday it happened. War. The extras were on our street just before noon, and my husband was on his way almost at once, after telephoning a brother officer, a Lieutenant Bozell, who picked him up and off they drove to Fort Leavenworth, their M-Day assignment. Brian did not wait for his telegram.

Brian Junior and George were home for lunch, waited until their father left—then were late for school for the first time ever. Nancy and Carol came home from their school—Central High School, just a few blocks away—just in time to kiss their father good-bye. I did not ask if they were cutting classes or school had closed early; it did not seem to matter.

Father exchanged salutes with Lieutenant Bozell and with Brian, then headed straight for the streetcar line without coming back into the house. He said to me, "You know where I'm going, and why. I'll be back when you see me."

I agreed that I knew. Father had been increasingly restless ever since his request for active duty had been turned down.

I turned everything over to Nancy and went back to bed . . . for the second time, as I had impressed Father as baby watcher earlier, so that Brian and I could go back to bed after breakfast; we both guessed that this would be *Der Tag*.

But this time I went to bed just to cry.

About three I got up and Nancy served me tea and milk toast; I ate some of it. While I was fiddling with it, Father returned home in the most towering rage I have ever seen him in. He offered no explanation. Nancy told him that Mr. Bronson had called and had asked for him . . . and that brought it out of him in a flood.

I think "poltroon" was the mildest term that he used about Mr. Bronson. "Pro-German traitor" may have been the bitterest. He did not use profanity, just words of rage and disappointment.

I had great trouble believing it. Mr. Bronson a coward? Pro-German? But Father was detailed in his account and

broken-hearted in his response. In my own confused grief—
my beloved country, my beloved husband, my secret lover,
all the same day—I had to force myself to remember that
Father was hit just as hard. His brother's boy—or was Theodore Bronson his own son? Father had hinted at the possibility.

I went back to bed, cried some more, then lay there, dry
eyed, with this triple ache in my heart.

Father tapped on my door. "Daughter?"

"Yes, Father?"

"Mr. Bronson is on the telephone, asking for you."

"I don't want to talk to him! Must I?"

"Certainly not. Is there anything you wish me to say to
him?"

"Tell him . . . not to call me. Not to come here. Not to
speak to any of my children . . . now or ever."

"I'll tell him. With a few words for myself, too. Maureen,
his sheer gall amazes me."

About six Carol brought me a tray. I ate some of it. Then
Justin and Eleanor came to see me and I cried on my big
sister and they consoled me. Later—I don't know the time
but it was after dark. Eight-thirty? Nine? I roused at some
commotion downstairs. Shortly my father came up, tapped
on the door. "Maureen? Mr. Bronson is here."

"What?!"

"May I come in? I have something to show you."

I didn't want to let Father in; I hadn't cleaned up and I
was afraid Father would notice. But . . . Mr. Bronson here?
Here? After what Father had said to him? "Yes, Father, come
in."

He showed me a piece of paper. I read it; it was a carbon
copy of an Army enlistment form . . . which stated that
"Bronson, Theodore" was enlisted at the rank of private in
the National Army of the United States.

"Father, is this some sort of bad joke?"

"No. He's here. That's authentic. He did it."

I got out of bed. "Father, will you start me a tub? I'll be
down quickly."

"Certainly."

He went into my bath; I peeled off my gown, went in after
him, thanked him. I didn't realize that I was naked in front

of him until he looked at me and looked away. "Ask Nancy to serve him something, please. Is Nancy still up?"

"Everyone is up. Get into that tub, dear; we'll wait for you."

Fifteen minutes later I went downstairs. I suppose my eyes were red but I was smiling and no longer stunk and I was dressed in Sunday best. I hurried to him and offered my hand. "Mr. Bronson! We are all so proud of you!"

I don't remember details of the next hour or two hours or whatever. I sat there in a golden haze of bittersweet happiness. My country was at war, my husband was off to war, but at least I knew the deeper meaning of "better death than dishonor"—I knew now why Roman matrons said, "With your shield or on it." Those hours of believing that my beloved Theodore was not what I had believed him to be but a coward who would refuse to defend his country—those hours had been the longest, most hateful hours of my life.

I had not really believed that there were such subhuman creatures. I had never known one. Then to have it turn out simply to be a bad dream, the result of a misunderstanding over words— I've read somewhere that pleasure is relief from pain. Psychologists are a silly lot, mostly, but that night I enjoyed that sort of ecstatic pleasure. Even my fires of libido were banked and, for the time, I did not worry about Briney, so joyed was I that Theodore was indeed what a man to be loved must be: a hero, a warrior.

My big girls did their best to stuff him full and Carol made him a sandwich and wrapped it to take with him. Father was full of man-to-man advice, old soldier to new recruit; my big boys were falling over each other to try to do things for him, and even Woodrow was almost well-behaved. At last they all lined up to kiss him good-bye, even Brian Junior, who had given up kissing save for an occasional peck on his mother's cheekbone.

They all went to bed but Father . . . and it was my turn.

I have always been of such rugged health that winning Testaments for perfect attendance at Sunday School was never any trouble to me—so wasn't it nice that I had two Testaments when I needed them? I did not even need to think up a new inscription; what I had written for my husband was right for any Lucasta to any warrior off to the wars:

> To Private Theodore Bronson
> Be true to self and country.
> Maureen J. Smith
> April 6, 1917

I gave it to him, saw him read it, then I said, "Father?" He knew what I wanted, a decent amount of privacy.

"No." (Damn him! Did he really think that I would drag Theodore down on the rug? With the children awake and only a flight of stairs away?)

(Well, perhaps I would.) "Then turn your back."

I put my arms up and kissed Theodore, firmly but chastely . . . then knew that a chaste kiss was not enough to say farewell to a warrior. I let my body grow soft and my lips come open. My tongue met his and I promised him wordlessly that whatever I had was his. "Theodore . . . take care of yourself. Come back to me."

13

"Over There!"

My father, having been refused a return to active duty in the Army Medical Corps, was then turned down again when he tried to enlist as an infantry private (he made the mistake of showing his separation papers . . . which showed his 1852 date of birth), and then tried to enlist in St. Louis with a claimed date of birth of 1872 but was tripped up somehow— and finally did manage to enlist in the Seventh Missouri, an infantry militia regiment formed to replace Kansas City's Third Missouri, which was now the 110th Combat Engineers training at Camp Funston and about to go "Over There."

This new home guard, made up of the too young, too old, too many dependents, too halt, or too lame, was not fussy about Father's age (sixty-five) in view of his willingness to accept a dull job as supply sergeant and the fact that he needed no training.

I greatly appreciated Father's decision to live with us for

the duration. For the first time in my life I had to be the head of the family, and it's really not Maureen's style. I like to work hard and do my best while the key decisions are left up to someone bigger, stronger, and older than I, and with a warm male odor to him. Oh, I'll be a pioneer mother if I must. My great-great-grandmother Kitchin killed three hostiles with her husband's musket after he was wounded—and Father did teach me to shoot.

But I would rather be a womanly woman to a manly man.

Brian was emphatic that I must not let Father dominate me, that *I* must make the decisions—that I was head of the family. "Use Ira to back you up—fine! But you are boss. Don't let him forget it, don't let our children forget it, and don't *you* forget it."

I sighed internally and said, "Yes, sir."

Brian Junior did nobly when he suddenly found himself in his father's shoes—but twelve is young for that job; it was well that his grandfather had agreed to stay with us. Brian Junior and his brother George kept on with their jobs, delivering the *Journal* and lighting street lamps, and still brought home straight A's. When the summer ended and the weather turned cold, I started getting up at four-thirty A.M. as they did, and served them hot cocoa before they started out. They enjoyed it and it made me feel better as I watched them start off to work before daylight. The winter of 1917–18 was bitter; they had to bundle up like Esquimaux.

I wrote to Betty Lou every week, and also to Nelson. My beastly, lovable cousin Nelson came home on the Monday following the declaration of war and told Betty Lou, "Hon, I've found a wonderful way to avoid going into the Army."

"How? Castration? Isn't that rather drastic?"

"Somewhat. At least I think so. Guess again."

"I know! You're going to jail."

"Even better than jail. I've joined the Marines."

So Betty Lou was managing our mine. I had no doubt that she could do it; she had been in on every detail from the day we acquired majority ownership. She was not a mining engineer but neither was Nelson. The minority owner was our mining superintendent—not a graduate engineer either but with over twenty-five years of white-metals experience.

It seemed to me that it would work. It would have to work. It was "Root, hog, or die."

During those war years people all over our beloved country were doing things they had never done before—doing them well or doing them badly, but trying. Women who had never driven even a team of horses were driving tractors, because their husbands had gone to "Hang the kaiser!" Student nurses were supervising whole wards because graduate nurses were in uniform. Ten-year-old boys such as my George were knitting squares for blankets for British Tommies and buying Baby Bonds with money earned from newspaper routes. There were dollar-a-year men, and four-minute speakers, and Salvation Army lassies (loved by every serviceman), and volunteers for every sort of special war work, from rolling bandages to collecting walnut shells and peach pits for gas masks.

Meanwhile what did Maureen do? Nothing much, I suppose. I cooked and kept house for a family of ten, with much help from my four oldest and even some from my eight-year-old, Marie. I never missed a Red Cross bandage rolling. I saw to it that my family observed all meatless, wheatless, sweetless days and other economies of scarce foods decreed by Mr. Herbert Hoover . . . while learning how to make candies and cookies and cakes with sorghum and corn syrup and honey (all unrationed) in place of sugar (rationed) as Corporal Bronson's buddies appeared to be capable of eating a whole bakeshop of such things.

Shortly Carol took over this attempt to fill hollow legs; she considered Corporal Bronson "her soldier." We all wrote to him, in rotation—and he wrote back, to all of us but especially to Father.

There arose a church-sponsored movement for families to "adopt" lonely servicemen. Carol wanted us to adopt Corporal Bronson—so we did, subject to Brian's approval, which came by return mail.

I wrote to my husband every day—and would tear up a letter and start again if, on rereading, I found in it bad news or a flavor of self-pity . . . which meant that I tore up letters again and again and again until I learned how to write a proper Lucasta letter, one to lift a warrior's morale, not drag him down.

That early in the war Brian was not far away, at Camp Funston, adjacent to Manhattan, Kansas, about a hundred miles west of Kansas City. After three months of not coming home at all Briney started coming home about once a month for short weekends—Saturday afternoons to Sunday evenings—when and if he could arrange to ride with another officer. It was a practical distance for a forty-four-hour pass (noon Saturday to eight A.M. Monday) by automobile, but not for travel by train.

In those days trains were ordinarily much faster than automobiles, as there were so few paved roads—none in Kansas that I can remember. There was a direct rail line, the Union Pacific. But on all railroads troop trains had first priority, freight trains headed east had second priority, other freight trains had third priority . . . and passenger trains could use the rails only when nobody else wanted them. Wartime precedence—Mr. McAdoo was strict about it. So Brian's trips home were infrequent as they depended on duty schedules of brother officers with automobiles.

I sometimes wondered whether or not Brian regretted having sold "El Reo Grande." But I did not say anything and neither did he. Count your blessings, Maureen! This is wartime and your husband is a soldier. Be glad he is able to come home occasionally and that he is not (yet) being shot at.

The carnage in Europe got worse and worse. In March 1917 the tsar was overthrown. In November 1917 the Communist Bolsheviki displaced President Kerensky's government, and the Communists immediately surrendered to the Germans.

From then on we were in for it. The German veterans from the Eastern Front were moving by whole division to the Western Front at a time when we had landed only a few of our troops in France. The Allies were in bad trouble.

I did not know it. Certainly my children did not. I suspect that they reckoned their father as equal to at least two German divisions.

In May 1918 I was able to tell my husband that we had "rung the cash register" on his last weekend at home; I was two weeks overdue. Yes, I know that with many women this is not a sure sign—but it is with Maureen. I felt so euphoric about it that I avoided reading the newspapers and just enjoyed being me.

Brian went into Manhattan and telephoned me from there, for privacy. "Is this Myrtle, the Fertile Turtle?"

I answered, "Not so loud, Claude; you'll wake my husband. No, I won't be fertile again for another eight months."

"Congratulations! I'll plan on coming home for Christmas; you won't need me sooner than that."

"Now you listen to me, Roscoe; I'm not taking the veil, I'm merely having a baby. And I do have other offers."

"From Sergeant Bronson, perhaps?"

I caught my breath and did not answer. Presently Brian said, "What's the matter, love? Children where they can overhear you?"

"No, sir. I've taken the phone into our bedroom and there is no one else upstairs. Beloved, that man is as stubborn as my father. I have invited him here, Father has invited him here, and Carol invites him at least once a week. He thanks us . . . and then says that he doesn't know when he'll be granted any leave. He's admitted that he is off duty alternate weekends but he says that the actual time on pass is not enough to go that far from camp."

"That's almost true. Since he doesn't have a car. Since he left his car with Ira. Or with Brian Junior."

"Pish and tosh. The Weston boy is home every other weekend and he's only a private. I think I'm a woman scorned."

"Nick Weston picks up his son in Junction City and you know why. But don't fret, Mabel; the money's on the table. I saw Carol's favorite soldier just today."

I reswallowed my heart. "Yes, Briney?"

"I find that I agree with Carol. And with *mon beau-père*. I already knew that Bronson is as fine a sergeant instructor as we have; I've checked his efficiency marks each week. As for Sergeant Bronson himself, he puts me in mind of Ira. As Ira must have looked at that age."

"Sergeant Bronson and I look like twins."

"So you do but on you it looks better."

"Oh, fiddle! You have always said that I look my best with a pillow over my face."

"I say that to keep you from becoming too conceited, beautiful. You are gorgeous and everybody knows it, and you look like Sergeant Bronson in spite of it. But he is most like Ira in his personality and in his Gung-Ho attitude. I fully understand your wish to trip him and beat him to the rug. If you still feel that way. Do you?"

I took a deep breath and sighed it out. "I do, sir. If our

daughter Carol doesn't crowd me out and beat me to it."

"No, no! By seniority, please; this is wartime. Make her wait her turn."

"Don't tell Carol it's okay unless you mean it, dear man—because she means it."

"Well, somebody's going to do it to Carol . . . and I think a lot better of Bronson than I do of that pimply young snot who broke in our Nancy. Don't you?"

"Oh, heavens, yes! But the matter is academic; I have given up all hope of getting Sergeant Bronson to enter this house. Until the war is over, at least."

"I told you not to fret. A little bird whispered in my ear that Bronson will soon receive a midweek pass."

"Oh, Brian!" (I knew what a midweek pass meant: orders overseas.)

"Ira was right; Bronson is eager to go Over There, so I put him on the list, a special requisition from Pershing's staff for sergeant instructors. Another little bird let me know that my own request was being acted on favorably. So I expect to be home about the same time. But— Listen closely. I think I can arrange it so that you will have a twenty-four-hour clear shot at him. Can you bring him down in that length of time?"

"Oh, goodness, Briney!"

"Can you, or can't you? I've known you to manage it in an hour with just a horse and buggy to work with; today you have at your disposal a guest bedroom with its own bath. What does it take? Cleopatra's barge?"

"Brian, Father supplied that horse and buggy knowing what was up and actively cooperating. But this time he considers it his bounden duty to stand over me with a shotgun. Except that it is a loaded thirty-eight and he would not hesitate to use it."

"Can't have that; General Pershing wouldn't like it—good sergeant instructors are scarce. So I had better brief Ira on the operation plan before I hang up—which I must soon; I am running out of nickels and dimes. Is Ira there?"

"I'll get him."

Sergeant Theodore did get that midweek pass, from just after Retreat on Monday to eight o'clock muster Thursday morning—and at last he did come to Kansas City. At that time the picture shows always included a comedy—John Bunty,

Fatty Arbuckle, Charlie Chaplin, or the Keystone Kops. That week I managed to outdo both Fatty Arbuckle and the Keystone Kops in always stepping into a bucket or falling over my feet.

To begin with, that difficult man, Sergeant Theodore, did not show up at our house until late Tuesday afternoon . . . when Brian had told me that Sergeant Theodore's pass should cause him to arrive at our house by midmorning at the latest.

"Where have you been? What took you so long?" No, I did not say anything of the sort. I may have felt like saying it . . . but I had learned the relative merits of honey and vinegar back when I was still a virgin—a long time ago indeed. Instead I took his hand, kissed his cheek, and said in my warmest voice, "Sergeant Theodore . . . it is so good to have you home."

I played Cornelia and her Jewels before and during dinner—held my peace and smiled while all my children vied for his attention . . . including Father, who wanted to talk soldier talk with him. At the end of dinner Father suggested (by prearrangement with me) that Staff Sergeant Bronson take me for a spin, and then squelched attempts by the younger children to come along—especially Woodrow, who wanted both to play chess and to be taken to Electric Park.

So at last Sergeant Theodore and I headed south just at sundown. In 1918 there was very little south of Thirty-ninth Street on the east side of Kansas City even though the city line had been pushed clear south to Seventy-seventh Street in order to include Swope Park. Swope Park had many popular lovers' lanes but I wanted a place much more private—and knew some, as Briney and I had searched all the back roads one time and another, looking for what Briney called "poontang pastures," grassy places private enough to evade the buzzard eye of Mrs. Grundy.

All along the east side of Kansas City runs the Blue River. In 1918 it held many delightful spots—as well as thick bushes, deep mud, chiggers, mosquitoes, and poison ivy; one had to know where to go. If you went south but not too far south, and knew where to cross the tracks of the St. Looie and Frisco, you could work your way into a wooded, grassy dell as nice as anything in Swope Park but utterly private, as it was surrounded by river and railroad embankment save for one narrow lane leading into it.

I wanted that particular spot; I was sentimental about it. When in 1912 we had become footloose through Briney's having purchased "El Reo Grande," that was the first place Briney had taken me for outdoor loving. That delightful picnic (I had fetched along a lunch) was the occasion on which I became pregnant with Woodrow.

I wanted to receive my new love into me first on that very spot—and then tell my husband about it in every detail, giggling with him over it while we made love. Briney did so enjoy my trips over the fence and always wanted to hear about them before, during, or after our own lovemaking, or all three, as a sauce to encourage us in more and heartier lovemaking.

Brian always told me about his own adventures, but what he liked best was to hear about mine.

So I took Sergeant Theodore to the spot marked X.

Time was short; I had promised Father that I would stay out, at most, only long enough to tumble him, then wait another half or three-quarters of an hour for that wonderful, relaxed second go at it—call it ten-thirty or eleven. "So I should be home about the time you get back from the Armory, Father."

Father agreed that my plans were reasonable . . . including our need for a second engagement if the first one went well.

"Very well, Daughter. If you have to be later, please telephone so that we won't worry. And— Maureen."

"Yes, Father?"

"Enjoy it, darling."

"Oh, *mon cher papa, tu es aimable! je t'adore!*"

"Go out there and adore Sergeant Ted. You will probably be his last piece for a long time . . . so make it a good one! Love you, best of daughters."

My usual method of letting myself be seduced is to decide ahead of time, create or help create the opportunity, then cooperate with whatever advances the nominal seducer makes. (Contrariwise, if I have decided against it, I simply see to it that no opportunity arises.) That night I did not have time for the ladylike pianissimo protocol. I had just this one chance and only two hours to make it work—and no second chance; Theodore was going overseas. A warrior's farewell had to be now.

So Maureen was not ladylike. As soon as we turned off Benton Boulevard and the gathering dusk had given us some privacy, I asked him to put his arm around me. When he did so, I reached up, took his hand and placed it on my right breast. Most men understand that.

Theodore understood it. He caught his breath. I said, "We haven't time to be shy, dear Theodore. Don't be afraid to touch me."

He cupped my breast. "I love you, Maureen!"

I answered soberly, "We have loved each other since the night we met. We simply could not say so." I raised his hand, then slid it down the full neck of my dress, felt scalding excitement as his hand touched my breast.

He answered huskily, "Yes. I didn't dare tell you."

"You would never have told me, Theodore. So I had to be bold and let you know that I feel it, too. The turn is just ahead, I think."

"I think so too. I'll need both hands to drive that lane."

"Yes, but only till we get there. Then I want *both* your arms . . . and *all* your attention."

"Yes!"

He drove in, turned his car around and headed out, turned off his lights and stopped his engine, set his hand brake and turned to me. He took me in his arms and we kissed, a fully-shared kiss, with our tongues exploring and caressing and talking wordlessly. I was in Heaven. I still think that a totally unrestrained kiss is more intimate than is coupling; a woman should never kiss that way unless she intends to couple at once in whatever way he wants her.

Without words I said this to Theodore. As soon as our tongues met I pulled up my skirt, took his hand and put it between my thighs. He still hesitated, so I moved his hand farther up.

No more hesitation— All Theodore needed was to be certain that I knew what I wanted and that his best attentions were welcome. He explored me gently, then slipped a finger inside. I let it enter, then squeezed it as hard as I could— and congratulated myself on never having skipped my exercises even a day since Ethel was born, two years earlier. I love to surprise a man with the strength of my vaginal sphincter. My passage is so baby-stretched that, if I did not work endlessly to overcome it, I would be "big as a barn door and loose as a goose"—so says my father, whose advice got me started on this routine years ago.

We were now past all shyness, any turning back. But I had something I had to tell him. I got my tongue back and took my mouth a half inch from his, chuckled against his mouth. "Surprised to find that I am not wearing bloomers? I took them off when I went upstairs . . . for I can't tell my gallant warrior a proper farewell with drawers in the way. Don't hold back, beloved soldier mine; you can't harm me, I'm expecting."

"What did you say?"

"Must I always be the bold one? I am pregnant, Theodore; no possible doubt, I am seven weeks gone. So don't use a rubber on me—"

"I can't, I don't have one."

"So? Then isn't it nice that you don't need one? But didn't you expect to have me?"

"No. I did not. Not at all."

"But you're going to have me. You can hardly get out of it now. You'll have me bare, darling, no rubber. Would you like me to be bare all over? I will be if you ask me to. I'm not afraid."

He stopped to kiss me fiercely. "Maureen, I don't think you are ever afraid of anything."

"Oh, yes, I am. I would not dare be alone on Twelfth Street at night. But afraid of sex and loving? No, not anything I can think of. So help yourself, my darling. If I know how, I'll do it. If I don't, show me and I'll try." (Theodore, stop talking and take me!)

"This seat is narrow."

"I hear that the young people take out the back seat and put it on the ground. There is a robe in the back seat, too."

"Um, yes."

We got out of his car—and ran into the most confounded Keystone Kops contretemps I have ever experienced.

Woodrow.

My favorite, Woodrow, whom I could happily have throttled at that moment, was in the back seat, and woke up as I opened the door. Well, I think he woke up; he may have been awake and listening the whole time—memorizing any words he did not know, for later investigation—and blackmail.

Oh, that boy! Would the world let him grow up? I wondered.

But what I said, in my happiest voice, was: "Woodrow, you're a scamp! Sergeant Theodore! See who is sleeping in the back seat." I reached behind me and tried to button Theodore's breeches.

"Sergeant Ted promised to take me to Electric Park!"

So we went to Electric Park, thoroughly chaperoned.

I wonder if other women have as much trouble getting themselves "ruined" as I do?

About twenty hours later I was in my own bed, my husband Captain Brian Smith on my right, my lover Captain Lazarus Long on my left. Each had an arm under my neck, each was using his free hand to caress me.

I was saying, "Brian beloved, when Lazarus completed the ritual by answering, 'But not "While the Evil Days Come Not," ' I almost fainted. When he said that he was descended from me—from us, you and me—from all three of us, you and me and Woodrow—I was convinced that I was losing my mind. Or had lost it."

Briney tickled my right nipple. "Don't worry about it, Swivel Hips; on a woman it hardly shows. As long as she can still cook. Hey! Stop that."

I eased up on him. "Sissy. I didn't do that very hard."

"I'm in a weakened condition. Captain Long, as I understand it, you decided to reveal yourself—against your own best interests, I believe—in order to tell me that I won't get hurt in this war."

"No, Captain, not that at all."

Briney sounded puzzled. "I must confess that I don't understand."

"I revealed that I am a Howard from the future in order to reassure Mrs. Smith. She's been worrying herself sick that you might not come back. So I told her that I was certain that you did come back. Since you are one of my direct ancestors, I studied your biographical résumé before I left Boondock. So I knew."

"Well— I appreciate your motives; Maureen is my treasure. But it is reassuring to me, too."

"Excuse me, Captain Smith. I did not say that you won't get hurt in this war."

"Eh? But you just did. So I thought."

"No, sir. I said that you will come back. You will. But I did not say that you won't get hurt. The Archives in Boondock are silent on that point. You may lose an arm. Or a leg. Or your eyes. Or even become a basket case; I don't know. I'm sure of just this much: you will live through it and won't lose your testicles and penis, because the Archives show that you two have several more children. Ones you will sire after you come back from France. You see, Captain, the Howard Family Archives are mostly genealogies, with few details otherwise."

"Captain Long—"

"Better call me 'Bronson' sir. Here I'm a staff sergeant; my ship is light-years away and far in the future."

"Then knock off calling me 'Captain,' for Pete's sake. I'm Brian; you're Lazarus."

"Or Ted. Your children call me 'Uncle Ted' or 'Sergeant Ted.' Calling me 'Lazarus' could involve all sorts of explanations."

I said, "Theodore, Father knows you are Lazarus and so do Nancy and Jonathan. And so will Carol when you take her to bed. You let me tell Nancy when you took her to bed; my big girls are too close to each other to keep such secrets from each other. So it seems to me."

"Maureen, I said that you could tell anyone because you would not be believed. Nevertheless each case involves long explanations. But why are you assuming that I am going to take Carol to bed? I did not say that I would. And I have not asked for that privilege."

I turned my face to the right. "Briney, do you hear this man? Do you see now why it has taken me more than a year to trip him? He didn't offer the slightest objection to screwing Nancy—"

"I'm not surprised; neither did I." My husband leered and licked his lips. "Nancy is special. I told you."

"You're an old goat, my beloved. I don't believe you've turned down anything female since you were nine—"

"Eight."

"You're boasting. And untruthful. And Theodore is just as bad. He let me think he was willing to satisfy Carol's greatest ambition once I cleared it with headquarters, meaning you . . . and I did, and then I told Carol not to despair, that Mama was working on it and it looked hopeful, quite hopeful. And now he acts as if he had never heard of the idea."

"But, Maureen, I expected Brian to object. And he has."

"Now wait a moment, Lazarus. I did not object. Carol is physically a grown woman and—I have today learned—no longer virgin . . . and not surprising; she's a year older than her mother was—"

"More nearly two," I put in.

"Shut up, you; I'm pimping for our daughter. All I did was lay down some reasonable rules for Carol's protection. Lazarus, you did agree that they were reasonable?"

"Oh, certainly, Captain. I simply refused to accept them. My privilege. Just as it is your privilege to make them. I have accepted that you do not want me to copulate with your daughter Carol other than by your rules. That settles it; I won't touch her."

"Very well, sir!"

"Gentlemen, gentlemen!" I almost let my voice rise. "You both sound like Woodrow. What are these rules?"

Theodore said nothing. Brian answered in a pained voice, "First, I asked him to use a rubber. Didn't matter with you or Nancy; both of you broads are knocked up. He refused. I then—"

"Are you surprised, my darling? I've often heard you refer to it as 'washing your feet with your socks on.' "

"Yes, but Carol does not need a baby this season. Certainly not a little bastard before she's considered her Howard options. But Mo', I did concede that Ted is himself a Howard. I simply said that, All right, if Carol got pregnant from giving him a soldier's farewell, I wanted him to promise that he would come back when the war is over and marry Carol and take her and her baby to— What's that you call your planet, Captain? Boondock?"

"Boondock is a city; my home is in its suburbs. The planet is Tellus Tertius, Earth Number Three."

I sighed. "Theodore, why wouldn't you agree to that? You tell us that you have four wives and three co-husbands. Why wouldn't you be willing to marry our Carol? She is a good cook, and she doesn't eat all that much. And she's very sweet-tempered and loving." I was thinking how dearly I would like to go to Boondock . . . and marry Tamara. Not that I ever would; I had Briney and our babies to take care of. But even an old woman can dream.

Theodore said slowly, "I abide by my own rules, for my own reasons. If Captain Smith does not trust me with respect to my behavior toward other people—"

"Not 'other people,' Captain! A particular sixteen-year-old girl named Carol. I am responsible for her welfare."

"So you are. I repeat, 'other people,' be they sixteen-year-old girls or whosoever. You don't trust me without promises; I don't give promises. That ends it and I am sorry the matter ever came up. *I* did not bring it up. Captain, I did not come here to bed your ladies; I came to say good-bye and thank-you to a whole family all of whom had been most generous and hospitable to me. I have not intended to disturb your household. I'm sorry, sir."

"Ted, don't be so damned stiff-necked. You sound just like my father-in-law when he gets his back up. You have not disturbed my household. You have pleased my wife enormously and for that I thank you. And I know that you were trapped by her; she told me months ago what she intended to do to you if she ever got you alone. This discussion is just over Carol, who has no claim on you. If you don't want her under what I see as minimum protection for her welfare, then let her stick to boys her own age. As she should."

"Agreed, sir."

"Damn it; knock off the 'sirs'; you're in bed with my wife. And me."

"Oh, dear!"

"Mo', it's the only sensible solution."

"Men! Always doing what you call 'sensible' and always so wrong-headed and stubborn! Briney, don't you realize that Carol doesn't give a hoot about promises? She just wants to spread her legs and close her eyes and hope that she catches. If she doesn't catch, a month from now she's going to cry her eyes out. If she does catch, well, I trust Theodore and so does Carol."

Briney said, "Oh, for God's sake, Mo'! Ted, ordinarily she is quite easy to live with."

Theodore said, "Maureen, you said, 'A month from now she's going to cry her eyes out.' Do you know her calendar?"

"Why, yes. Well, maybe. Let me think." My girls kept their own calendars . . . but old snoopy Mama kept her eyes open, just in case. "Today is Wednesday. If I recall correctly, Carol is due again three weeks from tomorrow. Why?"

"Do you remember the thumb rule I gave you to insure, uh, 'ringing the cash register,' you called it."

"Yes, indeed. You said to count fourteen days from onset of menses, then hit that day. And the day before and the day after, if possible."

"Yes, that is how to get pregnant, a thumb rule. But it works the other way, too. How not to get pregnant. If a woman is regular. If she is not abnormal in some way. Is Carol regular?"

"Like a pendulum. Twenty-eight days."

"Brian, stipulating that Maureen's recollection of Carol's calendar is accurate—"

"I would bet on it. Mo' hasn't made a mistake in arithmetic since she found out about two and two."

"—if so, Carol can't get pregnant this week . . . and I'll be on the high seas the next time she is fertile. But this week a whole platoon of Marines could not knock her up."

Briney looked thoughtful. "I want to talk to Ira. If he agrees with you, I'll drop all objections."

"No."

"What do you mean 'No'? No rules. Relax."

"No, sir. You don't trust and I don't promise. The situation is unchanged."

I was ready to burst into tears from sheer exasperation. Men's minds do not work the way ours do and we will never understand them. Yet we can't get along without them.

I was saved from making a spectacle of myself by a knock on the door. Nancy. "May I come in?"

"Come in, Nanc'!" Briney called out. "Come in, dear," I echoed.

She came in and I thought how lovely she looked. She was freshly shaved that morning, in preparation for a swap that Nancy and Jonathan had asked for—Jonathan into my bed, Nancy into Theodore's. Theodore had hesitated—afraid of hurting my feelings—but I had insisted, knowing what a treat our Nancy would be for Theodore (and Theodore for Nancy!) (and Jonathan for Maureen; I was flattered enormously that Jonathan had suggested it).

Father had taken the rest of my zoo to the Al G. Barnes Circus, playing in Independence—all but Ethel, too young for the circus, too young to notice; I had her crib in my bathroom, safe and in earshot.

That playful swap had gone beautifully and made me think even more highly of my prospective son-in-law. About three o'clock we four, Nancy and Theodore, Jonathan and I, had gathered in "Smith Field," my big bed, mostly to chat. As Briney often said, "You can't do it all the time, but there is no limit to how much you can talk about it."

We four were still lounging in Smith Field, talking and necking, when Brian telephoned—he had just arrived in town, on leave. I told him to hurry home and cued him in family code as to what he could expect. Nancy understood the coded message and looked wide-eyed but said nothing.

Thirty-odd minutes later she closed her eyes and opened her thighs and for the first time received her father—then opened her eyes and looked at Jonathan and me, and grinned. I grinned back at her; Jonathan was too busy to look.

What this world needs is more loving, sweaty and friendly and unashamed.

Then the children had gone downstairs; Nancy had sensed that I wanted time alone with my two men. She took the telephone with her, long cord and all. Now she stood by the bed and smiled at us. "Did you hear the phone ring? It was Grandpa. He said to tell you that the zoo wagon will arrive— that's your car, Ted-Lazarus darling—will arrive at exactly six-oh-five P.M. So Jonathan is bathing and I wanted him not to use all the hot water. He left his clothes up here; I'll take them down to him, then I'll bathe and dress up here. Ted-Lazarus dear, where are your clothes?"

"In the sewing room. I'll be right down."

"Cancel that," Brian said. "Nanc', fetch Ted's clothes when you come up, that's my sweet girl. Ted, in this family we spit in their eyes and tell 'em to go to hell. You don't need to dress until we do, after the doorbell rings. A husband is all the chaperon a wife needs, and I don't explain to my children why we choose to have a guest upstairs. As for *mon beau-père*, he knows the score and is our shut-eye sentry. If Carol guesses, she won't talk. Thanks, Nancy."

"*Pas de quoi, mon cher père.* Papa! Is it true that Ted doesn't have to go back tonight?"

"Ted goes back with me, Sunday night. Special duty, assigned to me—and I sold him, body and soul, to your mother, who may kill him by then—"

"Oh, no!" Both my daughter and I said it.

"Or not, but she'll try. Now get along, darling, and set that door to latch as you close it."

Nancy did so; my husband turned to me. "Flame top, it is now five-forty. Can you figure out a way to entertain Ted and me for the next twenty-five minutes?"

I took a deep breath. "I'll try."

14

Black Tuesday

WORLD-AS-MYTH   Much as I love Hilda, much as I love Jubal and respect his analytical genius, World-as-Myth doesn't explain anything.

As Dr. Will Durant would put it, it is an insufficient hypothesis. I studied philosophy under Dr. Durant in Kansas City in 1921 and '22, not long after he left the Catholic Church—and turned agnostic, socialist, and benedict, all through sniffing a fourteen-year-old girl half his age.

Dr. Durant must have been a disappointment to Mrs. Grundy—he married his jailbait sweetheart and stayed married to her till his death in his nineties, with never a breath of scandal. For Mrs. Grundy it must have been a case of "Some days it is hardly worthwhile to listen at keyholes."

The Church's loss was the World's gain. A horny young teacher's inability to keep his hands off a pretty, smart, and nubile student gave several universes a great teacher in history and philosophy . . . and gave Maureen her introduction to metaphysics—my greatest intellectual adventure since Father introduced me to Professor Thomas Henry Huxley.

Professor Huxley introduced me to the fact that theology is a study with no answers because it has no subject matter.

No subject matter? That's right, no subject matter whatever—just colored water with artificial sweetening. "Theo-" = "God" and "-logy" = word(s), i.e., any word ending in "-ology" means "talk about" or "discussion of" or "words concerning" or "study of" a subject named in the first part of the word, whether it is "hippology," or "astrology," or "proctology," or "eschatology," or "scatology," or something else. But to discuss any subject, it is first necessary to agree on what it is you are discussing. "Hippology" presents no problem; everybody has seen a horse. "Proctology"—everybody has seen an arsehole . . . or, if you have been so carefully brought up that you've never seen one, go down to your city hall; you will find the place full of them. But the subject tagged by the spell-symbol "theology" is a horse of another color.

"God," or "god," or "gods"—have you ever seen "God"? If so, where and when, how tall was She and what did She weigh? What was Her skin color? Did She have a belly button and, if so, why? Did She have breasts? For what purpose? How about organs of reproduction and of excretion—did She or didn't She?

(If you think I am making fun of the idea of a God fashioned in Man's image or vice versa, you have much to go on.)

I will agree that the notion of an anthropomorphic God went out of fashion some time ago with most professional godsmen . . . but that doesn't get us any nearer to defining the English spell-symbol "God." Let's consult fundamentalist preachers . . . because Episcopalians won't even let God into His sanctuary unless He shines His shoes and trims that awful beard . . . and Unitarians won't let Him in at all.

So let's listen to fundamentalists: "God is the Creator. He Created the World. The existence of the World proves that it was created; therefore there is a Creator. That Creator we call 'God.' Let us all bow down and worship Him, for He is Almighty and His works proclaim His might."

Will someone please page Dr. S. I. Hayakawa? Or, if he is busy, any student who received a B + or better in Logic

101? I'm looking for someone able to discuss the fallacy of circular reasoning and also the concatenative process by which abstract words can be logically defined by building on concrete words. What is a "concrete" word? It is a spell-symbol used to tag something you can point to and thereby agree on, e.g., "cat," "sailboat," "ice-skating"—agree with such certainty that when you say "sailboat" there is no chance whatever that I will think you mean a furry quadruped with retractile claws.

With the spell-symbol "God" there is no way to achieve such agreement because there is nothing to point to. Circular reasoning can't get you out of this dilemma. Pointing to something (the physical world) and asserting that it has to have a Creator and this Creator necessarily has such-and-such attributes proves nothing save that you have made certain assertions without proof. You have pointed at a physical thing, the physical world; you have asserted that this physical thing has to have a "Creator" (Who told you that? What's his mailing address? *Who* told *him?*). But to assert that something physical was created out of nothing—not even empty space—by a Thingamajig you can't point to is not to make a philosophical statement or any sort of statement, it is mere noise, amphigory, sound and fury signifying nothing.

Jesuits take fourteen years to learn to talk that sort of nonsense. Southern fundamentalist preachers learn to talk it in a much shorter time. Either way, it's nonsense.

Pardon me. Attempts to define "God" cause one to break out in hives.

Unlike theology, "metaphysics" does have a subject, the physical world, the world that you can feel, taste, and see, the world of potholes and beautiful men and railroad tickets and barking dogs and wars and marshmallow sundaes. But, like theology, metaphysics has no answers. Just questions.

But what lovely questions!

Was this world created? If so, when and by whom and why?

How is consciousness ("Me-ness") hooked to the physical world?

What happens to this "Me-ness" when this body I am wearing stops, dies, decays, and the worms eat it?

Why am I here, where did I come from, where am I going?

Why are you here? *Are* you here? Are you anywhere? Am I all alone?

(And many more.)

Metaphysics has polysyllabic words for all of these ideas but you don't have to use them; Anglo-Saxon monosyllables do just as well for questions that have no answers.

Persons who claim to have answers to these questions invariably are fakers after your money. No exceptions. If you point out their fakery, if you dare to say aloud that the emperor has no clothes, they will lynch you if possible, always from the highest of motives.

That's the trouble I'm in now. I made the mistake of flapping my loose lower jaw before learning the power structure here . . . so now I am about to be hanged (I hope it is as gentle as hanging!) for the capital crime of sacrilege.

I should know better. I didn't think anyone would mind (in San Francisco) when I pointed out that the available evidence tended to indicate that Jesus was gay.

But there were cries of rage from two groups: a) gays; b) non-gays. I was lucky to get out of town.

(I do wish Pixel would come back.)

On Friday we got my daughter Nancy and Jonathan Weatheral married. The bride wore white over a peanut-sized embryo that qualified her for Howard Foundation benefits, while the bride's mother wore a silly grin that resulted from her private activities that week and the groom's mother wore a quieter smile and a faraway look in her eyes from similar (but not identical) private activities.

I had gone to much trouble to slide Eleanor Weatheral under Sergeant Theodore. To their mutual joy, I know (my husband says that Eleanor is a world-class mattress dancer), but not solely for their amusement. Eleanor is a touchstone, able to detect lies when she is sexually linked and *en rapport*.

Let's go back two days— On Wednesday my "zoo" got home from the circus at 6:05 P.M.; we had a picnic dinner in our back yard at 6:30, the exact timing being possible through Carol's having prepared it in the morning. At sundown Brian lit the garden lights and the younger ones played croquet while we elders—Brian, Father, Theodore, and I—sat in the garden glider swing and talked.

Our talk started on the subject of human female fertility.

Brian told Father that he wanted him to hear something Captain Long had said about the matter.

But I must note first that I had gone to Father's room the night before (Tuesday) after the house was quiet, pledging him a King's X, then told him about a strange story Sergeant Theodore had given me earlier that night, after that silly unplanned visit to Electric Park, a story in which he claimed to be Captain Lazarus Long, a Howard from the future.

Despite my promise of King's X, Father left the door ajar. Nancy tapped on it and we invited her in. She perched on the other side of Father's bed, facing me, and listened soberly to my repetition.

Father said, "Maureen, I take it you believe him, time travel and ether ship and all."

"Father, he knew Woodrow's birth date. Did you tell him?"

"No. I know your policy."

"He knew your birthday, too, not just the year, but the day and the month. Did you tell him?"

"No, but it's no secret. I've set it down on all sorts of documents."

"But how would he know where to find one? And he knew Mother's birthday—day, year, and month."

"That's harder. But not impossible. Daughter, as you tell me he pointed out: Anyone with access to the Foundation's files in Toledo could look up all of these dates."

"But why would he know Woodrow's birthday and not Nancy's? Father, he came here knowing quite a bit about all his ancestors—those he claims as ancestors—that is to say, Woodrow and his ancestors but not the birthdays of Woodrow's brothers and sisters."

"I don't know. If he did have access to Judge Sperling's files, he could have memorized just those data needed to back up his story. But the most interesting item is his assertion that the war will end on November eleventh, this year. I would have guessed sometime this summer, with bad news for Britain and worse news for France, and humiliation for us . . . or not earlier than the summer of 1919, with victory for the Allies but a horribly expensive one. If it turns out that Ted is right—November 11, 1918—then I'll believe him. All of it."

Nancy said, suddenly, "I believe him."

Father said, "Why, Nancy?"

"Grandpa, do you remember— No, you weren't here. It was the day war was declared, a year ago. Papa had kissed us good-bye and left. Grandpa, you went out right after Papa left—"

Father nodded. I said, "I remember."

"—and, Mama, you had gone up to lie down. Uncle Ted telephoned. Oh, I know that he telephoned later and you talked to him, Grandpa. You— You were mean to him—"

"Nancy, I'm sorry about that."

"Oh, that was a misunderstanding, we all know that. This was before he talked to you, maybe an hour before, maybe longer. I was upset and crying a bit, I guess, and Uncle Ted knew it . . . and he told me to stop worrying about Papa, because he—Uncle Ted, I mean—had second sight and could tell the future. He told me that Papa would come home safely. And suddenly I quit worrying and have not worried since— not that way. Because I knew that he was telling the truth. Uncle Ted does know the future . . . because he is from the future."

"Father?"

"How can I tell, Maureen?" Father looked terribly thoughtful. "But I think we must assume as least hypothesis— Occam's Razor—that Ted believes his own story. Which of course does not exclude the hypothesis that he is as loony as a June bug."

"Grandpa! You know Uncle Ted isn't crazy!"

"I don't think he is. But his story sounds crazy. Nancy, I'm trying to be rational about this. Now don't scold Grandpa; I'm doing the best I can. At worst we'll know in about five months. November eleventh. Which is little comfort to you now, Maureen, but it may make up somewhat for the dirty trick Woodrow played on you. You should have clobbered him, on the spot."

"Not out in the woods at night, Papa, not a child that young. And now it's too late. Nancy, you remember that spot where Sergeant Theodore took you all on a picnic a year ago? We were there."

Nancy's mouth dropped open. "Woodie was with you? Then you didn't—" She chopped off what she was saying. Father put on his draw-poker face.

I looked from one to the other. "You darlings! I confided my plans to each of you. But did not tell either of you that

I had told the other. Yes, Nancy, I went out there with the precise purpose I told you about: to offer Sergeant Theodore the best warrior's farewell I could manage, if he would let me. And he was about to let me. And it turned out that Woodrow had hidden in the back seat of the car."

"Oh, how dreadful!"

"I thought so. So we got out of there quickly and went to Electric Park and never did have the privacy we needed."

"Oh, poor Mama!" Nancy leaned across Father's legs and grabbed my head and made mother-hen sounds over me, exactly as I had over her for all those years, whenever she needed sympathy.

Then she straightened up. "Mama, you should go do it right now!"

"Here? With a house full of children? My dear! No, no!"

"I'll jigger for you! Grandpa! Don't you think she should?"

Father kept quiet. I repeated, "No, dear, no. Too risky."

She answered, "Mama, if you're scared to, here in the house, I certainly am not. Grandpa knows I'm pregnant, don't you, Grandpa? Or I wouldn't be getting married. And I know what Jonathan would say." She sat up straight, started to get off the edge of the bed. "I'm going straight down and give Uncle Ted a soldier's farewell. And tomorrow I'll tell Jonathan. And— Mama, I have a message for you from Jonathan. But I'll tell you when I come back upstairs."

I said, weakly and hopelessly, "Don't stay down too long. The boys get up at four-thirty; don't get caught by them."

"I'll be careful. 'Bye."

Father stopped her. "Nancy! Sit back down. You are crowding in on your mother's prerogatives."

"But, Grandpa—"

"Pipe down! Maureen is going downstairs to finish what she started. As she should. Daughter, I will stand jigger and Nancy can help me if she wishes. But take your own advice; don't stay down too long. If you aren't upstairs by three, I'm coming down to tap on the door."

Nancy said eagerly, "Mama, why don't we both go down? I bet Uncle Ted would like that!"

"I'll bet Uncle Ted would like that, too," Father said grimly, "but he's not going to get it tonight. If you want to give him a soldier's send-off, that's fine. But not tonight, and not until after you have consulted Jonathan. Now git for bed, dear . . . and you, Maureen, go downstairs and see Ted."

I leaned over and kissed him and got quietly off the edge of the bed and started to leave. Father said, "Get along, Nancy; I'll take the first watch."

She shoved out her lower lip. "No. Grandpa, I'm going to stay right here and bother you."

I left, via the sleeping porch and my own room, then went downstairs barefooted and wearing just a wrapper, not stopping to see if Father threw Nancy out. If she had managed to tame Father when I had not been able to manage it in twice her years, I didn't want to know it. Not then. I thought about Theodore instead . . . so successfully that by the time I quietly opened the door to my sewing room I was as ready as a female animal can be.

Quiet as I was, he heard me and had me in his arms as I closed the door. I returned his embrace, then let go and shrugged off my wrapper, and reached up to him again. At last, at last I was naked in his arms.

Which led, inevitably, to my sitting with Theodore and Brian and Father in our back yard glider swing after our picnic dinner on Wednesday, listening to a discussion between Father and Theodore, while our young people played croquet around us. At Briney's request, Theodore had repeated his statements about when and how female *h. sapiens* could and could not get pregnant.

The conversation drifted off from reproduction to obstetrics and they started using ungrammatical Latin at each other— some difference of opinion about the best way to handle a particular sort of birth complication. They became more and more polite to each other the more they differed. I did not have any opinions as birth complications are something I know about only from reading, since I have babies about as easily as a hen lays eggs—one big ouch and it's over.

Briney finally interrupted them, somewhat to my relief. I don't even want to hear about the horrible things that can happen if a birthing goes wrong. "This is all very interesting," Brian said, "but, Ira, may I ask one question? Is Ted a medical doctor, or not? Sorry, Ted."

"Not at all, Brian. My whole story sounds phony, I know. That's why I avoid telling it."

Father said, "Brian, haven't you heard me addressing Ted

as 'Doctor' for the last thirty minutes? The thing that makes me so angry—so graveled, rather—is that Ted knows more about the art of medicine than I could ever possibly learn. Yet his shop talk makes me want to go back to the practice of medicine."

Theodore cleared his throat, sounding just like Father. "Mrrrrph. Dr. Johnson—"

"Yes, Doctor?"

"I think my superior knowledge of therapy—correction: my knowledge of superior therapy—bothers you in part because you think of me as being younger than you are. But, as I explained, I simply look young. In fact I am older than you are."

"How old?"

"I declined to answer that question when Mrs. Smith asked it—"

"Theodore! My name is Maureen." (That exasperating man!)

"Little pitchers with big ears, Maureen," Theodore said quietly. "Dr. Johnson, the therapy of my time is not harder to learn than is therapy today; it is easier, because less of it is empirical and more of it—most of it—is based on minutely developed and thoroughly tested theory. With correct and logical theory as a framework you could catch up on what new has been learned in jig time, then go quickly into clinical work under a preceptor. You would not find it difficult."

"Damn it, sir, I'll never have the chance!"

"But, Doctor, that's what I'm trying to offer you. My sisters will pick me up at an agreed rendezvous in Arizona on August 2, 1926, eight years from now. If you wish, I will be delighted to take you with me to my time and my planet, where, if you wish, you can study therapy—I am chairman of the board of a medical school there; no problem. Then you can either stay on Tertius, or return to Earth—to the exact spot and instant that you left, if that is your wish, but with your medical education updated and you yourself rejuvenated . . . and with renewed zest for life, that being merely a side effect but a fine bonus of rejuvenation."

Father looked strange, haunted. I heard him murmur, " '—unto an exceeding high mountain, and sheweth him all the kingdoms of the world—' " Sergeant Theodore answered, " '—and the glory of them.' Matthew, four, verse eight. But, Doctor, I am not the Devil and I am not offering you treasure or power—simply the hospitality of my home as I have enjoyed the hospitality of this home . . . plus an opportunity for a refresher course if you want it. But you don't have to make up your mind tonight; you have more than eight years for that. You can postpone your decision right up to the last minute. *Dora*—that's my ship—has ample room."

I turned and put my hand on Father's arm. "Father, do you remember what we did in 1893?" I looked across at Ted. "Father read medicine under a preceptor who never believed in germs. So, after Father had been in practice for many years, he went back to school at Northwestern University in 1893 to learn the latest knowledge about germ theory and asepsis and such things. Father, this is the same thing—and an incredible opportunity! Father accepts, Theodore—he's just slow to admit what he wants, sometimes."

"Mind your own business, Maureen. Ted said I could take eight years to answer."

"Carol would not take eight years to answer. And neither would I! If Brian permitted. If Theodore can bring me back to the same hour and day—"

"I can."

"Would I meet Tamara?"

"Of course."

"Oh, my! Brian? Just a visit and I come home the same day—"

Theodore put in, "Brian, you can come with her. A few days or a few months vacation, and back the same day."

"Uh— Oh, Heavens! Sergeant, you and I have a war to win first. Can we table this till we come back from France?"

"Certainly, Captain."

I don't recall how the talk got around to economics. First, I was sworn to silence about the periodic nature of female fertility . . . and took the oath with my fingers crossed. Fiddlesticks. Both doctors, Papa and Theodore, pointed out that my mucous membranes had never been invaded by bugs— *gonococci* and *spirochete treponema pallidum* and such—because I had been drilled and drilled in "Always use a rubber except when you want a baby," and my girls had been trained the same way. I didn't mention the far more numerous times when I had happily skipped those pesky sheaths because I was pregnant and knew it. Such as the night before. Avoiding disease does not depend on anything as trivial as a rubber purse; it depends on being very, very fussy about your intimates. A woman can catch something bad in her mouth or in her eyes just as quickly as in her vagina—and much easier. Am I going to copulate with a man without kissing him? Let's not be silly.

I can't recall ever using a rubber after Theodore explained exactly how to chart my fertile span. Or ever again failing to "ring the cash register" when I wished to.

Then I heard, "—October twenty-ninth, 1929."

I blurted, "Huh? But you said you were leaving in 1926. August second."

My husband said, "Pay attention, Carrot Top. There will be a quiz Monday morning."

Theodore said, "Maureen, I was speaking of Black Tuesday. That is what future historians will call the greatest stock market crash in all history."

"You mean like 1907?"

"I'm not sure what happened in 1907 because, as I told you, I studied closely only the history of the decade I planned to spend here—from the year after the end of this war until shortly before Black Tuesday, the twenty-ninth of October, 1929. That ten years, from after the First World War—"

"Hold it! Doctor, you said 'First World War—' First?"

"Doctor Johnson, except for this one Golden Age, from November eleventh, 1918, to October twenty-ninth, 1929, there are wars all through this century. The Second World War starts in 1939, and is longer and worse than this one. Then there are wars off and on—mostly on—the rest of this century. But the next century, the twenty-first century, is far worse."

Father said, "Ted. The day war was declared. You were simply speaking the truth as you saw it. Weren't you?"

"Yes, sir."

"Then why did you enlist? This isn't your war . . . Captain Long."

Theodore answered very softly, "To gain your respect, Ancestor. And to make Maureen proud of me."

"Mrrph! Well! I hope that you will never regret it, sir."

"I never will."

Thursday was a busy day indeed; Eleanor and I, with the aid of all my older children and all her older children, with much help from Sergeant Theodore as my aide de camp ("dog robber" he called it, and so did Father—I declined to let them get my goat), with some help from our spouses and from Father—Eleanor and I mounted a formal church wedding in only twenty-four hours.

Oh, I must admit that Eleanor and I had done spadework ahead of time—guest lists, plans, alerting of minister and janitor and caterer as soon as Brian's first phone call had made it possible, engraving of invitations on Tuesday, envelopes addressed on Wednesday by her two best penmen, invitations delivered by my two boys and two of hers, with RSVP to Justin's office by telephone, etc., etc.

We managed to have the bride dressed correctly and on time because Sergeant Theodore displayed another unexpected talent: ladies' sempstress—no, sempstor—no, I think it must be "ladies' tailor". I had already accomplished my prime purpose of using Eleanor's special telepathic talent by having Theodore drive me to Eleanor's house out south on Thursday morning and there putting my problem to her bluntly—speeding things up by peeling my clothes off the instant the door was locked on El and me in her private apartment, then bringing her up to date—then Eleanor had her maid show Theodore to El's private suite.

Never mind the sweaty details; in another thirty minutes Eleanor reported to me, "Maureen love, Theodore believes every word of what he has been telling us," which Theodore countered by pointing out that every Napoleon in every insane asylum believed his own story just as firmly.

"Captain Long," Eleanor had answered, "few males have a firm grip on reality; I can't see that it matters. You were telling me the truth as you know it when you told me about your home in the future and you were again telling the truth when you told me that you love Maureen. Since I love her, too, I hope to earn some portion of your love. Now, please, if you will let me up—and thank you, sir! you pleasured me immensely."

It was immediately after that we ran into a time conflict: how to get Eleanor's wedding dress and Nancy to Eleanor's sempstress at a time when Justin said that Jonathan must fetch Nancy and Brian to Justin's office so that all four could go to City Hall together to obtain the necessary special license, both principals being under age.

Theodore said, "Why do we need a sempstress? Eleanor,

doesn't that cabinet over there conceal a Singer sewing machine? And why do we need Nancy? Mama Maureen, didn't you tell me that you and Nancy can wear the same clothes?"

I agreed that Nancy and I could (and did) borrow clothes from each other. "I'm an inch more in the thighs and about the same bigger in the bust. But, Lazarus, we don't dare touch Eleanor's dress—wait till you see it."

Although Eleanor was taller and bigger than I, the wedding dress was close to my size as it had already been cut down once for her daughter Ruth, three inches shorter than her mother. It was a magnificent gown of white satin, lavishly beaded with seed pearls. It had a Belgian lace veil and a ten-foot train. It had originally had mutton-leg sleeves and a derrière cut for a bustle; these had vanished in the alteration for Ruth.

All the money in the world could not produce a wedding dress of that quality in the few hours until it would be needed; my Nancy was lucky that her Aunt El was willing to lend it to her.

Eleanor fetched it. Theodore admired it but did not seem intimidated by it. "Eleanor, let's fit it snugly to Mama Maureen, then there will be just room for its slip under it for Nancy. What other underclothes? Corset? Brassiere? Panties?"

I said, "I've never put a corset on Nancy and she says she's never going to start."

"Good for Nancy!" agreed Eleanor. "I wish I never had. Mau, Nancy doesn't need a brassiere. What about underpants? Can't wear bloomers with that dress. Both Emery Bird and Harzfeld carry sheer underpants . . . but they will still make lines under this dress if it is fitted as well as it should be."

"No pants," I ruled.

"Every old biddy there will know she's not wearing any," Eleanor said doubtfully.

I explained in Chaucerian terms my lack of interest in what old biddies thought. "I'll put round garters on her. She can shift to hose supporters when she changes to leave."

"At which time she can put on underpants," Theodore added.

I was startled. "Why, Theodore! I'm surprised. What need has a bride for pants?"

"The tiniest, scantiest, sheerest girl panties that are sold today, I mean—not bloomers. So Jonny can take them off when he gets her there, darling. Symbolic defloration, an old pagan rite. It tells her she's married."

El and I giggled. "I must be sure to tell Nancy that."

"And I'll tell Jonathan so that he will make it a proper ceremony. Eleanor, let's put Maureen up on that low table and start shoving pins into her. Mama Maureen, are you clean and dry all over? I'm about to turn this dress inside out. Satin shows water marks something 'orrible."

For the next twenty-five minutes Theodore was very busy, while I held still and Eleanor kept him supplied with pins. Presently El said, "Lazarus, where did you learn women's clothes?"

"In Paris, about a hundred years from now."

"I wish I hadn't asked. Are you descended from me? As well as from Maureen?"

"I wish I were. I'm not. But I'm married to three of your descendants . . . Tamara, Ishtar, and Hamadryad—and co-husband to another, Ira Weatheral. Probably—certainly—other connections, but Maureen was right; I checked the archives only for my own ancestors. I didn't guess that I would meet you, El of the beautiful belly. I'm almost through. Shall I go ahead and make the alterations? Or do we take this to your ladies' sempstress?"

El said, "Maureen? I'm willing to risk the dress; I have confidence in Lazarus—I mean M'sieur Jacques Noir. But I won't risk it for Nancy's wedding without your permission."

I answered, "I don't have any judgment about Theodore, or Lazarus, or whatever name he's using today—I mean this stud who's treating me like a dressmaker's dummy. But— Sergeant, didn't you tell me you have retailored your breeches yourself? Pegged them?"

"*Oui, Madame.*"

" '*Oui, Madame*' my tired back. Where did you leave your pants, Sergeant? You should always know where your pants are."

"I know where they are!" said El, and fetched them.

"Around the knees, El. Turn them inside out and look." I joined her in checking Theodore's tailoring. Shortly I said, "El, I can't see where they were altered."

"I can. See? The original thread is just barely faded; the

thread he used in altering is the same shade as the cloth of the outlets—the cloth that has not been in sunlight."

I agreed. "Mmm, yes, once I get it into stronger light. If I look closely."

El looked up. "You're hired, boy. Room, board, ten dollars a week, and all the tail you can use."

Theodore looked thoughtful. "Well . . . all right. Though I usually get paid extra for that."

El looked surprised, then laughed merrily, ran to him, and started rubbing tits against his ribs. "I'll meet your terms, Captain. What is your stud fee?"

"I usually get the pick of the litter."

"It's a deal."

The wedding was beautiful and our Nancy was dazzlingly lovely in a magnificent dress that fitted her perfectly. Marie was flower girl; Richard was ring bearer, both in Sunday white. Jonathan was (to my surprise) in formal cutaway, ascot in pearl gray with pearl stickpin, gray striped trousers, spats. Theodore was his best man, in uniform; Father was in uniform and wearing his many medals and acting as usher and groomsman; Brian was utterly beautiful in boots and Sam Browne and spurs and saber and his '98 medals and forest-green jacket and pinks.

Carol was maid of honor and almost as dazzling as the bride in lime-green tulle and her bouquet. Brian Junior was the other usher and groomsman and was dressed in his grammar-school graduation suit, brand new only two weeks earlier—double-breasted blue serge and his first long pants and very grown-up in his manner.

George was charged with just one duty, to see to it that Woodrow kept quiet and behaved himself, and was authorized to use force as necessary. Father gave George this instruction in Woodrow's presence . . . and Woodrow did behave himself; he could always be counted on to act in his own self-interest.

Dr. Draper did not indulge in any of the nonsense with which the Reverend Timberly had almost spoiled my wedding; he used the ME service right straight out of the 1904 Discipline, not a word more, not a word less . . . and in short order our Nancy was going back down the aisle on her husband's arm to the traditional strains of the Mendelssohn recessional, and I sighed with relief. It had been a perfect wedding, no rough spots whatever, and I thought to myself how dumbfounded Mrs. Grundy would have been had she seen a majority of the wedding party thirty-six hours earlier, behind locked doors, in a gentle orgy inaugurating Carol's Day.

It was the first celebration of the holiday that would spread at the wavefront of the Diaspora of the human race: Carol's Day, Carolmas, Carolita's Birthday (it was not!), Fiesta de Santa Carolita. Theodore had told us that it had become (would become) the midsummer fertility rite for all planets, anywhen. Then he had toasted Carol's graduation to womanhood in champagne, and Carol had answered his toast with great seriousness and dignity—and got bubbles up her nose and gagged and coughed and had to be consoled.

I did not know then and do not know now whether or not Theodore granted my second daughter the boon she craved. All I can say is that I gave them every opportunity. But with Theodore (stubborn, difficult man!) one never knows.

On Saturday afternoon there was a rump session of the trustees of the Ira Howard Foundation, Judge Sperling having come all the way from Toledo for that purpose: Judge Sperling, Mr. Arthur J. Chapman, Justin Weatheral, Brian Smith (by unanimous consent), Sergeant Theodore . . . and me. And Eleanor.

When Judge Sperling cleared his throat, I understood the signal and started to withdraw. Whereupon Theodore stood up to leave with me.

There was some backing and filling, but the result was that I stayed and Eleanor stayed because Theodore headed for the door when we did. He did explain that the Howard Families, in their permanent organization, used absolute equality of the sexes . . . and, as Howard chairman in his own time, attending this meeting as a courtesy to the twentieth-century Howard organization, he could not in conscience take part in any Howard meeting from which women were excluded.

Once they got past that hurdle, the meeting simply consisted of Theodore's repeating his prediction of November 11, 1918, as the day the war would end, followed by his prediction of Black Tuesday, October 29, 1929. On being questioned he embellished this latter, with mention of devaluation of the dollar, from twenty dollars to the ounce down to thirty-five dollars to the ounce. "President Roosevelt will do this by what amounts to decree, although Congress will ratify it . . . but this doesn't happen until early in 1933."

"Just a moment, Sergeant Bronson, or Captain Long, or whatever you call yourself, are you saying that Colonel Roosevelt makes a comeback? I find that hard to swallow. In 1933 he will be, uh—" Mr. Chapman stopped to think.

"Seventy-five years old," Judge Sperling put in. "What's so unusual about that, Arthur? I'm older than that, but I have no intention of retiring anytime soon."

Theodore said, "No, gentlemen, no. Not Teddy Roosevelt. Franklin Roosevelt. Now assistant secretary to Mr. Josephus Daniels."

Mr. Chapman shook his head. "I find that even harder to believe."

Theodore answered rather testily, "It does not matter what you believe, Counselor; Mr. Roosevelt will be inaugurated in 1933 and shortly after that he will close all the banks and call in all gold and gold certificates and devalue the dollar. The dollar never does regain its present value. Fifty years later an ounce of gold will fluctuate wildly, from around a hundred dollars an ounce to around a thousand dollars an ounce."

"Young man," Mr. Chapman pronounced, "what you describe is anarchy."

"Not quite. It gets worse. Much worse. Most historians call the second half of this century 'the Crazy Years.' Socially the Crazy Years start at the end of the next World War. But from a standpoint of the economy the Crazy Years start on Black Tuesday, October twenty-ninth, 1929. For the rest of this century you can lose your shirt if you don't maintain a strong cash position. But it is a century of great opportunity, too, in almost every field."

Mr. Chapman closed down his face. I could see that he had made up his mind not to believe anything. But Justin and Judge Sperling exchanged some side remarks, then the Judge said, "Captain Long, can you tell us what some of these 'great opportunities' will be?"

"I'll try. Commercial aviation both for passengers and for freight. Railroads will be in deep trouble and will not recover. The present picture shows will add sound—talking pictures. Television. Stereovision. Space travel. Atomic power. Lasers.

Computers. Electronics of every sort. Mining on the Moon. Asteroid mining. Rolling roadways. Cryonics. Artificial manipulation of genetics. Personal body armor. Sunpower screens. Frozen foods. Hydroponics. Microwave cooking. Do any of you know D. D. Harriman?"

Chapman stood up. "Judge, I move we adjourn."

"Sit down, Arthur, and behave yourself. Captain, you realize how shocking your predictions are, do you not?"

"Certainly," Theodore answered.

"The only way I can listen to your words with equanimity is to recall the changes I have seen in my own lifetime. If your prediction as to the day the war ends turns out to be accurate, then I feel that we must take your other predictions seriously. In the meantime, do you have anything more to tell us?"

"I guess not. Two things, maybe. Don't buy on margin after the middle of 1929. And don't sell short if a wrong guess could clean you out."

"Good advice at any time. Thank you, sir."

Carol and I and the children kissed them both good-bye on Sunday June thirtieth, then went back inside as Captain Bozell's car drove away, to cry in private.

The news got worse and worse all that summer.

Then in the late fall it began to be apparent that we were gaining on the Central Powers. The kaiser abdicated and fled to Holland, and then we knew we were going to win. The false armistice came along and my joy was shaded by the realization that it was not the eleventh of November.

And the real armistice did arrive, right on time, November the eleventh, and every bell, every whistle, every siren and horn, anything that could make noise all sounded at once.

But not in our household. On Thursday George fetched home from his route the Kansas City *Post.* In its casualties report it listed as "MISSING IN ACTION—Bronson Theo Cpl KCMo."

15

Torrid Twenties,
Threadbare Thirties

During the fifty-odd years on my personal time line from
my rescue in 1982 to the start of the Time mission which
aborted into my present predicament on this planet I spent
time equal to about ten years in study of comparative history,
in particular the histories of the time lines that the Circle of
Ouroboros attempts to protect, all of which appear to share
a single ancestral time line at least through A.D. 1900 and
possibly through about 1940.

This sheaf of universes includes my own native universe
(time line two, code Leslie LeCroix) and excludes the un-
counted but far more numerous exotic time lines—universes
in which Columbus did not sail for the Indies (or failed to
return), ones in which the Viking settlements succeeded and
"America" became "Great Vinland," ones in which the Mus-
covite empire on the West Coast clashed with the Hispanic
empire on the East Coast (worlds in which Queen Elizabeth

died in exile), other worlds in which Columbus found America already owned by the Manchu emperors—and worlds with histories so exotic that it is hard to find even a remote ancestral line in common with anything we can recognize.

I am almost certain that I have slipped into one of the exotics . . . but of a previously unsuspected sort.

I did not spend all my time studying histories; I worked for a living, supporting myself first as a nursing assistant, then as a nurse, then as a clinical therapist, then as a student rejuvenator (all the while going to school), before I shifted careers to the Time Corps.

But it was this study of histories that caused me to think about a career in Time.

Several of the time lines known to "civilization" (our name for ourselves) appear to split off about 1940. One cusp at which these splits show is the Democratic National Convention of 1940 at which Mr. Franklin Delano Roosevelt either was or was not nominated by the Democratic party for a third term as president of the United States, then either was or was not elected, then either did or did not serve through the end of the Second World War.

In time line one, code John Carter, the Democratic nomination went to Paul McNutt . . . but the election to Republican Senator Robert Taft.

In the composite time lines coded "Cyrano," Mr. Roosevelt had both a third and a fourth term, died in his fourth term and was succeeded by his vice-president, a former senator from Missouri named Harry Truman. In my own time line there was never a senator by that name but I do remember Brian speaking of a Captain Harry Truman whom he knew in France. "A fighting son of a gun," Briney called him. "A real buzz saw." But the Harry Truman whom Brian knew was not a politician; he was a haberdasher, so it seems unlikely that it could be the same man. Briney used to go out of his way to buy gloves and such from Captain Truman. Brian described him as "a dying breed—an old-fashioned gentleman."

In time line two, code Leslie LeCroix, my own native time line and that of Lazarus Long and Boondock, Mr. Roosevelt was nominated for a third term, in July 1940, then died from a stroke while playing tennis the last week in October, thereby creating a unique constitutional crisis. Henry Wallace, the Democratic nominee for vice-president, claimed that the electors from the states that went Democratic were bound by law to vote for him for president. The Democratic National Committee did not see it that way and neither did the Electoral College—and neither did the Supreme Court—three different points of view. Four, in fact, as John Nance Garner was president from October on . . . but had not been nominated for anything and had bolted his party after the July convention.

I will return to this subject as this was the world I grew up in. But note that Mr. Roosevelt was stricken "while playing tennis."

I learned while studying comparative history that in all other time lines but mine Mr. Roosevelt had been a poliomyelitis cripple confined to a wheelchair!

The effects of contagious diseases on history are a never-ending subject for debate among mathematico-historians on Tertius. I often wonder about one case, because I was there. In my time line Spanish influenza killed 528,000 U.S. residents in the epidemic of the winter of 1918–19, and killed more troops in France than had been killed by shot and shell and poison gas. What if the Spanish flu had struck Europe one year earlier? Certainly history would have been changed—but in what way? Suppose a corporal named Hitler had died? Or an exile who called himself Lenin? Or a soldier named Pétain? That strain of flu could kill overnight; I saw it happen more than once.

Time line three, code Neil Armstrong, is the native world of my sister-wife Hazel Stone (Gwen Campbell) and of our husband Dr. Jubal Harshaw. This is an unattractive world in which Venus is uninhabitable and Mars is a bleak, almost airless desert, and Earth itself seems to have gone crazy, led by the United States in a lemminglike suicide stampede.

I dislike to study time line three; it is so horrid. Yet it fascinates me. In this time line (as in mine) United States historians call the second half of the twentieth century the "Crazy Years"—and well they might! Hearken to the evidence:

a) The largest, longest, bloodiest war in United States history, fought by conscript troops without a declaration of war, without any clear purpose, without any intention of winning—

a war that was ended simply by walking away and abandoning the people for whom it was putatively fought;

b) Another war that was never declared—this one was never concluded and still existed as an armed truce forty years after it started . . . while the United States engaged in renewed diplomatic and trade relations with the very government it had warred against without admitting it;

c) An assassinated president, an assassinated presidential candidate, a president seriously wounded in an assassination attempt by a known psychotic who nevertheless was allowed to move freely, an assassinated leading Negro national politician, endless other assassination attempts, unsuccessful, partly successful, and successful;

d) So many casual killings in public streets and public parks and public transports that most lawful citizens avoided going out after dark, especially the elderly;

e) Public school teachers and state university professors who taught that patriotism was an obsolete concept, that marriage was an obsolete concept, that sin was an obsolete concept, that politeness was an obsolete concept—that the United States itself was an obsolete concept;

f) School teachers who could not speak or write grammatically, could not spell, could not cipher;

g) The nation's leading farm state had as its biggest cash crop an outlawed plant that was the source of the major outlaw drug;

h) Cocaine and heroin called "recreational drugs," felony theft called "joyriding," vandalism by gangs called "trashing," burglary called "ripping off," felonious assault by gangs called "muggings," and the reaction to all of these crimes was "boys will be boys," so scold them and put them on probation but don't ruin their lives by treating them as criminals;

i) Millions of women who found it more rewarding to have babies out of wedlock than it would be to get married or to go to work.

I don't understand time line three (code Neil Armstrong) so I had better quote Jubal Harshaw, who lived through it. "Mama Maureen," he said to me, "the America of my time line is a laboratory example of what can happen to democracies, what has eventually happened to all perfect democracies throughout all histories. A perfect democracy, a 'warm body' democracy in which every adult may vote and all votes count equally, has no internal feedback for self-correction. It depends solely on the wisdom and self-restraint of citizens . . . which is opposed by the folly and lack of self-restraint of other citizens. What is supposed to happen in a democracy is that each sovereign citizen will always vote in the public interest for the safety and welfare of all. But what does happen is that he votes his own self-interest as he sees it . . . which for the majority translates as 'Bread and Circuses.'

" 'Bread and Circuses' is the cancer of democracy, the fatal disease for which there is no cure. Democracy often works beautifully at first. But once a state extends the franchise to every warm body, be he producer or parasite, that day marks the beginning of the end of the state. For when the plebs discover that they can vote themselves bread and circuses without limit and that the productive members of the body politic cannot stop them, they will do so, until the state bleeds to death, or in its weakened condition the state succumbs to an invader—the barbarians enter Rome."

Jubal shrugged and looked sad. "Mine was a lovely world—until the parasites took over."

Jubal Harshaw also pointed out to me a symptom that, so he says, invariably precedes the collapse of a culture: a decline in good manners, in common courtesy, in a decent respect for the rights of other people. "Political philosophers from Confucius to the present day have repeatedly pointed this out. But the first signs of this fatal symptom may be hard to spot. Does it really matter when an honorific is omitted? Or when a junior calls a senior by his first name, uninvited? Such loosening of protocol may be hard to evaluate. But there is one unmistakable sign of the collapse of good manners: dirty public washrooms.

"In a healthy society public restrooms, toilets, washrooms, look and smell as clean and fresh as a bathroom in a decent private home. In a sick society—" Jubal stopped and simply looked disgusted.

He did not need to elaborate; I had seen it happen in my own time line. In the first part of the twentieth century right through the thirties people at all levels of society were habitually polite to each other and it was taken for granted that anyone using a public washroom tried hard to leave the place as clean and neat as he found it. As I recall, decent behavior concerning public washrooms started to slip during World War II, and so did good manners in general. By the sixties and the seventies rudeness of all sorts had become commonplace, and by then I never used a public restroom if I could possibly avoid it.

Offensive speech, bad manners, and filthy toilets all seem to go together.

America in my own time line suffered the cancer of "Bread and Circuses" but found a swifter way to commit suicide. I don't boast about the difference, as in time line two the people of the United States succumbed to something even sillier than Bread and Circuses: The people voted themselves a religious dictatorship.

It happened after 1982, so I did not see it—for which I am glad! When I was a woman a hundred years old, Nehemiah Scudder was still a small boy.

The potential for religious hysteria had always been present in the American culture, and this I knew, as my father had rubbed my nose in it from an early age. Father had pointed out to me that the only thing that preserved religious freedom in the United States was not the First Amendment and was not tolerance . . . but was solely a Mexican standoff between rival religious sects, each sect intolerant, each sect the sole custodian of the "One True Faith"—but each sect a minority that gave lip service to freedom of religion to keep its own "One True Faith" from being persecuted by all the other "True Faiths."

(Of course it was usually open season on Jews and sometimes on Catholics and almost always on Mormons and Muslims and Buddhists and other heathens. The First Amendment was never intended to protect such outright blasphemy. Oh, no!)

Elections are won not by converting the opposition but by getting out your own vote, and Scudder's organization did just that. According to histories I studied at Boondock, the election of 2012 turned out 63 percent of the registered voters (which in turn was less than half of those eligible to register); the True American party (Nehemiah Scudder) polled 27 percent of the popular vote . . . which won 81 percent of the Electoral College votes.

In 2016 there was no election.

The Torrid Twenties . . . Flaming Youth, the Lost Generation, flappers, cake eaters, gangsters and sawed-off shotguns and bootleg booze and needled beer. Hupmobiles and Stutz Bearcats and flying circuses. A joy hop for five dollars. Lindbergh and the *Spirit of St. Louis*. Skirts climbed unbelievably until, by the middle of the decade, rolled stockings permitted bare knees to be seen. The Prince of Wales Glide and the Finalé Hop and the Charleston. Ruth Etting and Will Rogers and Ziegfeld's Follies. There were bad things about the Twenties but on the whole they were good years for most people—and they were never dull.

I kept busy as usual with housewifely things of little interest to outsiders. I had Theodore Ira in 1919, Margaret in 1922, Arthur Roy in 1924, Alice Virginia in 1927, Doris Jean in 1930—and they all had the triumphs and crises that children have and aren't you glad that you don't have to look at their pictures and listen to me repeating their cute sayings?

In February of 1929 we sold our house on Benton Boulevard and leased with option to buy a house near Rockhill Road and Meyer Boulevard—an old farmhouse, roomy but not as modern as our former home. This was a hard-nosed decision by my husband, who always believed in making every dollar work twice. But he did consult me and not alone because title was vested in me.

"Maureen," he said to me, "do you feel like gambling?"

"We always have. Haven't we?"

"Some yes, some no. This time we would tap the pot, shoot the works, shout *Banco!* If I failed to bring it off, you might have to go out and pound a beat, just to keep potato soup on the table."

"I've always wondered if I could make a living that way. Here I am, forty-seven in July—"

"Wups! Your age is now thirty-seven. And I'm forty-one."

"Briney, I'm in bed with you. Can't I be truthful in bed?"

"Judge Sperling wants us to stick to our corrected ages at all times. And Justin agrees."

"Yessir. I'll be good. I've always wondered if I could make a living as a streetwalker. But how do I find a beat? I understand that a gal can get her eyes scratched out if she just goes out and starts soliciting without finding out who owns that territory. I know what to do in bed, Briney; it's the merchandizing of the product that I must learn."

"Don't be so eager, slippery bottom; it may not be necessary. Tell me— Do you still believe that Ted—Theodore—Corporal Bronson—came from the future?"

I suddenly sobered. "I do. Don't you?"

"Mo', I believed him as quickly as you did. I believed him before his prophecy about the end of the war proved true. Now I'm asking you this: Do you believe in Ted strongly enough that you are willing to risk every cent we own that his prediction of a collapse in the stock market will be right on the button exactly like his prediction of Armistice Day?"

"Black Tuesday," I said softly. "October twenty-ninth. This year."

"Well? If I take this gamble—and miss—we'll be broke. Marie won't be able to finish at Radcliffe, Woodie will have to scratch for a college education, and Dick and Ethel—well, we'll cross those bridges later. Sweetheart, I'm into this bull market up to my ears . . . and I propose to get deeper into it on the firm assumption that Black Tuesday takes place on the dot and exactly as Ted said it would."

"Do it!"

"Are you sure, Mo'? If anything goes wrong, we'll be right back to fried mush. Whereas it is not too late to hedge my bets—pull half of it out and stash it away. Gamble with the other half."

"Briney, I wasn't brought up that way. You remember Father's harness racer Loafer?"

"I saw him a few times. A beautiful beast."

"Yes. Just not quite as fast as he looked. Father regularly bet on himself. Always on the nose. Never to place or show. Loafer usually could come in second or third . . . but Father would not bet that way. I've heard him talk to Loafer before a heat, softly, gently: 'This time we're going to take 'em, boy! This time we're going to win!' Then later I've heard him say, 'You tried, old fellow! That's all I can ask. You're still a champion . . . and we'll take 'em next time!' And Father would pat him on the neck, and Loafer would whinny and nicker to him, and they would comfort each other."

"Then you think I should bet across the board? For there isn't going to be any next time."

"No, no! Shoot the works! You believe Theodore and so do I. So let's do it!" I added, as I reached down and grabbed his tool, "If it's fried-mush time again, it need not be for long. You can knock me up, uh, let me see"—I counted—"next Monday. Which would mean that I would unload about"—I stopped to count again—"oh, a couple of weeks after Black Tuesday. Then we will receive another Howard Foundation bonus shortly thereafter."

"No."

"Huh? I mean, 'Excuse me?' I don't understand."

"Mo', if Ted's prediction is wrong, the Foundation's principal assets may be wiped out. Justin and Judge Sperling are betting that Ted's prediction is correct; Chapman is bucking them. There are four other trustees . . . and two are Hoover Republicans, two were for Al Smith. Justin doesn't know which way it will go."

Selling our house when we did was part of the gamble. It was a hard-nosed decision as it involved what came to be known as "block busting." We lived in an all-white neighborhood, but Darktown was just north of us, not far away, and had been growing steadily closer in the twenty-odd years we had owned that house. (Dear, sweet house!—stuffed with happy memories.)

Brian had been approached by a white real estate agent who said he had an offer from an undisclosed client: How much did Brian want for his house?

"Darling, I did not ask about his client . . . because, if I had asked, it would turn out that the client was a white lawyer who, if pushed, would be acting for a client in Denver or Boston. In this sort of a deal the cover-up is about six levels deep . . . and the neighbors are not supposed to find out the color of the new owner's skin until the new owner moves in."

"What did you tell him?"

"I told him, 'Certainly I'm willing to sell my house if the price is right. But the price would have to be attractive, as we are comfortable where we are and moving is always expensive in time and in money. What price does your client offer? In cash, I mean—not a down payment and take back a mortgage. If I am going to have to find another house for my large family—eleven of us—I'll need cash to work with. I may have to build, rather than buy—not too many houses can handle big families today; I probably would have to build.

If I do this. So the price would have to be attractive and it would have to be in cash.

"This false face points out that any bank would discount the paper on such a property; a mortgage is as good as cash. 'Not to me, it isn't,' I told him. 'Let your client arrange the mortgage directly with his bank and bring the cash up front. My dear sir, I'm not anxious to sell. Give me a cash figure and, if it's big enough, we'll go straight to escrow. If it's not, I'll tell you No just as quickly.'

"He said that escrow would not be necessary, as they were satisfied that I could grant good title. Mo', that told me more than the words he said. It means that they have already run a title search on us . . . and probably on every house in our block. It means to me that this is probably the only house in this block that does not have a mortgage against it . . . or some other legal matter that would have to be cleared in escrow, such as lifetime tenancy under a will, or the property is currently in probate, or involved in a pending divorce, or there is a lien against it, or a judgment, or something. A man trying to put together this sort of a deal doesn't like escrow, because it is during that waiting period that the 'gentlemen's agreement' sort of people can find out what is going on, and move in to stop it . . . often with the connivance of a sympathetic judge."

"Briney, maybe you had better explain 'gentlemen's agreement' to me. I don't recall it from that course in commercial law we took."

"You would not have heard of it there because it is extralegal. Not against the law, just not covered by law. There is no covenant in your deed to this house that forbids you to sell to anyone you wish to, black, white, or green polka dots . . . and it might not stand up in court if there were. But, if you were to ask our neighbors, I guarantee that they would assure you that there is indeed a gentlemen's agreement binding you not to sell your house in this block to a Negro."

I was puzzled. "Have we ever agreed to anything of the sort?" My husband made all sorts of commitments, rarely told me. He simply assumed that I would back him up. And I always did. Marriage is not a sometime thing; it's whole hawg or you're not married.

"Never."

"Are you going to ask our neighbors what they think about this?"

"Mo', do you want me to? It's your house."

I don't think I hesitated as long as two seconds. But it was a new idea and I did have to decide. "Briney, several houses in this block have changed hands since we moved in here, uh, twenty-two years ago. I don't recall that we were ever asked our opinion about any of those transactions."

"That's right. We never were."

"I don't think it is any of their business to decide what a Negro can or can't buy. Or to tell us. What they do with their property is their business; what we do with ours is our business—as long as we obey the laws and abide by any open covenants that run with the land. That twenty-five-foot setback rule, for example. I can think of just one way they can legitimately keep us from selling this house to anyone who wants to buy it."

"What way is that, Mo'?"

"By coming to us before we are committed with the same sort of offer that Mr. False Face has made but with more money. If they buy this house from us, they can do with it as they wish."

"I'm glad you see it that way, my love. A year from now every house in this block will be occupied by a Negro family. Mo', I could see it coming. Population pressure works much like a rising river. You can put up dikes or levees, but the day comes when the river has to go somewhere. Kansas City's Darktown is terribly crowded. If the whites don't want to live next door to Negroes, then the whites must back off and give them room. I'm not especially concerned about Negro problems; I've got problems of my own. But I don't fight the weather and I don't bang my head against a stone wall. You and I will see the day when Darktown will run south all the way to Thirty-ninth Street. There is no use fussing about it; it is going to happen."

Briney did get a good price for our old house. After figuring in the rise in prices from 1907 to 1929 there was only a modest profit, but Briney did get the price in cash—gold certificates, not a check; the recorded price was "ten dollars and other valuable considerations"—and Briney put the money straight into the stock market. "Sweetheart, if Theodore's predictions are correct, in a year or so we'll be able to take our pick of big houses in the Country Club district at about a third of the going prices today . . . because it will turn out that Black Tuesday will leave about half of the nominal owners unable to meet their mortgage payments. In the meantime try to stay happy in this old farmhouse; Justin and I have to go to New York.''

I did not have any trouble staying happy in that farmhouse; it reminded me of my girlhood. I told Father so, and he agreed. ''But put that second bathroom in. Do you remember why we had two outhouses? You can't afford to encourage piles and constipation.''

Father was not formally living with us—he got his mail elsewhere—but, since 1916 and Plattsburg, Brian had insisted that we always keep a room for Father. When Brian went to New York to stay closer to his stock-market gambling, Father did agree to sleep (usually) at our house, just as he had when Brian was away in France. But by then I had that second bath installed and a washroom downstairs and the outhouse out back limed and filled.

My children readjusted to the change with little fret. Even our resident cat, Chargé d'Affaires, accepted it. He fretted on the long trip there, but he did seem to understand that the moving vans meant that home was no longer home. Ethel and Teddy kept him fairly well soothed during the move—I was driving that load; Woodrow had the rest of the family in his jalopy. Chargé looked over our land as soon as we got there, then came back, got me, took me with him while he went all the way around the inside of the fence. He sprayed all four corner posts, so I knew that he had accepted the change and his new responsibilities.

It was from Woodrow that I had expected the most fuss as he was due to enter his senior year at Central High School in September 1929 and was a likely candidate for cadet commander of the ROTC battalion at Central, especially as both Brian Junior and George had commanded the cadet battalion each in his senior year.

But Woodrow did not even insist on finishing out the second semester; he transferred in midterm to Westport High School—somewhat to my dismay, as I had counted on him to drive Dick and Ethel to Central, one in junior high there, the other just entering senior high. So, willy-nilly, they had to transfer in midterm, too, as I did not have time to drive them and it was an impossible trip by streetcar. Teddy and Peggy I put in Country Day School, an excellent private school, as Eleanor suggested that she could handle two more in her car along with the three she had in that school.

It was several years before I realized that Woodrow's willingness to switch schools abruptly had to do with a renovated cow pasture still farther south that had a sign on it: ACE HARDY'S FLYING SCHOOL. Woodrow had acquired (I think that is the right word) his unlikely automobile in the summer of 1928, and after that we had seen little of him other than at meals. But I learned later that Woodrow had learned to fly while still in high school.

As everyone knows, Black Tuesday arrived on the dot. Briney called me long distance a week later. "Frau Doktor Krausmeyer?"

"Elmer!"

"Children okay?"

"Everyone is fine but they miss their papa. As do I. Hurry home, dear; I'm honing to see you."

"Didn't that hired man work out?"

"No staying power. I let him go. I decided to wait for you."

"But I'm not coming home."

"Oh."

"Don't you want to know why?"

(Yes, Briney, I do want to know why. And someday I'm going to put itch powder into your jock strap for these guessing games.) "Buffalo Bill, you'll tell me when it suits you and whatever suits you."

"Rangy Lil, how would you like to go to Paris? And to Switzerland?"

"Hadn't you better make it South America? Some country where there is no extradition?" (Damn you, Briney! Quit teasing me.)

"I want you to leave tomorrow. Take the C and A to Chicago, then the Pennsy to New York. I'll meet your train and take you to our hotel. We sail for Cherbourg on Saturday."

"Yes, sir." (Oh, that man!) "About our children— Seven, I believe. Are you interested in the arrangements I make for them? Or shall I just use my judgment?" (What arrangements can I make with Eleanor?)

"Use your judgment. But if Ira is there, I'd like to speak to him."

"To hear is to obey, Effendi."

After Brian spoke to him, Father said to me, "I told Brian not to worry, as Ethel is a competent cook. If she needs help, I will hire help. So, Maureen, you two run along and have fun; the youngsters will be safe. Don't pack more than two bags, because—" The phone rang again.

"Maureen? Your big sister, dear. Did you hear from Brian?"

"Yes."

"Good. I have the train schedules and the Pullman reservations; Justin arranged them from New York. Frank will drive us to the station. You must be ready by ten tomorrow morning. Can you manage it?"

"I'll have to manage it. I may be barefooted and my hair in a bath knot—"

I became addicted to travel in a luxury liner in nothing flat. The *Île de France* was a wonderful shock to little Maureen Johnson whose idea of luxury was enough bathrooms for seven—usually seven; it varied—children and enough hot water. Briney had taken me to the Grand Canyon two years earlier and that was wonderful . . . but this was another sort of wonderful. A *concierge* who seemed anxious to swim back and fetch anything Madame wishes. A maid who spoke English but understood my French and did not laugh at my accent. A full orchestra at dinner, a chamber music trio for tea, dancing to live music every night. Breakfast in bed. A masseuse on call. A living room for our suite bigger and much fancier than Eleanor's at home, and two master bedrooms.

"Justin, why are we at the captain's table?"

"I don't know. Because we have this suite, maybe."

"And why do we have this suite? Everything in first class looks luxurious; I would not have complained if we had been in second class. But this is gilding the lily. Isn't it?"

"Maureen my sweet, I ordered two outside double staterooms, first class, which were confirmed and we paid for them. Then two days before sailing the agent telephoned and offered me this suite at the price we had paid plus a nominal surcharge, one hundred dollars. Seems the man who had reserved this suite had not been able to sail. I asked why he had canceled. Instead of answering he cut the surcharge to fifty dollars. I asked who had died in that suite and was it contagious. Again instead of answering he offered to eliminate the surcharge if we would just let the *New York Times* and *L'Illustration* photograph us in our suite—which they did, you remember."

"And was it contagious?"

"Not really. The poor fellow jumped out a twenty-story window—the day after Black Tuesday."

"Oh! I should keep my mouth shut."

"Mau darling, this suite was not his home, he was never in it in his life, it is not haunted. He was just one of many thousands of chumps who became paper wealthy gambling on margin. If it will make you feel any better, I can assure you that both Brian and I made no secret of our intention of getting out of the market when we did because we expected the market to collapse before the end of October. Nobody would listen." Justin shook his head, shrugged.

Brian added, "I almost had to strangle one broker to get him to execute my orders. He seemed to think it was immoral and possibly illegal to sell when the market was going steadily up. 'Wait till it tops,' he said. 'Then see. You're crazy to quit at this point.' I told him that my old grandmother had read the tea leaves and told me that now was the time to unload. He again said that I was crazy. I told him to execute those orders at once . . . or I was going straight to the governors of the Exchange and have him investigated for bucket shop operations. That really got him angry, so he sold me out . . . and then got still angrier when I insisted on a certified check. I took the check and cashed it at once. And changed the cash to gold . . . as I recalled all too clearly that Ted said that banks would start to go boom."

I wanted to ask where that gold was now. But I did not.

Zurich is a lovely city, prettier than any I had seen in the United States. The language there is alleged to be German but it is not the German spoken by my neighbor from Munich. But I got along fine once I realized that almost everyone spoke English. Our men were busy; Eleanor and I had a wonderful time being tourists.

Then one day they took us with them and I found myself

the surprised owner of a numbered bank account, for 155,515 grams of fine gold (which I had no trouble interpreting as one hundred thousand dollars, but it was not called such). Then I found myself signing powers of attorney over "my" bank account to Brian and to Justin, while Eleanor did the same with a similar account. And a limited power of attorney to someone I had never heard of in Winnipeg, Canada.

We were not placed in that fancy suite because we were high society; we were not. But the purser was carrying in his safe I do not know how many ounces of gold, most of which belonged to the Ira Howard Foundation, and some of which belonged personally to Brian, and to Justin, and to my father. That gold was moved by the Bank of France from Cherbourg to Zurich, and we rode with it.

In Zurich Brian and Justin, as witnesses and trustees for the Foundation, saw the shipment opened, saw it counted and weighed, and then deposited with a consortium of three banks. For the Foundation had taken very seriously Theodore's warning that Mr. Roosevelt would devalue the dollar, then make it illegal for American citizens to own or possess gold.

"Justin," I asked, "what happens if Governor Roosevelt does not run for the presidency? Or does but is not elected?"

"Nothing. The Foundation would be no worse off. But have you lost confidence in Ted? On his advice we rode the market up, and then cashed out before it crashed, and now the Foundation is about six times as wealthy as it was a year ago, all through depending on Ted's predictions."

"Oh, I believe in Theodore! I was just wondering."

Mr. Roosevelt was elected and he did indeed devalue the dollar and made it illegal for Americans to possess gold. But the assets of the Foundation had been placed out of reach of this confiscation. As was my own numbered bank account. I never touched it but Briney told me that it was not simply lying idle; he was using "my" money to make more money.

Brian was now a trustee of the Foundation, vice Mr. Chapman, who had been removed from the board for having lost his own money in the stock market. A trustee of the Foundation had to be himself qualified for Howard benefits (four living grandparents at time of marriage) and had to be himself a money-maker. If there were other requirements, I do not know what they were.

Justin was now chairman of the board and chief executive, vice Judge Sperling, who was still a trustee but was past ninety and had elected not to work quite so hard. When we got back to Kansas City, Justin and Brian set up offices in the Scarritt Building as "Weatheral and Smith, Investments" while "Brian Smith Associates" took an office on the same floor.

We never again had money worries but the decade of the Depression was not a time when it was fun to be rich. We strove to avoid the appearance of being rich. Instead of buying a fancy house in the Country Club district we bought that farmhouse at a bargain price, then rebuilt it into a more satisfactory structure. It was a period when skilled craftsmen were eager to get work at wages they would have sneered at in 1929.

The nation's economy was stuck on dead center and no one seemed to know why and everyone from bootblack to banker had a solution he wanted to see tried. Mr. Franklin Roosevelt took office in 1933 and, yes, the banks did close but the Smiths and the Weatherals had cash under the mattress and groceries squirreled away; the bank holiday did us no harm. The country seemed invigorated by the energetic actions of "The New Deal," the new president's name for a series of nostrums that came pouring out of Washington.

In retrospect it seemed that the "reforms" that constituted the New Deal did nothing to correct the economy—yet it is hard to fault emergency measures that put food into the mouths of the destitute. The WPA and the PWA and the CCC and the NRA and the endless make-work programs did not cure the economy and may well have done damage . . . but in Kansas City in the 1930s they almost certainly served to avoid food riots by desperate people.

On September first, 1939, ten years after Black Tuesday, Nazi Germany invaded Poland. Two days later Britain and France declared war against Germany. World War II had started.

16

The Frantic Forties

In the summer of 1940 Brian and I were living in Chicago at 6105 Woodlawn, an address just south of the Midway. It was a large apartment building, eighty units, owned by the Howard Foundation through a dummy. We occupied what was called "the Penthouse"—the west end of the top floor, a living room and balcony, a kitchen, four bedrooms, two baths.

We needed the extra bedrooms, especially in July during the Democratic National Convention. For two weeks we had from twelve to fifteen people sleeping in an apartment intended for a maximum of eight. I do not recommend this. The apartment did not have airconditioning, it was an exceptionally hot summer, and Lake Michigan a few hundred yards away turned our flat into a Turkish bath. At home I would have coped with it by walking around in my skin. But I could not do so in the presence of strangers. One of the real benefits of Boondock is that skin is just skin—means nothing.

I had not been in Chicago other than to change trains since 1893. Brian had frequently visited Chicago without me, as this flat was often used for Howard Foundation board meetings, the Foundation having moved its registered address from Toledo to Winnipeg in 1929. As Justin explained it to me, "Maureen, while we don't advertise what we're doing, we won't be breaking any laws about private ownership of gold; we are simply planning for whatever develops. The Foundation is now restructured under Canadian law, and its registered secretary is a Canadian lawyer, who is in fact a Howard client himself and a Foundation trustee. I never touch gold, even with gloves on."

(Brian expressed it otherwise. "No intelligent man has any respect for an unjust law. Nor does he feel guilt over breaking it. He simply follows the Eleventh Commandment.")

This time Brian was not in Chicago for a board meeting; he was there to watch the Chicago commodities market and to deal in it, because of the war in Europe—while I was in Chicago because I wanted to be. Much as I enjoyed being a brood mare, after forty years of it and seventeen babies, I relished seeing something other than wet diapers.

There was indeed much to see. The parkway a hundred yards north of us, stretching from Washington Park to Jackson Park and called the Midway Plaisance, was in fact a midway the last time I had seen it, with everything from Little Egypt's belly dance to pink cotton candy. Now it was a beautiful grassy park, with the matchless Fountain of Time by Lorado Taft at the west end and the lovely Fifty-seventh Street beach at the east end. The main campus of the University of Chicago, great gray Gothic buildings, dominated its north side. The university had been founded the year before I had come here as a girl, but none of these buildings had been built by then—as near as I could recall several major exhibit halls had occupied the ground now constituting the campus. I could not be certain, as nothing looked the same.

The elevated trains were much more widespread and now they were powered by electricity instead of steam. On the surface there were no longer horse cars or even cable cars; electric trolley cars had replaced them. No more horses anywhere—autos bumper to bumper, a dubious improvement.

The Field Museum, three miles to the north and on the lake, had been founded after my long visit in '93; its Malvina Hoffman exhibit, The Races of Man, was in itself worth a trip to the Windy City. Near it was the Adler Planetarium, the first one I ever visited. I loved the shows at the planetarium; they let me daydream of traveling among the stars like Theodore—but I did not dream that I would ever really do so. That hope was buried, along with my heart, somewhere in France.

Chicago in '93 had kept eleven-year-old Maureen Johnson round-eyed; Chicago in 1940 kept Maureen Smith, now officially forty-one years old, still more round-eyed, there were so many new wonders to see.

One change I did not like: in 1893 if I happened to be out after dark, Father did not worry and neither did I. In 1940 I was careful never to be caught out after dark, other than on Brian's arm.

Just before the 1940 Democratic convention the "Phony War" ended and France fell. On June sixth at Dunkirk, France, the British evacuated what was left of their army and that was followed by one of the greatest speeches in all histories: "—we shall fight them on the beaches, we shall fight them in the streets, we shall never surrender—"

Father telephoned Brian, told him that he was signing up with the AFS. "Brian, this time even the Home Guard says I'm too old. But these folks are signing up medics the Army won't accept. They want them for support service in war zones and they'll take anybody who can saw off a leg—meaning me. If this is the only way I can fight the Huns, then this is what I'll do—I owe that to Ted Bronson. Understand me, sir?"

"I quite understand."

"How soon can you put somebody else here to watch the youngsters?"

I could hear both sides, so I took the phone. "Father, Brian can't come home now but I can. Although I may be able to put Betty Lou there in my place even quicker. Either way, you can go ahead with your plans. But, Father, listen to me. You take care of yourself! Do you hear me?"

"I'll be careful, Daughter."

"Please do so, please! I'm proud of you, sir. And Theodore is proud of you, too. I know."

"I shall try to make both you and Ted proud of me, Maureen."

I said good-bye quickly and hung up before my voice broke. Briney was looking thoughtful. "I'll have to get busy right away and correct my age with the Army. Or they might start saying that I am too old."

"Briney! Surely you don't expect to convince the Army that you are your Howard age? They have years and years of records on you."

"Oh, I wouldn't try to tell the adjutant general my Howard age. Although I don't think I look any older than the forty-six it says on my driver's license. I mean that I want to correct the little white lie I told in 1898. When I was actually fourteen but swore that I was twenty-one so that they would let me enlist."

"Fourteen indeed! You were a senior at Rolla."

"I was precocious, just like our children. Yes, dearest, I was a senior at Rolla in '98. But there is nobody left in the War Department who knows that. And nobody is likely to tell them. Maureen, a reserve colonel fifty-six years old is a lot more likely to be ordered to duty than one who is sixty-three. About one hundred percent more likely."

I'm using a Time-agent's field recorder keyed to my voice and concealed in a body cavity. No, no, not concealed in the tunnel of love; that would not do, as Time agents aren't nuns and are not expected to be. I mean an artificial cavity about where my gall bladder used to be. This gadget is supposed to be good for a thousand hours and I hope it is working properly because, if these spooks scrag me—better make that "when they scrag me"—I hope that Pixel can lead somebody to my corpse and thereby let the Time Corps retrieve the record. I want the Circle to understand what I was trying to do. I should have done it openly, I suppose, but Lazarus would have grabbed it away from me. I have perfect hindsight—not so good in the other direction.

Brian did manage to "correct" his War Department age, simply because his general wanted him. But he did not manage to get himself ordered to a combat command. Instead combat came to him—he was holding down a desk at the Presidio and we were living in an old mansion on Knob Hill when the Japanese pulled their sneak attack on San Francisco, December 7, 1941.

It is an odd feeling to look up into the sky, see planes overhead, feel their engines deep in your bones, see their bellies give birth to bombs, and know that it is too late to run, too late to hide, and that you have no control whatever over where those bombs will hit—on you or on houses a block away. The feeling was not terror; it was more a sense of déjà vu, as if I had been there a thousand times before. I don't care to feel it again but I know why warriors (real ones, not wimps in uniform) always seek combat assignments, not desk jobs. It is in the presence of death that one lives most intensely. "Better one crowded hour of life—"

I have read that in time line three this sneak attack was made on Hawaii, not San Francisco, and that California Japanese were thereafter moved back from the coast. If so, they were extremely lucky, for that spared them the blood bath that took place in time line two, where more than sixty thousand Japanese-Americans were lynched or shot or (in some cases) burned alive on Sunday through Tuesday, December 7–9, 1941. Did this affect what we did to Tokyo and Kobe later? I wonder.

Wars that start with sneak attacks are certain to be merciless; all the histories prove it.

As one result of those lynch mobs President Barkley placed California under martial law. In April 1942 this was eased off and only the twenty-mile strip inland from the mean high-tide line was militarized, but the zone was extended up the coast to Canada. In San Francisco this caused no special inconvenience—it was much like living on a military reservation and a marked improvement over San Francisco's usual civic corruption—but after dark on the coast itself there was always a danger that some sixteen-year-old boy in a National Guard uniform, armed with a World War I Springfield, might get nervous and trigger happy.

Or so I heard; I never risked it. The beach from Canada to Mexico was a combat zone; anyone on it after dark was risking sudden death and many found it.

I had my youngest with me, Donald, four, and Priscilla, two. My school-age children—Alice, Doris, Patrick, and Susan—were in Kansas City with Betty Lou. I had thought of Arthur Roy as being school age (born 1924), but his cousin Nelson swore him into the Marine Corps the day after the bombing of San Francisco, along with his older brother Richard (born 1914); they went to Pendleton together. Nelson was on limited duty, having left a foot in Belleau Wood in 1918. Justin was on the War Production Board, based in Washington but traveling rather steadily; he stayed with us on Knob Hill several times.

Woodrow I did not see even once until the war was over. I received a Christmas card from him in December 1941, postmarked Pensacola, Florida: "Dear Mom and Pop, I'm hiding out from the Nips and teaching Boy Scouts how to fly upside down. Heather and the kids are stashed for the duration at Avalon Beach, PO Box 6320, so I sleep home most nights. Merry Christmas and have a nice war. Woodrow."

The next we heard from Woodrow was a card from the Royal Hawaiian at Waikiki: "The service here is not quite up to peacetime standards but it is better than that at Lahaina. Despite any rumors to the contrary the sharks in Lahaina Roads are not vegetarians. Hoping you are the same. W.W."

That was our first intimation that Woodrow had been in the Battle of Lahaina Roads. Whether he was in the *Saratoga* when she was sunk, or whether he ditched from the air, I do not know. But his card implies that he was in the water at some point. I asked him about this after the war. He looked puzzled and said, "Mom, where did you get that notion? I spent the war in Washington, D.C., drinking Scotch with my opposite number in the British Aircraft Commission. His Scotch, it was—he had worked out a scam to fly it in from Bermuda."

Woodrow was not always strictly truthful.

Let me see— Theodore Ira, my World War I baby, went to active duty with Kansas City's 110th Combat Engineers and spent most of the war in Noumea, building air strips and docks and such. Nancy's husband and Eleanor's son, Jonathan, had stayed in the Reserve but not in the Guard; he was a column commander in Patton's Panzers when they drove the Russians out of Czechoslovakia. Nancy helped organize the WAAC and finished the war senior to her husband, to the vast amusement of all of us—even Jonathan. George started out in the Thirty-fifth Division HQ but wound up in the OSS, so I don't know what he did. In March 1944 Brian Junior made the landing at Marseilles, caught a piece of shrapnel in his left thigh, and wound up back in Salisbury, England, an executive officer in the training command.

My letters to Father were returned to me in 1942, along with a formal letter of regret from the national headquarters of the AFS.

Richard's wife, Marian, stayed in nearby San Juan Capistrano while Richard was at Camp Pendleton. When he shipped out, I invited her to move in with us, with her children—four, and one that was born shortly after she arrived. We could make room for them and it was actually easier for us two women to take care of seven children than it had been for each of us to cope with our own unassisted. We worked things out so that one of us could assist at Letterman Army Hospital every afternoon, going to the Presidio by bus (no gasoline ration expended) and coming back with Brian. I was fond of Marian; she was as dear to me as my own daughters.

So it came about that she was with us when she received that telegram; Richard had earned the Navy Cross on Iwo Jima—posthumously.

A little over five months later we destroyed Tokyo and Kobe. Then Emperor Akihito and his ministers shocked us all by ritually disemboweling themselves, first the ministers, then the emperor, after the emperor announced to them that his mind had been quieted by President Barkley's promise to spare Kyoto. It was especially shocking in that Emperor Akihito was just a boy, not yet twelve, younger than my son Patrick Henry.

We will never understand the Japanese. But the long war was over.

I am forced to wonder what would have happened if the emperor's father, Emperor Hirohito, had not died in the "Star Festival" air strike, July seventh? He was reputed to be so "Westernized." The other pertinent histories, time lines three and six, give no firm answers. Hirohito seems to have been the captive of his ministers, reigning but not ruling.

Once Japan surrendered Brian asked for early separation, but was sent to Texas—Amarillo, then Dallas—to assist in contract terminations (the only time, I think, that he regretted having passed his bar examinations back in 1938). But moving away from San Francisco at that time was a good idea—a change of background to a place where we knew no one—because on arrival in Texas Marian became "Maureen J.

Smith" and I dyed my hair and became her widowed mother, Marian Hardy. None too soon; she was already showing—four months later she gave birth to Richard Brian. We kept it straight with the Foundation, of course, and registered Marian's new baby correctly: Marian Justin Hardy + Brian Smith, Sr.

What happened next is difficult for me to talk about, because there are three points of view and mine is only one of those three. I am certain that the other two are each as fair-minded as I am, if not more so. "More so," I think I must concede, as Father had warned me, more than half a century earlier, that I was an amoral wretch who could reason only pragmatically, not morally.

I had not tried to keep my husband out of my daughter-in-law's bed. Neither Briney nor I had ever tried to own each other; we both approved of sex for fun and we had established our rules for civilized adultery many years earlier. I was a bit surprised that Marian had apparently made no effort to keep from getting pregnant by Brian . . . but only in that she did not consult me ahead of time. (If she consulted Briney, he never mentioned it. But men do have this tendency to spray sperm around like a fire hose while letting the females decide whether or not to make practical use of the juice.)

Nevertheless I was not angry, just mildly surprised. And I do recognize the normal biological reflex under which the first thing a freshly bereft widow does, if she can manage it, is to spread her legs and sob bitterly and use her womb to replace the dear departed. It is a survival mechanism, one not limited to wars but more prevalent in wartime, as statistical analysis demonstrates.

(I hear that there are men who watch the newspapers for funerals, then attend those of married men in order to meet new widows. This is shooting fish down a well and probably merits castration. On the other hand, those widows might not thank us.)

So we moved to Dallas and everything was satisfactory for a while. Brian was simply a man with two wives, a situation not unknown among Howards—just pull the shades against the neighbors, like some Mormons.

A short time after the birth of Marian's new baby Brian came to me with something on his mind, something he had trouble articulating. I finally said, "Look, dearest, I am not a mindreader. Whatever it is, just spill it."

"Marian wants a divorce."

"Huh? Briney, I'm confused. If she's not happy with us, all she needs to do is to move out; it doesn't take a divorce. In fact I don't see how she could get one. But I'm terribly sorry to hear it. I thought we had gone to considerable trouble to make things happy for her. And for Richard Brian and her other children. Do you want me to talk to her? Try to find out what the trouble is?"

"Uh— Damn it, I didn't make myself clear. She wants you to get a divorce so that she can marry me."

My jaw dropped, then I laughed. "Goodness, Briney, what in the world makes her think I would ever do that? I don't want to divorce you; you're the nicest husband a gal ever had. I don't mind sharing you—but, darling, I don't want to get rid of you. I'll tell her so. Where is she? I'll take her to bed and tell her so as sweetly as possible." I reached up, took his shoulders and kissed him.

Then I continued to hold his shoulders and look up at him. "Hey, wait a minute. *You* want a divorce. Don't you?"

Briney didn't say anything; he just looked embarrassed.

I sighed. "Poor Briney. Us frails do make your life complicated, don't we? We follow you around, climb into your lap, breathe in your ear. Even your daughters seduce you, like—what was his name? Old Testament. And even your daughters-in-law. Stop looking glum, dear man; I don't have a ring in your nose, and never have had."

"You'll do it?" He looked relieved.

"Me? Do what?"

"Divorce me."

"No. Of course not."

"But you said—"

"I said that I didn't have a ring in your nose. If you want to divorce me, I won't fight it. But I'm not the one who wants a divorce. If you like, you can simply do it to me Muslim style. Tell me 'I divorce you' three times, and I'll go pack my clothes."

Perhaps I should not have been stubborn about it but I do not see that I owed it to either of them to go through the fiddle-faddle—the trauma—of finding a lawyer and digging up witnesses and appearing in court. I would cooperate . . . but let them do the work.

Brian gave in once he saw that I meant it. Marian was

vexed with me, stopped smiling, and avoided talking with me. Finally I stopped her when she was about to leave the living room when I came in. "Marian!"

She stopped. "Yes, Mother?"

"I want you to stop pretending to be aggrieved. I want to see you smile and hear you laugh, the way you used to. You have asked me to turn my husband over to you and I have agreed to cooperate. But you must cooperate, too. You are acting like a spoiled child. In fact, you are a spoiled child."

"Why, how utterly unfair!"

"Girls, girls!"

I turned and looked at Brian. "I am not a girl. I am your wife of forty-seven years. While I am here, I will be treated with respect and with warmth. I don't expect gratitude from Marian; my father taught me years ago never to expect gratitude because there is no such thing. But Marian can simulate gratitude out of politeness. Or she can move out. At once. Right this minute. If you two expect me not to fight this divorce, you can both show me some appreciation."

I went to my room, got into bed, cried a little, then fell into a troubled sleep.

A half hour later, or an hour, or longer, I was awakened by a tap on my door. "Yes?"

"It's Marian, Mama. May I come in?"

"Certainly, darling!"

She came in, closed the door behind her, looked at me, her chin quivering and tears starting. I sat up, put out my arms. "Come to me, dear."

That ended any trouble with Marian. But not quite with Brian. The following weekend he pointed out that the *sine qua non* of an uncontested divorce was a property settlement agreed to by both parties. He had fetched home a fat brief-case. "I have the essential papers here. Shall we look them over?"

"All right." (No use putting off a trip to the dentist.)

Brian put the briefcase down on the dining table. "We can spread them out here." He sat down.

I sat down on his left; Marian sat down opposite me. I said, "No, Marian, I want to go over these in private. So you are excused, dear. And do please keep the children out."

She looked blank and started to stand up. Brian reached

out, stopped her. "Maureen, Marian is an interested party. Equally interested."

"No, she's not. I'm sorry."

"How do you figure?"

"What you have there, what is represented by those papers, is our community property, yours and mine, what you and I have accumulated in the course of our marriage. None of it is Marian's and I don't care to go over it in the presence of a third party. At a later time, when she divorces you, she'll be present at the divvy-up and I will not be. Today, Brian, it is between you and me, no one else."

"What do you mean?—when she divorces me."

"Correction: If she divorces you." (She did. In 1966.) "Brian, did you fetch home an adding machine? Oh, all I really require is a sharp pencil."

Marian caught Brian's eye, left the room, closed the door behind her. He said, "Maureen, why do you always have to be rough on her?"

"Behave yourself, Briney. You should not have attempted to have her present for this and you know it. Now . . . do you want to do this politely? Or shall we wait until I can call in a lawyer?"

"I see no reason why it can't be done politely. And even less reason why a lawyer should look at my private business."

"And still less reason why your fiancée should look at mine. Briney, stop behaving like Woodie at age six. How did you plan on whacking this up?"

"Well, first we must plan on the marriage allotments for the kids. Seven, that is. And Marian's five. Six, now."

(Each time we had "rung the cash register"—received a baby bounty from the Ira Howard Foundation—Brian had started a bookkeeping account for that child, letting that amount enhance on his books at 6 percent compounded quarterly, then passed on the enhanced amount to that child as a wedding present—about three times the original baby bounty. In the meantime Brian had the use of the money as working capital for eighteen or more years . . . and, believe me, Brian could always make working capital pay more than 6 percent, especially after 1918 when he had Theodore's predictions to guide him. Just one word—"Xerox" or "Polaroid"—could mean a fortune, known ahead of time.)

"Wups! Not out of this pile, Briney. Richard received his

marriage allotment from us when he married Marian. Her
children by Richard are our grandchildren. What about our
other grandchildren? I haven't counted lately but I think we
have fifty-two. Are you planning to subsidize all fifty-two out
of what we own today?"

"The situation is different."

"It certainly is. Brian, you are trying to favor five of our
grandchildren at the expense of all our other grandchildren
and all our remaining unmarried children. I won't permit it."

"I'll be the judge of that."

"No, you will not. It will be a real judge, in a real court.
Or you will treat all our children equally and not attempt to
favor five grandchildren while ignoring forty-seven others."

"Maureen, you've never behaved this way in the past."

"In the past you never broke up our partnership. But now
that you have done so, that breakup will be on terms that
strike both of us as equitable . . . or you can tell it to the
judge. Brian, you can't cast me off like an old shoe and then
expect me to continue to accept your rulings as docilely as I
have done all these years. I say again: Quit behaving like
Woodie as a child. Now . . . stipulating that we have agreed,
or will agree, on what is earmarked for marriage allowances,
how do you want to divide up the rest of it?"

"Eh? Three equal portions. Of course."

"You're giving me two portions? That's generous of you,
but more than I had expected."

"No, no! A share for you, a share for me, a share for
Marian. Even all the way around."

"Where is the fourth share? The one for my husband."

"You're getting married again?"

"No immediate plans. I may."

"Then we'll cross that bridge when we come to it."

"Briney, Briney! Your needle is stuck in a groove. Can't
you get it through your head that you cannot force me to
accept your fiancée as co-owner of the property you and I
have accumulated together? Half of it is mine. Fair is fair."

"Damn it, Mo', you cooked and kept house. I am the one
who got out there and struggled to build up a fortune. Not
you."

"Where did the capital come from, Briney?"

"Huh?"

"Have you forgotten? How did we 'ring the cash register'?

For that matter how did it come about that you knew ahead of time the date of Black Tuesday? Did I have something to do with it? Briney, I'm not going to argue it because you don't want to be fair about it. You keep trying to hand over to your new love some of my half of what you and I accumulated together. Let's take it into court and let a judge decide. We can do it here, a community property state, or in California, another community property state, or in Missouri where you can count on it that a judge would give me more than half. In the meantime I will ask for temporary alimony—"

"Alimony!"

"—and child support for six children while the court determines what my share, plus alimony, plus child support, adds up to."

Brian looked astounded. "You intend to strip me bare? Just because I knocked up Marian?"

"Certainly not, Brian. I don't even want alimony. What I do want . . . and expect . . . and insist on—or we go to court over it—is this: after an equitable arrangement for support of the children and for their marriage allowances, based on what we have done for our married children in the past and based on what you are now sending to Betty Lou for our children in Kansas City . . . once the kids are taken care of, I want exactly half, right down the middle. Otherwise we let a judge settle it."

Brian looked grim. "Very well."

"Good. Make up two lists, two halves, and then we can draw up a formal property settlement, one we can file with the court. Where do you intend to divorce me? Here?"

"If you have no objection. Easiest."

"All right."

It took Brian all that weekend to make the two property lists. On Monday night he showed them to me. "Here they are. Here is a summary list of my half, and here is yours."

I looked at them and could see at once that the totals matched . . . And I suppressed a need to whistle at the totals. I had not guessed even to the nearest million how wealthy we were.

"Brian, why is this list mine and that list yours?"

"I've kept on my list the properties I want to handle. On your list are things that don't require my expertise, such as commercial bonds and municipals. It doesn't matter; it's an even split."

"Since it is even, let's just swap them. I'll take everything on your list, you take the half you listed for me."

"Look, I explained to you why I—"

"Then, if there are properties on my list that you really want, you can buy them from me. At a mutually agreeable price."

"Mo', do you think I am trying to cheat you?"

"Yes, dear, you have been trying to cheat me from the moment this matter of a divorce and property settlement came up." I smiled at him. "But I shan't let you; you would regret it later. Now take those two lists and rearrange them. Make the division so meticulously fair that you really do not care which list I take, which list I leave to you. Or, if you prefer it, I will make the division and you can take your choice. But you are not going to put all of the goodies into one list and then claim that the list with the goodies is yours. So— Do I make the lists and you choose? Or do you make them and I choose?"

It took him a week to do it, and the poor man almost died of frustration. But at last he produced new lists.

I looked at them. "This suits you, Briney? You now have our community property divided so perfectly that you really don't care which list I choose?"

He smiled wryly. "Let's say that I will wince and shudder and bleed equally either way."

"Poor Briney. You remind me of the donkey and the two piles of hay. There are ample liquid assets in each list; you can buy from me anything dear to your heart." I reached for one list while watching his eyes—then picked up the other list. "Here's my half. Let's start in on the paperwork."

Brian squawked again when he wanted to buy from me some of the items on my list and I agreed to sell but insisted on dickering over the prices. But my memory serves me well, and I had made a point of remembering and looking up the name "D. D. Harriman" after I heard Theodore mention it on that sad, glad, mad Sunday he went away and never came back. At the time we divided our property I knew exactly which companies Mr. Harriman controlled, whether they were listed on the NYSE or not.

So I sold Brian what he wanted, but not at nominal book

value. At replacement value, plus a reasonable profit. I'm not totally ignorant about business. But Brian had never left enough cash in my hands for me to treat it as capital. However, for years I had found it entertaining to speculate on paper. The game made reading the *Wall Street Journal* quite entertaining.

Brian divorced me the middle of 1946 and I went back to Kansas City. He did not hold a grudge and neither did I and neither did Marian. Briney had not truly been a bad boy; he had simply fought as hard for Marian as he had once fought for me . . . and I had done the same, once I realized that I was on my own and that my beloved husband was no longer my champion.

No point in holding grudges. Once the ship lifts, all bills are paid.

17

Starting Over

My daughter Susan married Henry Schultz on Saturday, August second, 1952, in Saint Mark's Episcopal Church, The Paseo at Sixty-third in Kansas City. Brian was there and gave his daughter in marriage; Marian stayed behind in Dallas, with her children . . . and, I must add, with an acceptable excuse: She was at or near term with her latest baby, and could reasonably have asked Brian to stay home. Instead she urged him not to disappoint Susan.

I'm not sure Susan would have noticed, but I would have.

Over half of my children were there, most of them with their spouses, and about forty of my grandchildren and their spouses, along with a sprinkling of great-grandchildren—and one great-great-grandchild. Not bad, for a woman whose official age was forty-seven. Not bad even for a woman whose actual age was seventy years and four weeks.

Impossible? Not quite. My Nancy gave birth to her Roberta

on Christmas Day 1918. Roberta married at sixteen (Zachary
Barstow) and bore Anne Barstow on November 2, 1935. Anne
Barstow married Eugene Hardy and had her first child, Nancy
Jane Hardy, on June 22, 1952.

Name	Birth Date	Relationship
Maureen Johnson (Smith)	Jul. 4, 1882	great-great-grandmother
Nancy Smith (Weatheral)	Dec. 1, 1899	great-grandmother
Roberta Weatheral (Barstow)	Dec. 25, 1918	grandmother
Anne Barstow (Hardy)	Nov. 2, 1935	mother
Nancy Jane Hardy	Jun. 22, 1952	daughter

According to the archives Nancy Jane Hardy (Foote) gave
birth to Justin Foote, first of that name, on the last day of
the twentieth century, December 31, 2000. I married his (and
my) remote descendant, Justin Foote the forty-fifth, in marrying into the Lazarus Long family in Gregorian A.D. 4316,
almost twenty-four centuries later—my hundred-and-first year
by my personal time line.

The Schultz family was almost as well represented at Susan's wedding as the Johnson family, even though most of
them had to fly in from California or from Pennsylvania. But
they could not show five generations, all in one room. I was
delighted that we could, and I did not hang back when the
photographer, Kenneth Barstow, wanted a group picture of
us. He seated me in the middle with my great-great-granddaughter in my lap, while my daughter, granddaughter, and
great-granddaughter hovered around us, like angels around
Madonna and Child.

Whereupon we got scolded. Ken kept shooting pictures
until Nancy Jane got bored with it and started to cry. At that
point Justin Weatheral moved in and said, "Ken, may I see
your camera?"

"Certainly, Uncle Justin." (Honorary uncle—first cousin
twice removed, I believe. The Howard Families were beginning to reach the point where everyone was related to everyone else . . . with those inevitable defects through inbreeding
that later had to be weeded out.)

"You can have it back in a moment. Now, ladies—you especially, Maureen—what I have to say is strictly among ourselves, persons registered with the Foundation. Look around you. Is the lodge tyled? Are there any strangers among us?"

I said, "Justin, admission to this reception is by card only. Almost anyone could have been at the wedding. But it takes a card to get inside this room. I sent them out for our family; Johanna Schultz handled it for Henry's relatives."

"I got in without a card."

"Justin, everybody knows you."

"That's my point. Who else got in without a card? Good old Joe Blow, whom everybody knows, of course. Is that Joe behind that table, ladling out punch?"

I answered, "Of course there are hired staff inside. Musicians. The caterer's people. And such."

"'And such.' Exactly." Justin lowered his voice, spoke directly to us five and to Ken. "You all know the efforts all of us are making to keep our ages optimized. You, Maureen, how old are you?"

"Uh . . . forty-seven."

"Nancy? Your age, dear?"

Nancy started to say, "Fifty-two." She got out the first syllable, bit it off. "Oh, shucks, Papa Weatheral, I don't keep track of my age."

"Your age, Nancy," Justin insisted.

"Let me see. Mama had me at fifteen, so— How old are you, Mama?"

"Forty-seven."

"Yes, of course. I'm thirty-two."

Justin looked at my granddaughter Roberta, my great-granddaughter Anne, and my great-great-granddaughter Nancy Jane, and said, "I'm not going to ask the ages of you three, because any way you answer would emphasize the impossibility of reconciling your very existence with Nancy's claimed age and Maureen's. Speaking for the trustees I can say how pleased we are with how thoroughly all of you are carrying out the purpose of Ira Howard's will. But, again speaking for the trustees, I must again emphasize the necessity of never calling attention to our peculiarity. We must try to avoid having anyone notice that we are in any way different." He sighed, then went on:

"So I am forced to say that I am sorry to see you five ladies all in one room at one time, and to add that I hope that it will never happen again. And I shiver at the idea that you are being photographed together. If that photograph wound up in the society section of next Sunday's *Journal Post*, it could ruin the careful efforts of all our cousins to avoid calling attention to ourselves. Ken, don't you think it would be well to kill that picture?"

Ken Barstow was outgunned; I could see that he was about to let the Foundation's chief officer have his own way.

But I was not outgunned. "Hey! Justin, you stop that! You're chairman of the board, surely. But nobody appointed you God. Those photos were taken for me and my kids. You kill them, or get Ken to, and I'm going to beat you over the head with his camera."

"Now, Maureen—"

" 'Now Maureen' my tired feet! We'll keep it out of the papers, certainly. But I want five copies of Ken's best shot, one for each of us. And Ken is entitled to a copy for his own files, if he wants it."

We agreed on that and Justin asked for one to place in the archives.

I thought at the time that Justin was being unnecessarily cautious. I was wrong. Justin, in instituting and stubbornly pressing the policy later known as the Masquerade, caused our cousins to enter the Interregnum of the Prophets with 80 percent having public ages under forty, only 3 percent with public ages over fifty. Once the Prophet's thought police were active it became both difficult and dangerous to switch backgrounds and change identities; Justin's foresight made it usually unnecessary to attempt it.

According to the archives Brian died in 1998 at age 119—a newsworthy age in the twentieth century. But his public age at that time was 82, which is not newsworthy at all. Justin's policies let almost all Howard clients enter the Interregnum (2012) with reduced public ages that let them live and die without living conspicuously too long.

Thank God I didn't have to cope with it! No, not "thank God"—Thank Hilda Mae, Zeb, Deety, Jake, and a wonderful, lovable machine named "Gay Deceiver." I would like to see all five of them right now; Mama Maureen needs rescuing again.

Maybe Pixel will find them. I think he understood me.

•   •   •

Several out-of-towners stayed over the weekend, but by Tuesday morning the fifth of August I was alone—truly alone for the first time in my seventy years of life. My two youngest—Donald, sixteen, and Priscilla, fourteen—were still unmarried. But they were no longer mine. In the divorce settlement, they had elected to stay with the children they had been living with as brothers and sisters—and who now were legally their brothers and sisters as Marian had adopted them.

Susan was the youngest of the four who had lived with Betty Lou and Nelson during the war, and the last to marry. Alice Virginia had married Ralph Sperling right after the war ended; Doris Jean married Roderick Briggs the following year; and Patrick Henry, my son by Justin, had married Charlotte Schmidt in 1951.

Betty Lou and Nelson moved to Tampa shortly after I returned home, taking with them their three who were still at home. Her parents and Nelson's mother Aunt Carole were in Florida; Betty Lou wanted to look after all of them. (How old was Aunt Carole in 1946? She was the widow of Father's older brother, so she— Goodness! In 1946 she must have been on or near her century mark. Yet she looked the same as ever the last time I had seen her, uh—shortly before Japan's sneak attack in '41. Did she dye her hair?)

On Saturday I had been *triste* not only because my last chick was getting married and leaving home but also (and primarily) because Susan's wedding day was Father's century day; he was born August second, 1852.

Apparently no one associated the date with Father, and I mentioned it to no one because a wedding day belongs to the couple getting married and no one should bring up any subject, say or do anything, that might subtract from the joyfulness of the occasion. So I had kept quiet.

But I was constantly aware of the date. It had been twelve years and two months since Father had gone to war . . . and I had missed him every one of those four thousand, four hundred, and forty-one days—and most especially during the years after Brian turned me in on a newer model.

Please understand me; I am not condemning Brian. I had stopped being fertile around the beginning of World War II, whereas Marian was still decidedly fertile—and children are the purpose of a Howard-sponsored marriage. Marian was willing and able to bear him more children but she wanted that marriage license. That's understandable.

Neither of them tried to get rid of me. Brian assumed that I would stay, until I made it clear that I would not. Marian begged me to stay, and cried when I left.

But Dallas is not Boondock, and the unnatural practice of monogamy is as rooted in the American culture of the twentieth century as group marriage is rooted in the quasi-anarchistic, unstructured culture of Tertius in the third millennium of the Diaspora. At the time I decided not to stay with Brian and Marian, I had no Boondock experience to guide me; I simply knew in my gut that, if I stayed, Marian and I would be locked, willy-nilly, in a struggle for dominance, a struggle that neither of us wanted and that Brian would be buffeted by our troubles and made unhappy thereby.

But that does not mean that I was happy about leaving. A divorce, any divorce no matter how necessary, is an amputation. For a long time I felt like an animal that has gnawed off its own leg in order to escape from a trap.

By my own time line all this happened more than eighty years ago. Am I still resentful?

Yes, I am. Not at Brian—at Marian. Brian was a man with no malice in him; I am sure in my heart that he did not intend to mistreat me. At worst, one may say that it was not too bright of him to impregnate his son's widow. But how many men are truly wise in their handling of women? In all history you can count them on the fingers of one thumb.

Marian— She is another matter. She rewarded my hospitality by demanding that my husband divorce me. My father had taught me never to expect that imaginary emotion, gratitude. But am I not entitled to expect decent treatment from a guest under my roof?

"Gratitude": An imaginary emotion that rewards an imaginary behavior, "altruism." Both imaginaries are false faces for selfishness, which is a real and honest emotion. Long ago Mr. Clemens demonstrated in his essay "What Is Man?" that every one of us acts at all times in his own interest. Once you understand this, it offers a way to negotiate with an antagonist in order to find means to cooperate with him for mutual benefit. But if you are convinced of your own "altruism" and you try to shame him out of his horrid selfishness, you will get nowhere.

So, in dealing with Marian, where did I go wrong?

Did I lapse into the error of "altruism"?

I think I did. I should have said, "Listen, bitchie! Behave yourself and you can live here as long as you like. But forget this idea of trying to crowd me out of my own home, or you and your nameless babe will land out there in the snow. If I don't tear out your partition instead." And to Brian: "Don't try it, buster! Or I'll find a shyster who will make you wish that you had never laid eyes on that chippie. We'll take you for every dime."

But those are just middle-of-the-night thoughts. Marriage is a psychological condition, not a civil contract and a license. Once a marriage is dead, it is dead, and it begins to stink even faster than dead fish. What matters is not who killed it but the fact of its death. Then it becomes time to divvy up, split up, and run, with no time wasted on recriminations.

So why am I wasting time eighty years later brooding over the corpse of a long-dead marriage?—when I am having enough trouble from these murderous spooks? I feel sure that Pixel does not fret over the ghosts of long-dead tabby cats. He lives in the eternal now . . . and I should, too.

In 1946, as soon as I was back in Kansas City, the first thing I wanted to do was to register as a college student. Both the University of Kansas City and Rockhurst College were a mile north of us at Fifty-third Street, each a block off Rockhill Boulevard, Rockhurst to the east and KCU to the west—five minutes by car, ten by bus, or a pleasant twenty-minute walk in good weather. The Medical School of the University of Kansas was just west of Thirty-ninth and State Line, ten minutes by car. The Kansas City School of Law was downtown, a twenty-minute drive.

Each had advantages and shortcomings. Rockhurst was very small but it was a Jesuit school and therefore probably high in scholarship. It was a school for men but not totally so. I had been told that its coeds were all nuns, school teachers improving their credentials, so I was not sure that I would be welcome. Father McCaw, president of Rockhurst, set me straight:

"Mrs. Johnson, our policies are not set in stone. While most of our students are men, we do not exclude women who seriously desire what we offer. We are a Catholic school but we welcome non-Catholics. Here at Rockhurst we do not actively proselytize but perhaps I should warn you that Episcopalians, such as yourself, exposed to sound Catholic doctrine, often wind up converted to the true Church. If, while you are among us, you find yourself in need of instruction in faith and dogma, we will be happy to supply it. But we will not pressure you. Now— Are you degree-seeking? Or not?"

I explained to him that I had registered as a special student and potential candidate for a bachelor's degree at KCU. "But I am more interested in an education than I am in a degree. That is why I have come here. I am aware of the reputation of the Jesuits for scholarship. I hope to learn things here that I would not learn on the other campus."

"One may always hope." He scribbled something on a pad, tore it off and gave it to me. "You are a special student now, entitled to audit any lecture course. There are additional fees for some courses, such as laboratory courses. Take this to the bursar's office; they'll accept your tuition fee and straighten you out on other charges. Stop in and see me in a week or two."

The next six years, 1946–52, I spent in school, including summer sessions. My household had no babies in it and no small children. There is not much work in such a household and what there was, I delegated—to Doris, sixteen and just starting to check her Howard list under my protective chaperonage, and to Susan, who was only twelve and still virgin (I felt fairly sure) but an outstanding cook for her age. So I started in on her sex education, I being aware of the strong correlation between good cooking and high libido . . . only to find that Aunt Betty Lou had done well by my girls in bringing them up as innocent sophisticates, well informed about their bodies and their female heritage long before they would have to face that heritage emotionally.

I had just one son at home, Pat, fourteen in '46. I decided, somewhat reluctantly, that I was going to have to check on his knowledge of sex—before he contracted some silly disease, or impregnated a twelve-year-old moron with big breasts and a small brain, or got caught in a public scandal. I had never had to cope with this before; either Brian, or Father, or both, had taught my sons.

Patrick was patient with me.

Finally he said, "Mama, is there something special you want to ask me? I'll try. Auntie B'Lou gave me the same examination she gave Alice and Doris . . . and I missed only one question."

(Shut my mouth.) "What was the question you missed?"

"I couldn't define 'ectopic pregnancy.' But I can now. Shall I?"

"Never mind. Did Aunt Betty Lou or Uncle Nelson discuss the Ira Howard Foundation with you?"

"Some. When Alice started courting, Uncle Nel got me aside and told me to mind my own business and keep my mouth shut . . . then to see him again when I wanted to start courting myself. If I did. I didn't think I would. But I did. So I did . . . and he told me about baby subsidies. For Howard babies. For Howard babies only."

"Yes. Well, dear, Aunt Betty Lou and Uncle Nelson seem to have told you everything I could tell you. Uh— Did Uncle Nelson ever show you the Forberg etchings?"

"No."

(Damn it, Briney; why aren't you here? This is your job.) "Then I must show them to you. If I can find them."

"Auntie B'Lou showed them to me. They're in my room." He smiled shyly. "I like to look at them. Shall I get them for you?"

"No. Well, at your convenience. Patrick, you seem to know all about sex a boy your age needs to know. Is there anything I can tell you? Or do for you?"

"Uh . . . I guess not. Well—Auntie B'Lou used to keep me supplied with fishskins. I promised her that I would always use them . . . but Walgren's won't sell them to anyone my age."

(What else has Betty Lou done for him? Is intercourse with an aunt incest? Correction: Is an aunt-in-law incest? They are certainly no blood relation. Maureen, mind your own business.)

"All right, I'll keep you supplied. Uh, Patrick, where have you been using them? Not 'who,' but where?"

"Right now I only know one girl that well . . . and her mother is very fussy. Her mother has told her to do it only at home, in their basement playroom. Or else."

(I did not ask about "Or else.") "Her mother seems very sensible. Well, dear, you can do it safely here at home, too. But nowhere else, I hope. Not in Swope Park, for example. Too risky." (Maureen, who are you to talk?)

All three were good children and I had no trouble with

them. Aside from some mild supervision the household ran itself and I had plenty of time for school. By the time Susan married in August 1952 I had not one but four degrees: bachelor of arts, bachelor of laws, master of science, and doctor of philosophy. Preposterous!

But here is how the rabbit got into the hat:

I could not claim a high school education because a high school diploma dated 1898 would have been horribly inconsistent with my claimed Howard age forty-four in 1946. Oh, whenever possible I listed my age as "over twenty-one" but, if pinned down, I claimed my Howard age and avoided situations that could possibly tie me into anything that happened before about 1910. Mostly I did this by keeping my lips zipped— no "Did you know so-and-so?" and no "Remember whens."

So, when I registered at KCU it was not as a freshman, but as a special student, then I asked for advanced standing and degree-seeking status, through examinations, and did not boggle at the high fees quoted to me for special examinations to discover just where I stood in English and American literature, American history, world history, mathematics, Latin, Greek, French, German, Spanish, anatomy, physiology, chemistry, physics, and general science. All during the remainder of that semester I took examinations steadily, cramming for the next one at night and sometimes auditing lectures across the boulevard for dessert.

Toward the beginning of the summer session I was called to the office of the dean of academics, Dr. Bannister. "Please sit down, Mrs. Johnson."

I sat down and waited. In appearance he reminded me of Mr. Clemens, even though he did not wear white suits and did not smoke (thank goodness!) those horrible cigars. But he had that untidy halo of white hair and that look of a jovial Satan. I liked him on sight.

He went on: "You have completed your special examinations. May I ask what standing you expected to receive here?"

"I had no expectations, Doctor. I asked to be examined in order to find out where I belong."

"Hmmm. Your application shows no schools."

"I was privately tutored, sir."

"Yes, so I see. You've never attended school?"

"I have attended a number of schools, sir. But briefly, never long enough for academic credit. My father traveled a great deal."

"What did your father do?"

"He was a doctor of medicine, sir."

"You used the past tense."

"He was killed in the Battle of Britain, Doctor."

"Oh. Sorry. Mrs. Johnson, your correct advanced standing is that of bachelor of arts—no, no, attend me. We do not award that degree or any degree simply on the basis of examinations with no time in residence. Do you expect to be on campus for the next two semesters? The academic year of 1946–47?"

"Certainly. And this present summer session as well. And then some, as I purpose asking to be accepted as a candidate for a doctor's degree if and when I achieve a baccalaureate."

"Indeed. In what field?"

"Philosophy. Metaphysics, in particular."

"Well. Mrs. Johnson, you amaze me. In your application you describe yourself as 'housewife.' "

"The description is correct, Doctor. I still have three children at home. However, two of them are adolescent girls; both are good cooks. With cooking and housekeeping divided among us we all have time to go to school. And, I assure you, there is nothing basically incompatible between dishwater and curiosity about noumena. I am a grandmother who never had time to go to college. But I cannot believe that I am too old to learn. This granny refuses to sit by the fire and knit." I added, "Dr. Will Durant lectured here in 1921. That was my initial exposure to metaphysics."

"Yes, I heard him myself. An evening series at the Grand Avenue Temple. A charming speaker. Goodness, you hardly seem old enough. That was twenty-five years ago."

"My father took me. I promised myself that I would resume the study of philosophy when I had time. Now I do."

"I see. Mrs. Johnson, do you know what I taught before I went into administration?"

"No, sir." (Of course I know! Father would be ashamed of me if I failed to scout the territory.)

"I taught Latin and Greek . . . and the Hellenic philosophers. Then the years moved along, and Latin was no longer required and Greek no longer offered, and Greek philosophers were ignored in favor of 'modern' ideas, such as Freud and Marx and Dewey and Skinner. So I was faced with a need to find something else to do on campus . . . or go look for a job somewhere in the busy marts of trade." He smiled ruefully. "Difficult. A professor from the physical sciences can find work with Dow Chemical or with D. D. Harriman. But a teacher of Greek? Never mind. You say you plan to take this summer session."

"Yes, sir."

"Suppose we call you a senior now . . . and graduate you at the end of the first semester, January '47, as a bachelor of arts, uh, major subject, modern languages, minor in—oh, what you will. Classical languages. History. But you can use the summer session and the first semester to support your real purpose, metaphysics. Um. I'm a grandfather myself, Mrs. Johnson, and an obsolete teacher of forgotten subjects. But would it suit you to have me as your faculty advisor?"

"Oh, would you?"

"I find an interest in your purpose . . . and I feel sure that we can assemble a committee sympathetic to that purpose. Mmm—

" 'Old age hath yet his honor and his toil;
" 'Death closes all; but something ere the end,
" 'Some work of noble note, may yet be done,
" 'Not unbecoming men that strove with Gods."

I picked it up:
" 'The lights begin to twinkle from the rocks;
" 'The long day wanes; the slow moon climbs; the deep
" 'Moans round with many voices. Come, my friends,
" ' 'Tis not too late to seek a newer world."

He smiled widely, and answered:
" 'Push off, and sitting well in order smite
" 'The sounding furrows; for my purpose holds
" 'To sail beyond the sunset, and the baths
" 'Of all the western stars, until I die.' "

He stood up. "Tennyson wears well, does he not? And if Odysseus can challenge age, so can we. Come in tomorrow and let's start planning a course of study toward your doctorate. Most of it will have to be independent study but we will look over the catalog and see what courses could be useful to you."

In June 1950 I was awarded the degree of doctor of philosophy in metaphysics, my dissertation being titled "A Comparison of the World Pictures of Aristocles, Arouet, and Dzhugashvili Considered Through Interaction of Epistemology, Teleology, and Eschatology." The actual content was zero, as honest metaphysics must be, but I loaded it with Boolean algebra, which (if solved) proved that Dzhugashvili was a murdering scoundrel . . . as the kulaks of Ukraina knew too well.

I gave a copy of my dissertation to Father McCaw and invited him to my convocation. He accepted, then glanced at the dissertation and smiled. "I think Plato would be pleased to be in the company of Voltaire . . . but each of them would shun the company of Stalin."

Over the course of many years the only person to translate correctly at first glance all three of those names was Father McCaw . . . except Dr. Bannister, who thought up the joke.

The dissertation was not important. But the rules required that I submit enough pounds of scholarly manuscript to justify the degree. And for four years I had a wonderfully good time, both there and across the boulevard.

The same week I got my Ph.D. I registered at KU Medical School and at Kansas City School of Law—little conflict as most lectures at the Law School were at night, whereas the courses I took at the Medical School were in the daytime. I was not a candidate for M.D. but for a master's degree in biochemistry. I had to register for a couple of upper division courses, but was allowed to do so while being accepted as a candidate for M.S. (I think I would have been turned down had I not walked in with a still-damp doctorate.) I did not really care whether or not I received the master's degree; I simply wanted to treat an excellent applied-science school as an intellectual smorgasbord. Father would have loved it.

I could have had that degree in one year; I stayed longer because there were still more courses I wanted to audit. In the meantime the KC School of Law was supposed to require four years . . . but I had been there before, having audited several of their courses while Brian was getting his law degree, 1934–38. The dean was willing to credit me with courses simply by examination as long as I paid full fees for each course—it was a proprietary school; fees were a prime consideration.

I took the bar examinations in the spring of 1952—and passed, to the surprise of my classmates and professors. It may have helped that my papers read: "M. J. Johnson" rather than "Maureen Johnson." Once I was admitted to the bar there was no fuss about my law degree; the school boasted about the percentage of its students that made it all the way into the bar—a much tougher hurdle than the degree.

That is how I legitimately got four academic degrees in six years. But I honestly think that I learned the most at the tiny little Catholic college at which I was only an auditor, never a candidate for a degree.

Especially from a Japanese-American Jesuit priest, Father Tezuka.

For the first time in my life I had an opportunity to learn an Oriental language and I jumped at the chance. This class was for prospective missionaries to replace those liquidated in the war; it had both priests and seminarians. I was welcome for just one reason, I think: Japanese language structure and idiom and Japanese culture make even greater differences between male and female than does American culture and American language. I was an "instructional tool."

In 1940, the summer we spent in Chicago, I took advantage of the opportunity to study semantics under Count Alfred Korzybski and Dr. S. I. Hayakawa, as the Institute for General Semantics was close to where we lived—across the Mall and east a couple of blocks at 1234 E. Fifty-sixth. One thing that stuck in my mind was the emphasis both scholars placed on the fact that a culture was reflected in its language, that indeed the two were so interblended that another language of a different structure (a "metalanguage") was needed to discuss the matter adequately.

Now consider the dates. President Patton was elected in November 1948 and succeeded President Barkley in January 1949.

The Osaka Incident took place in December 1948, between President Patton's election and his inauguration. So President Patton was faced with what amounted to open rebellion in the Far Eastern Possessions formerly known as the Japanese Empire. The secret society, the Divine Wind, seemed willing to exchange ten of their number for one of ours indefinitely.

In his inauguration address President Patton informed the Japanese and the world that this exchange was not acceptable. Starting at once, it was one American dead, one Shintoist shrine destroyed and defiled, with the price going up at each incident.

18

Bachelorhood

I am not an expert on how to rule a conquered country, so I will refrain from criticizing President Patton's policies concerning our Far Eastern Possessions. My dear friend and husband, Dr. Jubal Harshaw, tells me (and the histories at Boondock confirm) that on his time line (code Neil Armstrong) the policies were utterly different—supportive rather than harsh to the conquered foe.

But both policies (both time lines) were disastrous for the United States.

In the years from 1952 to 1982 I never had any real occasion to use my study of Japanese language and writing. But twenty-four centuries later my knowledge of Japanese caused Jubal to ask me to accept an odd assignment, after I had shifted from rejuvenation apprentice to the Time Corps. The outcome of the long and bitter war between the United States and the Japanese Empire had been disastrous for both sides on all time lines supervised by the Circle of Ouroboros, both those in which the United States "won" and those in which the Japanese Empire "won"—such as time line seven (code Fairacres), in which the emperor and the *Reichsführer* split the continent down the middle along the Mississippi River.

The Time Corps mathematicians, headed by Libby Long, and their bank of computer simulators, supervised by Mycroft Holmes (the computer who led the Lunar Revolution on time line three) attempted to determine whether or not a revised history could be created in which the Japanese-American war of 1941–45 never took place. If so, would that avoid the steady deterioration of planet Earth that had occurred after that war on all explored time lines?

To this end the Corps needed agents before 1941 in Japan and in the United States. Agents for the United States were no problem, as there were lavish records in Boondock of American language, history, and culture in the twentieth century Gregorian as well as residents of Tertius who had actually experienced that culture at or near the target dates: Lazarus Long, Maureen Johnson, Jubal Harshaw, Richard Campbell, Hazel Stone, Zeb Carter, Hilda Mae Burroughs, Deety Carter, Jake Burroughs, and others—most especially Anne, a Fair Witness. I know that she was sent. And probably others.

But residents of Tellus Tertius familiar with Japanese language and culture of the twentieth century Gregorian were between zero and nonexistent. There were two residents of Chinese ancestry, Dong Xia and Marcy Choy-Mu, who were physically similar to Japanese norms, but neither knew any Japanese or anything of Japanese culture.

I could not possibly pass for Japanese—red-haired Japanese are as common as fur on fish—but I could speak and write Japanese, not like a native but like a foreigner who has studied it. So a reasonable decision was made: I would go as a tourist—an exceptional tourist, one who had taken the trouble to learn something of the language, culture, and history of Nippon before going there.

A tourist who bothers to study these aspects of a country before visiting it will always be welcome, if he is polite by their rules of politeness. It is easy to say, glibly, that every tourist ought to do this, but in fact this is difficult, expensive in time and money. I have a knack for languages and enjoy studying them. So, by age seventy, I knew five modern languages including my own.

That left over a thousand languages I did not know and around three billion people with whom I had no common language. The job is too big—a labor of Tantalus.

But I was well equipped to be an inoffensive tourist in Japan for the decade preceding the great war of 1941–45. So I went, and was put down in Macao, a place where bribery is the norm and money will accomplish almost anything. I was armed with lavish amounts of money and three very sincere passports; one said that I was Canadian, another said that I was American, and the third said that I was British.

I went by ferry to Hong Kong, a place much more nearly honest but where nevertheless money is highly respected. By then I had learned that neither British nor Americans were well thought of in the Far East at that time but that Canadians had not yet inspired any special dislike, so I started using the passport that showed that I was born in British Columbia and lived in Vancouver. A Dutch ship, the MV *Ruys,* took me from Hong Kong to Yokohama.

I spent a lovely year, 1937–38, tramping around Japan, sleeping in native inns, feeding the tiny deer at Nara, being breathless at the sight of Fuji-San at dawn, cruising the Inland Sea in a dinky little steamer, relishing the beauties of one of the most beautiful countries and cultures in all histories—all the while gathering data that I recorded in an implanted, voice-operated recorder much like the one I am now using.

I was also wearing, internally, a finder such as I am wearing now, and the fact that I haven't been found indicates to me that Time Corps HQ does not know what planet I am on, as the equipment is supposed to be delicate enough to track down an agent who has missed a rendezvous no matter where he is, as long as he is on the planet of drop.

That's the bad news. Here is the good news. During that year in Japan I heard several times of another redheaded English (American)(Canadian) woman who was touring the empire, studying Japanese gardens. She speaks Japanese and she is said to look like me . . . although the latter means little; we round-eyes all look alike to them, except that red hair would always be noticed, and speaking Japanese is decidedly noticed.

Have I been (will I be) sent back on another visit to prewar Japan? Am I time-looped on myself? The paradox does not bother me; Time agents are used to loops—I am already looped for the year 1937–38; I spent that year the first time

in Kansas City, except for two weeks in July after the birth
of Priscilla and after Brian's bar exams; we celebrated both
events with a trip to the Utah Canyons—Bryce, Cedar Breaks,
North Rim.

If I am also looped on myself (tripled) in Japan in the year
1937-38, then the tripling will happen on my personal time
line after my present now . . . which means that Pixel will
carry the message and I will be rescued. There are no paradoxes in time; all apparent paradoxes can be untangled.

But it is a thin thread on which to hang my hope.

Tuesday, August 5, 1952, time line two, started as a sad
day for Maureen . . . utterly alone for the first time in my
life, alone with the tedious chore of cleaning out and closing
up our old farmhouse and getting rid of it. But a glad day in
one way. My married life had ended when Brian divorced
me; my widowhood ended when Susan got married; this chore
marked the start of my bachelorhood.

The difference between widowhood and bachelorhood?
Please look at it historically. When I married, at the end of
the nineteenth century, women were unmistakably second-
class citizens and everyone took it for granted. In most states
a woman could not vote, or sign contracts, or own real estate,
or sit on juries, or do any number of other mundane acts
without the consent of some man—her father, her husband,
or her eldest son. Most professions, trades, and occupations
were closed to her. A woman lawyer, a woman doctor, a
woman engineer aroused the same surprise as a waltzing bear.

"The wonder is not how well the bear waltzes but that it
waltzes at all." That is from Dr. Samuel Johnson, I believe—
a man who regarded women as no better than third-class
citizens, lower than Scotsmen or Americans—two groups quite
low in his esteem.

All through the twentieth century the legal status of women
slowly improved. By 1982 almost all the laws discriminating
against women had been repealed.

More subtle but at least as important and beyond repeal
were the cultural biases against women. An example:

In the summer of 1940 when we were living on Woodlawn
Avenue in Chicago, we were especially loaded with house
guests during the two weeks bridging the Democratic National
Convention. One Howard trustee, Rufus Briggs, said to me

one morning at breakfast, "I left my laundry on that balcony couch where I slept. I need twenty-four-hour service on it and tell them to soft starch the collars—no other starch."

I said briskly, "Tell them yourself." I was not feeling overly sweet-tempered, as I had been up late the night before, arranging shake-downs for late arrivals, such as Briggs himself—he was one of the cheerful idiots who had arrived in Chicago oblivious to the fact that for this period all hotel space as far away as Gary, Indiana, had been booked solid months earlier. Then I dragged myself out of bed early and ate in the kitchen in order to cook and serve breakfast to a dozen other people.

Briggs looked at me as if he could not believe his ears. "Aren't you the housekeeper?"

"I'm the housekeeper. But I'm not your servant."

Briggs blinked his eyes, then turned to Brian. "Mr. Smith?"

Brian said quietly, "You have made a mistake, Mr. Briggs. This lady is my wife. You met her last night but the lights were dimmed and we were whispering because others were asleep. So apparently you did not recognize her this morning. But I am sure Mrs. Smith would be happy to send your laundry out for you as a favor to a guest."

I said, "No, I would not."

It was Briney's turn to look startled. "Maureen?"

"I won't send out his laundry and I will not cook his breakfast tomorrow morning. His only comment this morning was to complain about his eggs; he did not even say thank-you when I put his breakfast in front of him. So he can go out for breakfast tomorrow. I imagine he'll find something open on Sixty-third Street. But I have this announcement for all of you," I added, looking around. "We have no servants here. I am just as anxious to get to Convention Hall on time as you are. Yesterday I was late because I was making beds and doing dishes. Only one of you made your own bed—thanks, Merle! I'm not going to make beds today; if you don't make your own bed, you will find it still unmade when you get back. Right now I want volunteers to clear the table and do the dishes . . . and if I don't get them, I am not going to cook breakfast for anyone tomorrow."

An hour later Brian and I left to go to the convention. While we were walking to the El station he said to me, "Mo', this is the first time I've had a chance to speak to you privately.

I really did not appreciate your failure to back me up in dealing with another trustee."

"How?" I asked (knowing quite well what he meant).

"I told Mr. Briggs that you would be happy to send out his laundry, and then you flatly refused, contradicting me. My dear, I was humiliated."

"Briney, I was humiliated when you attempted to reverse me after I had told him to send out his laundry himself. I simply stuck by my guns."

"But he had made a mistake, dear; he thought you were a servant. I tried to smooth it over by saying that of course you were happy to do it as a favor to a guest."

"Why didn't you say that you would be happy to send out his laundry?"

"Eh?" Brian seemed truly puzzled.

"I can tell you why you didn't offer to do it. Because both you men regard sending out laundry as women's work. And it is, when it's your laundry and I am the woman. But I'm not Rufus Briggs's wife and I will not do servant's work for him. He's a clod."

"Maureen, sometimes I don't understand you."

"You're right; sometimes you don't."

"I mean— Take this matter of making beds and washing dishes. When we are at home we never expect house guests to wash the dishes or to make their own beds."

"At home, Briney, I always have two or three big girls to help me . . . and never a dozen house guests at a time. And our women guests usually offer to help and if I need their help, I let them. Nothing like this mob I'm faced with now. They are not friends; they aren't relatives; most are total strangers to me and all act as if we were running a boarding house. But most of them at least say thank-you and please. Mr. Briggs does not. Briney, at bottom you and Mr. Briggs have the same attitude toward women; you both think of women as servants."

"I don't see that. I don't think you are being fair."

"So? Then I ask you again: If you wanted to be gracious to a guest, why did you not offer your own services to take care of his laundry? You can use a telephone and the yellow section quite as well as I can, then you can arrange for or do whatever is necessary. There is nothing about sending out laundry that requires special womanly skills; you can do it as easily as I. Why did you see fit to volunteer my services in the face of my stated opposition?"

"I thought it was the gracious thing to do."

"Gracious to whom, sir? To your wife? Or to the business associate who was rude to her?"

"Uh— We'll say no more about it."

That incident was not unusual; it was exceptional only in that I refused to accept the conventional subordinate role under which a woman, any woman, was expected to wait on men. Repealing laws does not change such attitudes because they are learned by example from earliest childhood.

These attitudes can't be repealed like laws because they are usually below the conscious level. Consider, please, who makes the coffee. You are in a mixed group, business or quasi-business: a company conference, a public interest group, a PTA meeting. As a lubricant for the exchange of ideas, coffee is a good idea, and the means to make it is at hand.

Who makes the coffee? It could be a man. But don't bet on it. Ten to one you would lose.

Let's move forward thirty years from the incident of Rufus Briggs the soft-starched clod, from 1940 to 1970. By 1970 most legal impediments to equality between the sexes were gone. This incident involved a board meeting of Skyblast Freight, a D. D. Harriman enterprise. I was a director and this was not my first meeting. I knew all the directors by sight and they knew me or at least had had opportunity to know me.

However I admit that I was looking younger than the last time they had seen me. I had had my pendulous baby-chewed breasts reshaped, and at the same Beverly Hills hospital I had tucks taken up under the hairline to take the slack out of my face, then I had gone to an Arizona health ranch to get into top condition and to lose fifteen pounds. I had gone next to Vegas and splurged on ultra chic, very feminine, new clothes—not the tailored pantsuits most female executives wore. I was smugly aware that I did not look the eighty-eight years I had lived, nor the fifty-eight years I admitted. I think I looked a smart forty.

I was waiting in the foyer outside the boardroom, intending not to go in until called—board meetings are dull rituals . . . but a crisis is sure to come up if you skip one.

Just as the light outside the boardroom started to blink a man came slamming in from outside, Mr. Phineas Morgan, leader of a large minority bloc. He headed straight for the blinking light while shucking off his overcoat. As he passed me, he chucked it at me. "Take care of it!"

I ducked aside, let his coat land on the floor. "Hey! Morgan!" He checked himself, looked back. I pointed at the floor. "Your coat."

He looked surprised, amazed, indignant, angry, and vindictive, all in one second. "Why, you little bitch! I'll have you fired for that."

"Go right ahead." I moved past him into the boardroom, found my place card, and sat down. A few seconds later he sat down opposite me, at which point his face managed still another expression.

Phineas Morgan had not intentionally tried to use a fellow director as a servant. He saw a female figure who, in his mind, must be hired staff—secretary, receptionist, clerk, whatever. He was late and in a hurry and assumed that this "subordinate employee" would as a matter of course hang up his coat so that he could go straight to roll call.

The moral? In 1970 on time line two the legal system assumed that a man is innocent until proved guilty; in 1970 on time line two the cultural system assumed that a female is subordinate until proved otherwise—despite all laws that asserted that the sexes were equal.

I planned to kick that assumption in the teeth.

August 5, 1952, marked the beginning of my bachelorhood because that was the day on which I resolved that from that time on I would be treated the way a man is treated with respect to rights and privileges—or I would raise hell about it. I no longer had a family, I was no longer capable of childbearing, I was not looking for a husband, I was financially independent (and then some!), and I was firmly resolved never again "to send out the laundry" for some man merely because I use the washroom intended for setters rather than the one set aside for pointers.

I did not plan to be aggressive about it. If a gentleman held a door for me, I would accept the courtesy and thank him. Gentlemen enjoy offering little gallantries; a lady enjoys accepting them graciously, with a smile and a word of thanks.

I mention this because, by the 1970s, there were many females who would snub a man unmercifully if he offered a gallantry, such as holding a chair for a woman, or offering to help her in or out of a car. These women (a minority but a ubiquitous, obnoxious one) treated traditional courtesy as if it were an insult. I grew to think of these females as the "Lesbian Mafia." I don't know that all of them were homosexual (although I'm certain about some of them) but their behavior caused me to lump them all together.

If some of them were not Lesbians, then where did they find heterosexual mates? What sort of wimp would put up with this sort of rudeness in women? I am sorry to say that by 1970 there were plenty of wimps of every sort. The wimps were taking over. Manly men, gallant gentlemen, the sort who do not wait to be drafted, were growing scarce.

The principal problem in closing the house lay in the books: what to store, what to give away, what to take with me. The furniture and the small stuff, from pots and pans to sheets, would mostly be given to Good Will. We had been in that house twenty-three years, 1929 to 1952; most of the furniture was that old, or nearly so, and, after being worked over by a swarm of active children all those years, the market value of these chattels was too low to justify placing them in storage—since I had no intention of setting up a proper household in the foreseeable future.

I hesitated over my old upright piano. It was an old friend; Briney had given it to me in 1909—second (third?) hand even then; it was the first proof that Brian Smith Associates was actually in the black. Brian had paid fourteen dollars for it at an auction.

No! If my plans were to work out, I must travel light. Pianos can be rented anywhere.

Having resolved to give up my piano other decisions were easy, so I decided to start with the books. Move all books from all over the house into the living—no, into the dining room; pile them on the dining table. Pile them high. Pile the rest on the floor. Who could believe that one house could hold so many books?

Roll in the big utility table; start stacking on it books to be stored. Roll in the little tea table; place on it books to take with me. Set up card tables for books to go to Good

Will. Or to the Salvation Army? Whichever one will come and get the stuff, soonest, can have the lot—clothes, books, bed clothes, furniture, whatever. But they've got to come get it.

An hour later I was still telling myself firmly: No! Don't stop to read anything! If you just must read it, then put that book in the "take with" pile—you can thin it down later.

When I heard the mewing of a cat.

I said to myself, "Oh, that girl! Susan, what have you done to me?"

Two years earlier we had become catless through the tragic demise of Captain Blood, grandson of Chargé d'Affaires—sudden death from a hit-and-run driver on Rockhill Boulevard. In the preceding forty-three years I had never tried keeping house without a cat. I tend to agree with Mr. Clemens, who rented three cats when he moved into his home in Connecticut in order to give a new house that lived-in feeling.

But this time I resolved to struggle along without a cat. Patrick was eighteen, Susan was sixteen; each had received his Howard list. It was predictable that each would be leaving the nest in the near future.

Cats have one major shortcoming. Once you adopt one, you are stuck for life. The cat's life, that is. The cat does not speak English; it does not understand broken promises. If you abandon it, it will die and its ghost will haunt your nights.

At dinner the day Captain Blood was killed none of us ate much and we were not talkative. At last Susan said, "Mama, do we start watching the want-ads? Or do we go to the Humane Society?"

"For what, dear?" (I was intentionally obtuse.)

"For a kitten, of course."

So I laid it on the line: "A kitten could live fifteen years, or longer. When you two leave home this house will be sold, as I have no intention of rattling around in a fourteen-room house, alone. Then what happens to the cat?

"Nothing. Because there is not going to be a cat."

About two weeks later Susan was a bit late getting home from school. She came in and said, "Mama, I must be gone a couple of hours. An errand." She was carrying a brown paper sack.

"Yes, dear. May I ask why and where?"

"This." She put the sack on my kitchen table. It tilted and a kitten walked out. A jellicle cat, small and neat and black and white, just as described in Mr. Eliot's poem.

I said, "Oh, dear!"

Susan said, "It's all right, Mama. I've already explained to her that she can't live here."

The kitten looked at me, wide-eyed, then sat down and started pin-pleating its white jabot. I said, "What is her name?"

"She doesn't have one, Mama. It wouldn't be fair to give her one. I'm taking her down to the Humane Society so that she can be put to sleep without hurting. That's the errand I have to do."

I was firm with Susan. She must feed the kitten herself. She must clean and refill its sand box as long as it needed one. She must train it to use the cat door. She must see to its shots, taking it back and forth to the veterinary hospital at the Plaza as necessary. The kitten was hers and hers alone, and she must plan on taking it with her when she married and left home.

Kitten and girl listened to this, round-eyed and solemn, and both agreed to the terms. And I attempted not to get friendly with this cat—let her look entirely to Susan, bond only with Susan.

But what do you do when a square ball of black and white fluff sits up on its hind legs, sticks out its little fat belly, waves its three-inch arms beside its ears, and says, plain as anything, "Please, Mama. Please come fight with me."

Nevertheless Susan remained committed to taking her kitten with her. We did not discuss it but the deal was never renegotiated.

I went to the front door—no cat. Then I went to the back door. "Come in, your Highness."

Her Serene Highness, Princess Polly Ponderosa Penelope Peachfuzz, paraded in, tail high. ("It's about time! But thank you anyway and don't let it happen again what's for lunch?") She sat down, facing the kitchen cupboard where canned cat food was kept.

She ate a six-ounce can of tuna and liver, demanded more and did equally well on veal in gravy, then ate some crunchies for dessert, stopping from time to time to head-bump my ankles. At last she stopped to clean.

"Polly, let me see your pads." She was not her usual immaculate self and I had never seen her so hungry. Where had she been the past three days?

I was certain from examining her paws that she had been on the road. I thought of some grim questions to ask Susan when she telephoned. If she did. But in the meantime the cat was here and this was home and the responsibility was now mine, by derivation. When I moved out of this house, the cat had to go with me. Unavoidable. Susan, I wish you were unmarried just long enough for me to spank you.

I rubbed Vaseline on her paws and got back to work. Princess Polly went to sleep on a pile of books. If she missed Susan, she didn't say so. She seemed willing to pig it with just one servant.

About one in the afternoon I was still sorting books and trying to decide whether to make do with a cold sandwich or go all out and open a can of tomato soup—when the front door chimed. Princess Polly looked up. I said, "You're expecting someone? Susan, maybe?" I went to the door.

Not Susan. Donald and Priscilla.

"Come in, darlings!" I opened the door wide. "Are you hungry? Have you had lunch?" I did not ask them any questions. There is a poem by Robert Frost, well known on that time line in that century: "The Death of the Hired Man," which contained this definition: "Home is the place where, when you have to go there, they have to take you in." Two of my children had come home; they would tell me what they wished to tell me when they got around to it. I was simply glad that I had a house to let them into and that I still had bed clothes for them. Cat and children had not changed my plans—but those plans could wait. I was glad that I had not managed to clear out the day before, Monday the fourth—I would have missed all three. Tragic!

I got busy rustling lunch for them—fancy cooking; I did open Campbell's tomato soup, two cans. "Let me see. We have quite a lot of not too stale cake left over from the reception, and a half gallon of vanilla ice cream that has not been opened. How much can you two eat?"

"Plenty!"

"Priss is right. We haven't eaten anything today."

"Oh, my goodness! Sit down. Let's get some soup into you

fast, then we'll see what else you want. Or would you rather have breakfast things, seeing that this is breakfast for you? Bacon and eggs? Cereal?"

"Anything," answered my son. "If it's alive, I'll bite its head off."

"Behave yourself, Donnie," said his sister. "We'll start with soup, Mama."

While we were eating Priscilla said, "Why are the books piled all around, Mama?"

I explained that I was getting ready to close the house, preparatory to selling it. My children exchanged looks; they both looked solemn, almost woebegone. I looked from face to face. "Take it easy," I advised. "There is nothing to look sad about. I'm not faced with any deadlines and this is your home. Do you want to fill me in?"

Most of it was fairly obvious from their condition—dirty, tired, hungry, and broke. They had had some sort of trouble with their father and their stepmother and they had left Dallas "forever"—"But, Mama, this was before we knew that you were planning to sell this house. We'll have to find somewhere else to go . . . because Donnie and I are not going back there."

"Don't be in a hurry," I said. "You are not out on the street. I'm going to sell this house, yes—but we'll put another roof over our heads. This is the right time to sell this place because I let George Strong—he's in real estate—know that this place would be available once Susan was married. Hmm—" I went to the screen and punched up Harriman and Strong.

A woman's face came on screen. "Harriman and Strong, Investments. Harriman Enterprises. Allied Industries. How may I help you?"

"I am Maureen Johnson. I would like to speak to Mr. Harriman or to Mr. Strong."

"Neither is available. You may record a message—scramble and hush are on line if needed. Or our Mr. Watkins will speak to you."

"No. Relay me to George Strong."

"I am sorry. Will you speak to Mr. Watkins?"

"No. Just get this message to Mr. Strong: George, this is Maureen Johnson speaking. That parcel is now available, and I punched in to offer you first refusal as I promised. I have carried out my promise but I am going to deal today. So now I will call the J. C. Nichols Company."

"Will you hold, please?" Her face was replaced by a flower

garden, her voice by a syrupy rendition of "In an Eighteenth-Century Drawing Room."

George Strong's face came on. "Greetings, Mrs. Johnson. Good to see you."

"Maureen to you, old dear. I called to say that I am moving. Now is the hour if you want to bid on it. Do you still want it?"

"I can use it. Do you have a price in mind?"

"Yes, certainly. Just twice what you are willing to pay."

"Well, that's a good start. Now we can dicker."

"Just a moment. George, I need another house, a smaller one. Three bedrooms, within walking distance of Southwest High. Got something like that?"

"Probably. Or across the line and close to Shawnee Mission High. Want to swap?"

"No, I'm planning to skin you on the deal. I want to lease by the year, automatic renewal unless notice given, ninety days."

"All right. Pick you up tomorrow morning? Ten o'clock? I want to look over your parcel, point out to you its short-comings and beat your price down."

"Ten o'clock, it is. Thank you, George."

"Always a pleasure, Maureen."

Donald said, "Dallas phones are all tanks now. How come KC still uses flatties? Why don't they modernize?"

I answered, "Money. Donald, any question that starts out 'Why don't they—' the answer is always 'Money.' But in this case I can offer more details. The Dallas try-out turns out not to be cost effective and the three-dee tanks will be phased out. For the full story see the *Wall Street Journal*. The back issues for the past quarter are stacked in the library. It's a six-part series, front page."

"I'm sorry I brought it up. They can use smoke signals for all of me."

"Be glad you brought it up and make use of the opportunity I offered you. Donald, if you intend to cope with the jungle out there, you need to make the *Wall Street Journal* and similar publications such as the *Economist* your favorite comic books." I added, "Ice cream and cake?"

I put Priscilla into Susan's room, and Donald into the room Patrick had had, just beyond my bath. We went to bed early.

About midnight I woke up, then got up to pee, not bothering with a light, as there was moonlight streaming in. I was about to flush the pot when I heard an unmistakable rhythmic sound—bed squeaks. Suddenly I was goose flesh all over.

Priss and Donnie had left here almost as babies, two years old and four; they probably didn't realize that this old house was about as well soundproofed as a tent. Oh, dear! Those poor children.

I kept very quiet. The rhythm speeded up. Then I heard Priscilla start to keen and Donald to grunt. Shortly the squeaks stopped and they both sighed. I heard Priscilla say, "I needed that. Thanks, Donnie."

I was proud of her. But it was time for me to hurry—much as I hated to, I must catch them in the act. Or I couldn't help them.

Seconds later I tapped on Donald's door. "Darlings? May I come in?"

19

Cats and Children

It was after one o'clock before I left the children; it had taken that long to convince them that I was not angry, that I was on their side, that my only concern was to see that they did not get hurt—because what they were doing was exceptionally dangerous in all sorts of ways, some of which I was sure they knew but some of which they might not know about or at least had not thought about.

When I had gone in to see them, I had not grabbed a robe. Instead I had gone in as I was, bare naked, because a fully dressed authority figure such as a parent, walking in on two children caught in delectable flagrente, is all too likely to scare it out of them—cause bladder and bowel to cut loose. But another human as naked and vulnerable as they were themselves simply could not be a "cop." As Father had taught me years earlier, to know which way the frog will jump, you have to put yourself in the frog's place.

They still would not like being caught—they didn't!—but, if I did not catch them in bed together, they would lie about it later if I tried to question them. It is parallel to the old rule about puppies: If you don't catch a puppy at it, it is useless to bring the matter up later.

So I tapped and asked to come in, and waited.

A suppressed gasp, then dead silence—

I waited awhile longer, then counted ten chimpanzees and tapped again. "Donald! Priscilla! Please! May I come in?"

There was a whispered conference, then Donald's strong, manly baritone called out—and cracked. "Come in—Mother."

I opened the door. There were no lights on, but there was moonlight and my eyes were adjusted to low light level. They were in bed together, sheet pulled up, and Donald was simultaneously protecting his sister against all dangers with his strong right arm around her while pretending hard that she was not there at all and that he was just waiting for a streetcar—and my heart went out to him.

The room reeked of sex—male musk, female musk, fresh ejaculate, sweat. I am expert in the odors of sex, with many years of wide experience. Had I not known better I would have judged that this was the site of a six-person orgy.

I must add that some of the odor came from me. Perhaps it is perverse that I should be sexually excited by catching my son and daughter in the most scandalous of all sex offenses. But volition does not enter into it. From the moment I recognized those squeaks and deduced what and who, I had been flowing. If King Kong had wandered by, he would have found me a pushover. Paul Revere I would have pulled from his horse.

But I ignored my state, reminding myself that they could not possibly smell me. "Hello, dears! Is there room in the middle for me?"

Silence, then they moved apart. I went quickly to them before they could change their minds, pushed down the sheet, crawled over Donald, got between them on my back, snaked my right arm under Priscilla's neck, reached for Donald. "Have a shoulder pillow, Donald. Turn toward me, dear."

He did so, stiffly, then remained tense. I said nothing and cuddled both my children, breathed deeply and tried to slow my heart. It began to work, and my youngsters seemed to relax somewhat, too.

Presently I said softly, "How sweet to have both my darlings in bed with me," and gave them each a quick squeeze and relaxed, still holding them.

Priscilla said timidly, "Mama, you're not mad at us?"

"Mad at you? Heavens, no! I'm worried about your welfare. But not angry. I love you, dear. Love you both."

"Oh. I'm glad you're not mad." Then curiosity got her. "How did you catch us? I was very careful. I listened at your door, made sure you were asleep before I snuck in here and woke Donnie."

"I probably wouldn't have noticed anything if I hadn't been drinking lemonade before going to bed. I woke up, dear, and had to pee. That wall on Donald's side of the bed is a wall of my bathroom. Sound goes right through it. So I heard you." I hugged her to me. "It sounded like a dandy!"

Brief silence— "It was."

"I believe you. There is nothing, just nothing, as good as a gut-wrenching orgasm when you really need one. And you seemed to need that one. I heard you thank Donald."

"Uh . . . he deserved thanks."

"And smart of you to tell him so. Priscilla, there is nothing a man likes more than to be appreciated for his lovemaking. So keep it up all your life; it will make both you and your love happy. Mark my words. Remember them."

"I'll remember."

Donald apparently had trouble believing what he was hearing. "Mother? Do I have this straight? You don't mind what we were doing?"

"Tell me what you were doing."

"Uh— We were screwing!" He said it defiantly.

" 'Screwing' is something dogs do. You were loving, you were making love to Priscilla. Or, if you like long medical words, you two were copulated and engaging in coition to climax . . . which is about like describing a gorgeous sunset in wavelengths of the electromagnetic spectrum. You were loving her, dear, and Priscilla is lovable. She was a lovable baby and she is even more lovable as a grown woman."

I decided that now was the time to grasp the nettle, so I went on, "Loving is sweet and good. Just the same, I'm extremely worried about you two. I suppose you both realize that the society around us strongly disapproves of what you were doing, has severe, cruel laws against it, and would punish you both horribly if they caught you. Priscilla, they would take you away from Donald and me, and put you in a home for delinquent girls, and you would hate every minute of it. Donald, if you were lucky, they might try you as a legal infant and do to you something like what they would do to Priscilla— reform school until you are twenty-one, then registration and supervision as a sex offender. Or they might decide to try you as an adult—statutory rape and incest, and about twenty years at hard labor . . . and then supervision the rest of your life. Do you know that, dear ones?"

Priscilla did not answer; she was crying. Donald said gruffly, "Yes, we know that."

"Well? What's the answer?"

"But, Mother, we love each other. Priss loves me and I love Priss."

"I know you do and I respect your love. But you didn't answer me; you avoided answering. What is the answer to your problem?"

He took a deep breath, let it out in a long sigh. "I guess we've got to quit."

I patted his ribs. "Donald, you are a gallant knight and I'm proud of you. But now I must ask a frank question. When you started masturbating, did you ever swear off? Resolve never to do it again?"

"Uh, yes."

"How long did you stay stopped?"

He answered sheepishly, "About a day and a half."

"How long are you going to leave Priscilla alone, when you happen on a perfect, utterly safe opportunity and she rubs up against you and tells you not to be a sissy, and she smells good and feels even better?"

"Why, Mama, I wouldn't do that!"

Donald heaved a quick sigh. "The hell you wouldn't, Slugger. You have, near enough. Mama, you've got me. What do you do? Nail me into a barrel? Or send me to Kemper?"

"Kemper isn't far enough; it had better be the Citadel. Children, that's not the answer. Instead— I really meant it when I said I wasn't angry. Let's all engage in a conspiracy to keep you two from being hurt. First, what contraception are you using?"

I had addressed the question to both of them. There was

an extended silence, as each (I think) waited for the other to answer.

At last Donald said, "We had some rubbers. But they're all gone and I don't have any money."

(Oh, my God!) "A clear reason why you should include me in your plans. There are both rubbers and fishskins in this house, and you can always have all you want. Priscilla, when did you menstruate last? Starting date?"

"On Monday the fourteenth, so—"

"No, it wasn't, Priss. The fourteenth was the day we went to Fort Worth. And we passed the French consulate—"

"Trade mission."

"Well, something French, and they had a lot of bunting and flags out because it was Bastille Day, and you certainly didn't start the curse that day because—well, you remember. So it must have been the following Monday. If it was a Monday."

I said, "Priscilla, don't you keep a calendar?"

"Of course I do! Always."

"Will you run get it, please? Let's turn on a light."

"Uh— It's in Dallas."

(Oh, damn!) "Well, I don't want to call Marian this late at night. Perhaps you two can compare notes and be certain and we won't have to call. Priscilla, do you know why I want that date?"

"Well, I think I do. You want to count up and tell if I'm fertile tonight."

"Good. Now both of you listen carefully. Marching orders. Laws of the Medes and the Persians, chiseled in stone. Once we figure it out, Priscilla, you will sleep with me the day you ovulate and three days each side . . . and each month you will stay in my sight during your fertile week. All the time. Every minute. We aren't going to trust to good resolutions."

I went on, "I'm not moralizing; I'm just being practical. The other three weeks of each month I will not try to keep you two apart. But you will use fishskins, not rubbers, and you will use them every time . . . because there are thousands of Catholic mothers and quite a few non-Catholic ones who depended solely on 'rhythm.' You will not make love anywhere but in this house, with me in the house, with no one else in the house, and with all outside doors locked.

"In public you will always behave like most brothers and

sisters, friendly but a little bored with each other. You will never show jealousy over each other; jealousy, possessive behavior, is a dead giveaway. However, Donald, you can always be your sister's gallant knight, empowered to poke anyone in the jaw or give him a karate chop if that's what it takes to protect her from some oaf. That's both a brother's duty and his proud privilege."

"That's what happened," he said gruffly.

"What, Donald?"

"Gus had her down and was giving her a bad time. So I pulled him off and beat the tar out of him. And he lied about it and Aunt Marian believed him and didn't believe us and told Dad and Dad backed up Aunt Marian and— Anyhow we cut out that night. And didn't have money enough for the bus. So we hitchhiked and saved what money we had for eating. But—" Donald started to shake. "There were three of them and they took what money I had left and, and— But Priss got away!" I could hear him suppressing sobs that I pretended not to hear.

"Donnie was wonderful," Priscilla said solemnly. "It was last night as we were leaving Tulsa, Mama, on Forty-four. They came at us and Donnie yelled for me to run and he stood up to them while I ran down the street to a filling station that was still open. I told the station owner and begged him to call the cops. He was doing so when Donnie showed up and the station owner helped us get a hitch into Joplin, and there we stayed in an all-night Laundromat till it got light, and then we came straight here, in two hitches."

(Dear Lord, if there is Anybody up there, why do You do this to children? Maureen Johnson speaking and You're going to have to answer to me.)

I squeezed his shoulder. "I'm proud of you, Donald. It sounds like you took a licking and got robbed to keep your sister from being raped. Did they hurt you? Besides that bruise on your face?"

"Uh, maybe I've got a cracked rib. One of 'em kicked me when I was down."

"Tomorrow we'll get hold of Dr. Rumsey. You're both going to need physical exams anyhow."

"Donnie ought to have that rib looked at, but I don't need a doctor. Mama, I don't like to be poked at."

"You don't have to like it, dear, but as long as you are

under my roof, you do have to hold still for it when I think it is necessary. That is not open to argument. But you've met Dr. Rumsey before. He delivered you, right in this bed."

"Really?"

"Really. His father was our first family doctor, and the present Dr. Rumsey has been my doctor since Alice Virginia was born, and he delivered both of you two. His son has just finished his internship, so it could happen that his son will deliver your first baby. Because the Rumseys are Howards, too, and practically members of our family. What have Marian and your father told you about the Ira Howard Foundation?"

"The Ira what?"

"I've heard of it," Donald told me. "But just barely. Dad told me to forget what I had heard and wait a couple of years."

"I think a couple of years have passed. Priscilla, how would you like to be sixteen, and you, Donald, eighteen? Now, I mean. Not two years from now."

"Mama, what do you mean?"

I told them what the Foundation is, in a handful of words or less. "So a Howard often needs to adjust his birthday to keep from being noticed. We'll discuss it further in the morning; I'm going back to bed. Mama needs the rest—busy day tomorrow. Kiss me goodnight, dears—again."

"Yes, Mama. And I'll go back to my bed . . . and I'm sorry I worried you."

"We'll handle the worries. You needn't go back to your bed. Unless you want to."

"Really?"

"Really truly. I do not believe in burning the horse after the barn has been stolen." (If the first billion little wigglers did not shoot you down, dear, the next billion will never get close to the target. So enjoy it while you can—because, if you're pregnant, we'll have a whole new crop of worries. We haven't discussed the real, utterly practical reason to avoid incest . . . but you are going to have to have Old Granny Maureen's Horror Lecture on reinforced harmful recessives, the one I've been giving every little while for centuries, seems like.)

I'm not sure whether this is the frying pan or the fire. Not very many minutes ago I was sitting here in this jail, petting

Pixel (he had been gone three days and I had been worried about him) and watching a stupid grope opera for lack of anything else to do, when a squad of spooks—well, four—robed and masked, came in, grabbed me, put their usual dog collar on me, and secured me by four leashes, then snapped them to rings in the walls instead of leading me away by them.

Pixel took one look at them and skittered away. Two of them, one on each side, started shaving the skin behind my ears.

"What's going on?" I demanded. "May one ask?"

"Hold still. This is for the electrodes. You have to be animated for the ceremony."

"What ceremony?"

"After your trial and execution. Quit wiggling."

So I wiggled harder and he backhanded me across the face, and four others came in and suddenly the first four were dead and shoved under my cot. Then they unsnapped my leashes from the walls. One said quietly, just above a whisper,

"We're from the Committee for Aesthetic Deletions. Look scared and don't make it too easy for us to lead you out of here."

Looking scared I could do, with no practice. They took me out into the corridor, on down and past the "courtroom" door, then a sharp left and through a freight door onto a loading dock, where I was shoved into a lorry and the door clanged shut. Then it opened again; somebody chucked in a cat. The door slammed shut and the lorry started up with a jerk. I fell down with a cat on top of me. "Is that you, Pixel?"

"Mrrow!" (Don't be silly!)

We're still in the lorry and rolling. Now where was I? Oh, yes—I woke up early from a nightmare in which one of my sons was humping his sister and I was saying, "Dear, you really ought not to do that on the front lawn; the neighbors will notice—" when the dream woke me and I heaved a sigh of relief; it was just a dream. Then I realized that it had not been all that much a dream; the essence of it was too, too solid flesh—and came wide awake with a shot of adrenaline. Oh, Christ! Oh, Mary's drawers! Donald, did you knock up your sister? Children, I do want to help you—but, if you have let that happen, it won't be easy.

I got up and peed, and sat there and again heard the rhythmic music I had heard in the night . . . and it had the same effect on me; it turned me on. And I felt better as in all my life I have never been able to feel both horny and depressed at the same time. Had those kids been at it all night?

When the squeaks stopped, I flushed the pot, not having wanted to disturb them until they were through. Then I used the bidet, so that I would not start the day whiffing of rut. I brushed my teeth and gave my face and hair a lick and a promise.

I dug out of my wardrobe an old summer bathrobe of Patrick's that I had confiscated when I gave him a new one for his honeymoon. For Priscilla I found a wrap of mine. And one for me.

Then I tapped on their door. Priscilla called out, "Come in, Mama!" She sounded happy.

I opened the door and held out the robes. "Good morning, darlings. One for each of you. Breakfast in twenty minutes."

Priscilla bounced out of bed and kissed me. Donald approached more slowly but did not seem much troubled at being caught in his skin by fierce old Mama. The room reeked even more than I remembered.

Something brushed past my legs—Her Serene Highness. She jumped up on the bed and started purring loudly. Priscilla said, "Mama, she bumped against the door last night, making a terrible racket, so I got up and let her in. She stayed with us a short while, then she jumped down, and demanded that I open the door again. So I did, and closed it behind her. It could not have been a half hour before she was banging on the door again. This time I ignored her. Uh . . . we were busy."

"She resents closed doors," I explained. "Any closed door. I leave mine ajar and she spent the rest of the night with me. Or most of it. Mmm— She's Susan's cat and you have Susan's room. Do you want to move? Otherwise she is likely to wake you at any hour."

"No, I'll just train Donnie to get up and hold the door for her."

"Now see here, Slugger—"

I left.

I stirred up muffins and popped a Pyrex pan of them into the oven on a six-minute cycle. While the muffins were baking

I set up baked eggs wrapped in bacon in another muffin pan. When the oven pinged, I transferred the muffins to the warmer, reset the cycle and put in the bacon and eggs. While they cooked, I poured orange juice and milk, and started the samovar to cycle. That left me time to set the breakfast table with happy mats and gaudy Mexican crockery—a cheerful table.

Priscilla appeared. "Donnie will be right down. May I help?"

"Yes, dear. Go out into the back yard and cut some yellow roses for that bowl in the middle. Make it quick; I am about to serve the plates. Polly! Down off that table! Take her with you, please. She knows better but she always crowds the limits."

I served the plates and sat down just as Donald appeared. "May I help?"

"Yes, you can keep the cat off the table."

"I mean, really help."

"You'll find that a full-time job."

Thirty minutes later I was working on my second cup of tea while Priscilla served another pan of muffins and more bacon, and opened another jar of Knott's Berry Farm marmalade. I was feeling as contented as Princess Polly looked. When you come right down to it, children and cats are more fun than stocks, bonds, and other securities. I would get these two married (but not to each other!) and then it would be soon enough for Maureen, the Hetty Green of the fast new world, to tackle the Harriman empire, force it to stand and deliver. "Polly! Get out of that marmalade! Donald, you are supposed to be watching that cat."

"I am watching her, Mama. But she's faster than I am."

"And smarter."

"Who said that? Who said that? Slugger, you'll rue the day."

"Stop it, children. Time we talked about the Howard Foundation."

Quite a while later Donald said, "Let me get this straight. You're saying that I have to marry a girl on my list and Priss has to marry a man on her list?"

"No, no, no! Nothing of the sort. Nobody has to marry anybody. If you do marry, it will be your own free choice and it need not be another Howard. There is just one marriage you can't make and that is to each other. Oh, you could marry each other; there are thousands of incestuous marriages in this country—so some Kinseys have calculated. You could do it by cutting out on your own again, supporting yourselves somewhere else and somehow until you both look old enough to convince a county clerk that you are both over twenty-one. You could do that and I would make no effort to stop you.

"But I would not help you. Not a thin dime. I'm not going to try to give you a course in genetics this morning, but I will later. Just let it stand for the moment that close incest isn't just against the Bible, and against the laws of Missouri and all the other fifty-five states, it's against natural laws because it makes unhealthy babies."

"I know that. But I could get a vasectomy."

"So you could. What are you going to use for money? I certainly won't pay for it! Donald, I hate to hear you talk that way. I would rather pay to have your eyes removed than see you submit to sterilization. You are here not only to live your life but to pass that life along. Your genes are very special; that is why the Foundation will subsidize any offspring of yours that you share with a female Howard. The same applies to you, Priscilla; you both have the genes for long life. Barring accidents, each of you will live to be more than a hundred. How much more we can't tell but it has been stretching longer each generation.

"Now here is how the Howard Foundation system works. If you ask for it, the Foundation will supply each of you with a list of Howard eligibles near your age, while your name and address will be supplied to each person on your list. When I was young, it used to be eligibles close by, say fifty or a hundred miles or inside one state. Today, with glide rockets spanning North America in thirty minutes and everybody moving around like disturbed ants, you can elect to have your name supplied to every bachelor or spinster Howard in North America if you like and get back a list like a phone book. Not quite true; I understand that they dole them out a couple of dozen at a time, grouped geographically . . . but you can go on shopping until you find the man—or woman—with whom you want to spend the rest of your life."

I continued, "Just one thing. When you date another Howard, while it can be fun, it is dead serious, too. You'll be looking him over as a prospective husband, Priscilla. If he is utterly impossible, for any reason or none, you must tell him so and tell him not to come back . . . or tell me and I'll tell him so. But if he appeals to you and better acquaintance causes you to think of him as a possible husband, then it's time to take him to bed. Right here at home and I'll arrange things so that you can do so comfortably and without embarrassment."

"Wait a minute! Make love to somebody else? With Donnie right upstairs and knowing what I'm doing?"

"No. One—Donnie is not likely to be upstairs. He is likely to be at the home of a girl on his list. Two—nobody is urging you to have intercourse with anyone. That is strictly, totally, and utterly up to you. I am saying only that if he is a young man whose name has been sent to you by Uncle Justin, and you decide you want to try him, you can do so safely at home . . . and if, after sober consideration, you and he decide to marry, then you can get pregnant right at home. Howard brides are almost always pregnant—always, so far as I know—because it would be sad indeed to marry a man and discover, too late, that you and he are not fertile together. Oh, divorce is easy today . . . but it is better to have a seven-month, seven-pound baby than to have a divorce before you are twenty."

I added, "You're going to have plenty of time to think about it. I want to check on some basics today. Priscilla, will you stand up and take off your wrap? We can ask Donald to leave the room if you wish. I want to guess how old you are, biologically."

"I'll go upstairs, Slugger."

"Don't be silly. You've seen me before and Mama knows you slept with me last night." My daughter stood up, took off my wrap, hung it on her chair. "Any special way, Mama?"

"No." No baby fat left that I could see and hers was not a baby face. A young woman, physically mature, functioning as such and enjoying it. Well, we'll get an expert opinion from Dr. Rumsey. "Priscilla, it seems to me that you look about the way I did at seventeen. We will see what Dr. Rumsey says. For the sooner you start shopping your Howard list, the sounder I will sleep."

I turned to my son. "I'm sure you can be listed as eighteen,

Donald, if you wish, and receive a list of eligible girls. And—I may be prejudiced; you're my son—but it is my guess that you can spend the next couple of years, if you choose to, traveling around the country, meeting Howard couples, eating at their tables and sleeping with their daughters—a different bedmate every week, until you find the right one. That program would be safest for your sister."

"Mama! What a nasty idea! Donnie! You wouldn't! Would you?"

"Son, don't make any promises you can't keep."

20

Soothsayer

"Priscilla, you have not yet admitted to yourself that you can't marry your brother. Until you realize that, right down in your gizzard, you aren't mature enough to start courting no matter how grown up your body is. But you must not try to interfere with Donald's right to a-wooing go."

"But I love him!"

"What do you mean by 'love'?"

"Oh, you're just being mean to me!"

"Quit blubbering and try to behave like a grown woman. I want you to tell me what you mean by the word 'love.' That you are horny about him, so hot for him that you would couple with him behind any bush if he would let you, I will concede. It doesn't surprise me; I find him just as attractive, he's as pretty as a collie pup. But I have more sense about it than you have. Any woman is going to find Donald sexually attractive; if you try to keep other women away from him, you'll be piling up more grief for yourself than you will ever be able to handle.

"But being in sexual heat over a man is not love, my sweet daughter. I am willing to believe that Donald loves you as he stood up to three muggers to protect you. But tell me what you mean when you say that you love him . . . other than your hot pants—an irrelevant concurrent phenomenon."

"Uh . . . everybody knows what love is!"

"If you can't define a word, you don't know what it means. Priscilla, this is a fruitless discussion and today is a busy day. We have established that you have hot pants over Donald. We have established that Donald loves you but we have not established that you love him. And I have pointed out what all of us know, that you can't marry your brother . . . which your brother has conceded but you are not willing to admit. So we'll continue this discussion on some later date when you've grown up a bit." I stood up.

"But— Mama, what do *you* mean by 'love'?"

" 'Love' means a number of things but it always means that the other person's happiness and welfare come first. Come, let's get bathed and dressed, so—"

The telephone sounded. I said, "Catch it, will you, Donald?"

"Yes, Mum; thankee, Mum." The screen was in the living room; Donald went there still carrying Princess Polly in his left arm. He flipped the switch. "Start talking; it's your money."

I heard Susan's voice. "Mama, I— Polly! Oh, you bad, bad girl!"

Polly turned up her nose, wiggled and jumped down, stalked away. I must add that she had never taken any interest in telephone images and voices. I think it may have been the lack of living odor but I must admit that feline reasoning is not for mortal man to comprehend. Or woman.

Donald said, "Susie, am I going to have to show you the strawberry mark on my shoulder? I'm your brother, Mrs. Schultz, the handsome one. How's married life? Boring?"

"Married life is just dandy and what are you doing in Kansas City and why didn't you come four days ago for my wedding and where's Mother?"

"Mama is around here somewhere and you didn't invite me."

"I did so!"

I moved in. "Yes, you did invite him, Sweet Sue, and all the rest of his family, all eight. Nine. But only Brian was able to come, as you know, so don't needle Donald. Good to see you, dear. How is Henry?"

"Oh, Hanky's all right. He says I can't cook the way you do but that he has decided to keep me for other reasons—I rub his back."

"That's a good reason."

"So he says. Mama, I called for two reasons . . . and the first reason no longer applies. I've been screwing up my courage since Sunday to tell you that I lost Princess Polly. And now she's not lost. How did she get there?"

"I don't know. How did you lose her?"

"I'm not sure. We were all the way to Olathe before we found a filling station that also serviced Shipstones. While Hank was trading his stone for a fully charged one, I opened Polly's cage to change her sand box—she had made a mess and the dragon wagon was stinking.

"I'm not clear just what happened then. I thought that I shut her back in. Hank says that I told him it was all right to let her ride free in the back. Anyhow we left and picked up the control road at Olathe and Hank turned it over to the bug, and we eased back the seats and went right to sleep. Oh, we were tired!"

"I'll bet you were!" I agreed, thinking about my own wedding.

"The alarm woke us when we reached Wichita and we were just getting our baggage out at the Holiday Inn when I saw that Polly was missing. Mama, I almost had a heart attack."

"What did you do?"

"What could we do? We turned around and rolled back to Olathe. And the station was closed. And we played kitty, kitty, here, Polly! for a half hour and the station owner's name was on the building and we asked a policeman and found his house and woke him and he wasn't pleased."

"I find myself unsurprised."

"But, yes, he had seen a little black and white cat, about the time we were there, but not later, which means she wasn't there all the time it took us to drive four hundred miles. So we left your telecode and asked him to call you if she showed up and we started back to Wichita but the bug quit and we took turns keeping each other awake while we rode the wire

by hand . . . or we would have had to get onto a slow road.
Just the same it was three in the morning by the time we got
to Wichita again and they hadn't held our room and we slept
in the car till morning. Mama, it was not the most successful
wedding night on record. I think Hanky was ready to toss
me back . . . and I wouldn't have blamed him."

"Are things better now?"

"Oh, yes! But— Finding Princess Polly at home raises another point."

"Do you want me to ship her to you?"

Susan suddenly stopped smiling. "Mama . . . pets are not
permitted in married students' dormitories. I didn't know. So
I guess I've got to go out into Tempe and find us somewhere
else to live . . . and I'm not sure we can afford it. You won't
let her stay there? Yes, she's my cat, but—Please?"

"Susan, I'm selling this house today."

She looked blank. "Yes, Mama. Uh, if you put her in a
kennel . . . with her doctor, I guess . . . I'll come and get
her. As fast as I can make arrangements. We'll have to cash
a bond. I'll have to work it out with Henry. But I won't let
you down. I promised. I know it."

"My good Susan. Dear, Princess settled it, I think, when
she managed to find her way home in only three days, when
she's never been anywhere before. Yes, I'm selling this house
but we are moving only a mile or so. I want a smaller house
and not all this acreage. I can persuade Princess to accept a
new home that close by, I think; it is a problem I've coped
with before."

Susan let out a deep sigh. "Mama, have I told you lately
that you're wonderful?"

"No."

"You're wonderful!"

"Thank you. Is that all?" (The clock was crowding me.)

"Just one thing. Aunt Eleanor was here today—"

"She was? I thought she was in Toronto. On Saturday she
didn't say anything about going to Arizona."

"Uncle Justin went to Toronto; she came here. To Scottsdale, I mean. She's going to Toronto. Right away, if this
works. She's had caretaker trouble two seasons now, she tells
me, and she wants Hanky and me to move into their place
and take care of it. What do you think?"

(I think you would be out of your mind to move into the

luxurious summer palace of a supermillionaire; you'll learn bad habits and fancy tastes—that's no way to start a marriage. And that commute up and down Scottsdale Road—six miles? Seven?—might take up enough time each day to interfere with your studies.) "Susan, what I think does not matter. What does your husband think?"

"He suggested that I talk to you."

"But what does he think?"

"Uh . . . I'm not sure. Will you talk to him?"

"Have him call me back. Susan, I have a business appointment and I'm late; I've got to switch off. Bye!"

Whew! Nine-thirty-five— I punched up Harriman and Strong, got the same female zombie as yesterday. "Maureen Johnson speaking. Let me speak to George Strong."

"Mr. Strong is not available. Will you record—"

"We went through that routine yesterday. I'm Maureen Johnson and he has an appointment with me at my house in twenty minutes and you know it! Catch him before he leaves the building or phone him in his car. Move, damn it!"

"I'm here, Maureen." George's face replaced hers. "I've been held up. Will you forgive me if I make it ten-thirty instead of ten?"

"Quite all right, George. You recall those envelopes I left with you in 1947?"

"Certainly. In my personal safe. Never mingled with business papers."

"Would you, please, bring with you envelopes numbers one and two?"

"Certainly, dear lady."

"Thank you, sir."

I switched off. "Up we go, darlings, and bathe and dress. Priscilla, come share my bath"—and my bidet; you smell like a whorehouse and don't realize it, dear—"and we'll put you into something of mine. Something summery, the day is going to be a scorcher. Shorts and a halter, probably. Donald, Patrick left some clothes behind, so look around. Shorts and a T-shirt, maybe. Or Levi's. We'll stop at the Plaza later and do some fast shopping. Don't use all the hot water—three baths at once. Be ready by ten-twenty. On your mark, get set, go!"

• • •

George had two houses to show me. One was near Seventy-fifth Street and Mission Road in Johnson County, close to Shawnee Mission East High School. It belonged to New World Homes, a Harriman Enterprise, and had all the newer-than-tomorrow touches New World Homes are famous for—and it reminded me of a Bauhaus flat.

My youngsters loved it.

The other was on the Missouri side of the line, about half-way between our old house and Southwest High School, off Linden Road. It was not as new. The appearance of the development and my memory told me that it had been built in 1940, give or take a year. "George, this is a J. C. Nichols subdivision."

"The Nichols organization always builds excellent houses. This came into our hands because I bought it from one of our executives in a compassionate move, following a tragic accident. He lost his wife and two children. When he got out of hospital, we shipped him to Tucson to recuperate, then put him to work in Paradise, at the power plant. Complete change of work, scene, people—my partner's notion of how to rehabilitate a good man who has had his very life chopped off. Delos—Mr. Harriman—takes care of his people. Shall we go in?"

It was a pleasant house, with good landscaping and a fenced back yard—and it was furnished. Mr. Strong said, "All he asked to have shipped to him were his books and his clothes. Her clothes and those of his youngsters and their personal possessions all went to the Salvation Army. The rest—bed linens, blankets, rugs, towels, drapes—have all been cleaned and the mattresses sterilized. The house is for sale furnished or unfurnished, and you can have it either way on lease."

It had a master bedroom and two smaller ones upstairs, each with bath. The master bedroom was on the west and had a "sunset" balcony, like the flat we had in 1940 on Wood-lawn in Chicago. Downstairs was both a parlor and a family room, an arrangement I strongly favor for any family having children at home. Youngsters need a place where they can be less than neat, without disturbing Mother when she has someone in for tea.

Off the back hallway, balancing the kitchen, was a maid's room and bath. The kitchen had a GE dishwasher and a Raytheon electronic cooking unit of the same sort that I had in my old farmhouse—and in both cases the equipment was new, not the age of either house. A feature that struck my eye was an abundance of built-in bookcases . . . added later, it seemed to me, except a pair of small ones flanking the fireplace in the family room. Most houses didn't even have that much, as most people don't read.

(Before the twentieth century was out that could be worded, "—most people can't read." One of the things I learned in studying the histories of my home planet and century on various time lines was that in the decline and fall that took place on every one of them there was one invariant: illiteracy.

In addition to that scandalous flaw, on three time lines were both drug abuse and concurrent crime in the streets, plus a corrupt and spendthrift government. My own time line had endless psychotic fads followed by religious frenzy; time line seven had continuous wars; three time lines had collapse of family life and marriage—but every time line had loss of literacy . . . combined with—riddle me this—more money per student spent on education than ever before in each history. Never were so many paid so much for accomplishing so little. By 1980 the teachers themselves were only semiliterate.)

The house had—*mirabile visu!*—two hot water heaters, one for upstairs, one for kitchen, laundry room, and maid's bath. I tried a tap and was amazed to discover that the water was hot. George Strong said, "After you called yesterday I instructed our maintenance foreman to have services turned on and the house aired. You could sleep here tonight if you so wished."

"We'll see." I took a quick look in the basement and we left.

George Strong treated us to a lovely lunch in The Fiesta Patio in the Plaza, then at my request we were taken to Dr. Rumsey's office. I spoke to Jim Rumsey and told him what in particular I wanted him to look for—I can be truthful with Dr. Rumsey, thank goodness, since he understands Howard problems. "Don't tell her whether or not she is pregnant; tell me. She's a difficult case; I need leverage. Do you want to know her real age?"

"You forget that I know it. I'll try not to let that fact affect my judgment."

"Jim, you're a comfort." I kissed him good-bye, went out and spoke to my youngsters:

"Just sit tight and wait. He has other patients ahead of you. When you are through, make your best of way home."

"You're not picking us up?" Priscilla seemed amazed. "I thought we were going shopping?"

"No, we've run out of time. Perhaps we'll go to the Plaza after dinner; I believe Sears is open late."

" 'Sears.' "

"Do you have something against Sears?"

"Aunt Marian never shops at Sears."

"That's interesting. I'll see you at home. You can walk or take the bus."

"Wait a moment! Did you tell the doctor that I don't want to be poked?"

"On the contrary, I told him that if you gave him any lip or showed any lack of cooperation, I wanted him to tell me."

Priscilla pouted. "I thought that you were going to pick us up and go shopping and then we were going back and decide which house to rent."

"I am about to decide that right now, while you two take your physicals."

"You mean we don't get a vote?"

"Did you think that we were going to vote on it? All right, we'll vote by the rules of the Republic of Gondor. For each dollar each interested party invests in the deal he or she gets one vote. How many votes do you want to buy?"

"Huh? Why, I think that's mean!"

"Priscilla, it has never been in the Bill of Rights that minor dependents get to pick the family domicile. And, while I do not know how Aunt Marian ran things, in my household I make such decisions. I may consult others; I may not. If I do consult others, I am not bound by their opinions. Understand me?"

Priscilla did not answer. Donald said quietly, "Slugger, you're crowding your luck."

I rejoined George at his car; he handed me in. "Where now, dear lady?"

"I would like to look again at the furnished house."

"Good."

We rode in silence. George Strong was a comfortable man to be with; he had no small talk. Presently I said, "Did you bring those two envelopes?"

"Yes. Do you want them now? If so, I had better park.

They are in a concealed zipper pocket, rather hard to reach."

"No, I was just checking, before we got too far from your office."

When we reached the house, I went upstairs with George at my heels, and into the master bedroom. I started undressing; his face lit up. "Maureen, I had hoped that you had this in mind." He sighed happily and started reaching for fastenings himself. "It's been a long time."

"Too long. I've been overwhelmed with mother problems and with school. But school is over for me, for a long time at least, and my mothering problems I have under control— I hope—and I'll have more time, if you want me."

"I'll always want you!"

"I've been thinking about you and your sweet ways all day. But I had to park the children first. Do you want to undress me? Or shall we both hurry and see how quickly we can be in bed?"

"What a choice to have to make!"

George wasn't the greatest bedroom artist in the world, but in the six years I had been his now-and-then mistress, he had never left me hanging on the fence. He was an attentive and considerate lover and he took as his prime purpose being certain that his partner in bed reached orgasm.

If he was no Adonis, I was no Venus. When I was Priscilla's age, I looked pretty good—as tasty as she did, I think. But now (1952) I was seventy and a simulated forty-seven, and did look past forty despite special effort. An older woman must work at it, just as George worked at it (and I did appreciate his efforts). She must keep her breath sweet, her inner muscles in good tone, her voice low and mellow, her smile ready and her frown never, and her attitude friendly and cooperative. Father had told me, "Widows are far better than brides. They don't tell, they won't yell, they don't swell, they rarely smell, and they're grateful as hell."

That's Maureen Johnson from 1946 to 1982. When I first heard Father's bawdy formula I was simply amused by it and never expected it to apply to me . . . until that sour day that Brian let me know that his younger concubine had displaced me. Then I found that Father's joking description was the simple truth. So I became an available "emergency squaw." I worked hard at being agreeable and smelling good. And I didn't insist on Adonis, just a friendly fair exchange with a gentleman. (Never an oaf, never a wimp!)

I always left time for a second one, if he wanted it. He wants it, if you have done the job on him you should do. The reason American men are such lousy lovers is that American women are such lousy lovers. And vice versa, and around and around. "Garbage in, garbage out." You get what you pay for.

That twenty minutes to an hour between goes is the best time in the world for intimate talk.

"Want first crack at the bathroom?" I asked.

"No hurry," George answered, his voice rumbling in his chest (I had my right ear against it). "How about you?"

"No rush. George, that was a goody. And just what I needed. Thank you, sir."

"Maureen, you're the one Shakespeare had in mind. '— Where other women satiate, she most makes hungry.' "

"Go along with you, sir."

"I mean it."

"Tell me enough times and I'll believe it. George, when you do get up, would you please get those envelopes? Wait a moment. Do you have time today for a second one?"

"I have time. That is what time is for."

"All right. I did not want to waste time in bed talking business if you were in a hurry. Because I do know ways to get you up again quickly if you are in a hurry."

"You do indeed! But I got a day's work done before ten in order to devote the rest of the day to Maureen." He got up, got the two envelopes, came back, offered them to me.

I said, "No, I don't want to touch them. George, please examine them. Is there any way I could have tampered with them?"

"I don't see how you could have. They have been in my possession continuously since July fourth, 1947." He smiled at me, and I smiled back—that was the date of the second time we had been in bed together. "Your birthday, girl, and you gave me a present."

"No, we exchanged presents, to our mutual profit. Examine the envelopes, George—have they been tampered with? No, don't come closer. I might bewitch them."

He looked them over. "The flap seal has both our signatures written across it, on each envelope. I know my signature and I saw you sign under mine. I do not see how even Houdini could have opened them."

"Please open number one, George, and read it aloud . . . and keep it. Put it back into your zipper pocket."

"Whatever you say, dear girl." He opened it and read, " 'July 4, 1947. In the spring of 1951 a man calling himself "Dr. Pinero" will infuriate both scientists and insurance men by claiming to be able to predict the date of any person's death. He will set up in business in this sort of fortunetelling. For several months he will enjoy great business success. Then he will be killed or die in an accident and his apparatus will be destroyed. Maureen Johnson.' "

(As George read aloud, I thought back to that Saturday night, the twenty-ninth of June, 1918. Brian slept part of the time; Theodore and I not at all. Every now and then I ducked into the bath, recorded in crisp Pitmann everything Theodore had told me—many details that he had not given to Judge Sperling and Justin and Mr. Chapman.)

George said, "Interesting. I never did believe that this Doctor Pinero could do what he claimed to do. It must have been some complex hoax."

"That's not the point, George." (I did not speak sharply.)

"Eh?"

"It does not matter now whether he was a charlatan or not; the man is dead, his apparatus destroyed, none of his notes remains. So said *Time* magazine and all the newspapers. All this happened last year, 1951. That envelope has been in your custody since July 1947, four years ago. How did I do it?"

He answered mildly, "I wondered about that. Are you going to tell me?"

(Certainly, George. This man from the stars and the future came to me and made love to me and told me these things because he thought they could help me. And then he died, killed in a war that wasn't his. For me. [Only now I know that he went back to the stars and I lost him . . . and found him . . . and now I'm lost again, in a darkened lorry with a screwball cat. Pixel, don't go away again!])

"George, I'm a soothsayer."

"A soothsayer. That's a fortuneteller."

"Literally it means one who speaks the truth. But I am a prophet, rather than a fortuneteller. All those envelopes contain prophecies. Now for envelope number two. Don't open it quite yet. George, have I been in your office in the past month?"

"Not to my knowledge. The only time you were ever in it, that I can recall, was about two years ago. We had a dinner date and it suited you to stop by my office rather than be picked up."

"That's right. You read the *Wall Street Journal,* I'm sure. You are a director of the corporation managing the paradise atomic power plant; I suspect that you read the *Journal* pretty carefully concerning public power matters."

"That's true. Managing business involves studying all sorts of finicky details."

"What is new in the public power business lately?"

"Nothing much. The usual ups and downs."

"Any new power sources?"

"No, nothing significant. Some experimental windmills, but windmills, even improved ones, can't be classed as new."

"How about sunpower, George?"

"Sunpower? Oh! Yes, there was a feature story in the *Wall Street Journal.* Eh . . . sunpower screens. Direct conversion of sunlight to electricity. Uh, two long-hair scientists, Dr. Archibald Douglas and Dr. M. L. Martin. Maureen, their gadget will never amount to anything. If you are considering it, don't risk any money on it. Do you realize how much of the time it is cloudy, how many hours are dark, how smog cuts into the potential? You wind up with—"

"George. Open the second envelope."

He did so. " 'Two scientists, Douglas and Martin, will develop conversion of sunlight into electricity at high efficiency. Douglas-Martin Sunpower Screens will revolutionize public power and strongly affect everything else for the rest of the twentieth century.' Maureen, I just can't see how such an inefficient source—"

"George, George! How did I know, in 1947, about these sunpower gadgets disclosed just this year? How did I get the names right? Douglas. Martin."

"I don't know."

"I told you and now I'll repeat it. I am a prophet. Envelope number three tells Harriman Industries how to cash in on the Douglas-Martin Sunpower Screens. The next three envelopes concern power, public power, big power—and the changes coming that you won't believe. But you will have to believe when we open those envelopes one by one. The question is:

Will we open them after the fact, as with these two—and then all I could say is 'I told you so'—or do we open each one long enough before the fact that my prophecy is useful to you?"

"I'm getting chilly. Shall I get dressed, or come back to bed?"

"Oh, dear! I've talked business too long. Come to bed, George, and let me try to make it up to you."

He did and we cuddled, but the essential miracle did not take place. At last I said, "Shall I apply a little direct magic? Or would you rather rest?"

"Maureen, what is it you want from Harriman Industries? You have not done this just to perplex me."

"Of course not, George. I want to be elected a director of Harriman Industries, the holding company. Later on you will need me on the board of some of the corporations being held by it. However, I will continue to decide how to time prophecies . . . as timing is everything."

"A director. There are no women on the board."

"There will be when you nominate me and I am elected."

"Maureen, please! All directors are major stockholders."

"How much stock does it take to be eligible?"

"One share complies with the rules. But company policy calls for major ownership. In the holding company or any of its subsidiaries."

"How much? Shares. No, dollar value by the market; the various corporate shares are not all the same value per share. Not any, I should say."

"Uh, Mr. Harriman and I think a director should own, or acquire soon after election, at least half a million in market value of shares. It fixes his attention on what he is voting on."

"George, on Monday at the close of market my summed up position in all of your companies was $872,039.81—I can bring that up to an even million in a few days if it would help to smooth the way."

George's eyebrows went way up. "Maureen, I didn't know that you owned any of our stock. I should have spotted your name in connection with any large block."

"I use dummies. Some in Zurich, some in Canada, some in New York. I can get it all into my own name if there is any reason to."

"We'll need some intelligences filed with us, at least. Maureen, am I free to tell Mr. Harriman about your envelopes? Your prophecies?"

"How would he feel about them?"

"I'm not sure. He and I have been in business together since the twenties . . . but I don't know him. He's a plunger . . . I'm a plough horse."

"Well, let's keep it a bedroom secret for now. Perhaps you will want to open the next envelope in his presence. Or perhaps not. George, if the public, particularly the Street, got hold of the idea that you were making business decisions on the advice of a soothsayer, it might damage Harriman Industries, might it not?"

"I think you're right. All right, bedroom secret." He suddenly smiled. "But if I said that I consulted an astrologer, half of those knotheads would consider it 'scientific.' "

"And now let's drop it, and let me see if I can get our plough horse interested in ploughing me. George, do all the men in your family have oversize penises?"

"Not that I know of and I think you are trying to flatter me."

"Well, it seems big to me. Hey! It's getting bigger!"

21

Serpent's Tooth

My problems for the next ten years were Princess Polly, Priscilla, Donald, George Strong . . . and a curious metaphysical problem I still don't know how to resolve—or how I should have resolved it, although I have talked it over in depth with my husband and friend Dr. Jubal Harshaw and with some of the finest mathematico-manipulative cosmologists in any universe, starting with Elizabeth "Slipstick Libby" Long. It involves the age-old pseudo-paradox of free will and predestination.

Free will is a fact, while you are living it. And predestination is a fact, when you look at any sequence from outside.

But in World-as-Myth neither "free will" nor "predestination" have meaning. Each is semantically null. If we are simply patterns of fictions put together by fabulists, then one may as well speak of "free will" for pieces in a chess game. After the game is history and the chessmen have been placed back in the box, does the Red Queen lose sleep moaning, "Oh, I should never have taken that pawn!"

Ridiculous.

I am not an assemblage of fictions. I was not created by a fabulist. I am a human woman, daughter of human parents, and mother of seventeen boys and girls in my first life and mother of still more in my first rejuvenation. If I am controlled by destiny, then that destiny lies in my genes . . . not in the broodings of some near-sighted introvert hunched over a roboscriber.

The trouble was that there came a time as we neared the end of the decade that I realized that Theodore had told me about a tragedy that possibly could be prevented. Or could it? Could I use my free will to break the golden chains of predestination? Could I use my foreknowledge that something was going to happen to cause it not to happen?

Let's turn it upside down— If I keep something from happening, how could I have foreknowledge of something that never happened?

Don't try to sort that out; you'll bite your own tail.

Is it ever possible to avoid an appointment in Samarra?

I knew that the power satellite was going to blow up, killing everybody aboard. But in 1952 no one else knew there ever would be a power satellite. In 1952 it was not even a blueprint.

What was my duty?

On Friday Dr. Rumsey told me that Priscilla was not pregnant and that she was physically old enough to be bred and that he was willing to support a delayed birth certificate, if I wanted her to have one, showing an age anywhere from thirteen to nineteen . . . but that in his opinion she was childish in her attitudes.

I agreed. "But I may have to phony an age of at least sixteen."

"I see. Her brother is screwing her, isn't he?"

I answered, "Is this room soundproofed?"

"Yes. And so is my nurse. We've heard everything, dear, much of it worse than a little brother-sister incest. We had a case last week—not Howards, thank God—of 'His brother is screwing him.' Be glad your kids are normal. With brother-sister games all that is usually needed is to see to it that she doesn't get pregnant and that they get over it in time to marry somebody else. Which they almost always do. Haven't you run into this before?"

"Yes. Before you took over your father's practice. Didn't he tell you?"

"Are you kidding? Pop treats the Hippocratic Oath as handed down from on high. How did it work out?"

"Okay in the long run, although it worried me at the time. Older sister taught younger brother and then younger brother taught still younger sister. I walked on eggs for a while, wondering whether to catch them or just to keep an eye out for trouble. But they never let it get intense; they just enjoyed it. My kids are a horny lot, all of them."

"And you aren't?"

"Shall I take off my panties? Or shall we finish this discussion?"

"I'm too tired. Go on."

"Sissy. Eventually they all took the Howard shilling, and now all three couples are friendly, with, I think, occasional Westchester weekends. But they keep such things out of my sight to keep from shocking poor old strait-laced Mama. But these two don't have that easygoing attitude. Jim, I've got to get that girl married."

"Maureen, Priscilla isn't ready to get married. The cure would be worse than the disease. You would ruin some man's life while spoiling hers, not to mention the damage to possible children. Hmm— Priscilla told me she had just moved here from Dallas. I don't know Marian. Hardy family—right? What sort of a person is Marian?"

"Jim, I am not an unprejudiced witness."

"That from the woman who can always see the good side in the Devil himself tells me all I need to know. Well, Marian may have had good intentions but she did not do a good job on Priscilla. At least not good enough to risk letting her marry at fourteen no matter how mature her pelvic measurements are. Maureen, I'll fake any age you say—but don't let her get married so young."

"I'll try, dear. I've got a tiger by the tail. Thank you."

He kissed me good-bye. Shortly I said, "Stop that; you said you were too tired. And you've got a waiting room full of patients."

"Sissy."

"Yup. Some other time, dear. Give my love to Velma. I

want to get you both over for dinner next week to see my new house. Maybe then."

Princess Polly took a while to accept the move. For two weeks I kept her indoors and using a sand box. Then I let her out. An hour later, not being able to find her, I drove slowly back the eight blocks to our old house. When I was almost there, I spotted her, parked quickly and called her. She stopped and listened, let me approach her, then scampered away, straight for her old home. No, her only home.

I watched in horror as she crossed diagonally at Meyer and Rockhill—two busy boulevards. She made it safely and I breathed again and went back for my car and drove to our old house, arriving as she did because I conformed to traffic rules while she did not. I let her sniff around inside an empty house for a few minutes, then picked her up and brought her home.

For the next ten days this was repeated once and sometimes twice a day. Then came a day—the day after Labor Day, I believe—when a wrecking crew arrived to clear the site. George had warned me, so that day I did not let her out; I took her there—let her go inside as usual and sniff around, then the crew arrived and started tearing the house down. Princess came running to me and I let her sit in my lap in the car, at the curb.

She watched, while the Only Home was destroyed.

Aside from fixtures, which had been removed earlier, nothing was salvaged. So they tore down that fine old nineteenth-century frame structure in only a morning. Princess Polly watched, unbelieving. When the wreckers hitched bulldozers to the north wing and pulled it down, made it suddenly rubbish, she hid her face against me and moaned.

I drove us home. I did not like watching the death of that old house, either.

I took Polly back the next day. There was nothing but soil scraped bare and a basement hole where our home had been. Princess Polly would not get out of the car; I am not sure she recognized the site. She never ran away again. Sometimes gentleman friends came to call on her, but she stayed home. I think that she forgot that she had ever lived anywhere else.

But I did not forget. Never go back to a house you once lived in—not if you loved it.

*   *   *

I wish that Priscilla's problems had been as easy to cope with as Polly's. It was Friday before I saw Dr. Rumsey; Thursday we moved to our new house and any such move is exhausting, even though I used professional packers and handlers, not just their vans. It was simplified, too, by the fact that most of the furniture was not moved to our new house, but given to Good Will—I told both Good Will and the Salvation Army that a houseful of furniture, plus endless minor chattels, were to be donated to charity but they must send a truck. The Salvation Army wanted to come over and select what they wanted, but Good Will was not so fussy, so they got the plunder.

We kept only the books, some pictures, my desk and my files, clothing, some dishes and flatware, an IBM typewriter, and a few oddments. About eleven I sent Donald and Priscilla over to the new house with all salvaged food from pantry and freezer and refrigerator. "Donald, please come back for me after you unload. Priscilla, see what you can find for lunch; I think they will be loaded by noon. But don't fix anything for which timing is critical."

"Yes, Mother." Those were almost the only words she spoke to me that morning. She had done whatever I told her to do but made no attempt to use initiative, whereas Donald tackled the job with imagination.

They drove away. Donald came back for me at noon, just as the crew was breaking for lunch. "We'll have to wait," I told him, "as they are not quite finished. What did you do with Princess?"

"I shut her into my bathroom for now, with her sand box and food. She resents it."

"She'll just have to put up with it for a while. Donald, what is eating on Priscilla? Last night and this morning she has been acting as if someone—me, I think—had broken her little red wagon."

"Aw, Mother, that's just the way she is. Doesn't mean anything."

"Donald, it's not the way she is going to be, not if she stays here. I will not cater to sullenness. I have tried to give all my sons and daughters a maximum of freedom consistent with civilized behavior toward other people, especially toward their own family. But civilized behavior is required of everyone at all times. This means politeness and a cheerful demeanor, even if simulated rather than felt. No one is ever exempt from these rules, no matter how old. Do you think you can influence her? If she's sulky, I am quite capable of telling her to leave the table . . . and I don't think she would like that."

He laughed without mirth. "I'm sure she wouldn't like it."

"Well, perhaps you can put it over to her. Possibly she won't resent it from you."

"Uh, maybe."

"Donald, do you feel that there is anything I have said or done—or required of her—or of you—that she is justified in resenting?"

"Uh . . . no."

"Be frank with me, son. This is a bad situation; it can't go on."

"Well . . . she never has liked to take orders."

"What orders have I given that she doesn't like?"

"Well . . . she was pretty upset when you told her she couldn't come along and help decide which house we would take."

"That was not an order. I simply told her that it was my business, not hers. And so it is."

"Well, she didn't like it. And she didn't like being told that she had to be what she calls 'poked at.' You know."

"Yes, a pelvic examination. That was indeed an order. An order not subject to discussion. But tell me, what did you think of my requiring her to submit to a pelvic examination? Your opinion won't change my mind; I would just like to know what you think about it."

"Uh, none of my business."

"Donald."

"Well . . . I guess girls have to have them. If her doctor is going to know whether she's healthy or not. Yeah, I suppose so. But she sure didn't like it."

"Yes, girls do have to have them for their own protection. I don't like them and never did and I've had them so many, many times that I couldn't begin to count. But it's just a nuisance, like getting your teeth cleaned. Necessary, so I put up with it . . . and Priscilla must put up with it, too, and I won't take any nonsense out of her about it." I sighed. "Try to make her see it. Donald, I'm going to drive you back and drop you, while they are still eating, and then I'll turn right around and hurry back, or something will wind up in the wrong truck."

I got to the house about two, then supervised where things went while carrying a sandwich in my hand. It was after five by the time the van left and still later before the house was arranged—if you can call it arranged when the back yard was strewn with cardboard cartons and clothes were dumped on beds and books were simply shoved into any bookcase to get them off the floor. Was it Poor Richard who said that "Two removes equal one fire?" Yet this was an easy move.

By eight I got some supper into them. We all were quiet. Priscilla was still sullen.

After supper I had us all move into the family room for coffee—and a toast. I poured thimble glasses of Kahlua . . . because you can't get drunk on Kahlua; you'll get sick first. I held up a glass. "Here's to our new home, dears."

I took a sip; so did Donald. Priscilla did not touch hers. "I don't drink," she said flatly.

"This is not a drink, dear; it is a ceremony. For a toast, if one does not wish to drink it, it is sufficient to lift the glass, say, 'Hear, hear!' and touch the glass to your lips, put it down and smile. Remember that. It will serve you well at other times."

"Mother, it is time we had a serious talk."

"All right. Please do."

"Donald and I are not going to be able to live here."

"I'm sorry to hear that."

"I'm sorry, too. But it's the truth."

"When are you leaving?"

"Don't you want to know why we are leaving? And where we are going?"

"You will tell me if you wish to tell me."

"It's because we can't stand being treated like prisoners in a jail!"

I made no answer. The silence stretched out, until finally my daughter said, "Don't you want to know how you've been mistreating us?"

"If you wish to tell me."

"Uh . . . Donnie, you tell her!"

"No," I objected, "I'll hear from Donald any complaint he has about how I have treated him. But not about how I have treated you. You are right here, and I am your mother and the head of this house. If you have complaints, make them to me. Don't try to fob it off on your brother."

"That's it! Orders! Orders! Orders! Nothing but orders, all the time . . . like we were criminals in a prison!"

I recited to myself a mantra I learned in World War II: *Nil illegitimi carborundum.* I said it three times, under my breath. "Priscilla, if that is what you mean by orders, nothing but orders, I can assure you that I won't change it. Any complaints you have I will listen to. But I won't listen to them second-hand."

"Oh, Mother, you're impossible!"

"Here is another order, young lady. Keep a civil tongue in your head. Donald, do you have any complaints about my treatment of you? You. Not your sister."

"Uh . . . no, Mama."

"Donnie!"

"Priscilla, do you have any specific complaints? Anything but a general objection to taking orders?"

"Mother, you— There is no point in trying to reason with you!"

"You haven't tried reason as yet. I'm going to bed. If you leave before I get up, please leave your latchkeys on the kitchen table. Goodnight."

"Goodnight, Mama," Donald answered.

Priscilla said nothing.

Priscilla did not come down for breakfast. "She said to tell you she doesn't want any breakfast, Mama."

"Very well. Fried eggs and little sausages this morning. How do you want your eggs, Donald? Broken yolks and vulcanized? Or just chased through the kitchen?"

"Uh, however you have yours, I guess. Mama, Priss doesn't really mean she doesn't want breakfast. Shall I go up and tell her that you said she has to come to breakfast?"

"No. I usually have my eggs up and easy but not sloppy. Suits?"

"Huh? Oh, sure! Please, Mama, can't I at least go up and tell her that you said breakfast is ready and she should come eat?"

"No."

"Why not?"

"Because I have not said that and I do not say it. The first child to try a hunger strike on me was your brother Woodrow. He lasted several hours but he cheated—he had stashed vanilla wafers under his pillow. When he finally gave up and came downstairs, I did not permit him to eat until dinnertime, which was several hours away. He did not try it again." (But he tried everything else, with lots of imagination!) "I don't coddle hunger strikers, Donald, or tantrums of any sort . . . and I think no government should. Coddle hunger strikers, I mean, or people who chain themselves to fences or lie down in front of vehicles. Grown-up tantrums. Donald, you've objected to my orders twice this morning. Or is it three times? Are you catching this from Priscilla? Don't you have it through your head yet that I do not give unnecessary orders, but those I do give, I expect to have carried out? Promptly and as given. If I tell you to go jump in the lake, I expect you to return wringing wet."

He grinned at me. "Where is the nearest lake?"

"What? Swope Park, I guess. Unless we count a water hazard at the golf club. Or a landscaping pond at Forest Hills. But I don't recommend disturbing either corpses or golfers."

"There's a difference?"

"Oh, certainly, some at least. Donald, I don't mind that Priscilla chooses to skip breakfast this morning, as I need to talk with you without having her hanging over you and putting words in your mouth. When do you two plan to leave? And where do you plan to go, if you don't mind telling me?"

"Shucks, Mama, that was never serious. How can we leave? No money, and no place to go. Except back to Aunt Marian and we won't do that. We'll never go near her again."

"Donald, just what is it you find so poisonous about Aunt Marian? Six years ago you both elected to stay with her when you could have come with me. What happened? Did she punish you endlessly? Or what?"

"Oh, no! She hardly ever punishes anybody. Sometimes she would have Pop work us over. Like this last hooraw with Gus."

"What happened there? Gus is a year older than you are and bigger . . . or was the last time I saw him. You said, 'He had her down and was giving her a bad time.' How bad a time? Was he raping her? Or trying to?"

"Uh . . . Mama, I'm in a prejudiced position. Jealous, I guess."

"So I would guess, too. Was it really rape? Or— What is it you young people call it today? They were 'getting it on'?"

He sighed and looked hurt. "Yeah, they were. I— I got sore."

I patted his hand. "Poor Donald! Dear, are you beginning to realize that you aren't doing yourself any good by falling in love with your sister? Or doing her any good? You are probably harming her even more than you are harming yourself. Do you see that, dear?"

"But, Mama, I couldn't leave her there. Uh, I'm sorry we didn't come with you six years ago. But you were so strict and Aunt Marian wasn't, and— Oh, I'm sorry!"

"How was Marian about housework? I am about to assign each of you your share of the work. But Priscilla seems to be clumsy in the kitchen. Yesterday she filled the freezer, dumping stuff in any which way, then didn't turn it on. I just happened to catch it or we could have lost the whole load. Did she take her turn at cooking along with Mildred and Sara and whoever is the right age now?"

"I don't think so. No, I know she didn't. Granny Bearpaw does all the cooking . . . and doesn't like having anyone else in her kitchen."

"Who is Granny Bearpaw?"

"Aunt Marian's cook. Black as coal and a hook nose. Half Negra, half Cherokee. And a swell cook! Always willing to fix you a bite. But you had better ask for it from the door. If you step inside, she's likely to wave a frying pan at you."

"She sounds like quite a gal. And it sounds like I'm going to have to teach Priscilla to cook."

Donald made no comment. I went on, "In the meantime we must get transcripts and get you two into the city school system. Donald, what would you think of going to Westport High instead of Southwest? Say yes and we might find you a jalopy, four wheels of some sort, so that it would not be too difficult. I really don't want you in the same school Priscilla is in. She hasn't any judgment, dear; I'm afraid she would get into fights with other girls over you."

"Yeah, she might. But, Mama, I don't need to go to Westport."

"I think you do. For the reason I named."

"I don't need to go to high school. I graduated in June."

I had lived with children all my life; they had never ceased to surprise me.

"Donald, how did I miss this? I had you tagged for next year, and I don't recall receiving an announcement."

"I didn't send out any . . . and, yeah, I was classed as a junior this past year. But I've got the required hours and then some, because I took summer session last year to make sure I got all the math they offered. Mama, I figured on being ready to go either way . . . didn't decide to graduate until May, when it was too late for the yearbook and all that jazz. Mr. Hardecker—he's the principal—wasn't pleased. But he did check my record and agreed that I had the option of graduating at the end of my junior year if I wanted to. But he suggested that he just arrange to issue my diploma quietly and I should not attend graduation or try to convince the Class of '52 that I was in their class since I wasn't in their yearbook and didn't wear their class ring and all the rest. I agreed. Then he helped me apply for the schools I was interested in. The really good technical schools, I mean, like MIT and Case and Cal Tech and Rensselaer. I want to build rocketships."

"You sound like your brother Woodrow."

"Not quite. He flies 'em; I want to design them."

"Have you heard from any of your applications?"

"Two. Case and Cal Tech. Turned me down."

"There may be good news waiting for you in Dallas. I'll check with your father—I must call him today anyhow; I have yet to tell him that you two wanderers showed up here. Donald, if you are turned down this year for the schools you have applied to, don't lose hope."

"I won't. I'll apply next year."

"Not quite what I meant. You should go to school this year. Dear, it is not necessary to go to one of the world's top technical schools for your lower-division courses. Any liberal arts college with high scholastic standards is okay for lower division. Such as Claremont. Or any of the so-called Little Ivy League. Or Grinnell College. Lots of others."

"But this is August, Mama. It's too late to apply anywhere."

"Not quite." I thought hard. "Donald, I want you to let me promote you to eighteen; we'll start by getting you a Missouri driver's license that shows that age for you, then we'll get you a delayed birth certificate when you need one. Not soon, unless you need a passport. Then you'll go to . . . Grinnell, I think"—one of the committee for my doctorate was now dean of admissions there and I had known him rather well—"for one or two years. Make up your mind just which engineering school you want and we'll work on getting you into it next year or the year after . . . while you work hard for top grades. And—"

"Mama, what am I going to use for money?"

"My dear son, I am ready to go to almost any expense to get you separated from your sister before you two get into real trouble. I won't pay for an abortion, but I will pay for your education over and above what you can earn yourself, working part time. Which you should do, for self-discipline and for your own self-respect. At Grinnell a male student can often wash dishes in a sorority house."

I went on, "Those cornfed coeds are luscious; I've seen them. But you may not notice them too much as I want to submit your name to the Howard Foundation, and ask for the Iowa list of the youngest age group of girls."

"But, Mama, I'm not anxious to get married and I can't support a wife!"

"You don't have to get married. But are you totally un-interested in meeting a select list of girls about your age, all of whom are healthy, all long-lived—as you are—all desirable girls by all the usual criteria . . . and all of them guaranteed not to scream if you make a polite, respectful, but unmistak-able pass at her? And won't get indignant—What kind of a girl do you think I am?—when it turns out you have a fishskin or a Ramses in your pocket.

"Son, you do not have to do anything whatever about your Howard list. But if you get horny or lonely or both, shopping your Howard list surely beats hanging around bars or at-tending prayer meetings; all the preliminary work has been done for you. Because the Howard Foundation does indeed want Howards to marry Howards, and spends millions of dollars to that end."

"But, Mama, I can't possibly get married until I'm out of school. That's five years away, at least. I need an M.S. A Ph.D. wouldn't hurt."

"You talked to your sister Susan yesterday. Did you won-der how Susan and Henry were able to go to college, right straight from their wedding? Quit worrying, Donald. If you will just pick a college not too close to Kansas City, all your problems can be worked out. And your mother can quit wor-rying."

•   •   •

Priscilla blew all her fuses when she learned that Donald was going to go to school somewhere else. We kept her from knowing about it until the last minute; the day she registered at Southwest High was the day he left for Grinnell. Donald packed while his sister was at school, then waited until she got home to break the news. Then he left at once, driving a Chevrolet so old that it could not be used on a control road; it had no bug.

She threw a fit. She insisted that she was going with him. She made silly noises about suicide. "You're deserting me! I'll kill myself, I will! Then you'll be sorry you did this to me!"

Donald looked glum but he left. Priscilla went to bed. I ignored the fact. Threats of suicide are just another tantrum to me, blackmail to which I will not submit.

Besides, if a person wants to take his own life, it is (I think) his privilege. Also, if he is dead serious about it, no one can stop him.

(Yes, I am a cruel and heartless scoundrel. Stipulated. Now go play with your dolly somewhere else.)

Priscilla came downstairs about ten P.M. and said that she was hungry. I told her that dinner was long over but that she could fix herself a sandwich and a glass of milk—which she did, and then joined me in the family room . . . and started in on recriminations.

I cut her short. "Priscilla, you will not sit there and call me names while eating my food. Stop one or the other."

"Mama, you're cruel!"

"That counts as name calling."

"But— Oh, I'm so unhappy!"

That was self-evident and did not call for comment, it seemed to me, so I went back to watching Walter Cronkite and listening to his sonorous pronouncements.

She gloomed around for some days, then discovered the advantages of living close to school, of having a family room that was hers to use as she liked, and of a mother who permitted almost any racket and muss as long as it was cleaned up afterward—or at least once or twice a week. The house started to be filled with young people. I found that as Priscilla became happy, so did I.

In late September I came downstairs one Friday night about eleven for a glass of milk and a midnight snack, and heard those giveaway squeaks coming out of the maid's room across from the kitchen. I was not tempted to disturb them as I felt relief rather than worry, especially as the sound effects proved that Priscilla had learned to have orgasms as readily with another male as with her brother. But I went up and checked a calendar in my bathroom, one that duplicated the one in hers—and saw that it was a "safe" day for her and then felt nothing but relief. I never expected Priscilla to give up sex. Once they start and find they like it, they never quit. Or perhaps I should say that I would worry if one did.

The next day I called Jim Rumsey and asked him to take a smear and a blood test each time I sent Priscilla in, as I did not trust her judgment and knew that she might be exposed. He snorted. "Do you think I'm not on the ball? I check everybody. Even you, you old bag."

"Thanks, dear!" I threw him a kiss through the screen.

It was shortly after that cheerful occasion that George Strong called me. "Dear lady, I'm just back in town. I have good news." He smiled shyly. "Delos agrees that you must be on the board. We can't put it to the stockholders until the annual meeting but an interim appointment can be made by the directors if a vacancy occurs between stockholders' meetings. It so happens that one of my assistants is about to resign. As a director, not as my assistant. Could you attend a directors' meeting in Denver on Monday the sixth of October?"

"Yes, indeed. I am enormously pleased, George."

"May I pick you up at ten? A company rocketplane will take us to Denver, arriving there at ten, mountain time. The directors' meeting is at ten-thirty in the Harriman Building, followed by luncheon at the top of the same building—a private dining room with a spectacular view."

"Delightful! George, are we returning later that day?"

"We can if you wish, Maureen. But there are some beautiful drives around that area, and I have a car and a driver available. Does that appeal to you?"

"It does indeed! George, be sure to fetch envelope number three."

"I will be sure to do so. Until Monday, then, dear lady."

I moved around in a happy fog, wishing that I could tell my father about it—how little Maureen Johnson of Muddy Roads, Mizzourah, was about to be named a director of the Harriman empire, through an unlikely concatenation: first, an adulterous love affair with a stranger from the stars; second, because her husband left her for another woman; and third, an autumn affair between an immoral grass widow and a lonely bachelor.

If Brian had kept me, I could never have become a director in my own person. While Brian had not begrudged me any luxury once we were prosperous, aside from my household budget, I had actually controlled only "egg money"—even that numbered Zurich bank account had been only nominally mine. Brian was a kind and generous husband . . . but he was not even remotely a proponent of equal rights for women.

Which was one reason I refused George Strong's repeated proposals of marriage. Although George was twenty years younger than I (a fact I never let him suspect), his values were rooted in the nineteenth century. As his mistress I could be his equal; were I to marry him, I would at once become his subordinate—a pampered subordinate, most likely . . . but subordinate.

Besides, it would be a dirty trick to play on a confirmed old bachelor. His proposals of marriage were gallant compliments, not serious offers of civil contract.

Besides, I had become a confirmed old bachelor myself— even though I found myself unexpectedly rearing one more child and a problem child at that.

My problem child— What to do about Priscilla while I was in Colorado overnight? Or possibly over two nights—if George suggested staying another day, at Estes Park, or Cripple Creek, would I say no?

Were I living alone with only Princess Polly to worry about, I could stuff her into a kennel and ignore her protests. Would that I could do so with a strapping big girl who outweighed me! . . . but who lacked sense enough to boil water.

What to do? What to do?

"Priscilla, I am going to be away from home overnight, possibly two nights. What would you prefer to do while I am gone?"

She looked blank. "Why are you going away?"

"Let's stick to the point. There are several possibilities. You could stay overnight or over two nights with a chum from school, if you like. Or you could stay with Aunt Velma—"

"She's not my aunt!"

"True and you need not call her that. It is simply customary among Howards to use such terms among ourselves to remind us of our common membership in the Howard families. Suit yourself. Now please let's get back to the main question: What do you prefer to do while I'm away?"

"Why do I have to do anything? I can stay right here. I know you think I can't cook . . . but I can rustle my grub for a couple of days without starving."

"I'm sure you can. Staying here was the next possibility that I was about to mention. I can find someone to come stay with you so that you won't have to be alone. Your sister Margaret, for example."

"Peggy's a pill!"

"Priscilla, there is no excuse for your calling Margaret by a derogatory slang name. Is there someone you would like to have here to keep you company?"

"I don't need any company. I don't need any help. Feed the cat and bring in the *Star*—what's hard about that?"

"Have you stayed alone in a house before?"

"Oh, sure, dozens of times!"

"Really? What were the occasions?"

"Oh, all sorts. Papa and Aunt Marian would take the whole family somewhere, and I would decide not to go. Family outings are a bore."

"Overnight trips?"

"Sure. Or more. Nobody in the house but me and Granny Bearpaw."

"Oh. Mrs. Bearpaw is live-in help?"

"I just got through saying so."

"That isn't quite what you said and your manner is not as polite as it could be. Staying with Mrs. Bearpaw in the house is not the same as staying alone . . . and I have gathered an impression that Granny with a frying pan could intimidate an intruder."

"She wouldn't use a frying pan; she's got a shotgun."

"I see. But I can't get her to stay with you . . . and apparently you have never stayed alone before. Priscilla, I can arrange for a couple to stay here—strangers to you but reliable."

"Mother, why can't I simply stay here by myself? You act like I'm a child!"

"Very well, dear, if that is what you prefer." (But I'm not

going to leave it entirely up to your good judgment. I'm going to hire the Argus Patrol to do more than cruise slowly past three times a night—I'll place the next thing to a stakeout on this house. I shan't leave you vulnerable to some night prowler just because you think you are grown up.)

"That's what I prefer!"

"Very well. Everyone has to learn adult responsibility at some time; I simply was reluctant to thrust it on you if you did not want it. I'll be leaving at ten o'clock Monday morning, the sixth, for Colorado—"

" 'Colorado'! Why didn't you say so? Take me along!"

"No, this is a business trip."

"I won't be any trouble. Can I take the train up to the top of Pikes Peak?"

"You aren't going; you're going to stay here and go to school."

"I think that's mean."

I was gone two days and I had a wonderful time. Being a director was a bit dazzling the first time, but when it came time to vote, I simply voted the way George did, for the nonce—later I would have opinions.

At lunch Mr. Harriman had me placed at his right. I didn't touch the wine and I noticed that he didn't either. He had been all business at the meeting but was most charming at lunch—no business talk. "Mrs. Johnson, Mr. Strong tells me that you and I share an enthusiasm—space travel."

"Oh, yes!" We talked about nothing else then and were last to leave the table; the waiters were clearing it around us.

George and I spent the night at a guest house halfway between Denver and Colorado Springs, on the inner road, not the highway. We discussed envelope number three in bed:

"The Douglas-Martin Sunpower Screens will cause the greatest change in the American countryside since the first transcontinental railroad. Moving roadways will be built all over the country, powered by D-M screens. These will follow in general the network of federal highways now in existence— Highway One down the East Coast, Route Sixty-Six from Chicago to L.A., and so forth.

"String cities will grow up along these moving roads and the big cities now in existence will stop growing and even lose population.

"The moving roads will dominate all the rest of the twentieth century. Eventually they will die out, like the railroads—but not until next century."

"Maureen," George said soberly, "this is awfully hard to believe."

I said nothing.

"I don't see how they could be made to work."

"As a starter, try multiplying a thousand miles by two hundred yards, to get square yards, then call it horsepower. Use a ten percent efficiency factor. Save the surplus power in Shipstones when the Sun is high and bright; use that surplus to keep the roads rolling when the Sun doesn't shine." (I could be glib about it; I had done the arithmetic many times in thirty-four years.)

"I'm not an engineer."

"Then discuss it with your best engineer—Mr. Ferguson?—when you get home."

"You stand by this?"

"It's my prophecy. It won't happen quickly—the first roadcity—Cleveland to Cincinnati—won't roll for several years. I'm telling you now so that Harriman Industries can get in on the ground floor."

"I'll talk to Ferguson."

"Good. And now let me be nice to you because you have been so very nice to me."

I returned on Wednesday and stopped at the office of Argus Patrol before I went home. I spoke to Colonel Frisby, the president of the company. "I'm back; you can take the special watch off my home. Do you have a report for me?"

"Yes, Mrs. Johnson. Your house is still there, no fires, no burglars, no intruders, nothing but a noisy party on Monday night, and one not quite so noisy last night—kids will be kids. Your daughter did not go to school yesterday—slept in, we think; the party Monday night ran quite late. But she's at school today and looks none the worse. Shall we put this on your bill or do you want to pay for this special service now?"

I paid it and went home, feeling relieved.

I let myself in and sniffed; the place needed airing.

And a thorough house cleaning. But those were minor matters.

Priscilla got home a little after four, looking apprehensive, but smiled when I did. I ignored the mess the house was in, took her out to dinner, and told her about my trip. Some of it.

On Friday I picked her up at school and we went to Jim Rumsey's office, by appointment. Priscilla wanted to know why.

"Dr. Rumsey wanted to see you again after a couple of months. It has been just two months."

"Do I have to be poked?"

"Probably."

"I won't!"

"Say that again. Say it loud enough to be heard in Dallas. Because, if you mean that, then I'll have to bring your father into it. He has still legal custody of you. Now say it."

She shut up.

About an hour later Jim called me into his private office. "First, the good news. She doesn't have crabs. Now the bad news. She does have syphilis and clap."

I used a heartwarming expletive. Jim tut-tutted. "Ladies don't talk that way."

"I'm not a lady. I'm an old bag with an incorrigible daughter. Have you told her?"

"I always tell the parent first."

"All right, let's tell her."

"Slow down. Maureen, I recommend putting her into a hospital. Not just for gonorrhea and syphilis, but for what her emotional condition will be after we tell her. She's cocky at the moment, almost arrogant. I don't know what she'll be ten minutes from now."

"I'm in your hands, Jim."

"Let me call Bell Memorial, see if I can get an immediate admission."

22

The Better-Dead List

A noise woke me up. I was still in that pitch-dark lorry, clutching Pixel to me. "Pixel, where are we?"

"*Kuhbleeert!*" (How would I know?)

"Hush!" Someone was unlocking the lorry.

"*Meeroow?*"

"I don't know. But don't shoot till you see the whites of their eyes."

A side door rolled back. Someone was silhouetted against the open door. I blinked.

"Maureen Long?"

"I think so. Yes."

"I am sorry to have left you in the dark so long. But we had a visit from the Supreme Bishop's proctors and we have just finished bribing them. And now we must move; they don't stay bribed. Second-order dishonesty. May I offer you a hand?"

I accepted his hand—bony, dry, and cold—and he handed me down while I held Pixel in my left arm. He was a small man, in a dark siren suit, and the nearest thing to a living skeleton I have ever seen. He appeared to be yellowed parchment stretched over bones and little else. His skull was completely hairless. "Permit me to introduce myself," he said. "I am Dr. Frankenstein."

" 'Frankenstein,' " I repeated. "Didn't we meet at Schwab's on Sunset Boulevard?"

He chuckled, a sound like dry leaves rustling. "You are jesting. Of course it is not my original name but one I use professionally. You will see. This way, if you please."

We were in a windowless room, with a vaulted ceiling glowing with what seemed to be Douglas-Martin shadowless skyfoam. He led us to a lift. As the door closed with us inside Pixel tried to get away from me. I clung to him. "No, no, Pix! You've got to see where they take me."

I spoke just to Pixel, almost in a whisper, but my escort answered, "Don't worry, Milady Long; you are now in the hands of friends." The lift stopped at a lower(?) level; we got out and we all got into a tube capsule. We zoomed fifty yards, five hundred, five thousand, who knows?—the capsule accelerated, decelerated, stopped. We got out. Another lift took us up this time. Shortly we were in a luxurious lounge with about a dozen people in it and more coming in. Dr. Frankenstein offered me a comfortable seat in a large circle of chairs, most of them occupied. I sat down.

This time Pixel would not be denied. He wiggled out of my arms, jumped down, explored the place and examined the people, tail up and poking the little pink nose into everything.

There was a wheelchair in the circle, occupied by an excessively fat man, who had one leg off at the knee, the other amputated higher up. He was wearing dark glasses. He felt like a diabetic to me, and I wondered how Galahad would approach the case. He spoke up:

"Ladies and gentlemen, shall we get started? We have a new sister." He pointed with his whole hand at me, like a movie usher. "Lady MacBeth. She is—"

"Just a moment," I put in. "I am not Lady MacBeth. I am Maureen Johnson Long."

He trained his head and dark glasses at me slowly, like a

battleship's turret. "This is most irregular. Dr. Franken-stein?"

"I am sorry, Mr. Chairman. The contretemps with the proctors spoiled the schedule. Nothing has been explained to her."

The fat man let out a long sibilant sigh. "Incredible. Madam, we apologize. Let me introduce our circle. We are the dead men. All of us here are enjoying terminal illness. I say 'enjoying' because we have found a way—hee, hee, hee, hee!—to relish every golden moment left to us . . . indeed to extend those moments because a happy man lives longer. Each companion of the Committee for Aesthetic Deletions—at your service, Madam!—spends his remaining days in insuring that scoundrels whose removal will improve the human breed predecease him. You were elected *in absentia* to our select circle not merely because you are a walking corpse yourself but as a tribute to the artistic crimes you committed in attaining that status.

"With that synoptic explanation out of the way, permit me to introduce our noble companions:

"Dr. Fu Manchu." (A burly Irishman or Scot. He bowed without getting up.)

"Lucrezia Borgia." (Whistler's Mother, with tatting in her lap. She smiled at me and said, "Welcome, dear girl!" in a sweet soprano.)

"Lucrezia is our most accomplished expunger. Despite inoperable cancer of the liver she has counted coup more than forty times. She usually—"

"Stop it, Hassan," she said sweetly, "before you tempt me to put you on your proper track."

"I wish you would, dear. I grow weary of this carcass. Beyond Lucrezia is Bluebeard—"

"Hiyah, babe! What are you doing after?"

"Don't fret, Madam; he is disarmed. Next we have Attila the Hun—" (A perfect Caspar Milquetoast, in shorts and singlet. He sat utterly still, save that his head nodded steadily, like a nursery toy.) "—next to him, Lizzie Borden." (She was a young and beautiful woman, in a provocative evening gown. She looked quite healthy and she smiled happily at me.) "Lizzie is kept alive by an artificial heart . . . but the fuel that powers it is killing her slowly. Lizzie was formerly a Sister of the Order of Santa Carolita, but she fell out of favor at the Cathedral and was assigned to medical and surgical research. Hence her heart. Hence her fate. Hence her commitment, for Lizzie is a specialist; she terminates only the priesthood of the Church of the Divine Inseminator. Her teeth are very sharp.

"Next is Jack the Ripper—"

"Call me 'Jack.' "

"—and Dr. Guillotine."

"Your servant, Madam."

"Professor Moriarty is lurking back there, and with him is Captain Kidd. That completes our circle tonight, save for myself, chairman for life if I may be permitted a jest. I am the Old Man of the Mountain, Hassan the Assassin."

"Where is Count Dracula?"

"He asked to be excused, Lady MacBeth; he is indisposed—something he drank, I believe."

"I warned him that Rh negative would poison him. Hassan, you pretentious old fraud, this is ridiculous. My name is not Lady MacBeth and I am not a walking corpse; I am in perfect health. I'm lost, that's all."

"You are indeed lost, my lady, for there is no spot on the globe where in the long run you can escape the Supreme Bishop's proctors. All we offer you, all we can offer you, are some moments of exquisite pleasure before they find you. As for a name, do please pick one that pleases you. Bloody Mary, perhaps? But surely it is prudent to suppress your real name when it is posted in every post office in the realm? But come— enough of business for the nonce. Let sweet music play and good wine flow. *Carpe diem*, my cousins! Drink up, enjoy the moment. Later, when we again come to order, we will hear nominations of new candidates for termination." He touched a control on the arm of his wheelchair, spun around, and rolled to a bar in one corner.

Most of the others followed him. "Lizzie Borden" came over to me as I stood up.

"Let me welcome you personally," she said in a gentle, warm contralto. "I do especially appreciate what you did that got you condemned, as it is much like my own case."

"Really?"

"I think so. I was a simple temple prostitute, a Sister of Carolita, when I fell from grace. I had always been attracted to the religious life and believed that I had a true vocation while I was still in high school." She smiled and showed dimples. "Eventually I learned that the Church is run solely for the benefit of the priesthood, not for the good of our people. But I learned it too late."

"Uh, are you really dying? You look so healthy."

"With luck I can expect to live another four to six months. Here all of us are dying, including you, my dear. But we don't waste time thinking about it; instead we study our next client and plan the details of his final moment. May I get you something to drink?"

"No, thank you. Have you seen my cat?"

"I saw him go out onto the balcony. Let's go look."

We did—no Pixel. But it was a beautiful clear night; we stopped to look. "Lizzie, where are we?"

"This hotel is near the Plaza, and we're looking north. That's the downtown district, and beyond it, the Missouri River."

As I expected, Priscilla set new highs for screaming irrelevancy. She blamed everyone—me, Dr. Rumsey, Donald, President Patton, the Kansas City school board, and unnamed others, for the conspiracy against her. She did not blame herself for anything.

While she was ranting, Jim shoved an injector against her—a tranquilizer, Thorazine, I think, or something about as powerful. We got her into my car and over to the hospital. Bell Memorial used the bed-first-paperwork-later check-in method, so Jim got her treatment started at once. That done, he ordered a barbiturate for nine P.M. and authorized a wet pack if she failed to quiet down.

I signed all sorts of papers, showed my American Express card, and we left—back to Jim's office, where he took a sample of my blood and a vaginal smear. "Maureen, where was it you sent the boy?"

"I don't think he had anything to do with it, Jim."

"Don't talk like your daughter, you stupid little broad. We don't guess; we find out."

Jim dug into a reference listing, called a doctor in Grinnell. "Doctor, we'll find the lad and send him to you. Are you equipped to do the Morgan test? Do you have fresh reagents and a polarizer at hand?"

"In a college town, Doctor? You can bet your last dollar I do!"

"Good. We'll track him down and chase him right over to your office, then I'll wait at this telecode for you to call me back."

We were lucky; Donald was in his dormitory. "Donald, I want you to go straight to Dr. Ingram. His office is downtown, across from Stewart Library. I want you to go right now, this instant."

"Mama, what is this all about?" He looked and sounded upset.

"Call me at home, tonight, from a secure phone, and I'll tell you. I won't discuss it over a screen in the hallway of a dormitory. Go straight to Dr. Ingram and do what he tells you to. Hurry."

I waited in Jim's private office for Dr. Ingram's call. While I was waiting Jim's nurse finished my tests. "Good news," she said. "You can go to the Sunday School picnic after all."

"Thanks, Olga."

"Too bad about your youngster. But with the drugs we use nowadays she'll be home in a couple of days, as healthy as you are."

"We cure 'em too fast," Jim said gruffly. "Catching something nasty used to teach 'em a lesson. Now they figure it's no worse than a hangnail, so why worry?"

"Doctor, you're a cynic," Olga countered. "You'll come to a bad end."

After an agonizing wait, Dr. Ingram called back. "Doctor, did you have reason to suspect that this patient was infected?"

"No. But he had to be eliminated, under a VD trace required by Missouri state law."

"Well, he's negative on both of those and on two or three other things I checked while I was at it. He doesn't even have dandruff. I don't see why he would be included in a VD search; I think he's still a virgin. How shall I bill this?"

"To my office."

They switched off. I asked, "Jim, what was that about Missouri state law?"

He sighed. "Clap and pox are among the many diseases I must report, but for venereal diseases I not only have to report them but also I must cooperate in an effort to find out where the patient contracted the disease. Then public health officers try to follow each infection back to its source—impossible, since the original source is somewhere centuries back in history. But it does serve to thin it out. I know of one case here in town where spotting one dose of clap turned up thirty-seven other cases before it ran off the map, to other cities or states. When the track does that, our public health officers pass along the data to those other jurisdictions and we drop that search.

"But locating and curing thirty-seven cases of gonorrhea is worthwhile in itself, Maureen. The venereal diseases are ones we stand a chance of stamping out, the way we did smallpox, because—do you know the definition of a venereal disease?"

(Yes, I do, but go ahead, Jim.) "No."

"A venereal disease is one that is so terribly difficult to catch that only intercourse or deep kissing is likely to pass it on. That's why we stand a chance of stamping them out . . . if only the idiots would cooperate! Whereas there is no chance, none whatever, of stamping out the so-called common cold. Yet people pass on respiratory infections with utter careless-ness and aren't even apologetic about it." He was explosively profane.

I said, "Tut, tut! Ladies don't talk that way."

The screen was blinking and its alarm was sounding as I got home. I dropped my handbag and answered it—Donald. "Mama, what's this all about?"

"Secure phone?" I could not see what was behind him—just a blank wall.

"I'm in one of the soundproof booths at the phone com-pany."

"All right." I know of no gentle way to tell a boy that his sister has big and little casino, a full house. So I put it bluntly. "Priscilla is ill. She has gonorrhea and syphilis."

I thought he was going to faint. But he pulled himself together. "Mama, this is awful. Are you sure?"

"Of course I'm sure. I was there when she was tested and I saw the test results. That's why you were tested. I was greatly relieved to learn that you are not the one who gave them to her."

"I'll be there at once. Uh, it's about two hundred and forty miles. Coming up, it took me—"

"Donald."

"Yes, Mama?"

"Stay where you are. We sent you to Grinnell to get you away from your sister."

"But, Mama, these are special circumstances. She needs me—"

"She does *not* need you. You are the worst possible influence on her; can't you get that through your head? She doesn't need sympathy; she needs antibiotics and that is what she is getting. Now leave her alone and give her a chance to get well . . . and to grow up. And you grow up, too!"

After inquiring about how he was doing with his studies, I shut him off. Then I did something I avoid doing as a matter of principle but sometimes must do through pragmatic necessity; I searched a child's room.

I think a child has a right to privacy but that right is not absolute; his parents have an overriding responsibility for everything under their roof. If the circumstances require it, the child's right to privacy may have to be temporarily suspended.

I am aware that some libertarians (and all children) disagree with me. So be it.

Priscilla's room was as untidy as her mind, but that was not what I was after. I worked slowly through her bedroom and bathroom, trying to check every cubic inch, while leaving her clothes and other possessions as much as possible the way I had found them.

I found no trace of liquor. I found a stash of what I thought was marijuana but I was not sure how to tell "grass" when I saw it. That it probably was "grass" was made almost certain in my mind by two things: two little packets of cigarette papers under the bottom liner of another drawer, and a lack of any tobacco of any sort, loose or in cigarettes. Are cigarette papers used for any purpose other than rolling cigarettes of some sort?

The last odd thing I found was at the very bottom of a catch-all drawer in her bathroom: a small rectangular mirror, and with it a Gem single-edge blade. She had a big make-up mirror that I had given her, as well as a three-way that was part of her dressing table; why had she bought this mirror? I stared at those two items, mirror and razor blade, then looked elsewhere in her bath, and found, as my memory led me to expect, a Gillette razor that required double-edged blades, and an opened packet of double-edged blades—but no Gem razor. I then searched both bath and bedroom a second time. I even searched the room and bath that had been Donald's, although I knew them to be as bare as Mother

Hubbard's cupboard; I had cleaned after he left. I did not find a stash of white powder having the appearance of powdered sugar . . . which proves only that I did not find such a stash.

I put everything back the way I had found it.

About one A.M. the front door chimed. I answered it from bed. "Who is it?"

"It's me, Mama. Donald."

(Dirty names!) "Well, come in."

"I can't, it's bolted."

"Sorry, I'm not awake yet. I'll be down." I grabbed a robe, found some slippers, went downstairs and let my youngest son in. "Come in, Donald. Sit down. When did you eat last?"

"Uh, I grabbed a Big Mac in Bethany."

"Oh, Lordy." I fed him first.

When he had polished off all of a giant Dagwood and had eaten a big dish of chocolate ice cream, I said, "All right, why did you come here?"

"You know why, Mama. To see Priss. I know you said she didn't need me . . . but you're mistaken. Ever since she was a baby girl, when she was in trouble, she came to me. So I know she needs me."

(Oh, dear! I should have fought it in court. I should not have left my two youngest in the custody of— Regrets, regrets! Father, why did you have to go get yourself killed in the Battle of Britain? I need your advice. And I miss you dreadfully!) "Donald, Priscilla is not here."

"Where is she?"

"I won't tell you."

Donald looked stubborn. "I won't go back to Grinnell without seeing her."

"That's your problem. Donald, you two have outworn both my patience and my resourcefulness. You ignore my advice and disobey necessary orders and you are each too big to spank. I have nothing else to offer."

"You won't tell me where she is?"

"No."

He heaved a big sigh. "I'm going to stay here until I see her."

"That's what you think. Son, you are not the only stubborn member of this family. Any more of your lip and I'll call your

father and tell him to come get you because I can't handle
you—"

"I won't go!"

"—and then close this house and take an apartment for
myself at the Kansas Citian—a single apartment, big enough
for a sand box for Polly, not big enough for another person.
I was about to move into an apartment when you and your
sister showed up . . . so I changed my plans and rented this
house, especially for you two. But neither of you have treated
me decently and I'm sick of trying. I'm going to bed. You
can stretch out on that couch and get a nap. But if you are
not gone when I get up, I intend to call your father and tell
him to come get you."

"I won't go with him!"

"Your problem. The next step could be juvenile court but
that is up to your father. As a result of your choice, six years
ago, he has custody." I stood up, then recalled something.
"Donald, do you know marijuana when you see it?"

"Uh . . . maybe."

"Do you, or don't you?"

"Yeah . . . I do."

"Wait here." I was back in a few moments. "What is this?"

"That's marijuana. But, shucks, Mama, everybody does
marijuana now and then."

"I don't. And no one living in this house is permitted to.
Tell me what this is for." I reached into one pocket of my
robe, got out that mirror so inappropriate to a girl's room,
reached more carefully into the other pocket, got out that
single-edged razor blade, placed it on the mirror. "Well?"

"What am I supposed to say?"

"Did you ever cut a line of cocaine?"

"Uh . . . no."

"Have you seen it done?"

"Uh . . . Mama, if you are trying to tell me that Priss is
hooked on coke, all I can say is that you must be out of your
mind. Of course, most kids these days have tried it once or
twice, but—"

"You have tried it?"

"Well, sure. The janitor at our school sold it. But I didn't
like it. It rots your nose out—did you know that?"

"I knew that. Has Priss tried it?"

He looked at the mirror and blade. "I suppose so. It looks
like it."

"Have you seen her try it?"

"Uh . . . once. I chewed her out about it. Told her not to do it again."

"But, as you have told me and as she says herself, she doesn't like to take orders. And apparently did not take yours. I wonder if it's the janitor at her present school?"

"Uh, it could be a teacher just as easily. Or one of the seniors, a Big Man on Campus. Or a bookstore. Lots of places. Mama, they clean up the neighborhood dealers every now and then—doesn't make the least bit of difference; there's a new pusher the next week. The way I hear it, it's the same everywhere."

I sighed. "It beats me, Donald. I'll get you a blanket to pull over you."

"Mama, why can't I sleep in my own bed?"

"Because you're not supposed to be here at all. The only reason you're being indulged even this much is that I don't think it is safe to let you go back on the road without something to eat and a few hours sleep."

I went back to bed, could not sleep. After about an hour I got up and did something I should have done earlier: I searched the maid's room.

I found the stash. It was between the mattress and the mattress cover, at the foot of the bed. I was tempted to taste the least trace of it, having some notion from biochemistry of what cocaine should taste like, but I had sense enough—or was chicken enough—not to risk it; there are street drugs that are dangerous in the tiniest amounts. I took it back up with me, locked it, the "grass" and the cigarette papers, and the mirror and blade, into a lock box I keep in my bedroom.

They won. I lost. They were too much for me.

I brought Priscilla home, cured but sullen as ever. Two Public Health officers, a man and a woman, called on us (Jim's doing, with my cooperation) almost as we were taking off our coats. They wanted to know, gently and politely, Priscilla's "contacts"—who could have given the bugs to her and to whom she could have passed them on.

"What infections? I'm not ill, I never was ill. I've been held against my will in a conspiracy! Kidnaped and held prisoner! I'm going to sue somebody!"

"But, Miss Smith, we have copies of your lab tests and your medical history. Here, look at them."

Priscilla brushed them aside. "Lies! I'm not going to say another word without my lawyer."

At which point I made still another mistake. "But, Priscilla, I am a lawyer; you know that. What they're asking is quite reasonable, a matter of public health."

I have never been looked at with such contempt. "You're not my lawyer. You're one of the ones I'm going to sue. And these two characters, too, if they don't quit heckling me." She turned her back and went upstairs.

I apologized to the two Public Health officers. "I'm sorry, Mr. Wren and Mrs. Lantry, but I can't do anything with her, as you can see. I'm afraid you'll have to get her on the witness stand and under oath to get anything out of her."

Mr. Wren shook his head. "It would not work. In the first place, we have no way to put her on the stand; she has not broken any laws that we know of. And we don't know of anyone who has. In the second place, a youngster with her attitude simply takes the Fifth Amendment and shuts up."

"I'm not sure she knows what the Fifth Amendment is."

"You can bet she does, Mrs. Johnson. Today all these kids are street smart and every one of them is a chimney-corner lawyer, even in a rich neighborhood like this one. Put one on the stand and he'll holler for a lawyer and the ACLU will supply one pronto. The ACLU figures it is more important to protect a teenager's right to clam up than it is to protect some other teenager from infection and sterility."

"That's ridiculous."

"Those are the conditions we work under, Mrs. Johnson. If we don't get voluntary cooperation, we have no way to force it."

"Well . . . I can do one thing. I can go talk to her principal, tell him that he has VD running around loose in his school."

"It won't do any good, Mrs. Johnson. You will find that he is extremely leery of being sued."

I thought about it . . . and had to admit (the lawyer in me) that I had nothing to tell the principal if Priscilla refused to cooperate. Ask him to run "short arm inspection" (Brian's Army slang for it) on all his older boys? He would have hundreds of parents on his neck before dark.

"What about drugs?"

"What about drugs, Mrs. Johnson?"

"Does Public Health deal with drugs?"

"Some. Not much. Drugs are usually a police matter."

I told them what I had found. "What should I do?"

"Does your daughter admit that these items are hers?"

"I haven't had a chance to talk to her about them yet."

"If she won't admit it, you may have great trouble proving that the key items—the *cannabis* and the powder that may be cocaine—are hers, rather than yours. I know you are a lawyer . . . but perhaps you need to see a lawyer who specializes in such matters. There is an old saw about that, is there not?"

("A man who is his own lawyer has a fool for a client.") "Indeed there is! All right, I'll take advice first."

Donald showed up right after that. He had not been on the couch on Saturday morning; I had assumed that he had gone back to Grinnell. It was now evident from the speed with which he showed up once I fetched Priscilla home from the hospital that he had stayed in Kansas City and placed himself somewhere near to watch for her return. Evident, but not true. He had learned somehow what hospital she was in—I could think of three simple ways—then arranged for someone to let him know when she was dismissed—again, three simple ways, including bribery if he could afford it. Never mind; he showed up.

The door chimed.

I buzzed the door phone. "Announce yourself, please."

"It's Donald, Mama."

"What are you doing here?"

"I've come to see Priss."

"You can't see her."

"I'll see her if I have to bust this door down!"

I reached up and set off the Argus Patrol's "Mayday!"

"Donald, I will not let you enter this house."

"Try and stop me!" He started kicking the door.

Priscilla came running downstairs, started to open the front door. I grabbed at her; there was a scuffle, we both went down.

I'm no fighter. Fortunately Priscilla was not trained, either. Brian had taught me just one thing: "If you have to do it, do it fast. Don't wait."

As she was getting up, I punched her in the stomach—no, the solar plexus. She went down and lay there, trying to gasp air.

I heard from outside, "Mrs. Johnson! Argus is here."

"Nab him and take him away! I'll call you."

"Nab who?"

"Uh—" Priscilla was trying to get up again. I punched her in the same spot; she went down the same way. "Can you wait around for twenty minutes or a half hour? He might come back."

"Certainly. We'll stay as long as you need us. I'll call in."

"Thank you, Rick. It is 'Rick,' is it not?"

"Rick it is, Ma'am."

I turned around, grabbed my daughter by the hair, lifted her head, and snarled at her. "Crawl upstairs, go to your room, and stay there! If I hear another peep out of you, I'll punch you again."

She did exactly as I told her to, crawled away, sobbing, and crept upstairs, slowly. I made sure all doors and windows on the ground floor were locked, then I called Dallas.

I explained to Brian in bitter detail what had happened since I had last called him to report on our children, what I had tried to do, what had actually happened. "Brian, I can't cope with them. You must come get them."

"I want no part of either one of them. I was relieved when they ran away. Good riddance."

"Brian, they are your children and you have custody."

"Which I happily turn over to you."

"You can't; it takes a court to do that. Brian, since I can't handle them, if you won't come for them—or send someone for them—all I can do is have them arrested—"

"On what charges? Sassing you?"

"No. Delinquency. Incest. Use of drugs. Possession of drugs. Running away from custodial parent, Brian Smith of Dallas, Texas." I watched his face as I read off what I would tell the juvenile court. He did not flinch when I said "Incest" so I concluded that it was no news to him. He did not flinch until I named his name and city.

"What! The newspapers would have a field day!"

"Yes, in Dallas I imagine both the *News* and the *Times Herald* would feature it. I don't know whether the *Kansas City Star* would touch it or not. Incest is a bit whiff for their editorial policies. Particularly incest involving a sister with two of her brothers, August and Donald."

"Maureen, you can't mean this."

"Brian, I'm at the end of my rope. Priscilla knocked me down not twenty minutes ago and Donald has been trying to break down the front door. If you won't come here by the very next rocketplane, I am calling the police and swearing out warrants, all those charges—enough to get them locked up at least long enough for me to close this house and get out of town. No half measures, Brian. I want your answer, right now."

Marian's face appeared beside his. "Mother, you can't do that to Gus! He didn't do anything. He told me so, on his honor!"

"That isn't what they say, Marian. If you don't want them saying it on the witness stand, under oath, Brian will come here and get them."

"They're your children."

"They are Brian's children, too, and he has custody. Six years ago, when I left them with you, they were well-behaved children, polite, obedient, and no more given to naughty spells than any growing child. Today they are incorrigible, uncivilized, totally out of hand." I sighed. "Speak up, Brian. What will you do?"

"I can't come to K.C. today."

"Very well, I'll call the police and have them arrested. Have them taken in and then swear out the warrant, the criminal charges."

"Now wait a minute!"

"I can't, Brian. I'm holding them off temporarily with the patrol, the private police who watch this neighborhood. But I can't keep them here tonight; she's bigger than I am and he's twice as big. Good-bye; I've got to call the cops."

"Now hold it! I don't know how soon I can get a ship."

"You can hire one; you're rich enough! How soon will you be here?"

"Uh . . . three hours."

"That's six-twenty, our time. At six-thirty I'm calling the cops."

Brian got there at six-thirty-five. But he had called me from the field in North Kansas City well before the deadline. I was waiting for him in my living room with both children . . . and with Sergeant Rick of the Argus Patrol and Mrs. Barnes, the Patrol's office manager, who doubled as matron. It had not been a pleasant wait; both rent-a-cops had been forced to demonstrate that they were tougher than teenage children and would brook no nonsense.

Brian had taken the precaution of fetching four guards with him, two men, two women, one pair from Dallas, one pair from Kansas City. That did not make it legal but he got away with it because no one—I least of all!—cared to argue technicalities.

I saw the door close behind them, went upstairs and cried myself to sleep.

Failure! Utter and abject failure! I don't see what else I could have done. But I will always carry a heavy burden of guilt over it.

What should I have done?

23

The Adventures of
Prudence Penny

It took the opening of the Cleveland-Cincinnati rolling road to nail down in George Strong's mind that my prophecies really were accurate. I was always most careful not even to hint the source of my foreknowledge because I had a strong hunch that the truth would be harder for George to take than leaving it all a mystery. So I joked about it: my cracked crystal ball—a small time machine I keep in the basement next to my Ouija Board—my séance guiding spirit, Chief Forked Tongue—tea leaves, but it has to be Black Dragon tea, Lipton's Orange Pekoe doesn't have the right vibrations.

George smiled at each bit of nonsense—George was a gentle soul—and eventually quit asking me how I did it and simply treated the message in each envelope as a reliable forecast—as indeed it was.

But he was still chewing the bit at the time the Cleveland-Cincinnati road opened. We attended the opening together, sat in the grandstand, watched the ~~governor~~ of Ohio cut the ribbon. We were seated where we could talk privately if we kept our voices down; the speeches over the loudspeakers covered our words.

"George, how much real estate does Harriman and Strong own on each side of the roadway?"

"Eh? Quite a bit. Although some speculator got in ahead of us and took options on the best commercial sites. However, Harriman Industries has a substantial investment in D/M power screens—but you know that; you were there when we voted it, and you voted for it."

"So I did. Although my motion to invest three times that amount was first voted down."

George shook his head. "Too risky. Maureen, money is made by risking money . . . but not by wildly plunging. I have trouble enough keeping Delos from plunging; you mustn't set him a bad example."

"But I was right, George. Want to see the figures on a We-Woulda-Made if my motion had carried?"

"Maureen, one can always do a We-Woulda-Made on a wild guess that happens to hit. That doesn't justify guessing. It ignores the other wild guesses that did not hit."

"But that's my point, George—I don't guess; I know. You hold the envelopes; you open them. Have I ever been wrong? Even once?"

He shook his head and sighed. "It goes against the grain."

"So it does and your lack of faith in me is costing both Harriman and Strong and Harriman Industries money, lots of money. Never mind. You say some speculator optioned the best land?"

"Yes. Probably somebody in a position to see the maps before the decisions were public."

"No, George, not a speculator—a soothsayer. Me. I could see that you weren't moving fast enough so I optioned as much as I could, using all the liquid capital I could lay hands on, plus all the cash I could raise by borrowing against non-liquid assets."

George looked hurt. I added hastily, "I'm turning my options over to you, George. At cost, and you can decide how much to cut me in after the special position we have begins to pay back."

"No, Maureen, that's not fair. You believed in yourself; you got there first; the profits are yours."

"George, you didn't listen. I don't have the capital to exploit these options; I put every cent I could raise into the options themselves—if I had been able to lay hands on another million, I would have optioned still more land farther out and for longer terms. I just hope you will listen to me next time. It distresses me to tell you that it is going to rain soup, then have you show up with a teaspoon rather than a bucket. Do you want me to warn you about the next special position? Or shall I go straight to Mr. Harriman and try to persuade him that I am an authentic soothsayer?"

He sighed. "I'd rather you told me. If you will."

I said most quietly, "Do you have a place where we can shack up tonight?"

He answered just as quietly, "Of course. Always, dear lady."

That night I gave him more details. "The next road to be converted will be the Jersey Turnpike, an eighty-mile-per-hour road as compared with this fiddling thirty-mile-per-hour job we saw opened today. But the Harriman Highway—"

" 'Harriman'?"

"The D. D. Harriman Prairie Highway from Kansas City to Denver will be a hundred-mile-per-hour road that will grow a strip city thirty miles wide from Old Muddy to the Rocky Mountains. It will boost Kansas from a population of two million to a population of twenty million in ten years . . . with endless special positions for anyone who knows it is going to happen."

"Maureen, you frighten me."

"I frighten myself, George. It's rarely comfortable to know what is going to happen." I decided to take the plunge. "The rolling roads will continue to be built at a frantic pace, as fast as sunpower screens can be manufactured to drive them—down the East Coast, along Route Sixty-six, on El Camino Real from San Diego to Sacramento and beyond—and a good thing, too, as the sunpower screens on the roofs of the road cities will take up the slack and fend off a depression when the Paradise power plant is shut down and placed in orbit."

George kept quiet so long I thought he had fallen asleep. At last he said, "Did I hear you correctly? The big atomic power pile in Paradise, Arizona, will be placed in orbit? How? And why?"

"By means of spaceships based on today's glide rockets.

But operating with an escape fuel developed at Paradise. But, George, George, it must not happen! The Paradise plant must be shut down, yes; it is terribly dangerous, it is built wrong—like a steam engine without a relief valve." (In my head I could hear Sergeant Theodore's dear voice saying it: "They were too eager to build . . . and it was built wrong—like a steam engine without a relief valve.") "It must be shut down but it must not be placed in orbit. Safe ways will be found to build atomic power plants; we don't need the Paradise plant. In the meantime the sunpower screens can fill the gap."

"If it's dangerous—and I know some people have worried about it—if it is placed in orbit, it won't be dangerous."

"Yes, George, that's why they will put it in orbit. Once in orbit, it would not be dangerous to the town of Paradise, or the state of Arizona . . . but what about the people in orbit with it? They will be killed."

Another long wait— "It seems to me that it might be possible to design a plant to operate by remote control, like a freighter rocket. I must ask Ferguson."

"I hope you are right. Because you will see, when you return to Kansas City and open my envelope number six and also number seven, that I prophesy that the Paradise power plant will be placed in orbit, and that it will blow up and kill everybody on board, and destroy the rocketship that services it. George, it must not be allowed to happen. You and Mr. Harriman must stop it. I promise you, dear, that if this can be stopped—if my prophecy can be proved wrong—I will break my crystal ball and never prophesy again."

"I can't make any promises, Maureen. Sure, both Delos and I are directors of the Power Syndicate . . . but we hold a minor position both in stock and on the board. The Power Syndicate represents practically all the venture capital in the United States; the Sherman Anti-Trust Law was suspended to permit it to be formed in order to build the Paradise plant. Mmm . . . a man named Daniel Dixon controls a working majority, usually. A strong man. I don't like him much."

"I've heard of him, haven't met him. George, can he be seduced?"

"Maureen!"

"George, if I can keep fifty-odd innocent people from being killed in an industrial accident, I'll do considerably more than offer this old body as a bribe. Is he susceptible to women?

If I am not the woman he is susceptible to, perhaps I can find her."

Dixon didn't cotton to me at all (nor I to him, but that was unimportant) and he did not seem to have any cracks in his armor. After the Power Syndicate voted to shut down the Paradise plant "in the public interest" I was successful only in getting George and Mr. Harriman to vote against reactivating that giant bomb in orbit—theirs were the only dissenting votes. The death scenario rolled on and I could not stop it: Power satellite and spaceship *Charon* blew up together, all hands killed—and I stared at the ceiling for nights on end, reflecting on the bad side of knowing too much about the future.

But I did not stop working. Back in 1952, shortly after I had given George my earliest predictions, I had gone to Canada to see Justin: 1) to set up a front to handle business for my "Prudence Penny" column, and 2) to offer Justin the same detailed predictions I was giving to George.

Justin had not been pleased with me. "Maureen, do I understand that you have been holding all these years additional information you got from Sergeant Bronson—or Captain Long, whatever—the Howard from the future—and did not turn it over to the Foundation?"

"Yes."

Justin had shown an expression of controlled exasperation. "I must confess to surprise. Well, better late than never. Do you have it in writing, or will you dictate it?"

"I'm not turning it over to you, Justin. I will continue to pass on to you, from time to time, data that I have conserved, item by item as you need to know it."

"Maureen, I really must insist. This is Foundation business. You got these data from a future chairman of the Foundation—so he claimed and so I believe—so I am their proper custodian. I am speaking not as your old friend Justin, but as Justin Weatheral in my official capacity as chief executive officer of the Foundation and conserver of its assets for the benefit of all of us."

"No, Justin."

"I must insist."

"Insist away, old dear—it's good exercise."

"That's hardly the right attitude, Maureen. You don't own

that data. It belongs to all of us. You owe it to the Foundation."

"Justin, don't be so tediously male! Data from Sergeant Theodore saved the Foundation's bacon on Black Tuesday, in 1929. Stipulated?"

"Stipulated. That's why—"

"Let me have my say. And that same data also saved your arse and made you rich—and made the Foundation rich. Why? How? Who? Old busy bottom Maureen, that's who! Because I'm an amoral wench who fell in love with this enlisted man and kicked his feet out from under him—and got him to talking. That had nothing to do with the Foundation, just me and my loose ways. If I hadn't cut you in on it, you would never have met Theodore. Admit it! True? False? Answer me."

"Well, when you put it that way—"

"I do put it that way and let's have no more nonsense about what I owe the Foundation. Not until you've counted up what the Foundation owes me. I still promise to pass on data as needed. Right now, the Foundation should get heavily into Douglas-Martin Sunpower Screens, and if you don't know about them, see your files of the *Economist* or the *Wall Street Journal* or the *Toronto Star*. After that, the hottest new investment as soon as it opens up will be rolling roads and real estate near them."

"Rolling roads?"

"Damn it, Justin, I know Theodore mentioned them in that rump meeting of the board on Saturday the twenty-ninth of June, 1918, as I took notes and typed them out and gave you a copy, as well as the original to Judge Sperling. Look it up." So clear back in 1952 I showed Justin where the principal roadtowns would be, as told to me by Theodore. "Watch for them, get in early. Enormous profits to the early birds. But get rid of all railroad stock."

At that time I decided not to bother Justin with my "Prudence Penny" venture—not when he was feeling bruised on his maleness bump. Instead, I had taken it up with Eleanor. Entrusting a secret to Eleanor was safer than telling it to Jesus.

"Prudence Penny, The Housewife Investor" started out as a weekly column in country newspapers of the sort we had

had in Thebes, the *Lyle County Leader*. I always offered the first six weeks free. If a trial period stirred any interest, a publisher could continue it for a very small fee—those small-town weeklies can't pay more than peanuts; there was no sense in trying to make money on it at first.

In fact my purpose was not to make money. Or only indirectly.

I set the format in 1953 with the first column and never varied it:

Prudence Penny
THE HOUSEWIFE INVESTOR

TODAY'S DEFINITION: (Each column I gave at least one definition. Money people have their own language. If you don't know their special words, you can't play in their poker game. Some of the words I defined for my readers were: Common stock, preferred stock, bonds, municipal bonds, debentures, margin, selling short, puts and calls, living trust, joint tenancy, tenants in common, float, load, points, deficiency judgment, call money, prime rate, gold standard, fiat money, easement, fee simple, eminent domain, public domain, copyright, patent, etc., etc.

(Trivial? To you, perhaps. If so, you did not need "Prudence Penny." But to most people these elementary terms might as well be ancient Greek. So I offered one definition each column, in one-syllable Anglo-Saxon words that could be misunderstood only by a professor of English.)

Next I offered a discussion of something in the news of the day that might affect investing. Since everything, from weather to elections to killer bees, affects investing, this was easy. If I could include a little juicy gossip, I did. But not anything hurtful, or cruel, and I was most careful not to offer anything actionable.

My next item each week was TODAY'S RECOMMENDED INVESTMENT. This was a sure thing, based directly or indirectly on Theodore's predictions. The same recommendation might be repeated many times, alternated with others from the same source.

I always closed with Prudence Penny's Portfolio:

Ladies, we started this portfolio with one thousand dollars ($1,000.00) in January 1953. If you invested the same amount and at the same time, investing and changing investments just as we did, your portfolio is now worth $4,823.17.

If you invested $10,000.00, your portfolio is now worth $48,231.70.

If you invested $100,000, today your portfolio is worth $482,317.00.

But it is never too late to start prudent investing with Penny. You can start today with $4,823.17 (or any multiple or fraction), which you then place as follows:

(List of investments that add up to $4,823.17.)

If you want to see for yourself the details of how a thousand dollars grows to (current figure) in only (fill in) years and (blank) months, send ($1.00, $2.50, $4.00—the price went steadily up) to Pinch-Penny Publications, Suite 8600, Harriman Tower, New York, N.Y. HKL030 (that being a drop box that caused mail to be routed, eventually, to Eleanor's stooge in Toronto) or buy it at your local book store: *The Housewife's Guide to Thrifty Investing* by Prudence Penny.

The hugger-mugger about the address was intended to keep the Securities Exchange Commission from learning that "Prudence Penny" was a director of Harriman Industries. The SEC takes a jaundiced view of "inside information." So far as I could tell, it would matter not at all to them that my advice was truly beneficial to anyone who followed it. In fact, that might get me beheaded even more quickly.

The column spread from country weeklies to city dailies and did make money after the first year, and quite a lot of money in the thirteen years that I wrote it. Women read it and followed it—so my mail indicated—but I think even more men read it, not to follow my advice, but to try to figure out how this female bear could waltz at all.

I knew that I had succeeded when one day George Strong quoted "Prudence Penny" to me.

My ultimate purpose was not to make money and not to impress anyone but to establish a reputation that let me write a special column in April 1964, one headed "THE MOON BELONGS TO EVERYONE—but the first Moonship will belong to Harriman Industries."

I advised them to hang on to their Prudence Penny portfolio . . . but to take every other dime they could scrape up and bet it on the success of D. D. Harriman's great new venture, placing a man on the Moon.

From then on "Prudence Penny" always had something to say about space travel and Harriman Industries in every column. I freely admitted that space was a long-term investment (and I continued to recommend other investments, all backed by Theodore's predictions) but I kept on pounding away at the notion that untold riches awaited those farsighted investors who got in early in space activities and hung on. Don't buy on margin, don't indulge in profit-taking—buy Harriman stock outright, put it away in your safety deposit box and forget it—your grandchildren will love you.

In the spring of 1965 I moved my household to the Broadmoor Hotel south of Colorado Springs because Mr. Harriman was building his Moonship on Peterson Field. In 1952 I had tried half-heartedly to drop my lease in Kansas City after Brian had taken Priscilla and Donald back to Dallas (another story and not a good one). But George had outflanked me. Title to that house was in George, not Harriman and Strong, not Harriman Industries. When I told him that I no longer needed a four-bedroom house (counting the maid's room), he asked me to keep it, rent free.

I pointed out that, if I was to become his paid mistress, it wasn't enough, but if I was to continue the pretense of being a respectable woman, it was too much. He said, All right, what was the going rate for mistresses?—he would double it.

So I kissed him and took him to bed and we compromised. The house was his and he would put his driver and wife in the house, and I could stay in it any time I wished . . . and the resident couple would take care of Princess Polly.

George had spotted my weak point. I had once subjected this little cat to the trauma of losing her Only Home; I grabbed this means of avoiding doing it to her again.

But I did take an apartment at the Plaza, moved my most necessary books there, got my mail there, and occasionally took Polly there—subjecting her to the indignity of a litter box, true, but she did not fuss. (The new clay pellets were a vast improvement over sand or soil.) Moving back and forth this short distance got her used to a carrying cage and to being away from home now and then. Eventually she got to be a true traveling cat, dignified and at home in the best hotels, a sophisticated guest who would never think of scratching the furniture. This made it much easier for Elijah and Charlene to take vacations, or go elsewhere if George needed them elsewhere.

So in the spring of 1965 a few weeks before the historic first flight to the Moon, Princess Polly and I moved into the Broadmoor. I arrived with Polly in her carrying case, baggage to follow from the terminal of the Harriman Prairie Highway fifty miles north of there—I hated those rolling roads from the first time I rode one; they gave me headaches. But I had been told that the noise problem had been overcome on the Prairie Highway. Never trust a flack!

The desk clerk at the Broadmoor told me, "Madam, we have an excellent kennel back of the tennis club. I'll have a bellman take your cat there."

"Just a moment." I got out my Harriman Industries card— mine had a gold band.

The clerk took one look at it, got the assistant manager on duty. He hurried over, gardenia and striped pants and professional smile. "Mrs. Johnson! So happy to welcome you! Do you prefer a suite? Or a housekeeping apartment?"

Princess Polly did not have to go to a kennel. She dined on chopped liver, courtesy of the management, and had her own cat bed and litter box, both guaranteed sterilized—so said the paper band around each of them, like the one around the toilet seat in my bath.

No bidet—aside from that the Broadmoor was a first-class hotel.

After a bath and a change—my luggage arrived while I was in the bath (of course)—I left Princess Polly to watch television (which she liked, especially the commercials) and went to the bar, to have a solitary drink and see what developed.

And found my son Woodrow.

He spotted me as I walked in. "Hi, Mom!"

"Woodrow!" I was delighted! I kissed him and said, "Good to see you, son! What are you doing here? The last I heard you were at Wright-Patterson."

"Oh, I quit that; they didn't appreciate genius. Besides, they expected me to get up too early. I'm with Harriman Industries now, trying to keep 'em straight. It ain't easy."

(Should I tell Woodrow that I was now a director of Harriman Industries? I had avoided telling anyone who did not need to know—so wait and see.) "I'm glad you're keeping them straight. This Moonship of theirs— Do you have something to do with it?"

"Sit down first. What'll you drink?"

"Whatever you're having, Woodrow."

"Well, now, I'm having Manitou Water, with a twist."

"It looks like vodka tonic. Is that what it is?"

"Not exactly. Manitou Water is a local mineral water. Something like skunk, but not as tasty."

"Hmm— Make mine a vodka tonic with lime. Is Heather here?"

"She doesn't like the altitude. When we left Wright-Patterson, she took the kids back to Florida. Don't raise your eyebrows at me; we get along just fine. She lets me know when it's time for her to get pregnant again. About every three years, that is. So I go home, stay a month or two, get reacquainted with the kids. Then I go back to work. No huhu, no sweat, no family quarrels."

"Sounds like a fine arrangement if it suits you two."

"It does." He paused to order my drink. I had never learned to drink but I had learned how to order a tall drink and make it last all evening, while ice cubes diluted it. I looked Woodrow over. His skin seemed tight on his face and his hands quite bony.

The waitress left; he turned back. "Now, Mom, tell me what you're doing here."

"I've always been a space travel buff—remember how we read Roy Rockwood's Great Marvel series together? *Lost on the Moon, Through Space to Mars—*"

"Sure do! I learned to read because I thought you were holding out on me."

"Not in those. A little in the Barsoom books, perhaps."

"I've always wanted a beautiful Martian princess . . . but not the way you had to get one on Barsoom. Remember how they were always spilling each other's blood? Not for me! I'm the peaceful type, Mom. You know me."

(I wonder if any mother ever knows her children. But I do feel close to you, dear. I hope you and Heather really are all right.) "So when I heard about the Moonship, I made plans to come here. I want to see it lift off . . . since I can't go in it. What do you think of it, Woodrow? Will it do the job?"

"Let's find out." Woodrow looked around, then called out

to someone sitting at the bar. "Hey, Les! Bring your redeye over here and come set awhile."

The man addressed came over. He was a small man, with the big hands of a jockey. My son said, "May I present Captain Leslie LeCroix, skipper of the *Pioneer*? Les, this is my daughter Maureen."

"I'm honored, Miss. But you can't be Bill's daughter; you're too young. Besides, you're pretty. And he is— Well, look at him."

"Stop it, boys. I'm his mother, Captain. You really are the captain of the Moonship? I'm impressed."

Captain LeCroix sat down with us. I saw that his "redeye" was another tall, clear drink. He said to me, "No need to be impressed; the computer pilot does it all. But I'm going to ride her . . . if I can avoid Bill long enough. Have a chocolate éclair, Bill."

"Smile when you say that, stranger!"

"A cheeseburger? A jelly doughnut? A stack of wheats with honey?"

"Mom, do you see what that scoundrel is doing? Trying to keep me from dieting just because he's scared I might break his arms. Or his neck."

"Why would you do that, Woodrow?"

"I wouldn't. But Les thinks I would. He weighs just one hundred and twenty-six pounds. My best weight, in training, is one forty-five, you may remember. But by liftoff day and H-hour I have to weigh exactly what he does . . . because, if he catches a sniffle or slips in the shower and breaks something, God forbid, I have to sit there in his place and pretend to pilot. I can't avoid it; I accepted their money. And they have a large, ugly man following me around, making sure I don't run."

"Don't believe him, Ma'am. I'm very careful going through doors and I won't eat anything I don't see opened. He intends to disable me at the last minute. Is he really your son? He can't be."

"I bought him from a Gypsy. Woodrow, what happens if you don't make the weight?"

"They slice off one leg, a bit at a time, until I'm down to exactly one twenty-six. Spacemen don't need feet."

"Woodrow, you always were a naughty boy. You would need feet on the Moon."

"One is enough there. One-sixth gravity. Hey, there's that big, ugly man they got watching me! He's coming this way."

George Strong came over and bowed. "Dear lady! I see you have met our Moonship captain. And our relief pilot, Bill Smith. May I join you?"

"Mom, do you know this character? Did they hire you to watch me, too? Say it ain't so!"

"It ain't so. George, your relief pilot is my son, Woodrow Wilson Smith."

Later that night George and I had a chance to talk privately and quietly. "George, my son tells me that he must get his weight down to one hundred and twenty-six pounds in order to qualify as relief pilot. Can that be true?"

"Yes. Quite true."

"He hasn't weighed that little since his junior year in high school. If he did get his weight down to that and if Captain LeCroix fell ill, I suspect that Woodrow would be too weak to do the job. Wouldn't it make more sense to adjust weights the way they do with race horses? Add a few lead weights if Captain LeCroix flies; take them out if the relief pilot must go?"

"Maureen, you don't understand."

I admitted that I did not.

George explained to me just how tight was the weight schedule for the ship. The *Pioneer* was stripped down to barest essentials. She carried no radio—only indispensable navigational instruments. Not even a standard pressure suit—just a rubber acceleration suit and a helmet. No back pack—just a belt bottle. Open the door, drop a weighted flag, grab some rocks, get back in.

"George, this doesn't sound to me like the way to do it. I won't tell Woodrow that—after all, he's a big boy now"—assumed age, thirty-five; true age, fifty-three— "but I hope Captain LeCroix stays healthy."

Another of those long waits in which George pondered something unpleasant— "Maureen, this is utter, Blue Star secret. I'm not sure anyone is going to fly that ship."

"Trouble?"

"Sheriff trouble. I don't know how much longer I can hold off our creditors. And we haven't anywhere else to turn. We've pawned our overcoat, so to speak."

"George, let me see what I can do."

He agreed to live in my apartment and look after Princess Polly while I was away—okay with Princess Polly, as she was used to him. I left for Scottsdale in the morning, to see Justin.

"Look at it this way, Justin. How bad will the Foundation be hurt if you let Harriman Industries collapse?"

"The Foundation would be hurt. But not fatally. We would be able to resume full subsidy in five years, ten at the outside. Maureen, one thing is certain: A conservator of other people's money must never throw good money after bad."

Eight million was the most I could squeeze out of him, and I had to guarantee it. Half of it was in CDs, some of which had due dates as long as six months away. (But a certificate of deposit can always be used in place of cash, although it may cost you points.)

To accomplish that much I had to tell Justin, first, that he would never get another "Theodore" tip out of me if he didn't produce the money, and, second, that if he laid the money on the table, I would place beside it a full and complete transcript of those notes I had taken in the middle of the night on the twenty-ninth of June, 1918.

In the Broadmoor the next morning George would not accept the money from me but took me to Mr. Harriman, who seemed detached, barely able to recognize me, until I said, "Mr. Harriman, I want to buy some more participation in the Lunar launching."

"Eh? I'm sorry, Mrs. Johnson; there is no more participation stock for sale. That I know of."

"Then let me put it this way. I would like to lend you eight million dollars as a personal loan without security."

Mr. Harriman looked at me as if seeing me for the first time. He had grown gaunt since the last time I had seen him and his eyes burned with fanatic fervor—he made me think of those Old Testament prophets.

He studied me, then turned to George. "Have you explained to Mrs. Johnson what a risk she would be taking?"

George nodded glumly. "She knows."

"I wonder. Mrs. Johnson, I'm cleaned out and Harriman Industries is a hollow shell—that's why I haven't called a directors' meeting lately. I would have to explain to you and to the other directors the risks I've been taking. Mr. Strong and I have been trying to hold things together on jaw-bone and sheer nerve, long enough to get the *Pioneer* off her pad and into the sky. I haven't given up hope . . . but, if I take your money and I am forced into bankruptcy and my senior company into receivership, my note to you could not be in a preferred position. You might get three cents on the dollar; you might not get anything."

"Mr. Harriman, you are not going to be bankrupt and that tall ship out there will fly. Captain LeCroix will land on the Moon and return safely."

He smiled down at me. "It's good to know that you have faith in us."

"It's not just faith; I'm certain. We can't fail now for the lack of a few pennies. Take that money and use it. Pay it back when you can. Not only will *Pioneer* fly, you also will send many ships after her. You are manifest destiny in person, sir! You will found Luna City . . . freeport for the Solar System!"

Later that week George asked me if I wanted to be in the blockhouse during the launching—Mr. Harriman had said to invite me. I had already considered it, knowing that I could demand it if I cared to push it. "George, that's not the best place to watch the liftoff, is it?"

"No. But it's the safest. It's where the VIPs will be. The governor. The president if he shows up. Ambassadors."

"Sounds claustrophobic. George, I've never been much interested in the safest place . . . and the few VIPs I've met struck me as hollow shells, animated by PR men. Where are you going to be?"

"I don't know yet. Wherever Delos needs me to be."

"So I figured. You are going to be too busy to have me hanging on your arm—"

"It would be a privilege, dear lady. But—"

"—you are needed elsewhere. Where is the best view? If you weren't busy, where would you watch it?"

"Have you visited the Broadmoor Zoo?"

"Not yet. I expect to. After the liftoff."

"Maureen, there is a parking lot at the zoo. From it you would have a clear view to the east from a spot about fifteen hundred feet higher than Peterson Field. Mr. Montgomery has arranged with the hotel to place some folding chairs there.

And a radio link. Television. Coffee. If I weren't busy, that's where I would be."

"So that's where I will be."

Later that day I ran across my son Woodrow in the lobby of the Broadmoor. "Hi, Mom! They got me working."

"How did they manage that?"

"I didn't read my contract carefully enough. This is 'educational and public communication activity associated with the Moonship'—meaning I have to set this thing up to show people how the ship works, where it will go, and where the diamonds are on the Moon."

"Are there diamonds on the Moon?"

"We'll let you know later. Come here a sec." He led me away from the crowd in the lobby into a side hall by the barbershop. "Mom," he said quietly, "if you want to do it, I think I have enough bulge around here to get you into the blockhouse for the liftoff."

"Is that the best place to see it?"

"No, it's probably the worst. It'll be hot as a June bride, because the airconditioning isn't all that good. But it's the safest place and it's where the high brass will be. Visiting royalty. Party chairmen. Mafia chiefs."

"Woodrow, where is the best place to watch? Not the safest."

"I would drive up Cheyenne Mountain. There is a big paved parking lot outside the zoo. Come back into the lobby; I want to show you something."

On a giant (four-foot) globe that made my mouth water, Woodrow showed me the projected path of the *Pioneer*.

"Why doesn't it go straight up?"

"Doesn't work that way. She goes east and makes use of the Earth's rotation . . . and unloads all those extra steps. The bottom one, the biggest one, number five, drops in Kansas."

"What if it landed on the Prairie Roadway?"

"I'd join the Foreign Legion . . . right behind Bob Coster and Mr. Ferguson. Honest, it can't, Mom. We start out here, fifty miles south of the road, and where it lands, over here, near Dodge City, is over a hundred miles south of it."

"What about Dodge City?"

"There's a little man with a switch, hired solely to push that switch and bring step five down in open country. If he makes a mistake, they tie him to a tree and let wild dogs tear him to pieces. Don't worry, Mom. Step four lands around here, off the coast of South Carolina. Step three lands in the Atlantic north of this narrowest place where the nose of South America faces the bulge of Africa. Step two lands in the South Atlantic near Capetown. If it goes too far, we'll hear some interesting cussing in Afrikaans. Step one—ah, that's the one. With luck it lands on the Moon. If Bob Coster made a mistake, why, it's back to the old drawing board.''

It will be no news to anyone that *Pioneer* lifted off to plan and that Captain Leslie LeCroix landed on Luna and returned safely. I watched from Cheyenne Mountain, the zoo parking lot, with such a fine, horizon-wide view to the east that it seemed to me that I could stand on my tiptoes and see Kansas City.

I'm glad that I got to see one of the great rockets while they were still in use—I know of no planet in any patrolled universe where the big rockets are still used—too expensive, too wasteful, too dangerous.

But oh, so magnificent!

It was just dark when I got up there. The full Moon was rising in the east. The *Pioneer* was seven miles away (I heard someone say) but the ship was easy to see, bathed in floodlights and standing tall and proud.

I looked at my chrono, then watched the blockhouse through binoculars. A white flare burst out its top, right on time.

Another flare split into a red and green fireball. Five minutes.

That five minutes was at least a half hour long. I was beginning to think that the launching was going to abort—and I felt unbearable grief.

White fire lapped out of the base of the ship and slowly, lumberingly, it lifted off the pad . . . and climbed faster and faster and faster and the whole landscape, miles and miles, was suddenly in bright sunlight!

Up, up, and up, to apparent zenith and it seemed to have bent back to the west and I thought it was falling on us—

—and then the light was not quite as bright and now we could see that this "sun" overhead was moving east . . . and was a moving bright star. It seemed to break up and a voice from a radio said, "Step five has separated." I remembered to breathe.

And the sound reached us. How many seconds does it take sound to go seven miles? I've forgotten and, anyhow, they weren't using ordinary seconds that night.

It was "white" noise, almost unbearable even at that distance. It rumbled on and on . . . and at last the turbulence reached us, whipping skirts and knocking over chairs. Someone fell down, cursed, and said, "I'm going to sue somebody!"

Man was on his way to the Moon. His first step to his Only Home—

George died in 1971. He lived to see every cent paid back, Pikes Peak Space Catapult operational, Luna City a going concern with over six hundred inhabitants, more than a hundred of them women, and some babies born there—and Harriman Industries richer than ever. I think he was happy. I know I miss him, still.

I'm not sure Mr. Harriman was happy. He was not looking for billions; he simply wanted to go to the Moon—and Daniel Dixon euchered him out of it.

In the complex maneuverings that got a man to the Moon Dixon wound up controlling more shares of voting stock than Mr. Harriman controlled, and Mr. Harriman lost control of Harriman Industries.

On top of that, in lobbying maneuvers in Washington and in the United Nations, a Harriman daughter firm, Spaceways, Ltd., became the "chosen instrument" for the early development of space, with a rule, "The Space Precautionary Act," under which the company controlled who could go into space. I heard that Mr. Harriman had been turned down physically, under this rule. I'm not certain what went on behind the scenes; I was eased off the board of directors once Mr. Dixon was in control. I didn't mind; I didn't like Dixon.

In Boondock, centuries later or about sixty-odd years ago on my personal time line, I listened to a cube, *Myths, Legends, and Traditions—The Romantic Side of History*. There was a tale in it concerning time line two that asserted that the legendary Dee Dee Harriman had managed, many years later, when he was very old and almost forgotten, to buy a pirate rocket, in which he finally made it to the Moon . . . there to die in a bad landing. But on the Moon, where he longed to be.

I asked Lazarus about this. He said that he did not know. "But it's possible. God knows the Old Man was stubborn."

I hope he made it.

24

Decline and Fall

I am not certain that my situation was improved when these ghouls grabbed me away from those spooks. I suppose that almost everybody has fantasies about making the punishment fit the crime or about some scoundrel who would look his best in the leading role at a funeral. It is a harmless way to kill time during a sleepless night.

But these weirdos mean it.

Murder is all they think about. The first night I was here they listed fifty-odd people who needed to be killed, itemized their crimes, and offered me the honor of being the next member to count coup—pick a client, do! One whose crimes are particularly offensive to you, Milady Johnson—

I admit that the listed miscreants were a scrofulous bunch over whom even their own mothers would not be likely to weep but, like Mr. Clemens's favorite son, Huckleberry Finn, I am not much interested in killing strangers. I am not opposed to the death penalty—I voted for it every time the matter came to a vote, which was frequently during the decline and fall of the United States—but in killing *pour le sport* I need to be emotionally involved. Oh, forced to a choice I would rather shoot a man than a deer; I can't see the "sport" in shooting a gentle vegetarian that can't shoot back.

But, given full choice, I would rather watch television than kill a stranger. Some, at least.

I said, "I don't see anyone on that list who is to my taste. Do you happen to have in your file of better-deads someone who abandons kittens?"

The fat chairman smiled at me under his dark glasses. "Now that's a delicious idea! No, I think not . . . unless by chance there is someone nominated for other reasons who also abandons kittens. I will have Research set up an inquiry at once. Madam, what would be an appropriate termination for such a client? Have you studied it?"

"No, I haven't. But his death should involve homesickness . . . and loneliness . . . and cold . . . and hunger . . . and fear . . . and utter despair."

"Artistic. But perhaps not practical. Such a death might stretch out over months . . . and we really do not have the facilities to permit a deletion to last more than a few days. Ah, Bluebeard—you have something to add?"

"Do what our sister suggests for as many days as we can afford the space. Then surround the client by a holo of enormous trucks, giant holos, the way traffic must look to a kitten. Have the images bear down on him, with overpowering sound effects. Then hit him with a real truck—a glancing blow to maim him. Let him die slowly, as is often the case with a road-killed animal."

"Madam, does that appeal to you?"

(It made me want to throw up.) "Unless something better comes along."

"If we can find such a client for you, he will be saved and held at your disposal. In the meantime we must find you someone else for coup, not let you sit among us naked of proper pride."

That was a week ago and I have begun to feel just a hint of the idea that if I do not promptly find on their list a client I wish to terminate, then . . . just possibly . . . we don't want to hurry you . . . but still . . . if I don't make blood coup soon, how can I be trusted not to betray them to the Supreme Bishop's proctors?

On that Time Corps mission I carried out in Japan in the 1930s, I wish I had investigated those reports of another woman who might be me. If I had proved to myself that I was indeed tripled for 1937–38, then I would sleep better here-now, as that third loop would have to be farther ahead on my personal time line . . . which would prove that I will get out of this mess still breathing.

That's the real trick: to keep breathing. Isn't it, Pixel? Pixel? Pixel! Oh, damn!

Changes— In 1972 Princess Polly died in her sleep—heart failure, I think, but I did not have an autopsy. She was a little old lady who had lived a long life and, I think, a happy one, on the whole. I said a prayer to Bubastis, asking Her to watch for the arrival in the eternal Catnip Fields of a little black and white cat who had never scratched or bitten without just cause and who had had the misfortune to have had only one kitten—by Caesarean section and the kitten never opened its eyes—and then she had lost her kitten factory by spaying because her surgeon said that she could never have a normal litter and could not safely risk another pregnancy.

I did not get another kitten. In 1972 I was ninety years old (although I admitted only to fifty-nine . . . and tried my darnedest—exercise and diet and posture and cosmetics and clothes—to look forty). Being ninety in fact, it was possible, even likely, that another kitten would outlive me. I chose not to risk that.

I moved to Albuquerque because it had no ghosts for me. Kansas City was choked with ghosts of my past, of every sort, both sad and happy. I preferred not to drive by a site, such as our old home on Benton Boulevard, or where our old farmhouse out south had once been, when driving past would cover the happy used-to-be with dreary or unrecognizable what-is.

I preferred to remember Central High School the way it had been when my children attended it. In those days the scholastic records of Central's graduates at West Point and Annapolis and MIT and other "tough" schools caused Central to be rated as the finest secondary school in the west, equal in academics to the best preparatory schools, such as Groton or Lawrenceville—instead of what it had become: mostly babysitting for overgrown infants, a place where police prowl cars gathered every afternoon to stop fights, to confiscate knives, and to shake down the "students" for drugs—a "high school" where half the students should never have been allowed to graduate from grammar school because they could not read or write well enough to get along in the world outside.

Albuquerque held no ghosts for me; I had never lived there, I had no children living there, no grandchildren. (Great-grandchildren? Well, maybe.) Albuquerque had had the good fortune (from my point of view) to be bypassed by moving roadway "Route Sixty-six." The old paved road numbered route 66 and once called "The Main Street of America" had run straight through Albuquerque, but roadcity "Route Sixty-six" was miles to the south; one could not hear it or see it.

Albuquerque was favored also by having been bypassed by many of the ills of the Crazy Years. Despite its size—180,000 and growing smaller because of the roadcity south of it; such shrinkage was usual—it continued to have the sweet small-town feeling so common in the early twentieth century, so scarce in the second half. It was the home of the main campus of the University of New Mexico . . . a school blessed with a chancellor who had not given in to the nonsense of the sixties.

Students there had rioted (some of them) just once; Dr. Macintosh kicked them out and they stayed kicked out. Parents screamed and complained at the state capital in Santa Fe; Dr. Macintosh told the trustees and the legislature that there would be order and civilized behavior on the campus as long as he was in charge. If they did not have the guts to back him up, he would leave at once and they could hire some masochistic wimp who enjoyed presiding over a madhouse. They backed him up.

In 1970 at campuses all over America half of all freshmen (or more) were required to take a course called "English A" (or something similar) but known everywhere as "Bonehead English." When Dr. Macintosh became chancellor, he abolished Bonehead English and refused to admit students who would have been required to take it. He announced, "It costs the taxpayers a minimum of seventeen thousand dollars a year to keep a student on this campus. Reading, writing, spelling, and grammar are grammar school subjects. If an applicant for admission to this university does not know these grammar school subjects well enough to get along here, let him go back to the grammar school that had dumped him untaught. He does not belong here. I refuse to waste tax money on him."

Again parents screamed—but the parents of these subliterate applicants were a minority, while the majority of voters and legislators were discovering that they liked what they heard from Chancellor Macintosh.

After Dr. Macintosh revised the university catalog, it carried a warning that students were at all times subject to surprise tests for drugs—urine, blood, whatever. If they were caught—expulsion, no second chance.

A student who flunked a drug test found his quarters searched at once, all legal and proper, as there were seven judges in town willing night and day to issue search warrants on "probable cause." No attention was paid to tender feelings; all who were caught in possession were prosecuted.

Especially for the benefit of drug dealers the legislature reinstituted a fine old custom: public hangings. Gallows were erected in plazas. To be sure, drug dealers sentenced to death always appealed to the state supreme court and then to Washington, but with five members including the chief justice of the Supreme Court of the United States having been appointed by President Patton, it worked out that drug dealers in New Mexico had little reason to complain of the "Law's Delays." One bright young entrepreneur lived exactly four weeks from arrest to Jack Ketch. The average time, once the system got rolling, was less than two months.

As usual, the ACLU had a fit over all these matters. Several ACLU lawyers spent considerable time in jail for contempt of court, not in the new jail, but in the drunk tank of the old jail, with the drunks, the hopheads, the wetbacks, and the quasi-male prostitutes.

These were some of the reasons I moved to Albuquerque. The whole country was losing its buttons, a mass psychosis I have never fully understood. Albuquerque was not immune but it was fighting back, and it had enough sensible men and women in key posts that it was a good place to live the ten years I was there.

At the very time that America's schools and families were

going to pieces the country was enjoying a renaissance in engineering and science, and not alone in such big items as space travel and roadcities. While students frivoled away their time, the research facilities of universities and of industry were turning out more good work than ever—in particle physics, in plasma physics, in aerospace, in genetics, in exotic materials, in medical research, in every field.

The exploitation of space flourished unbelievably. Mr. Harriman's decision to keep it out of government hands, let private enterprise go at it for profit, was vindicated. While Pikes Peak Spaceport was still new, Spaceways, Ltd., was building bigger, longer, and more efficient catapults at Quito and on the island of Hawaii. Manned expeditions were sent to Mars and to Venus and the first asteroid miners were headed out.

Meanwhile the United States went to pieces.

This decay went on not just on time line two but on all investigated time lines. During my fifty years in Boondock I read several scholarly studies of the comparative histories of the explored time lines concerning what was called "The Twentieth Century Devolution."

I'm not sure of my opinions. I saw it on only one time line, and that only to the middle of 1982 and in my own country. I have opinions but you need not take them seriously as some leading scholars have other opinions.

Here are some of the things I saw as wrong:

The United States had over six hundred thousand practicing lawyers. That must be at least five hundred thousand more than were actually needed. I am not counting lawyers such as myself; I never practiced. I studied law simply to protect myself from lawyers, and there were many like me.

Family decay: I think it came mainly from both parents working outside the home. It was said again and again that, from midcentury on, both parents had to have jobs just to pay the bills. If this was true, why was it not necessary in the first half of the century? How did laborsaving machinery and enormously increased productivity impoverish the family?

Some said the cause was high taxes. This sounds more reasonable; I recall my shock the year the government collected a trillion dollars. (Fortunately most of it was wasted.)

But there seems to have been an actual decline in rational thinking. The United States had become a place where entertainers and professional athletes were mistaken for people of importance. They were idolized and treated as leaders; their opinions were sought on everything and they took themselves just as seriously—after all, if an athlete is paid a million or more a year, he knows he is important . . . so his opinions of foreign affairs and domestic policies must be important, too, even though he proves himself to be both ignorant and subliterate every time he opens his mouth. (Most of his fans were just as ignorant and unlettered; the disease was spreading.)

Consider these:

1) "Bread and Circuses";

2) The abolition of the pauper's oath in Franklin Roosevelt's first term;

3) "Peer group" promotion in public school.

These three conditions heterodyne each other. The abolition of the pauper's oath as a condition for public charity insured that habitual failures, incompetents of every sort, people who can't support themselves and people who won't, each of these would have the same voice in ruling the country, in assessing taxes and spending them, as (for example) Thomas Edison or Thomas Jefferson, Andrew Carnegie or Andrew Jackson. Peer group promotion insured that the franchise would be exercised by ignorant incompetents. And "Bread and Circuses" is what invariably happens to a democracy that goes that route: unlimited spending on "social" programs ends in national bankruptcy, which historically is always followed by dictatorship.

It seemed to me that these three things were the key mistakes that destroyed the best culture up to that time in all known histories. Oh, there were other things—strikes by public servants, for example. My father was still alive when this became a problem. Father said grimly,

"There is a ready solution for anyone on the public payroll who feels that he is not paid enough: He can resign and work for a living. This applies with equal force to Congressmen, Welfare 'clients,' school teachers, generals, garbage collectors, and judges."

And of course the entire twentieth century from 1917 on was clouded over by the malevolent silliness of Marxism.

But the Marxists would not and could not have had much influence if the American people had not started losing the hard common sense that had won them a continent. By the sixties everyone talked about his "rights" and no one spoke of his duties—and patriotism was a subject for jokes.

I do not believe that either Marx or that cracker revivalist who became the "First Prophet" could have damaged the country if the people had not become soft in the head.

"But every man is entitled to his own opinion!"

Perhaps. Certainly every man had his own opinion on everything, no matter how silly.

On two subjects the overwhelming majority of people regarded their own opinions as Absolute Truth, and sincerely believed that anyone who disagreed with them was immoral, outrageous, sinful, sacrilegious, offensive, intolerable, stupid, illogical, treasonable, actionable, against the public interest, ridiculous, and obscene.

The two subjects were (of course) sex and religion.

On sex and religion each American citizen knew the One Right Answer, by direct Revelation from God.

In view of the wide diversity of opinion, most of them must necessarily have been mistaken. But on these two subjects they were not accessible to reason.

"But you must respect another man's religious beliefs!" For Heaven's sake, why? Stupid is stupid—faith doesn't make it smart.

I recall one candidate's promise that I heard during the presidential campaign of 1976, a campaign promise that seems to me to illustrate how far American rationality had skidded.

"We shall drive ever forward along this line until all our citizens have above-average incomes!"

Nobody laughed.

When I moved to Albuquerque I simplified my life in several ways. I simplified my holdings and split them among three conservative managements, in New York, in Toronto, and in Zurich. I wrote a new will, listing a few sentimental bequests, but leaving the major portion, over 95 percent, to the Howard Foundation.

Why? The decision resulted from some long, long midnight thoughts. I had far more money than one old woman could spend—Lawsy me, I could not even spend the income from it. Leave it to my children? They were no longer children and not one of them needed it—and each had received not only Howard bonuses but also the start-up money that Brian and I had arranged for each of them.

Leave it to "worthy causes"? That is thin gruel, my friend. Most of such money is sopped up by administration, i.e., eaten by parasites.

The original capital had come from the Ira Howard Foundation; I decided to send my accumulation back to the Foundation. It seemed fitting.

I bought a modern condo apartment near the campus, between Central Avenue and Lomas Boulevard, signed up for a course in pedagogy at the university, not with any serious intention of studying (it takes real effort to flunk a course in pedagogy) but to establish me on campus. There are all sorts of good social events on a campus—motion pictures, plays, open lectures, dances, clubs. Doctorates are as common on campus as fleas on a dog, but nevertheless a doctor's degree is a union card that gives entrée many places.

I joined the nearest Unitarian church and supported it with liberal donations, in order to enjoy the many social benefits of church membership without being pestered by straitjacket creeds.

I joined a square dance club, a Viennese Waltz club, a contract bridge club, a chess club, a current events supper club, and a civic affairs luncheon club.

In six weeks I had more passes than the Rocky Mountains. It let me be fussy about my bedmates and still get in far more friendly fornication than had been the case in the preceding quarter of a century. I had not limited myself to George Strong during those years, but I had kept too busy for serious pursuit of the all-time number-one sport.

Now I had time. As some old gal said (Dorothy Parker?), "There is *nothing* as much fun as a man!"

"Male and female created He them"—that's a good arrangement, and for ten years I made the most of it.

I did not spend all of my time chasing men . . . or in letting them chase me while I ran very slowly, the latter being my MO because it makes a man nervous for a woman to be overt about it—it is contrary to traditional protocol. Males are conservative about sex, especially those who think they are not.

We Howards were not inclined to keep in touch with all

our relatives; it was not feasible. By the year I moved to Albuquerque (1972) I had more descendants than there are days in the year—I should keep track of their birthdays? Heavens, I had trouble keeping track of their names!

But I did have some favorites, people I loved irrespective of blood relationship if any: My older sister Audrey, my older "sister" Eleanor, my brother Tom, my cousin Nelson and his wife Betty Lou, my father and I missed him always. My mother I did not love but I respected her; she had done her best for all of us.

My children? While they were at home I tried to treat them all alike and to lavish on each of them love and affection— even when my head ached and my feet hurt.

Once they were married— Now comes the Moment of Truth. I tried to do unto them as they did unto me. If one of my offspring called me regularly, I tried to call her (him) as often. To some I sent birthday cards, not much else. If a grandchild gave attention to Grandma, Grandma paid attention to that child. But there just isn't time to be both open-handed and evenhanded with 181 grandchildren, that being the number I had (unless I lost track) by my ninety-ninth birthday.

My special loves— Blood did not necessarily enter into it. There was little Helen Beck, who was just Carol's age, and the two little girls went to Greenwood school together in first and second grade. Helen was a lovely child and utterly sweet-natured. Because her mother was a working widow, Helen spent quite a bit of time in my kitchen until we moved too far away.

But she did not forget me and I did not forget her. She went into show business and traveled; we tried to keep each other advised of moves so that we could make rendezvous every year or six. She lived a long time for a non-Howard and was a beauty right up to her death—so much that she could afford to dance naked into her seventies, at which age she still gave every man present an erection. Yet her dancing was never styled to be provocative, nothing like the cootch dancer Little Egypt of an earlier generation.

Helen changed her name early in her show-biz career; most people knew her as Sally Rand. I loved Sally and Sally loved me, and we could be apart for several years, then manage to make rendezvous, and be right back where we had left off, intimate friends.

Sally and I shared one oddity: both of us went to school as often as we could manage it. She usually performed at night; in daytime she was a special student at whatever campus was nearest. By the time she died (1979) she had far more collegiate hours than most professors. She was a polymath; everything interested Sally and she studied in depth. Sally did not drink or smoke; her one weakness was big, thick textbooks.

Nancy stayed closer to me than did my other children, and I was her husband's sometime mistress for sixty-four years . . . because Nancy had decided it that way before she married Jonathan. Not often but always when we met and could find opportunity. I can't believe that Jonathan truly had much interest in this old carcass into its nineties—but he could lie about it delightfully. We really did love each other, and an erection is the most flattering compliment a man can pay to an old woman. Jonathan was a true Galahad, one who reminds me of my husband Galahad. Not too surprising, as Galahad is descended from Jonathan (13.2 percent, counting convergence)—and from me, of course, but all of my husbands are descended from me except Jake and Zeb, who were born on another time line. (Time line four, Ballox O'Malley.) (Oops! And Jubal, time line three.)

As a by-product of Nancy's offering Jonathan to me, Brian got Nancy's sweet, young body—the first incest in our family, I think. Whether it happened again on later occasions I do not know and it is none of my business. Nancy and I were much alike in temperament—both of us strongly interested in sex but relaxed about it. Eager but not tense.

Carol— For Carol I always tried to save June twenty-sixth, Carol's Day, Carolita's Day, Carolmas, and eventually Fiesta de Santa Carolita for millions of people who never knew her. After June twenty-sixth, 1918, she gave up her birthday entirely in order to celebrate Carol's Day.

During the decade that I spent mostly in Albuquerque she was star-billed several times in Reno or Vegas on Carol's Day. She always held her luau on June twenty-sixth even if a midnight show forced her to start it at four in the morning. No matter the hour her friends flocked to attend, coming from around the globe. It became a great honor to be invited to Carolita's annual party, something to boast about in London and Rio.

Carol married Rod Jenkins of the Schmidt family in 1920,

when he was just back from France—Rainbow Division and Rod picked up a Silver Star and a Purple Heart without losing anything. (One scar on his belly—) Rod had majored in mathematics at Illinois Tech, specializing in topology, then he had joined up between his junior and senior years, came back and shifted to theater arts. He had decided to try to shift from amateur magician to professional—stage magic, I mean. He told me once that being shot at had caused him to reassess his values and ambitions.

So Carol started her married life handing things to her husband on stage, while dressed in so little that she constituted misdirection every time she twitched. She tried to time it so that she had babies when Rod was resting. When that was not possible, she would go on working until a theater manager called a halt . . . usually as a result of complaints by females not as well endowed. Carol was one of those fortunate women who got more beautiful as her belly bulged.

She parked her children with Rod's mother when she and Rod were on the road, but she usually had one or two with her, a privilege her youngsters all loved. Then, in '55 (I think) Rod made a mistake in a bullet-catching illusion, and died on stage.

Carol did his act (or a magic act of some sort with his props) the next night. One thing was certain: she was not hiding props or rabbits in her costume. When she started working Reno and Vegas and Atlantic City, she trimmed it down to a G-string. She added juggling to her act.

Later, after coaching, she added singing and dancing. But her fans did not care what she did; they wanted Carol, not the gimmicks. Theaters in Las Vegas or Reno showed on their marquees just "CAROLITA!"—nothing more. Sometimes she would stop in the middle of juggling and say, "I'm too tired to juggle tonight and, anyhow, W. C. Fields did it better," and she would walk out on the runway and stop, hands on her hips, dressed in a G-string and a smile, and say, "Let's get better acquainted. You, there! Pretty little girl in a blue dress. What's your name, dear? Will you throw me a kiss? If I throw you one, will you eat it or throw it back to me?"—or, "Who has a birthday tonight? Hold up your hands."

In a theater crowd at least one in fifty is having a birthday, not one in three hundred and sixty-five. She would ask them to stand, and would repeat each name loudly and clearly—

then ask all the crowd to sing Happy Birthday with her, and when the doggerel reached "Happy Birthday, dear ———" the band would stop and Carol would sing out each first name, pointing at the owner: "—dear Jimmy, Ariel, Bebe, Mary, John, Philip, Amy, Myrtle, Vincent, Oscar, Vera, Peggy"— hand cue and the band would hit it—"Happy Birthday to you!"

If visitors had been allowed to vote, Carolita could have been elected mayor of Las Vegas by a landslide.

I once asked her how she remembered all those names. She answered, "It's not hard, Mama, when you want to remember. If I make a mistake, they forgive me—they know I've tried." She added, "Mama, what they really want is to think that I am their friend—and I am."

During those ten years I traveled now and then to see my special darlings, but mostly I stayed home and let them come to me. The rest of the time I enjoyed being alive and enjoyed new friends, some in bed, some out, some both.

As the decade wore on and I approached one hundred, I found that I was experiencing more frequently a slight chill of autumn—joints that were stiff in the mornings, gray hairs among the red, a little sagginess here and there—and, worst of all, a feeling that I was becoming fragile and should avoid falling down.

I didn't let it stop me; I just tried harder. I had one fairly faithful swain at that time, Arthur Simmons—and it tickled and pleased him when I referred to myself, in bed with him, as "Simmons' Mattress."

Arthur was sixty, a widower, and a CPA, and an absolutely reliable partner in bidding contract bridge—so dependable that I gave up Italian method and went back to Goren because he played Goren. Shucks, I would have reverted to Culbertson had Arthur asked me to; an utterly honest bridge partner is that pearl of great price.

And so is a perfect gentleman in bed. Arthur was no world-class stud—but I was no longer eighteen and I never had Carol's beauty. But he was unfailingly considerate and did his best.

He had one eccentricity; after our first time, in my apartment, he insisted on getting a motel room for each assignation. "Maureen," he explained, "if you are willing to make the effort to come where I am, then I know that you really want to. And vice versa, if I go out and rent a motel room, you know that I am interested enough to make an effort. When either of us stops making an effort, it is time to kiss and part, with no tears."

In June 1982 that time had arrived; I think each of us was waiting for the other to suggest it. On June twentieth I was headed on foot to an assignation with Arthur and was thinking that perhaps I had best bring up the matter during that quiet time after the first one . . . then a second one if he wanted it and say good-bye. Or would it be kinder to announce that I was making a trip back east to see my daughter? Or simply break sharp?

I had come to the intersection of Lomas and San Mateo boulevards. I had never liked that crossing; the timing of the traffic light was short and the boulevards were wide—and getting wider lately. And today, because of repairs in progress on the PanAmerican Highway, truck traffic had been routed around the repairs by sending it down San Mateo, then west on Central, and the reverse for northbound traffic.

I was halfway across when the lights changed and a solid mass of traffic started at me, especially one giant truck. I froze, tried to run back, tripped and fell down.

I caught sight of a policeman, knew that the truck would get me, wondered briefly whether Father would recommend prayer after my heathen lifetime.

Somebody scooped me up off the pavement and I fainted.

It seemed to me that I was taken out of an ambulance and placed on a gurney. I fainted again and woke up in bed. A pretty little dark woman with wavy hair was hovering over me. She spoke slowly and carefully in an accent that I thought was Spanish:

"Mama Maureen . . . Tamara am I. For . . . Lazarus . . . and for all . . . your children . . . I bid you . . . welcome to Tertius!"

I stared at her, not believing my eyes. Or ears. "You are Tamara? You really are Tamara? Wife to Captain Lazarus Long?"

"Wife am I to Lazarus. Tamara am I. Daughter am I, to you, our Mama Maureen. Welcome, Mama. We love you."

I cried and she gathered me to her breast.

25

Rebirth in Boondock

Let's review the bidding.

In 1982 on June twentieth I was in Albuquerque, New Mexico, on my way to a Sunday afternoon motel date for some friendly fornication . . . and that made me a scandal to the jaybirds as I was only days away from my hundredth birthday—while pretending to be much younger and, mostly, succeeding. My assignation was with a widowed grandfather who seemed willing to believe that I was his own age, give or take a bit.

Part of the orthodoxy of that time and place was that old women have no interest in sex and that old men have limp penises and no sex drive—except dirty old perverts with criminal and pathological interests in young girls. All young people were certain of these ideas through knowing their own grandparents, whom they knew to be interested only in singing hymns and in playing checkers or shuffleboard. But sex? *My* grandparents? Don't be disgusting!

(At that time and in that country, nursing homes for the elderly kept their guests chaperoned and/or physically segregated by sexes so that nothing "disgusting" could take place.)

So this dirty old woman on evil bent got caught in heavy traffic, panicked, fell down, fainted—and woke up in Boondock on the planet Tellus Tertius.

I had heard of Tellus Tertius. Sixty-four years earlier, when I was a modest young matron with a snow-white reputation, I had seduced a young sergeant, Theodore Bronson, who in pillow talk with me had revealed himself as a time traveler from the far future and a distant star, Captain Lazarus Long, chairman of the Howard Families in his time . . . and my remote descendant!

I had looked forward to years of happy adultery after the war was over, under the tolerant, shut-eye chaperonage of my husband.

But Sergeant Theodore went to France in the AEF and was missing in action in some of the heaviest fighting in the Great War. MIA = killed; it never meant anything else.

When I woke up and Tamara took me into her arms, I had great trouble believing any of it . . . especially the idea that Theodore was alive and well. When I did believe her (one cannot disbelieve Tamara), I was crushed with the grief of too late, too late!

Tamara tried to soothe me but we had language trouble; she is not a linguist, speaks broken English only—and I had not a word of Galacta. (Her first speech to me she had rehearsed most carefully.)

She sent for her daughter Ishtar. Ishtar listened to me, talked to me, finally got it through my head that being a hundred years old did not matter; I was about to be rejuvenated.

I had heard about rejuvenation from Theodore, long ago. But I had never thought of it as applying to me.

They both told me, over and over again. Ishtar said, "Mama Maureen, I am more than twice as old as you are. My last rejuvenation was eighty years ago. Am I wrinkled? Don't worry about your age; you will be no trouble at all. We'll start your tests at once; you will be eighteen again in a very short time. Months, I estimate, instead of the two or three years a really difficult case can take."

Tamara nodded emphatically. "Is true. Ishtar true word esspeak. Four century am I. Dying was I." She patted her belly. "Baby here now."

"Yes," agreed Ishtar, "by Lazarus. A baby I gene-plotted and required Lazarus to plant before he left to rescue you. We could not be sure that he would be back—these trips of his are always chancy—and, while I have his sperm on deposit, frozen sperm can deteriorate; I want as many warm-sperm babies sired by Lazarus as possible." She added, "And you, too, Mama Maureen. I hope you will gift us with many more babies. Our calculations show that what Lazarus has, his unique gene patterns, he got mainly from you. You need not bear babies yourself; there'll be host mothers standing in line for the privilege of bearing a Mama Maureen baby. Unless you prefer to bear them yourself."

"You mean I *can?*"

"Certainly. Once we have you made young again."

"Then I will!" I took a deep breath. "It has been . . . forty-four years—I think that is right. Forty-four years since last I became pregnant. Although I've always been willing and have not tried to avoid it." I thought about it. "Is it possible for me to postpone seeing Theodore—Lazarus, you call him—for a while? Could I be made younger before I see him? I dread the thought of his seeing me this way. Old. Not the way he knew me."

"Certainly. There are always emotional factors in a rejuvenation. Whatever a client needs to be happy is the way we do it."

"I would rather not have him see me until I look more as I looked then."

"It shall be done."

I asked to see a picture of Theodore-Lazarus. It turned out to be a moving holo, almost frighteningly lifelike. I was aware that Theodore and I looked enough alike to be brother and sister; that was what Father had first noticed about him. But this startled me. "Why, that's my son!" The holo looked just like my son Woodrow—my bad boy and always my favorite.

"Yes, he's your son."

"No, no! I mean that Captain Lazarus Long whom I knew as Theodore is a dead ringer—sorry, a twin-brother image—of my son Woodrow Wilson Smith. I hadn't realized it. Of course, in the brief time I knew Captain Long, my son Woodrow Wilson was only five years old; they did not look alike then, or nothing anyone would notice. So my son Woodrow grew up to look like his remote descendant. Strange. I find I'm touched by it."

Ishtar looked at Tamara. They exchanged words in a language I did not know (Galacta, it was). But I could hear worry in their voices.

Ishtar said soberly, "Mama Maureen, Lazarus Long is your son Woodrow Wilson."

"No, no," I said. "I saw Woodrow just a few months ago. He was, uh, sixty-nine at the time but looked much younger. He looked just as Captain Long looks in this picture—an amazing resemblance. But Woodrow is back in the twentieth century. I know."

"Yes, he is, Mama Maureen. Was, I mean, although Elizabeth tells me the two tenses are equivalent. Woodrow Wilson Smith grew up in the twentieth century, spent most of the twenty-first century on Mars and on Venus, returned to Earth in the twenty-second century and—" Ishtar stopped and looked up. "Teena?"

"Who rubbed my lamp? What'll you have, Ish?"

"Ask Justin for a printout in English of the memoirs he prepared on the Senior, will you, please?"

"No need to ask Justin; I've got 'em in my gizzard. You want them bound or scrolled?"

"Bound, I think. But, Teena, let Justin fetch them here; he will be delighted and honored."

"Who wouldn't? Mama Maureen, are they treating you right? If they don't, just tell me, 'cause I do all the work around here."

After a while a man came in who reminded me disturbingly of Arthur Simmons. But it was just a general resemblance combined with similar personality; in 1982 Justin Foote would have been a CPA, as Arthur Simmons had been. Justin Foote was carrying a briefcase. (*"Plus le change, plus la même chose."*) There was a degree of awkwardness as Ishtar introduced him; he seemed about to fall over his own feet from excitement at meeting me.

I took his hand. "My first great-great-granddaughter, Nancy Jane Hardy, married a boy named Charlie Foote. That was about 1972, I think; I went to her wedding. Is Charlie Foote any relation to you?"

"He is my ancestor, Mother Maureen. Nancy Jane Hardy Foote gave birth to Justin Foote the First on New Millennium Eve, December thirty-first, year 2000 Gregorian."

"Really? Then Nancy Jane had a nice long run. She was named for her great-grandmother, my first born."

"So the archives show. Nancy Irene Smith Weatheral, your first born, Ancestress. And I carry the first name of Nancy's father-in-law, Justin Weatheral." Justin spoke excellent English with an odd accent. Bostonian?

"Then I'm your grandma, in some degree. So kiss me, grandson, and quit being so nervously formal; we're family."

He relaxed and kissed me then, a firm buss on the mouth, one I liked. If we had not had company, I might have let it develop—he did remind me of Arthur.

He added then: "I'm descended from you and from Justin Weatheral another way, Grandma. Through Patrick Henry Smith, to whom you gave birth on July seventh, 1932."

I was startled. "Good heavens! So my sins follow me, even here. Oh, of course—you're working from the Foundation's records. I did report that case of bastardy to the Foundation. Had to keep it straight there."

Both Ishtar and Tamara were looking puzzled. Justin said, "Excuse me, Grandma Maureen"—and spoke to them in that other language. Then he added to me, "The concept of bastardy is not known here; issue from a coupling is either genetically satisfactory or not satisfactory. The idea that a child could be proscribed by civil statute is difficult to explain."

Tamara had looked startled, then giggled, when Justin explained "bastardy." Ishtar had simply looked sober. She spoke to Justin, again in Galacta.

He listened, then turned to me. "Dr. Ishtar says that it is regrettable that only once did you accept another father for one of your children. She tells me that she hopes to get many more children from you, each by a different father. After you are rejuvenated, she means."

" 'After,' " I repeated. "But I'm looking forward to it. Justin, you have a book for me?"

That book was titled *The Lives of Lazarus Long,* with a secondary title that started "The Lives of the Senior Member

of the Howard Families (Woodrow Wilson Smith . . . Lazarus
Long . . . Corporal Ted Bronson—[and a dozen other names])
Oldest Member of the Human Race—"

I didn't faint. Instead I teetered on the brink of orgasm.
Ishtar, aware somewhat of the customs of my time and place,
had hesitated to let me know that my lover of 1918 was actually my son. But she could not know that I had never felt
bound by the taboos of my clan and was as untroubled by
the idea of incest as a tomcat is. Indeed, the greatest disappointment of my life was my inability to get my father to
accept what I had been so willing to give him, from menarche
till I lost him.

I still haven't been able to do anything with Lizzie Borden's
disclosure that this city I'm in is Kansas City. Or one of its
permutations, that is. I don't think I am in one of the universes
patrolled by the Time Corps, although I can't be certain. So
far, all I have seen of the city is what can be seen from the
balcony off the lounge of the Committee for Aesthetic Deletions.

It's the correct geography all right. North of here, about
ten miles away, is the sharp bend in the Missouri River where
it swings from southwest to northeast at the point where the
Kaw River flows into it—a configuration that causes big floods
in the west bottoms every five or six years.

Between here and there is the unmistakable tall shaft of
the War Memorial . . . but it is not the War Memorial in this
universe; it is the Sacred Phallus of the Great Inseminator.

(It reminds me of the time Lazarus tried to check the his-
toricity of the man known as Yeshua or Joshua or Jesus. He
had not been able to track Him down through census or tax
records of that time at Nazareth or Bethlehem, so he went
looking for the most prominent event in the legend: the Cru-
cifixion. He did not find it. Oh, he found crucifixions on
Golgotha all right—but just common criminals, no political
evangelists, no godstruck young rabbis. He tried again and
again, using various theories to date it . . . and got so frustrated that he started calling it the "Crucifiction." His current
theory involves a really strong Fabulist of the second century
Julian.)

The only time I've been outdoors here was the night of
Fiesta de Carolita . . . and then I saw only the big park in

which the Fiesta was held (Swope Park?), with many bonfires and flambeaux, endless bodies wearing masks and body paint, and the most amazing gang bang I have ever heard of, even in Rio. And a witches' esbat, but you can see those anywhere if you hold the Sign and know the Word. (I was stooled in Santa Fe in 1976, Wicca rite.)

But it is amusing to see one held right out in public, on the one night of the year when correct dress for a sabbat or esbat wouldn't be noticed and odd behavior is the order of the day. What chutzpah!

Could this possibly be my own time line during the reign of the Prophets? (The twenty-first century, more or less—) The fact that they know of Santa Carolita lends plausibility to the idea, but this does not match too well any accounts that I have read of America under the Prophets. So far as I know the Time Corps does not maintain an office in Kansas City in the twenty-first century on time line two.

If I could hire a copter and a pilot I would search fifty miles south of here and attempt to find Thebes, where I was born. If I found it, it would give me an anchor to reality. If I failed to find it, that would tell me that after a while some husky nurses would take me out of this wetpack and feed me.

If I had any money. If I could get away from these ghouls. If I wasn't afraid of the Supreme Bishop's proctors. If I didn't think it would get my arse shot off in the air.

Lizzie has promised to buy me a harness for Pixel. Not to walk him on a leash (impossible!) but to carry a message. The bit of string around his neck that I used on my last attempt apparently did not work. He may have clawed away that bit of paper, or broken the string.

Ishtar set a date seventeen months after my arrival in Boondock for rendezvous with the persons involved in rescuing me in 1982: Theodore/Lazarus/Woodrow (I have to think of him as three persons in one, like another Trinity), his clone-sisters Lapis Lazuli and Lorelei Lee, Elizabeth Andrew Jackson Libby Long, Zeb and Deety Carter, Hilda Mae and Jacob Burroughs, and two sentient computers both animating ships, Gay Deceiver and Dora. Ishtar had assured Hilda (and me) that seventeen months would be long enough to make me young again.

Ishtar pronounced me done in only fifteen months. I can't

give details of my rejuvenation because I knew nothing of such details at the time—not until I was accepted as an apprentice technician years later, after I had become the Boondock equivalent of RN and M.D. At the medical school hospital and at the rejuvenation clinic they use a drug tagged "Lethe" that lets one do horrid things to a patient but have him not even recall that they happened. So I do not remember the bad days of my rejuvenation but only the pleasant, lazy ones during which I read Theodore's memoirs, as edited by Justin . . . and I spotted the authentic Woodie touch; the raconteur lied whenever he felt like it.

But it was fascinating. Theodore really had felt moral qualms about coupling with me. My goodness! You can take the boy out of the Bible Belt, but you can never quite take the Bible Belt out of the boy. Not even centuries later and after experiencing other and often better cultures utterly unlike Missouri.

One thing in those memoirs made me proud of my "naughty" son: He seems to have been always incapable of abandoning wife and child. Since (in my opinion) much of the decay that led to the decline and fall of the United States had to do with males who shrugged off their duty to pregnant women and young children, I found myself willing to forgive my "bad boy" for all his foibles since he never wavered in this prime virtue. A male must be willing to live and to die for his female and their cubs . . . else he is nothing.

Woodrow, selfish as he was in many respects, in this acid test measured up.

I was delighted to learn just how intensely Theodore had wanted my body. Since I had wanted him with burning intensity, it warmed me all through to read proof that he had wanted me just as badly. I had never been quite sure of it at the time (a woman in heat can be an awful fool) and was still less sure of it as the years wore on. Yet here was proof: eyes open, he shoved his head into the lion's mouth for me—for my sake he had enlisted in a war that was not his . . . and "got his arse shot off" as his sisters expressed it. (His sisters—*my* daughters. Goodness!)

In addition to Lazarus's memoirs, I read histories that Justin gave me. I also learned Galacta by the total-immersion method. After my first two weeks in Boondock I asked that no English whatever be spoken around me and asked Teena for the Galacta edition of Theodore's memoirs and reread them in that language. Soon I was fluent in Galacta and beginning to think in it. Galacta is rooted in Spanglish, the auxiliary language that was beginning to be used for trade and engineering purposes up and down the two Americas in the twentieth century, a devised language formed by taking as vocabulary the intersection of English and Spanish and manipulating that vocabulary by Hispanic grammar—somewhat simplified for the benefit of Anglophonic users of this lingua franca.

At a later time Lazarus told me that Spanglish had been adopted as the official language for space pilots clear back at the time of the Space Precautionary Act, when all licensed space pilots were employees of Spaceways, Ltd., or some other Harriman Industries subsidiary. He told me that Galacta was still recognizably the same language as Spanglish centuries, millennia, later—although with a much amplified vocabulary—much the same way and for the same reasons that the Latin of the Caesars had been conserved and augmented for thousands of years by the Church of Rome. Each language filled a need that kept it alive and growing.

"I always wanted to live in a world designed by Maxfield Parrish—and now I do!" These words open a journal I started to write, early in my rejuvenation, to keep my thoughts straight in the face of the culture shock I felt in being lifted bodily out of the Crazy Years of Tellus Prime and plunked down in the almost Apollonian culture of Tellus Tertius.

Maxfield Parrish was a romantic artist of my time and place (1870–1966) who used a realistic style and technique to paint a world more beautiful than any ever seen—a world of cloud-capped towers and gorgeous girls and breath-stopping mountain peaks. If "Maxfield Parrish blue" means nothing to you, go to the museum of BIT and enjoy the M.P. collection there, "stolen" by means of a replicating pantograph from twentieth-century museums on the East Coast of North America (and one painting in the lobby of the Broadmoor) by a Time Corps private mission paid for by the Senior, Lazarus Long— a birthday present to his mother on her 125th birthday to celebrate the silver anniversary of their marriage.

Yes, my naughty-boy son Woodrow married me, sandbagged into it by his co-wives and brother husbands, as a result of their having sandbagged me into it—a working majority of them; Woodrow had three of his wives with him, his twin clone-sisters and Elizabeth who used to be Andrew Libby before his reincarnation as a woman.

At that time (Galactic 4324) the Long family had seven adults in residence: Ira Weatheral, Galahad, Justin Foote, Hamadryad, Tamara, Ishtar, and Minerva. Galahad, Justin, Ishtar, and Tamara you have met; Ira Weatheral was the executive of such government as Boondock had (not much); Hamadryad was his daughter who had obviously made a pact with the Devil; Minerva was a slender, long-haired brunette who had had a career of more than two centuries as an administrative computer before getting Ishtar's assistance in becoming flesh and blood through an assembled-clone technique.

They picked Galahad and Tamara to propose to me.

I had no plans to get married. I had married once "till death do us part"—and it had turned out not to be that durable. I was most happy to be living in Boondock, my cup overflowed at growing young again, and I was looking forward with almost unbearable delight at the expectation of being again in Theodore's arms. But marriage? Why take vows that are usually broken?

Galahad said, "Mama Maureen, these vows will not be broken. We simply promise each other to share in taking care of our children—support them and spank them and love them and teach them, whatever it takes. Now believe me, this is how to do it. Marry us now; settle it with Lazarus later. We love him—but we know him. In an emergency Lazarus is the fastest gun in the Galaxy. But hand him a simple little social problem and he'll dither around about it, trying to see all sides to arrive at the perfect answer. So the only way to win an argument with Lazarus is to present him with an accomplished fact. He'll be home now in a few weeks—Ishtar knows the exact hour. If he finds you married into the family and already pregnant, he will simply shut up and marry you himself. If you will have him."

"In marrying all of you, am I not marrying Lazarus, too?"

"Not necessarily. Both Hamadryad and Ira were members of our founding family group. But it took several years before Ira admitted that there was no reason for him not to marry his own daughter—Hamadryad just smiled and outwaited him. Then we held a special wedding ceremony just for them and what a luau that was! Honest, Mama Maureen, our arrangements are flexible; the only invariant is that everybody guarantees the future of any babies you pretty little broads give us. We don't even ask where you got them . . . since some of you tend to be vague about such things."

Tamara interrupted to tell me that Ishtar watches such matters. (Galahad tends to joke. Tamara doesn't know how to joke. But she loves everybody.) So later that day I said my vows with all of them, standing in the middle of their beautiful atrium garden (*our* garden!)—crying and smiling and all of them touching me and Ira sniffling and Tamara smiling while tears ran down her face, and we all said, "I do!" together and they all kissed me, and I knew they were mine and I was theirs, forever and ever, amen.

I got pregnant at once because Ishtar had timed it so that our wedding and my ovulation matched—Ira and Ishtar had planned the whole thing. (When I had that baby girl, after the usual cow-or-countess gestation period, I asked Ishtar about the baby's paternity. She said, "Mama Maureen, that one is from all your husbands; you don't need to know. After you've had four or five more, if you are still curious, I'll sort them out for you." I never asked again.)

So I was pregnant when Theodore returned, which suited me just fine . . . as I was sure from past experience that he would greet me more heartily and with less restraint if he knew that it was certain that copulation with me would be solely for love—and sweet pleasure—and sheer, sweaty fun. Not for progeny.

And so it was. But at a party that started out with Theodore fainting dead away. Hilda Mae, the head of the task force that rescued me, had rigged a surprise party for Theodore, in which she had presented me to him dressed in a costume of high symbology to him—heeled slippers, long sheer hose, green garters—at a time when he thought that I was still in Albuquerque two millennia earlier and still in need of rescue.

Hilda did not intend to shock Theodore so sharply that he fainted—she loves him, and later she married Theodore and all of us, along with her husband and family—Hilda does not have a mean bone in her little elfin body. She caught Theodore as he fainted, or tried to, and he wasn't hurt and the party developed into one of the best since Rome burned. Hilda Mae has many other talents, in and out of bed, but she is the best party arranger in any world.

A couple of years later Hilda was director general of the

biggest party ever held anywhere, bigger than the Field of the Cloth of Gold: the First Centennial Convention of the Interuniversal Society for Eschatological Pantheistic Multiple-Ego Solipsism, with guests from dozens of universes. It was a wonderful party and the few people killed in the games went straight to Valhalla—I saw them go. From that party our family gained several more husbands and wives—eventually, not all in one day—especially Hazel Stone aka Gwen Novak who is as dear to me as Tamara, and Dr. Jubal Harshaw, the one of my husbands to whom I turn when I truly need advice.

It was to Jubal that I turned many years later when I found that despite all the wonders of Boondock and Tertius, all the loving happiness of being a cherished member of the Long Family, despite the satisfaction of studying the truly advanced therapy of Tertius and Secundus, and at last being apprenticed to the best profession of all, rejuvenator, something was missing.

I had never stopped thinking about my father, missing him always, with an ache in my heart.

Consider these facts:

1) Lib had been raised from dead, a frozen corpse, and reincarnated as a woman.

2) I had been rescued from certain death, across the centuries. (When an eighteen-wheeler runs over a person my size, they pick up the remains with blotting paper.)

3) Colonel Richard Campbell had twice been rescued from certain death and had had history changed simply to calm his soul, because his services were needed to save the computer that led the Lunar Revolution on time line three.

4) Theodore himself had been missing in action, chopped half in two by machine-gun fire . . . yet he had been rescued and restored without even a scar.

5) My father was "missing in action," too. The AFS didn't even get around to reporting him as missing until long after the fact and there were no details.

6) In the thought experiment called "Schrödinger's Cat" the scientists(?), or philosophers, or metaphysicians, who devised it, maintain that the cat is neither dead nor alive but simply a fog of probabilities, until somebody opens the box.

I don't believe it. I don't think Pixel would believe it.

•   •   •

But— Is my father alive? or dead? away back there in the twentieth century?

So I spoke to Jubal about it.

He said, "I can't tell you, Mama Maureen. How badly do you want your father to be alive?"

"More than anything in the world!"

"Enough to risk everything on it? Your life? Still worse, the chance of disappointment? Of knowing that all hope is gone?"

I sighed deeply. "Yes. All of that."

"Then join the Time Corps and learn how such things are done. In a few years—ten to twenty years, I would guess— you will be able to form an intelligent opinion."

" 'Ten to twenty years'!"

"It could take longer. But the great beauty about time manipulations is that there is always plenty of time, never any hurry."

When I told Ishtar that I wanted to take an indefinite leave of absence, she did not ask me why. She simply said, "Mama, I have known for some time that you were not happy in this work; I have been waiting for you to discover it."

She kissed me. "Perhaps next century you will find a true vocation for this work. There is no hurry. Meanwhile, be happy."

So for about twenty years of my personal time line and almost seven years of Boondock time I went where I was told to go and reported on what I was told to investigate. Never as a fighter. Not like Gretchen, whose first baby is descended both from me (Colonel Ames is my grandson through Lazarus) and from my co-wife Hazel/Gwen (Gretchen is Hazel's great-granddaughter)—Major Gretchen is a big, strong, strapping Valkyrie, reputed to be sudden death with or without weapons.

Fighting is not for Maureen. But the Time Corps needs all sorts. My talent for languages and my love of history makes me suitable to be sent to "scout the Land of Canaan"—or Nippon in the 1930s—or whatever country or planet needs scouting. My only other talent is sometimes useful, too.

So with twenty years of practice and some preliminary research in history of time line two, second phase of the Permanent War, I signed off for a weekend and bought a ticket on a Burroughs-Carter time-space bus, one with a scheduled stop in New Liverpool, 1950, intending to scout the history of the 1939–1945 War a little closer up. Hilda had developed a thriving black-market trade through the universes; one of her companies supplied scheduled services to the explored time lines and planets for a bracket of dates—exact date of choice available if you pay for it.

The bus driver had just announced "New Liverpool Earth Prime 1950 time line two next stop! Don't leave any personal possessions aboard"—when there was a loud noise, the bus lurched, a trip attendant said, "Emergency exit—this way, please"—and somebody handed me a baby, there was much smoke, and I saw a man with a bloody stump where his right arm should have been.

I guess I passed out, as I don't remember what happened next.

I woke up in bed with Pixel and a corpse.

26

Pixel to the Rescue

After that Mad Tea Party in which I woke up in bed with a cat and a corpse in Grand Hotel Augustus, Pixel and I wound up in the office of Dr. Eric Ridpath, house physician, where we met his office nurse, Dagmar Dobbs—a gal who was at once awarded Pixel's stamp of approval. Dagmar was giving me a GYN examination, when she told me that tonight was La Fiesta de Santa Carolita.

It is a good thing that just before she put me on the table she had required me to pee in a cup, or I might have peed in her face.

As I have explained in excessive detail, "Santa Carolita" is my daughter Carol, born in Gregorian 1902 at Kansas City on Tellus Prime, time line two, code Leslie LeCroix.

Lazarus Long had initiated "Carol's Day" on June twenty-sixth, 1918 Gregorian, as a rite of passage for Carol, marking her transition from childhood to womanhood. Lazarus toasted Carol in champagne, telling her what a wonderful thing it was to be a woman, naming for her both the privileges and the responsibilities of her new and exalted status, and declaring that June twenty-sixth should then and forever be known as "Carol's Day."

The notion of calling it "Carol's Day" had suggested itself to Lazarus from something he remembered from a thousand years in the future—or in the past, depending on your time frame. On the frontier planet New Beginnings he and his wife Dora had declared "Helen's Day" to celebrate puberty in their oldest child, Helen. That was their stated purpose. Their unstated purpose was to attempt to place some control over the sexual behavior of their growing sons and daughters, in order to head off the sort of tragedy I ran into with Priscilla and Donald.

Neither Lazarus nor I (nor Dora) had moralistic notions about incest, but all of us had feared the damage incest can do, both genetically and socially. "Helen's Day" and "Carol's Day" gave each set of parents some leverage in handling the touchy problems of sex in young people, problems that so easily can end in tragedy . . . but need not.

(I despise most in Marian her self-indulgent failure to carry out the parental duty of maintaining discipline. "Spare the rod and spoil the child" is not sadistic; it is hard common sense. You fail your children worst if you do not punish them when they need it. The lessons you fail to teach them will be taught later and much more harshly by a cruel world, the real world where no excuses are accepted, the world of TANSTAAFL and of Mrs. BeDoneByAsYouDid.)

Lazarus told me (centuries later or years later—a matter of viewpoint) that he was halfway through his toast to Carol when he suddenly realized that he was inaugurating the most widespread holiday of the human race: Carolita's Day—and that he has been trying ever since to decide which came first: the chicken or the egg.

Chicken or egg, Carol's Day did develop over the centuries and on many planets into a public holiday—this I learned when I was taken to Tertius. Usually it was celebrated just for the fun of it, the way the Japanese celebrate Christmas, as a secular holiday having nothing to do with religion.

But in some cultures it developed as a religious holiday peculiar to theocracies: the safety-valve holiday, the day of excesses, of sin without punishment, the saturnalia.

•   •   •

While I got out of those silly stirrups and down off that cold table and put on my "clothes" (a caftan rigged from a beach towel), Dr. Ridpath and Dagmar looked over my test results. They pronounced me healthy—merely out of my skull, which neither of them seemed to regard as important.

Dr. Ridpath said, "Explain things to her, Dag. I'm going to take a shower and get ready."

"What do you want to do, Maureen?" Dagmar asked me. "Doc tells me that your total assets are that terry cloth tent you're wearing and this orange cat. Pixel! Stop that! This is not a night you can go to a police station and ask your way to the county poor farm; tonight the cops skin down and join in the riot." She looked me up and down. "If you go out on the streets tonight—well—you'd have a quieter time in—a lion's den. Maybe you like such things—many do. Me, f'rinstance. But tonight a gal is either locked up or knocked up. You can stay here, sleep on the couch. I can find you a blanket. Pixel! Get down from there!"

"Come here, Pixel." I held out both hands; he jumped into my arms. "How about the Salvation Army?"

"The what?"

I tried to explain. She shook her head. "Never heard of it. Sounds like another of your daydreams, dear; nothing of that sort is ever authorized by the Church of Your Choice."

"What church is your choice?"

"Huh? Your choice, my choice, everybody's choice—the Church of the Great Inseminator, of course—what other church be there? If it's not your choice, a ride on a rail might clarify your thinking. It would mine."

I shook my head. "Dagmar, I'm more and more confused. Back where I come from there is total religious freedom."

"That's what we have here, ducks—and don't let a proctor hear you say anything else." She suddenly smiled like the Wicked Witch of the West. "Although there are always some proctors and some priests found stone cold dead in the dawn's early light, grinning in *risus sardonicus,* the morning after Saint Carol's feast; I am not the only widow with a long memory."

I must have looked stupid. "You're a widow? I'm sorry."

"I talk too much. Not all that tragic, luv. Marriages are made in Heaven, as everybody knows, and my patron priest picked for me just the man Heaven had in mind for me, no possible doubt and you'll never hear me say otherwise. But when Delmer—my appointed soulmate—fell out of favor at the throne and was trimmed, well, I cried but not too long. Delmer is an altar boy now and quite a favorite among the male sopranos, so I understand. The awkward part is that, since he isn't actually dead, just trimmed, I can't marry again." She looked bleak.

Then she shrugged and smiled. "So Santa Carolita's night is a big night for me, seeing how closely we are watched all the rest of the year."

I said, "I'm confused again. Are you saying that things are puritanical here?—except this one night?"

"I'm not sure I know what you mean by 'puritanical,' Maureen. And I have trouble staying with your 'Man from Mars' pose—if it is a pose—"

"It's not a pose! Dagmar, I truly am lost. I'm not on my own planet; I don't know anything at all about this place."

"All right, I'll throw in with you, I said I would. But it is hard to keep it in mind. Okay, the way things work here— Three hundred and sixty-four days of the year—sixty-five on leap years—everything is either required or forbidden. 'The Golden Rule,' the Supreme Bishop calls it—God's Plan. But on Carolita's feast day, from sundown to sunrise, anything goes. Carolita is the patron saint of street singers, whores, Gypsies, vagabonds, actors, of all who must live outside the city walls. So on her day— Boss! You're not going outdoors in *that* outfit!"

"And why not?"

Dagmar made retching noises; I turned to see what the fuss was about. The doctor had gone to shower, had returned still stripped down and sporting the most amazing phallus I have ever seen. It was standing straight up, rising out of a wide, dense briar patch of dark brown curls. It thrust up at least twelve inches from that curly base. Just back of the miter it was as thick as my wrist. It curved back slightly toward his hairy belly.

It "breathed" when he did, bowing an inch at each breath. I looked at it in horrified fascination the way a bird looks at a snake, and felt my nipples grow crisp. Take it away! Get a stick and kill it!

"Boss, take that silly toy right back to Sears Roebuck and demand your money back! Or I'll, I'll— I'll flush it down the pot, that's what I'll do!"

"You do and you'll pay the plumber's bill. Look, Dagmar, I'm going to wear it home and I want you to snap a pic of Zenobia's face when she sees it. Then I'll take it off . . . unless Zenobia decides she wants me to wear it to the mayor's orgy. Now get into your costume; we still have to pick up Daffy and his assistant. His goose, although he claims otherwise. Move. Shake your tail, frail."

"Pee on you, Boss."

"Has the sun gone down so soon? Maureen, if I understood you earlier, you have not eaten today. Come have dinner with us and we can discuss what to do with you later; my wife is the best cook in town. Right, Dagmar?"

"Correct, Boss. That makes twice this week you've been right."

"When was the other time? Did you find something for Cinderella to wear?"

"It's a problem, Boss. All I have here are jumpsuit uniforms, cut for me. On Maureen they would fit too soon in one direction, too late in the other." (She meant that I'm shaped like a pear while she is shaped more like celery.)

Dr. Ridpath looked at me, then at her, decided that Dagmar was right. "Maureen, we'll see what my wife has that you can wear. It won't matter between here and there; you'll be in a robocab. Pixel! Dinnertime, boy!"

"Now? *Wow!*"

So we had dinner at the home of the Ridpaths. Zenobia Ridpath is indeed a good cook. Pixel and I appreciated her, and she appreciated Pixel and was warmly hospitable to me. Zenobia is a dignified matron, beautiful, about forty-five, with premature white hair tinted with a blue rinse. Her face did not change when she saw the mechanical monstrosity her husband was sporting. He said, "What do you think this is, Zen?"

She answered, "Oh, at last! You promised it to me as a wedding present all these many years ago! Well, better late than never—I think." She stooped and looked at it. "Why does it have 'Made in Japan' printed on it?" She straightened up and smiled at us. "Hello, Dagmar, good to see you. Happy festival!"

"Bumper crops!"

"Big babies! Mrs. Johnson, it was sweet of you to come. May I call you 'Maureen'? And may I offer you some crab legs? Flown in from Japan, like my husband's new peepee. And what would you like to drink?" A polite little machine rolled up with crab legs and other tasty tidbits, and took my drink order—*Cuba Libre* but omit the rum.

Mrs. Ridpath congratulated Dagmar on her costume: a black, sheer body stocking covering even her head—but missing wherever presence of garment would get in the way at a Saturnalia: cutaway crotch, breasts bare, mouth bare. The result was glaringly obscene.

Zenobia's costume was provocative but pretty—a blue fog that matched her eyes and did not hide much. Daffy Weisskopf climbed right up her front, making jungle noises. She just smiled at him. "Have something to eat first, Doctor. And save some of your strength for after midnight."

I think Dr. Eric's suspicions about Dr. Daffy's assistant, Freddie, were justified; he did not smell right to me and I apparently did not smell right to him—and I was beginning to be whiff, as I was starting to get into a party mood. As I had requested, that *Cuba Libre* had no rum in it, but I had half of it inside me before I realized that it was loaded with vodka—one hundred proof, I feel certain. Vodka is tricky; it has no odor and no taste . . . and now I lay me down to sleep—

I think some of those appetizers had aphrodisiacs concealed in them . . . and Maureen does not need aphrodisiacs. Has never needed them.

There were three sorts of wine at dinner and endless toasts that rapidly progressed from suggestive to outrageous. The little robot that waited on my sector of the table kept the wine glasses filled but was not programed to understand "water"—and Mama Maureen got potted.

No use pretending anything else. I had too little to eat and too much to drink and too little sleep and I never have learned to drink like a lady. I had simply learned how to pretend to drink while avoiding alcohol. But on Carolita's night I let my guard down.

I had planned to ask Zenobia to permit me to stay overnight in her house . . . then on the morrow, festival over, I could tackle a city restored to its senses. First I needed a minimum of money and clothes . . . and there are ways to get both without actually stealing. A female can often wangle an unsecured loan if she hits a male for it who shows a tendency to pat her in a friendly fashion. She can hint pretty strongly as to the interest she is willing to pay . . . and every female Time Corps field agent has done something like that on occasion. We aren't nervous virgins; we don't leave Boondock without being vaccinated against pregnancy and nineteen other things you might catch if a trouser worm bit you. If you are too tender-minded for such emergency measures, you don't belong in the profession. Females are better than males as Time Corps scouts because they can get away with such things. My co-wife Gwen/Hazel could steal the spots off a leopard and never disturb his sleep. If she were sent after the Rheingold, Fafnir and his flaming halitosis would not stand a chance.

Having acquired that minimum of local money and local clothing, my next move would be a preliminary study to determine: 1) how to get more money in this culture without going to jail; 2) where, if anywhere, is the Time Corps message drop; 3) if the second point is null, where is the dummy front for Hilda's crosstime black-marketeers? Most of this can be researched unobtrusively either at a public library or in a telephone directory.

All very professional— Instead I got snagged by the proctors and did not do any of it.

Zenobia insisted that I go with them to the mayor's orgy, and by then I lacked the judgment to refuse. She selected costume for me, too, from her clothes: Long sheer hose, green round garters, high heels, and a cape . . . and somehow it seemed to me the perfect costume, just right, although I could not remember why I thought so.

I recall only vignettes of the mayor's party. Perhaps it will help to think of a party given jointly by Caligula and Nero, as directed by Cecil B. de Mille in gorgeous Technicolor. I remember telling some oaf (I can't remember his face; I'm not sure he had a face) that it was not impossible to lay me— many have tried and most succeeded—but it had to be approached romanticlike, not like a man grabbing a bite standing up at a fast-food joint.

That party and the rest of that night was rape, rape, rape, all around me . . . and I do not care for rape; one does not meet a better class of people that way.

I escaped from that party and found myself out in the park. My leaving had to do with a pompous ass dressed in a long robe (a cope?) of white silk heavily embroidered in cardinal and gold. It was open down the front with his *Flaggenstange* sticking out. He was so self-important that he had four acolytes to help him with the chore.

He grabbed me as I was trying to slide past—stuck his tongue in my mouth. I kneed him and ran, and jumped out an open window. Ground floor, yes—but I did not stop to find out.

Pixel caught up with me in about fifty yards, then slowed me somewhat as he criss-crossed ahead of me. We went into that big park and I slowed to a walk. I was still wearing the cape but I had lost one slipper going out the window, then had kicked off the other at once, being unable to run one shoe off, one shoe on. It did not matter as I had gone barefooted so habitually in Boondock that my feet were as tough as shoe leather.

I wandered around the park for a while, watching the action (amazing!) and wondering where I could go. I did not want to risk the mayor's palace again; my pompous boy friend with the fancy vestment might still be there. I did not know where the Ridpaths lived even though I had been there. It seemed to me that I must wait for dawn, then locate Grand Hotel Augustus (should be easy), go to Dr. Eric's office on the mezzanine, and hit him for a small loan. Hobson's choice, no other option—but not too unlikely as he had brailled me quite thoroughly during dinner. He wasn't being rude; similar things or more so were going on all around the table. And I had been warned.

I joined in briefly at that esbat—midnight, full moon overhead, and ritual prayers being said in Latin, Greek, Old Norse (I think), and three other languages. One woman was a snake goddess from ancient Crete. Authentic? I don't know. Pixel rode my shoulder at the service as if he were used to the role of witch's familiar.

As I left the altar, he jumped down, ran ahead of me as usual.

I heard a shout. "There's her cat! And there she is! Grab her!"

And they did.

As I've said, I don't like rape. I especially dislike it when four men hold me while a fat slob in an embroidered cope does things to my body. So I bit him. And discussed his ancestry and personal habits.

So I wound up in the hoosegow and stayed there until the crazies from the Committee for Aesthetic Deletions pulled a jailbreak and got me loose.

This is called, "Out of the frying pan and into the fire."

Last night the Committee was presided over by Count Dracula, the only case of type casting that I saw—this repulsively handsome creature not only wore the opera cloak associated with video vampires, he also had taken the trouble to have a mouthpiece fashioned for him by a prosthodontist; he had dog teeth that came down over his lower lip. At least I assume that they were artificial; I don't really believe that any humans or quasi humans have teeth like that.

I joined the circle and took the one remaining chair. "Good evening, cousins. And good evening to you, Count. Where is the Old Man of the Mountain tonight?"

"That is not a question one asks."

"Well, excuse me, please! And pray, why not?"

"We will leave that to you as an exercise in deduction. But don't ask such a question again. And do not be late again. You are the subject of our discussion tonight, Lady Mac-Beth—"

"Maureen Johnson, if you please."

"It does not please me. It is one more instance of your unwillingness to observe the rules necessary to the safety of the Dead Men. Yesterday you were observed exchanging words with one of the hotel staff, a chambermaid. What were you talking about?"

I stood up. "Count Dracula."

"Yes, Lady MacBeth?"

"You can go to hell. And I am going to bed."

"Sit down!"

I did not. But all those near me grabbed at me, and sat me down. I don't think any three could have managed it; they all were ill, deathly ill. But seven were too much for me— and I was reluctant to be rough in resisting them.

The chairman went on, "Milady MacBeth, you have been with us over two weeks now. During that time you have refused every mission offered you. You owe us for your rescue—"

"Nonsense! The Committee owes me! I would never have been in a position to need rescue had you not kidnaped me and shoved me into bed with a corpse, one of your killings, Judge Hardacres. Don't talk to me about what I owe the Committee! You returned some of my clothes—but where's my purse? Why did you drug me? How dare you kidnap an innocent visitor to dress up one of your assassinations? Who planned that job? I want to talk to him."

"Lady MacBeth."

"Yes?"

"Hold your tongue. You will now have a mission assigned to you. It has been planned and you will carry it out tonight. The client is Major General Lew Rawson, retired. He was in charge of the recent provocation incident in—"

"Count Dracula!"

"Yes?"

"Go hang by your heels!"

"Don't interrupt again. The operation has been fully planned. Jack the Ripper and Lucrezia Borgia will go with you, and coach you. You can kill him in his bed, or, if you balk, you will be killed as he is killed and the two of you arranged in a tableau that will give substance to the rumors about him."

The attention of everyone was on the row between the new chairman and me; proctors poured in off the balcony before they were seen. But a voice I recognized called out, "Watch it, Maureen!" and I dived for the deck.

The robes and hoods were the Ku Klux Klan ersatz of the proctors, but the voice was the voice of Dagmar. When I turned my head at her voice, I spotted Pixel with her.

Time Corps military units have stun guns they use when killing must be selective. They fanned the room with them. I got the edge of one charge, did not quite pass out but did not object when a big, husky proctor (one of my husbands!) scooped me up. Then we were all out on the balcony and into a small troop carrier hovering at the rail.

I heard the door close, felt it in my ears. "Ready?"

"Ready!"

"Has somebody got Pixel?"

"I've got him! Let's go!" (Hilda's voice)

And then we were home in Boondock, on the parking lawn at the Long residence.

A voice I know well said, "Secure all systems," and the pilot turned in his seat and looked at me. "Mama," he said mournfully, "you sure give me a lot of grief."

"I'm sorry, Woodrow."

"Why didn't you tell me? I would have helped."

"I'm sure you would, dear. But I was merely scouting."

"But you should have—"

Hilda interrupted. "Stop it, Lazarus. Mama Maureen is tired and probably hungry. Mama, Tamara has lunch ready. Two hours from now—local time fourteen hundred—is an operation briefing, all hands. Jubal in charge of the briefing and—"

" 'Operation briefing'? What operation?"

"Your operation, Mama," Woodrow answered. "We're going to go find Gramp. Either rescue him, or slip him into a body bag. But we're doing it right, this time. It's a Time Corps major operation, resources as needed; the Circle of Ouroboros is unanimous. Mama, why didn't you tell me?"

Hilda said, "Shut up, Woodie. And stay shut. We've got Mama Maureen back and that's all that counts. Right, Pixel?"

"Rrrrite!"

"So let's go to lunch."

27

At the Coventry Cusp

I didn't eat much.

The party was in my honor and I loved it. But I needed two mouths, one for eating, one for the fifty-odd people who wanted to kiss me—and I wanted to kiss them. I wasn't really hungry. Even when I was a prisoner in the Cathedral the food had been adequate, and when I was another sort of prisoner with the Committee for Aesthetic Deletions, I was quite well fed, within the limits of hotel cooking.

But I was starved for love, and warm and loving people.

Did I say the party was in my honor? Well, yes, but any party Pixel attends is primarily in his honor. He is sure of that and behaves accordingly. He zigzagged among the couches, tail high, accepting hand feeding, and rubbing against his friends and retainers.

Dagmar came over, asked Laz to make room, and squeezed in by me—hugged me and kissed me. I found that I was leaking tears. "Dagmar, I can't tell you how I felt when I heard your voice. Are you going to stay here? You'll like it here."

She grinned at me, hanging on to my neck. "Do you think I want to go back to Kansas City? Compared with Kay See, Boondock is Heaven."

"Good! I'll sponsor you." I had my arm around her, which caused me to add, "You've put on a few pounds and it becomes you. And such a beautiful tan! Or is it out of a spray bomb?"

"No, I did it the best way, lying in the sun and increasing the dosage slowly. Maureen, you won't believe what a treat sunbathing is to someone who would be risking a public flogging if she sunbathed in her home town."

Laz said, "Mama, I wish I could tan the way Dagmar does, instead of these kingsize freckles."

"You get that from me, Lapis Lazuli; I always freckle. It's the price we pay for red hair."

"I know. But Dagmar can sunbathe every day, month after month, and never get a freckle. Look at her."

I sat up straight. "What did you say?"

"I said she doesn't freckle. All our men are following her around." Laz tickled Dagmar in the ribs. "Aren't they, Dag?"

"Not so!"

"You said, 'Month after month—' Dagmar, I saw you last two weeks ago. Less than three. How long have you been here?"

"Me? Uh . . . slightly over two years. Yours was a tough case—or so they tell me."

After being in the Time Corps twenty years of my personal time, seven years of Boondock time, I should not have been surprised. Time paradox is no news to me; I keep a careful journal to keep me sorted out, Maureen's personal time versus times and time lines and dates for each of the places I scout. But this time I was the subject of the operation (Operation Triple-M = Mama Maureen is Missing). I had been gone (my personal time) five and a half weeks . . . but it had taken over two years to find me and rescue me.

Laz called Hilda over to straighten me out. She snuggled in between Lorelei Lee and me on my other side; the couch was getting crowded. But Hilda does not take up much space.

She said, "Mama Maureen, you told Tamara that you were just going away for a day's holiday. She knew you were fibbing, of course, but she never contradicts any of our little white lies. She thought you were just shuttling to Secundus for some private fun and maybe some shopping."

"Hilda Mae, I did intend to be back here the next day, no matter how long I spent in research. I planned to spend a few weeks in the British Museum in 1950, time line two, soaking up as much detail as possible about the Battle of Britain, 1940–41. I had a fresh recorder implant for that purpose. I didn't dare go to England during that war without careful preparation; England was a battle zone—easy to be shot as a spy. I would have done the research and been back the next day, in time for dinner . . . if that time-twister bus had not broken down."

"It didn't break down."

"Huh? I mean, 'Excuse me?' "

"It was sabotage, Mau. The Revisionists. The same pascoodnyoks who came so close to killing Richard and Gwen Hazel and Pixel on time line three. We don't know why they wanted to stop you, or why they chose that method; neither side was taking prisoners, and we killed too many too fast. By 'we' I don't mean me; I'm the drawing-room type as everybody knows. I mean the old pros, Richard and Gwen and Gretchen and a strike force from time line five commanded by Lensman Ted Smith. But the Circle had put me in charge of Operation Triple-M, and I did dig out information that led us to the Revisionists. I got most of it from one of my employees, the pilot of that bus. I made a bad mistake, Maureen, in hiring that evil maggot. My poor judgment almost cost your life. I'm sorry."

"Sorry about what? Hilda Mae, my precious, if you hadn't rescued me in Albuquerque, years ago, I would be dead, dead, dead! Don't ever forget it, because I never forget it."

"Spare me your gratitude, Mau; I had fun. Both times. I borrowed some snakes from Patty Paiwonski and hung this oaf upside down over a snake pit while I questioned him. That sharpened his memory and got us the correct time line, place, and date—Kansas City in Gregorian 2184 starting at June twenty-sixth, on a previously unexplored variant of time line two, one in which the Second American Revolution never took place. It is now designated time line eleven, and is a nasty enough place that the Circle put it in the Someday File for cleaning or cauterizing when we get around to it."

Hilda leaned down and twiddled her fingers at Pixel, spoke to him in cat language; he came at once and settled in her lap, purring loudly. "We put agents into that version of Kansas City but they lost you the same day you arrived. Or that night. They traced you from Grand Hotel Augustus to a private home, from there to the mayor's palace, and then outdoors into the carnival. And lost you. But we had established that Pixel was with you . . . even though he was here every day, too. Or almost—"

"How does he do that?"

"How does Gay Deceiver have two portside bathrooms without being lopsided? Maureen, if you insist on believing in World-as-Logic you will never understand World-as-Myth. Pixel knows nothing about Einsteinian space-time, or the speed of light as a limit, or the Big Bang, or any of those fancies dreamed up by theorists, so they don't exist for him. Pixel knew where you were, inside the little world that does exist for him, but he doesn't speak much English. In Boondock, that is. So we took him where he can speak English—"

"Huh?"

"Oz, of course. Pixel doesn't know what a cathedral is but he was able to describe that one fairly well once we were able to get his mind off all those wonderful new places to investigate. The Cowardly Lion helped us question him, and for the first time in his life Pixel was impressed—I think he wants to grow up to be a lion. So we hurried back and sent a task force to get you out of the Supreme Bishop's private jail. And you weren't there."

Dagmar picked it up. "But I was, and Pixel led them straight to me—looking for you. I was in the cell you had been in— the proctors came for me as soon as you escaped."

"Yes," agreed Hilda. "Dagmar had befriended you and that was not a safe thing to do, especially after the Supreme Bishop died."

"Dagmar! I'm sorry!"

"About what? 'All's Well That Ends Well,' to coin a phrase. Look at me now, ducks; I like it here. So back they went to Oz, taking me along this time, and after I listened to Pixel, I was able to tell Hilda that you were being held in Grand Hotel Augustus—"

"Hey! That's where I started!"

"And that's where you wound up, too, in a suite that isn't in the hotel directory and can be reached from inside only by a private elevator from the sub-basement. So we came in by the scenic route, and caught the Committee with their pants down."

Lazarus had joined us, and now sat on the grass at my knees, without interrupting—and I wondered how long his angelic behavior would last. Now he said, "Mama, you don't know how true your words are. You remember when we moved? I was in high school."

"Yes, certainly. To our old farmhouse, out south."

"Yes. Then after World War Two you sold it, and it was torn down."

(How well I remembered!) "Torn down to build the Harriman Hilton. Yes."

"Well, Grand Hotel Augustus is the Harriman Hilton. Oh, after more than two centuries not much is the same structure, but the continuity is there. We researched it, and that's how we located this VIP suite that is not known to the public." He rubbed his cheek against my knee. "That's all, I guess. Hilda?"

"I think so."

"Wait a moment!" I protested. "What became of that baby? And the man with the bloody stump? The one with his arm chopped off in that accident."

"But, Maureen," Hilda said gently, "I tell you three times: It was not an accident. That 'baby' was just a prop, a lifelike animation, to keep your hands busy and your attention distracted. The 'wounded' man was a piece of grisly misdirection while they injected you—an old amputee with makeup; he wasn't freshly maimed. When I had my driver hanging over the snakes, he became downright loquacious and told me many details, mostly nasty."

"I'd like to speak to that driver!"

"I'm afraid you can't. I don't encourage employees to sell me out, Maureen. You are a gentle soul. I'm not."

"The surgical teams will be"—we were gathered in a lecture room in Ira Johnson Hall, BIT, and Jubal had started his briefing—"matched as nearly as possible in professional background. Tentatively they are:

"Dr. Maureen with Lapis Lazuli as her scrub nurse;

"Dr. Galahad with Lorelei Lee;

"Dr. Ishtar with Tamara;

"Dr. Harshaw—that's me—with Gillian;

"Dr. Lafe Hubert aka Lazarus, with Hilda; and

"Dr. Ira Johnson with Dagmar Dobbs.

"Dagmar, your match with Johnson Prime is not too close; you are over-qualified by a century and a half, plus whatever you have learned here. But it's the best we can manage. Dr. Johnson will not know that you are assigned to him. However, we know from library research and from quite a lot of oral history research—interviews conducted by field agents in Coventry and elsewhere in the years 1947–50, recording the experiences of persons who served in civil-defense first-aid teams in that war—we know that team-up between surgeon and nurse could be last minute, scratch, either one of them not fully qualified. Battle conditions, Dagmar. If you get there first when the sirens sound—and you will—Dr. Johnson will simply accept you."

"I'll try."

"You will succeed. All of us assigned to first aid will be wearing gowns and masks that won't look odd in wartime England, 1941, and you'll be using surgical instruments and other gear that does not scream anachronism . . . although anachronisms won't matter much, we think, in the pressure of a heavy bombing raid."

Jubal looked around the hall. "Everyone in this operation is a volunteer. I can't emphasize too often that this is an actual battle you are going into. If you are killed in England in 1941, history may be revised—but *you* will be *dead*. Those so-called 'iron bombs' used by the Nazi Luftwaffe will kill you just as dead as an exotic weapon of a later century. For that reason all of us are volunteers and anyone can quit right up to H-hour. All of Major Gretchen's young ladies are volunteers . . . and are on max hazard pay, as well." Jubal stopped and cleared his throat, then went on,

"But there is one volunteer we don't need, don't want, and who is urgently requested to stay home."

Jubal looked around again. "Ladies and gentlemen, what in the hell are we going to do about Pixel? When the bombs start falling and the wounded start piling up at that field station, the last thing we need is a cat who can't be shut up and can't be shut out. Colonel Campbell? He's your cat."

My grandson Richard Ames Campbell answered, "You have that the wrong way around, Doctor. I don't own Pixel. Whatever ownership there may be points in the other direction. I agree with you that we can't afford to have him underfoot during battle. But I don't want him there on his own account; he's too unsophisticated to know that bombs can kill him. He got involved in another fire fight when he was just a kitten . . . and it did almost kill him. I don't want that ever to happen again. But I never have figured out how to lock him up."

"Just a moment, Richard." Gwen Hazel stood up. "Jubal, may I offer a suggestion?"

"Hazel, it says on the organization chart that you are in command of this operation, all phases. I think that entitles you to make a suggestion. One, at least."

"Come off it, Jubal. There is a third member of our family that has more influence over Pixel than either Richard or I. My daughter Wyoming."

"Does she volunteer?"

"She will."

"Stipulating that she will, can she control Pixel every second for about four hours? For technical reasons involving how we handle the time/space gates we will use about that much Boondock time. So Dr. Burroughs tells me."

I interrupted. "May I say something?"

"Hazel, do you yield?"

"Don't be silly, Jubal; of course I do."

"Certainly we should use Wyoh; the child is utterly reliable. But don't have her try to hang on to Pixel here; one sneeze and he's gone. Take both of them to Oz and have them stay with Glinda. With Betsy, rather, but with Glinda's magic to insure that Pixel doesn't walk through any walls."

"Hazel?" Dr. Harshaw inquired.

"They'll both love it."

"It is so ordered. Now back to the raid. Projection, please." An enormous live picture grew up behind Jubal and around him. "This holo is not Coventry itself but our Potemkin-Village practice ground that Athene has built for us, about eighty kilometers east of here. Take a bow, Teena."

The executive computer's voice came out of the air: "Thanks, Papa Jubal, but that's 'Shiva's' work—Mycroft Holmes and me linked in synergistic parallel, with Minerva waving the baton. Now that I've got you all gathered together, let me remind you that all of you are invited to our wedding, Minnie and me to Mike, after the conclusion of Operation Coventry Cusp. So you all had better start thinking about wedding presents."

"Teena, you are crassly materialistic and neither of your composite bodies can possibly be ready that soon."

"Gotcha! Ish okayed moving our bodies to Beulahland, so now we can be uncorked and animated on any date we pick. You better study up on the laws of temporal paradox, Jubal."

Dr. Harshaw sighed. "Conceded. I look forward to kissing the brides. Now will you please let us get on with the operation?"

"Don't sweat it, Pops. You know or should know that there is never any hurry in a time operation."

"True. But we're all a bit eager. Friends, Teena—or Shiva—built our practice field from photos, stereos, holos, and motion pictures taken at Coventry on the first of April, 1941. You will recognize 1941 as a date so far back that all time lines patrolled by the agents of the Circle of Ouroboros are, in 1941, a single time line. In short, anything we do in Coventry in 1941 affects all civilized time lines—'civilized' in a parochial sense, of course; the Circle is not unbiased.

"Research for this operation turned up an odd fact. Lazarus?"

My son stood up. "History of World War Two 1939–1945 as I recall it shows a more favorable outcome in England and in Europe than that which turned up in this operation's field research. For example, my oldest brother, Brian Smith, Jr., was wounded in the landing at Marseilles, whereupon he was sent to England, to the Salisbury Plains and the American training command. Mama?"

"Yes, surely, Woodrow."

"But the history we researched shows that this could not have happened. The Luftwaffe won the Battle of Britain and there never was a Marseilles landing, much less an American training command in England. Instead, Germany was smashed from the air by atomic bombs delivered from North Africa by American B29 bombers. Friends and family, I was in that war. No atomic bombs were dropped on Europe in the war I remember."

"Thank you, Lazarus. I was in that war, too, and in North Africa. No B29s operated from there as I recall it and no atomic bombs were used in the European theater—so this research startled me as much as it did Lazarus. This bad news changed Operation Johnson Prime—which had as its purpose locating and recovering Dr. Ira Johnson, the Prime of the Johnson family—to Operation Coventry Cusp . . . which includes Operation Johnson Prime as one of its phases, but has the far wider purpose of changing the outcome of that war through this one raid. The raid of April eighth, 1941, was selected not only because Dr. Johnson was known to have been in it, as an AFS surgeon in civil defense, but also because the four waves of bombers—giant Heinkels—that bombed Coventry that night were the largest number of Nazi bombers used in any one raid.

"The Circle's mathematicians, working with Shiva, all agree that this is a cusp event, where a handful of people can turn the course of a history. So it will be the purpose of Major Gretchen's ladies to destroy as many as possible of that air Armada—as near one hundred percent as superior technology can manage. With this one assist, the RAF can and will win the Battle of Britain. Without it, it can be—or was—too big a raid for the Spitfires to handle. An almost invisible additional purpose of Operation Coventry Cusp, three layers down, is to save the lives of Spitfire pilots, so that they will live to fight another day.

"This is the sort of nudge the Circle of Ouroboros specializes in, the minor assist that makes a major change in the outcome—and the Companions of the Circle feel sanguine about this one.

"Now please look at the picture behind me. Our view is from the spot in Greyfriars Green occupied by the dressing station where Johnson Prime served that night. Those three towers are all that was left standing in the central city after earlier raids—the towers of St. Michael's cathedral, Greyfriars church, and Holy Trinity church. Off to the left is a lesser tower that does not show; that tower is the only original part of a Benedictine monastery built by Leofric, earl of Mercia, and his wife, Lady Godiva, in 1043. We have leased that tower from the earl, and the gate that will deliver Gretchen's archers will be—has been—erected on it, as well as the time gate that will move them to 1941. It may amuse you to hear that, while the contract payment was in gold, a lagniappe was added, a magnificent white gelding that the Lady Godiva named 'Aethelnoth'—and our gift to the Lady is the very mount she used in her famous ride through the town for benefit of her townspeople."

Jubal cleared his throat and grinned. "Despite widespread popular demand coming mostly from Castor and Pollux, this operation will not be combined with a sightseeing trip to watch Lady Godiva ride through Coventry.

"That's all today, friends. To take part in this operation you need to be convinced of three things: first, that the Nazi regime under Adolf Hitler was so vile that it must not be allowed to win, and, second, that it is strongly desirable to defeat the Nazis without dropping scores of atomic bombs on Europe, and, third, that it is worth it to you to risk your neck to achieve the operation's objectives. The Circle answers Yes to these questions, but you must weigh them in your own conscience. If your answer is not a whole-hearted Yes on all points, then please do not volunteer.

"After you have thought it over, the remaining Gideon's Band will meet for first rehearsal at ten tomorrow morning at our Potemkin-Village Coventry. A transbooth shuttling directly to the practice village is located just north of this building."

In Coventry, England, on Tuesday the eighth of April, 1941, at 7:22 P.M. the sun was setting, glowing red in smog and coal smoke. Looking at this city gave me a weird feeling, so exactly had Shiva's simulation matched what I now saw. I was standing at the entrance of a civil-defense first-aid station, the one that research showed that Father had worked in (would work in) tonight. It was hardly more than walls of sandbags covered by canvas painted opaque to guard the blackout.

It had a jakes of sorts (Phew!), and an anteroom for the wounded, three pine tables, some cupboards, and duck boards on a dirt floor. No running water—a tank with a spigot. Gasoline lamps.

Greyfriars Green spread out around me, an untended park pocked with bomb craters. I could not see the monastery tower we had rented from Lady Godiva's husband, Leofric, earl of Mercia, but I knew that it was north of me, off to my left. Field Agent Hendrik Hudson Schultz, who had conducted the dicker with the earl, reported that Godiva's hair really was surprisingly long and beautiful but that it was inadvisable to be downwind from her, as she had apparently not bathed more than twice in her life. Father Hendrik had spent a hard sixteen months learning eleventh-century Anglo-Saxon and customs and medieval church Latin in preparation for the assignment—one he completed in ten days.

Tonight Father Hendrik was with Gretchen as her interpreter; it had not been judged cost effective to require the members of the military task force to learn an Anglic language a century older than Chaucer, when their working language was not English but Galacta, and their MOS involved shooting, not talking.

Northeast of me I could see the three spires that gave the city its nickname: Greyfriars, Holy Trinity, and St. Michael's. Saint Michael's and Greyfriars were gutted in earlier bombings and much of the center of the city was destroyed. When I had first heard of the bombing of Coventry, a century ago on my personal time line, I had thought that the bombing of this historic town was an example of the sheer viciousness of the Nazis. While it is not possible to exaggerate the viciousness of that regime and the stench of its gas ovens, I now knew that the bombing of Coventry was not simply *Schrecklichkeit,* as this was an important industrial city, as important to England as Pittsburgh was to the United States.

Coventry was not the bucolic town I had pictured in my mind. I could see that, if fortune favored us tonight, we might possibly not only destroy a major part of the Luftwaffe's biggest bombers but also save the lives of skilled craftsmen as necessary to military victory as are brave soldiers.

Behind me I heard Gwen Hazel checking her communications: "Blood's a Rover, this is Lady Godiva's Horse. Come in, Blood."

I answered, "Blood to Horse, roger."

We had a uniquely complex communication net tonight; one I did not even try to understand (I'm a diaper engineer and a kitchen chemist—I've never seen an electron), a system that paralleled an even more astounding temporary time/space hookup.

Like this— From outside, the west end of the aid station was a blank wall of sandbags. From inside, that end was curtained off, a putative storage space. But push aside the curtain and you would find two time/space gates: one from Coventry 1941 to the medical school hospital, BIT, Tertius 4376 Gregorian, and the other doing just the reverse, so that supplies, personnel, and patients could move either way without traffic problems—and at the Tertius end was another double set of gates to Beulahland, so that the worst cases could be shuttled to a different time axis for treatment, then returned to Coventry.

A similar but not identical double-gate arrangement served Gretchen's command. She and her girls (and Father Schultz) were waiting in the eleventh century on the monastery tower. The gate that would place them in the twentieth century would not be activated until Gwen Hazel notified Gretchen that the sirens had sounded.

Gwen Hazel could talk to the twentieth century, the forty-fourth century, and the eleventh century, each separately or all at once, using a buried throat mike, tongue switches, and a body antenna, whether she was at the Tellus Prime end or the Tellus Tertius end of the aid-station gates.

In addition to these hookups she was in touch with Zeb and Deety Carter, in the *Gay Deceiver,* at thirty thousand feet over the English Channel—too high for bombers, too high for Messerschmitts or Fokkers, too high for AA fire of that year. Gay had agreed to be there only if she was allowed to pick her own altitude. (Gay is a pacifist with, in her opinion, a deplorable amount of combat experience.) But at that altitude Gay was sure that she could spot Heinkels taking off and forming up long before the British coastal radar could see them.

As a result of rehearsals at "Potemkin Village," drills involving every casualty we could think of, the surgical teams had been rearranged, with most of them held back on the Boondock side of the gates. "Triage" of a sort would be practiced; the hopeless cases would be rushed through to Boondock, where no case is hopeless if the brain is alive and not too damaged. There Doctors Ishtar and Galahad would head their usual teams (who need not be volunteers for combat; they would never be in Coventry). The "hopeless" cases, repaired, would be gated to Beulahland for days or weeks of recovery, then gated back to Coventry before dawn.

(Tomorrow there would be miracles to be explained. But we would be long gone.)

Cas and Pol had been volunteered (by their wives, my

daughters Laz and Lor) as stretcher bearers, to move the worst cases from Coventry to gurney floats on the Boondock side.

It had been decided that too many surgical teams and too much equipment showing up out of nowhere as soon as the sirens sounded would alert Father unnecessarily, make him smell a rat. But, when the wounded started pouring in, he would be too busy to notice or care.

Jubal and Gillian were a reserve team, and would go through when needed. Dagmar would go through when Deety in *Gay Deceiver* reported that the bombers were on their way, so that Dagmar would meet Father—Dr. Johnson—as he first poked his head in. When the sirens sounded, Lazarus and I would go through, already masked and gowned, with me as his scrub nurse. I'm an adequate surgeon but I'm a whiz as an operating nurse—much more practice at it. We figured that three of us could do what might have to be done at "all clear," the end of the raid: Grab Father and kidnap him— drag him through the gate, sit him down in Boondock, and explain things to him there . . . including the idea that he could have the works—rejuvenation and expert tutoring in really advanced therapy and still be returned to Coventry April eighth, 1941. If he insisted. If he had any wish to.

But by then I hoped and expected that, with Tamara's help, Father could be made to see the Quixotic futility of going back to the Battle of Britain when that battle had been won more than two millennia earlier.

With Tamara's help— She was my secret weapon. By a concatenation of miracles I had married my lover from the stars . . . and thereby married my son, to my amazement and great happiness. Could more miracles let me marry the only man I have always loved, totally and without reservation? Father would certainly marry Tamara, given the chance—any man would—and Tamara would then see to it that Father married me. I hoped.

If not, it would be enough and more than enough simply to have Father alive again.

I had gone back through the gate to Boondock when I heard Gwen Hazel's voice: "Godiva's Horse to all stations. Deety reports bandits in the air and forming up. Expect sirens in approx eighty minutes. Acknowledge."

Gwen Hazel was standing beside me by the gates in the hospital, but this was a communication check as much as an intelligence. My own comm gear was simple: a throat mike not buried but merely under a bandage I did not need; a "hearing aid" that was not one and an antenna concealed by my clothes. I answered, "Blood's a Rover to Horse, roger."

I heard, "British Yeoman to Horse, roger. Eighty minutes. One hour twenty minutes."

I said, "Blood to Horse. I heard Gretchen's roger. Should I?"

Gwen Hazel shut off transmission and spoke to me, "You shouldn't hear her until you both shift to Coventry 1941. Mau, will you please go through to Coventry for a second comm check?"

I did so; we established that Gwen Hazel's link to me, 44th C to 20th C, was okay, and that I now could not hear Gretchen—both as they should be. Then I went back to Boondock, as I was not yet gowned or masked. There was one point in the transition where something tugged at one's clothes and my ears popped—a static baffle against an air-pressure inequality, I knew. But ghostly, just the same.

Deety reported that the bombers' fighter escort was becoming airborne. The German Messerschmitts were equal to or better than the Spitfires, but they had to operate at the very limit of their range—it took most of their gasoline to get there and get back; they could engage in dogfighting only a few minutes—or wind up in the Channel if they miscalculated.

Gwen Hazel said, "Dagmar. Take your station."

"Roger wilco." Dagmar went through, gowned, masked, and capped—not yet gloved . . . although God knows what good gloves would do in the septic conditions we would experience. (Protect us, maybe, if not our patients.)

I tied Woodrow's mask for him; he did so for me. We were ready.

Gwen Hazel said, "Godiva's Horse to all stations, sirens. British Yeoman, activate gate and shift time. Acknowledge."

"Yeoman to Horse, roger wilco!"

"Horse to Yeoman, report arrival. Good hunting!" Hazel

added to me, "Mau, you and Lazarus can go through now. Good luck!"

I followed Lazarus through . . . and swallowed my heart. Dagmar was gowning Father. He glanced at us as we came out from behind that curtain, paid us no further attention. I heard him say to Dagmar, "I haven't seen you before, Sister. What's your name?"

"Dagmar Dobbs, Doctor. Call me 'Dag' if you like. I just came up from London this morning, sir, with supplies."

"So I see. First time in weeks I've seen a clean gown. And masks—what swank! You sound like a Yank, Dag."

"And I am, Doctor—and so do you."

"Guilty as charged. Ira Johnson, from Kansas City."

"Why, that's my home town!"

"I thought I heard some tall corn in your speech. When the Heinies go home tonight, we must catch up on home town gossip."

"I don't have much; I haven't been home since I got my cap and pin."

Dagmar kept Father busy and kept his attention—and I thanked her under my breath. I didn't want him to notice me until the raid was over. No time for Old Home Week until then.

The first bombs fell, some distance away.

I saw nothing of the raid. Ninety-three years ago, or eight months later that same year, depending on how you count it, I saw bombs falling on San Francisco under circumstances in which I had nothing to do but look up and hold my breath and wait. I'm not sorry that I was too busy to watch the bombing of Coventry. But I could hear it. If you can hear it hit, it is too far away to have your name on it. So they tell me. I'm not sure I believe them.

Gwen Hazel said in my ear, "Did you hear Gretchen? She says they got sixty-nine out of seventy-two of the first wave."

I had not heard Gretchen. Lazarus and I were busy with our first patient, a little boy. He was badly burned and his left arm was crushed. Lazarus got ready to amputate. I blinked back tears and helped him.

28

Eternal Now

I am not going to batter your feelings or mine by describing the details of that thousand-year night. Anything agonizing you have ever seen in the emergency room of a big-city hospital is what we saw, and worked on, that night. Compound fractures, limbs shattered to uselessness, burns—horrible burns. If the burns weren't too bad we slathered them with a gel that would not be seen here for centuries, put dressings over the affected areas, and had them carried outside by civil-defense stretcher bearers. The worst cases were carried in the other direction by Cas and Pol—behind that curtain, through a Burroughs-Carter-Libby gate, to Ira Johnson Hospital in Boondock, and (for burn cases) shifted again to Jane Culver Burroughs Memorial Hospital in Beulahland, there to spend days or weeks in healing, then to be returned to Coventry at "All Clear" this same night.

All of our casualties were civilians, mostly women, children, and old men. The only military (so far as I know) around or in Coventry were Territorials manning AA guns. They had their own medical setup. I suppose that in London a first-aid station such as ours would probably be in the underground. Coventry had no tube trains; this aid station was merely sand-bags out in the open but it was safer, perhaps, than it would have been in a building—one that might burn over it. I'm not criticizing. Everything about their civil defense had a make-do quality about it, a people with their backs to the wall, fighting gallantly with whatever they had.

In our aid station we had three tables, operating tables by courtesy, in fact plain wooden tables with the paint scrubbed right off them between raids. Father was using the one nearest the entrance; Woodrow was using the one nearest the curtain; the middle one was used by an elderly Englishman who was apparently a regular for this aid station: Mr. Pratt, a local veterinary surgeon, assisted by his wife, "Harry" for Harriet. Mrs. Pratt had unkind things to say about the Germans during the lulls but was more interested in talking about the cinema. Had I ever met Clark Gable? Gary Cooper? Ronald Colman? Having established that I knew no one of any importance she quit trying to draw me out. But she agreed with her husband when he said it was decent of us Yahnks to come over and help out . . . but when were the States going to come into the war?

I said that I did not know. Father spoke up. "Don't bother the Sister, Mr. Pratt. We'll be along a bit late, just like your Mr. Chamberlain. In the meantime please be polite to those of us who are here and helping."

"No offense meant, Mr. Johnson."

"And none taken, Mr. Pratt. Clamp!"

(Mrs. Pratt was as good an operating nurse as I've ever seen. She was always ready with what her husband needed without his asking for it—long practice together, I suppose. She had fetched the instruments he used; I assume that they were tools of his animal practice. That might bother some people; to me it made sense.)

Mr. Pratt was at the table that we had expected would be used by Jubal and Jill. (Our research on fine details was less than perfect, since it came from questioning people after the war was over.) So Jubal went out into the anteroom where the wounded waited and worked on triage, tagging the cases

Cas and Pol were to carry through to Boondock—the ones who would otherwise have been allowed to die untreated, as being beyond hope. Jill gave a hand to both Dagmar and me, especially with anesthesia, such as it was.

Anesthesia had been a subject of much discussion at our Potemkin-Village drills. It was bad enough to show up in the twentieth century with anachronistic surgical instruments . . . but Boondock anesthetic gear and procedures? Impossible!

Galahad decided on pressure injectors supplying metered amounts of "neomorphine" (as good a name as any—a drug not available in the twentieth century). Jill moved around the station and in the anteroom, injecting the damaged and the burned, and thereby left Dagmar and me with our hands free for surgery assistance. She made one try at helping Mrs. Pratt, but was waved away—Mrs. Pratt was using something I had not seen since 1910 or thereabouts: a nose cone with drops of chloroform.

The work went on and on. I wiped off our table between patients, until the towel I was using was so soaked with blood that it was doing more harm than good.

Gretchen reported a spotty kill on the second wave—sixty bombers attacked, forty-seven shot down. Thirteen bombers dropped at least one stick before being hit. Gretchen's girls were using particle beams and night-sight gear; the usual effect was to blow up the plane's gasoline tanks. Sometimes the bombs went off at the same time; sometimes the bombs exploded on hitting the ground; sometimes the bombs did not explode, leaving a touchy problem for bomb-disposal experts the next day.

But we saw none of this. Sometimes we would hear a bomb drop nearby and someone would remark, "Close," and someone would answer, "Too close," and we would continue working.

A shot-down plane makes a different sort of explosion from a bomb . . . and a fighter from a bomber. Mr. Pratt said that he could tell the crash of a Spitfire from the crash of a Messerschmitt. Probably he could. I could not.

The third wave broke into two formations, so Gretchen reported, and came in from southwest and southeast. But her girls now had practice in using what was essentially an infantry weapon against targets they were not used to, under conditions where they must be sure that they had bombers in their sights, not Spitfires. Gretchen described this one as a "skeet shoot." I made note to ask her what that meant, but I never did.

There were lulls between waves, but not for us. As the night wore on we dropped farther and farther behind; they brought in victims faster than we could handle them. Jubal grew more liberal in tagging, and routed to Ishtar and her teams more and more of the less severely wounded. It made our help more blatant but it surely saved more lives.

During the fourth wave of bombing, sometime early in the morning, I heard Gretchen say, "Yeoman to Horse, emergency."

"What is it, Gretchen?"

"Something—a piece of plane, probably—hit our gate."

"Damage?"

"I don't know. It disappeared. Whoof! Gone."

"Horse to Yeoman, disengage. Evacuate via gate at aid station. Can you find it? Range and bearing?"

"Yes, but—"

"Disengage and evacuate. Move."

"But, Hazel, it is just our gate we've lost. We can still take out any bombers that come over."

"Hold. Bright Cliffs, answer. Deety, wake up."

"I am awake."

"Research showed four waves, no more. Is Gretchen going to have any more targets?"

"One moment—" (It was a long moment.) "Gay says she can't see any bombers warming up on the ground. We now have signs of dawn in the east."

"Horse to all stations, disengage. Blood, wait for Yeoman, then evacuate . . . bringing Prime with you. Use injector if necessary. All stations, report."

"Cliffs to Horse, roger wilco; here we come!"

"Yeoman to Horse, roger wilco. Father Schmidt is leading; I'm chasing."

"Blood to Horse, roger wilco. Hazel, tell Ishtar to get all cases back here now . . . or she's got some unscheduled immigrants."

The next few minutes were hilarious, in a Grand Guignol

fashion. First the terribly burned cases came pouring back through the incoming gate, on their own feet and now quite well. Surgery cases followed them, some with prostheses, some with grafts. Even the last cases, ones that Galahad and Ishtar and other surgical teams were currently working on, were patched up somehow, pushed through to Beulahland, there to be finished and to stay for days or weeks—and then sent back through to Coventry only minutes after Hazel ordered an end to the operation.

I know that it was only minutes because none of Gretchen's troops had arrived from less than a mile away. Those girls move at eight miles per hour at field trot (3.5 meters per second). They should have made it in about eight or nine minutes, plus whatever time it took to get down that tower. I heard later that some of the civil-defense wardens tried to stop them and question them. I don't think the girls hurt anyone very badly. But they didn't stop.

They came pouring in, Maid Marians with long bows (disguised particle projectors), dressed for Nottingham Forest, led by Friar Tuck complete with tonsure, and followed by Gretchen, dressed also for a Robin Hood pageant and wearing a big grin.

She paused to slap Dagmar on her fanny as she passed Father's table, nodded at the Pratts, who were already stupefied by the procession of recovered patients going the other way. She stopped at Woodrow's table. "We did it!"

All three tables were bare at that moment; we had reached that wonderful point where no more wounded were waiting. Jubal came in from the anteroom, said, "You did indeed."

Gretchen hugged me. "Maureen, we did it!" She pulled my mask down and kissed me.

I bussed her back. "Now get your tail through that gate. We're on minus minutes."

"Spoilsport." She went on through, followed by Jubal and Gillian.

"All Clear" started sounding. Mr. Pratt looked at me, looked at the curtain, said, "Come, Harry."

"Yes, Pa."

"Goodnight, all." The old man plodded wearily away, followed by his wife.

Father said in a gruff voice, "Daughter, why are you here? You should be in San Francisco." He looked at Woodrow.

"You, too, Ted. You're dead. So what are you doing here?"

"Not dead, Dr. Johnson. 'Missing in action' is not the same as dead. The difference was slight but important. A long time in hospital, a long time out of my head. But here I am."

"Mmrrph. So you are. But what is this charade? People in costumes. Other people trotting back and forth like Piccadilly Circus. Hell of a way to run an aid station. Am I out of my head? Did we take a direct hit?"

Hazel said in my ear, "Come through, all of you! Now!"

I subvocalized, "Right away, Hazel." Dagmar had moved until she was behind my father. She had her injector ready; she queried me with her eyes. I shook my head a quarter of an inch. "Father, will you come with me and let me explain?"

"Mrph. I suppose—"

The roof fell in.

It may have been part of a Spitfire, or perhaps a Messerschmitt. I don't know; I was under it. Gwen Hazel heard it through my mike; her grandsons Cas and Pol got themselves badly burned going back through to rescue us.

Everybody got burned—Castor, Pollux, Woodrow, Father, Dagmar, me—and gasoline burns are nasty. But Hazel got more help through, dressed in fireproofs (planning, not happenstance) and we were all dragged out.

All of this I got from later reports; at the time I was simply clobbered and then I woke up in hospital an unmeasured time later. Unmeasured by me, that is; Dagmar says that I was laid up three weeks longer than she was. Tamara won't tell me. It does not matter; Lethe keeps one comfortable and unworried as long as necessary to let one get well.

After a while I was allowed to get up and take walks around Beulahland, a beautiful place and one of the few truly civilized places in any world. And then I was transferred back to Boondock . . . and Woodrow and Father and Dagmar came to call on me.

They all leaned over my bed and kissed me and I cried awhile and then we talked.

It was a big wedding. There was Mycroft and Athene and Minerva of course, and my grandson Richard Colin, who had at last forgiven Lazarus (for being his father). My darling Gwen Hazel had no reason to remain on leave from the family when Richard Colin was willing and eager to join. My daughters Laz and Lor had decided to cancel the indentures of their husbands, Cas and Pol, in recognition of their heroism in diving back into the fire for us four laggards—and to allow them to marry into the family. And there was Xia and Dagmar and Choy-Mu and Father and Gretchen—and the rest of us who had been Longs for years—some more years, some less. Our new family members each had had one reason or another to hesitate, but Galahad and Tamara made it clear: We take just one vow, to safeguard the welfare and happiness of all our children.

That's our total marriage contract. The rest is just poetic ritual.

Whom you sleep with, whom you make love with, is your private business. Ishtar, as our family geneticist, controls pregnancy and progeny to whatever extent control is needed for the welfare of our children.

So we all joined hands in the presence of our children (of course Pixel was there!) and we pledged ourselves to love and cherish our children—those around us, those still to come, worlds without end.

And we all lived happily ever after.

People in This Memoir

Anna Kristina Hansen Larsen, great-grandmother,
   1810–1912   72

IRA JOHNSON'S SIBLINGS

Samantha Jane Johnson, 1831–1915   72
James Ewing Johnson, 1833–1884   57
   (married Carole Pelletier, 1849–1954)   57
Walter Raleigh Johnson, 1838–1862   72
Alice Irene Johnson, 1840   72
Edward McFee Johnson, 1844–1884   72
Aurora Johnson, 1850   72

MAUREEN'S SIBLINGS

Edward Ray Johnson, 1876   18
Audrey Adele Johnson, 1878   18
   (married Jerome Bixby, 1896)   48
Agnes Johnson, 1880   18
Thomas Jefferson Johnson, 1881   18
Benjamin Franklin Johnson, 1884   18
Elizabeth Ann Johnson, 1882   18
Lucille Johnson, 1894   18
George Washington Johnson, 1897   18

Nelson Johnson, cousin, 1884
   (son of James Ewing Johnson and Carole Pelletier)   2

MAUREEN'S DESCENDANTS AND THEIR SPOUSES

Nancy Irene Smith, December 1, 1899   95
   (married Jonathan Sperling Weatheral)   95
Carol Smith, January 1, 1902   15
   (married Roderick Schmidt Jenkins)   361
Brian Smith Junior, March 12, 1905   98
George Edward Smith, February 14, 1907   98
Marie Agnes Smith, April 5, 1909   98
Woodrow Wilson Smith/Lazarus Long, et al.
   November 11, 1912   39
   (first wife: Heather Hedrick)   245
Richard Smith, 1914–1945
   (married Marian Hardy)   244

MAUREEN'S SPOUSES, CO-SPOUSES, LOVERS, FRIENDS

THE COMMITTEE FOR AESTHETIC DELETIONS

PUBLIC FIGURES

PEOPLE OFF STAGE

Richard Heiser	35
Pop Green, druggist	37
Dr. Phillips	44
Jonnie Mae Igo	45
Mrs. Malloy, landlady	51
The Widow Loomis	60
Mr. Barnaby, principal	80
Major General Lew Rawson, target	402
Bob Coster, ship design	361
Elijah Madison, driver	354
Charlene Madison, cook	354
Anne, a Fair Witness	270
Sarah Trowbridge, dead	82
Miss Primrose	82
"Scrooge" O'Hennessy	106
Annie Chambers, madam	123
Mrs. Bunch, gossip	123
Mr. Davis, see "Fones"	131
Cowboy Womack, miner	135
The Jenkins girl	139
Mr. Wimple, bank teller	151
Nick Weston	192
Mr. Watkins	281
Mr. Hardecker, principal	321
Granny Bearpaw, cook	320
Mr. Ferguson, chief engineer	328

ASSOCIATED STORIES

The Man Who Sold the Moon and Other Stories
Persons in "The Man Who Sold the Moon"—D. D. Harriman, George Strong, Daniel Dixon, Chief Engineer Ferguson, Bob Coster, Leslie LeCroix. In "Requiem"— D. D. Harriman, George Strong.

Revolt in 2100 and Other Stories
In " 'If This Goes On—' "—Nehemiah Scudder. In "Misfit"—(Elizabeth) Andrew Jackson Libby (Long).

Methuselah's Children
Lazarus Long aka Woodrow Wilson Smith, Andrew Jackson Libby.

Time Enough for Love
Lazarus Long, Ira Weatheral, Hamadryad, Ishtar, Galahad, Tamara, Lapis Lazuli, Lorelei Lee, Justin Foote 45th, "Theodore Bronson," Dr. Ira Johnson, Maureen Johnson Smith, Brian Smith, Nancy Smith, Carol Smith, Brian Smith, Jr., George Edward Smith, Marie Agnes Smith, Woodrow Wilson Smith, Ethel Smith, Richard Smith, Justin Weatheral, Eleanor Weatheral, Jonathan Sperling Weatheral.

The Rolling Stones
Hazel Stone, Castor Stone, Pollux Stone.

The Moon Is a Harsh Mistress
Hazel Stone, Mycroft Holmes IV.

Stranger in a Strange Land
Gillian Boardman, Jubal Harshaw, Anne (Fair Witness), Patty Paiwonski.

The Number of the Beast
Deety Burroughs Carter, Zebadiah John Carter, Jacob Burroughs, Hilda Mae Corners Burroughs, Lazarus Long, Elizabeth Andrew Jackson Libby Long, Lapis Lazuli Long, Lorelei Lee Long, Maureen Johnson Long, Hamadryad Long, Tamara Long, Hazel Stone, Castor Stone, Pollux

Stone, Minerva Long, Jubal Harshaw, Athene, Anne (Fair Witness), Dr. Jesse F. Bone, Samuel Clemens.

The Cat Who Walks Through Walls

Hazel Stone aka Gwen Novak, Col. Richard Colin Campbell Ames, Gretchen Henderson, The Rev. Dr. Hendrik Hudson Schultz, Tamara, Athene, Dong Xia, Marcy Choy-Mu, Pixel, Lazarus Long, Wendy Campbell Ames, Maureen Johnson Long, Justin Foote 45th, Wyoming Long, Jacob Burroughs Long, Deety Burroughs Carter Long, Jubal Harshaw.

N.B.: *The Past Through Tomorrow* is an omnibus volume containing *The Man Who Sold the Moon and Other Stories, The Green Hills of Earth and Other Stories, Revolt in 2100 and Other Stories,* and *Methuselah's Children.*